ALSO BY JONATHAN L. HOWARD

CARTER &

LOVECRAFT

CARTER &
LOVECRAFT

JONATHAN L. HOWARD

Thomas Dunne Books
St. Martin's Press
New York

THOMAS DUNNE BOOKS.
An imprint of St. Martin's Press.

CARTER & LOVECRAFT. Copyright © 2015 by St. Martin's Press, LLC. All rights reserved. Printed in the United States of America. For information, address St. Martin's Press, 175 Fifth Avenue, New York, N.Y. 10010.

www.thomasdunnebooks.com
www.stmartins.com

The Library of Congress Cataloging-in-Publication Data
is available upon request.

ISBN 978-1-250-06089-1 (hardcover)
ISBN 978-1-4668-6665-2 (e-book)

Our books may be purchased in bulk for promotional, educational, or business use. Please contact your local bookseller or the Macmillan Corporate and Premium Sales Department at (800) 221-7945, extension 5442, or by e-mail at MacmillanSpecialMarkets@macmillan.com.

First Edition: October 2015

10 9 8 7 6 5 4 3 2 1

In memory of my father, Noel Howard, 1923–2014.

A better man than I shall ever be,
but that's no reason not to keep trying.

CONTENTS

CONTENTS

CARTER &

LOVECRAFT

Chapter 1

THE KILLER IN RED HOOK

Crying and laughing, Charlie put his S&W Model 5946 between his teeth, squeezed the trigger, and excused himself from life.

Carter watched him drop, unable to comprehend what he was seeing, unable to take in that his friend had just killed himself for no reason. No reason at all.

But there had to be a reason. There's *always* a reason. This was something to do with Suydam. This was Suydam's fault.

Carter turned to where Suydam sat propped against the wall, sitting in a pool of his own blood and piss, but there would be no answers coming from him. His eyes were open, and he was dead. He was smiling.

When the scene came back to Carter again and again over the following months, he would always remember the *clack* of the pistol's aluminum frame against Charlie's teeth, the smell of blood, and the smile on dead Suydam's face. It wasn't a malevolent smile, that was the worst of it. It wasn't cunning, or triumphant. It was happy. Suydam was happy Charlie had gutshot him, happy that he was dying, maybe even happy that Charlie had seen the joke, too, and followed him into darkness, a 9mm bullet as his invitation.

The kid was crying in the other room where Carter had left him, hopeless little jerking, mechanical sobs of a terror that had gone on too long. Carter looked at the bodies for a moment longer, holstered his Glock 19, and went to the boy, to stay with him until the backup arrived.

It was going to be a great day. They just knew it. It was going to be one of those Hollywood cop days when the clues line up and they'd just follow them straight to the perp. And what a perp. What an arrest it would be.

The United States had a disproportionately high number of serial killings compared to other developed countries, a result of wide spaces, ease of procuring weapons, and—just maybe—it looking so damn cool on TV and in the movies. Want your fifteen minutes? Here's how you do it, sport. Just be sure to score at least five victims. You're not a real serial killer unless you've got at least five kills, just like a World War I fighter ace. Five's the trick, sport.

Not all at once, either. That makes you a mass killer, not a serial killer, and mass killers are just douches. Those Columbine kids? That dickwad in Norway? Fuck 'em. Delayed gratification is the mark of the intelligent mind. That's how you get into the forensic pathology books. That's how you get a movie made about you. Mass killers, the movie gets made about the *victims*. Fuck that. Mass killers are just children who want all the candy *now*. A serial killer is a spider in a web, see? Now *that's* juice.

Despite which, there still aren't enough serial killers to go around, and the FBI tends to run down the most high profile, both because serials often break federal laws along the way and because they're the Feds. Simple as that. Even a city as large as New York doesn't get many serial killers, but that's largely because the higher the population density, the tougher it is to get away with a string of killings. Too many eyes, too many ears.

This one had been getting away with it somehow, though, and that made him special. He took children, always male, always between the ages of six and eleven, and chose targets purely on the basis of opportunity, according to the FBI profile. Opportunity meant that kids from poorer families, larger families that just couldn't keep an eye on all their children, tended to be targeted. But a middle-class white-bread kid from Greenwich Village was taken, too. So, the profiler concluded, class and race were unimportant to the killer. Only gender and age.

Seven abductions over a period of fifteen months, and four bodies recovered. The CSU reports turned up little of use apart from a *modus operandi*. None of the boys had suffered sexual assault, but all had suffered amateur surgery that had ultimately resulted in their deaths. All the surgery was to the brain, and to the eyes. The techniques used showed no training whatsoever, and only the slightest understanding of the aims of brain surgery. Sections of skull were removed without reference to the structure of the plates, simply cut and torn away to reach areas of the parietal and occipital lobes. No attempt to preserve the meninges layers across the surface of the brain had been made; the perp clearly had no interest in preserving the victims' lives post-operation.

Tox screens showed traces of Rohypnol and ethanol, presumably used as a makeshift anesthetic, but also stronger traces of amphetamines. The conclusion was that the surgery was carried out while the victim was drugged and incapacitated and, once complete, the victim was brought to a high state of awareness. Cops who had seen a lot read the reports and were silent, the kind of heavy silence made by a little bit more of a human soul dying.

The LDC had been very clear that he did not want this son of a bitch to get a name. He was not to be tagged with some cool-sounding title that the press would get ahold of and, somewhere down the line, use as the title of a best seller.

Within half an hour, the detective-investigators were quietly calling the unknown subject "The Child-Catcher."

The Child-Catcher sucked as a surgeon, but he was doing all right for himself as killer. The abductions occurred all over the city and its suburbs, and the body dumps found so far were spread out. Analysis showed no pattern, which made the detectives think the unsub himself was analyzing possible abduction and dump sites before using them. There was *always* a pattern. Even attempts to leave no pattern left a pattern of their own. This was different; there really was nothing. All the analysis could say was that the killer was based in New York, probably. The detectives nodded slowly; they'd kind of figured that themselves.

All they could do was hope for the Child-Catcher to make a mistake, careful though he'd been up till then. Historically, all serial killers get sloppy. While their MOs might evolve, repeated success made them overconfident. Some psychologists were of the opinion that this was because they wanted to be caught, but the practical nature of the police made them think it was just likely to be human nature, the desire to do just enough and no more.

For the first crime, the unsub would pull out all the stops, cover all the bases, dot every "i." It would be difficult and nitpicking, but they didn't want to be caught, so they would go to any trouble. Then, if they got away with it, next time they might think—even if only subconsciously—*I didn't need to do that one thing on the list. That didn't make any difference.* So they skip it, and they get away with it again. With every iteration, they shave away a little bit of security, until they shave that bit too much and let the hounds have a sniff of them. Then it's all over, even if not straightaway. The fuse is lit, though; they're as good as apprehended.

The thought that the Child-Catcher had probably shed several onion skins of security since his first crime gave the detectives hope. Maybe there was already a clue out there. Maybe next time he would fuck up spectacularly and give himself up on a plate. They could only keep the net tight, scrape up every fragment of evidence from the first killings, look for the missing, and watch for anything new.

"Anything new" turned out to be the eighth abduction. Detective First Grade Charlie Hammond and his partner of two years, Detective Third Grade Dan Carter, were on the scene seven minutes after the 911 came in, only thirty seconds behind the beat car. The 76th Precinct covers Red Hook, which doesn't have the concentrations of Hispanic citizens found elsewhere in the city. The uniformed officers were trying to get the story out of the missing boy's mother, but their Spanish wasn't proving equal to the job.

Charlie Hammond showed his badge and said, "*Señora, ¿cuándo fue la última vez que vio a su hijo?*"

Carter thought her face would stay with him—the dull shock, the drained color, the flickers of rising panic as she realized her boy's picture might end up on the evening news for all the wrong reasons. He thought her face would join the other flashes, other images that stick with every cop, but he was wrong. After what was to come, he couldn't remember her face at all. When her son was returned to her later, he only recognized her in the way he might if he'd seen her in a picture.

She replied slowly, as if just awoken. "*El hombre del camión. De pronto agarró a Thiago y lo tiró por dentro.*" She said it in a near monotone, as if disbelieving her own words.

Carter's Spanish was still at the night school stage, but he understood enough to follow the gist of it. She'd actually seen the unsub?

She'd done better.

She held out a crumpled and ragged piece of paper, a receipt she'd found in her pocket when she had needed something to write on in a hurry. And there it was, in jagged, anxious figures, traced and retraced over in her anxiety for there to be no mistake in their reading: a license plate number.

* * *

The pickup's registered address wasn't even a mile away. Hammond and Carter went there, leaving the uniforms with the mother, and called for backup en route.

Hammond drove. Once Carter had put in the call, it grew quiet in the car. It wasn't just nerves or excitement, although that was there, too. There was a strong sense that something was not right. Carter could feel it, and he was damn sure Hammond could, too. There was always the chance it wasn't the Child-Catcher, they had to allow for that. There was always the chance it was just some happy-go-lucky pedo who'd decided to try it on when the city was on high alert for a serial child abductor.

But neither of them believed it wasn't the Child-Catcher for a second. Even if it wasn't, it was still a serious crime, and they were more than happy to deal. But it was him. It so *was* him.

"He's been pretty smart up to now," said Carter. The suspect even had a name now, but they still said "he" and knew what they meant. According to the license number, his name was Martin Suydam. He had no criminal record.

Hammond said nothing, didn't even grunt. Carter said nothing else.

They traveled without lights or sirens, hopeful of catching the unsub unawares, and Hammond slowed the car a hundred yards from the address and parked out of sight. They walked the remaining distance, talking as if they were just walking around the corner to get a sandwich and a coffee, just two guys. As they walked, they covered the angles between them, looking without appearing to look, sensitive to the sight of a dark blue pickup or a man with a seven-year-old boy with him. Always at the edge of vision. Always at the corner of the eye.

The house, when they cleared the corner, was larger than expected. It looked like it had been a hardware store at some time in the last few years, with maybe a couple of rooms to live in on the second story. Those days had gone, all the stock dispersed, and—unless the interior had seen a lot of work that left the exterior untouched—its sole current resident must have had a lot of space to call his own.

The street corner belonging to the building was occupied by an open yard behind a chain-link fence. Sitting there was the dark blue pickup. It was out in the open, its rear plate easily readable from the street, no attempt to hide or disguise it at all. Carter wondered if maybe there was something in the forensic psychology theory about serials wanting to be caught after a while. If Suydam was their man, he hadn't just shed a layer or two of protective caution, he'd dumped the whole thing.

They still had no direct cause to enter the property, however, although they knew that even as they moved out of the redbrick building's arcs of vision, a warrant was being prepared. They would just have to wait until it arrived with a whole posse of other officers, and probably a SWAT team. Of course, while all that was going on, Suydam could be quietly peeling Thiago Mata's skull like a hardboiled egg.

Carter and Hammond reached a side door on the alley. The same thoughts were going through both their minds, along with the same misgivings.

"I thought I heard a kid cry out just then," said Hammond, but he said it without emphasis. There had been no cry. "Did you hear it?"

Carter looked at Charlie Hammond, then across the street. The place was quiet. He breathed out heavily through his nose. He didn't want to leave the kid alone with Suydam a second longer than he had to, but if they fucked this up, the Child-Catcher might walk.

He drew breath to speak.

The shrill squeal of a young child in pain came to them through the door.

Hammond led in. There was no sign the door was reinforced, and there was no time to go around to another door in any case. He quickly and quietly tried the handle, but it was locked.

"Knock, knock," he said under his breath, landed a flat-footed kick against the lock that tore the striking plate clear out of the frame, and followed through immediately, allowing himself to be skylined against the daylight only for a second. Carter was next, moving across and by, into the shadows of the other side of the door.

Their guess that the place was a former store was borne out by the open floor plan, tall shelves still in place, and an exposed area of concrete where a counter had once stood. Sunlight streamed through narrow horizontal slits left unpainted at the top of the blacked-out windows. To the left, a wide staircase angled up through a left-hand turn to the second story. They heard movement up there, feet on bare boards, and a child's subdued sobbing.

There was little cover on the first floor, but they should still have cleared it before moving on. Hammond wasn't for waiting, though; their eyes had barely adjusted to the darker interior before he was moving to the foot of the stairs. There were a few crates toward the windows at the far end that it was possible somebody might hide behind. Hammond angled his head at them for a second, as if that was a good enough search. It was a fair reading of the ground that there would be no ambush from that direction, but it bothered Carter then and later that they didn't do it by the book. No reason—there was nobody hiding there—but it bothered him. One of those little things that nags irrationally. Maybe if they'd done it properly, things would have turned out differently.

With Carter covering him, Hammond was first up the stairs. He moved quietly, but not silently; anyone upstairs would have heard him if they were listening, and after the kicking in of the door, how could they not be listening? Carter was a few steps behind him, so he saw Suydam second.

Hammond called, "NYPD! Drop your weapon!" and Carter knew right then that it was all going to turn to shit, though he didn't truly know how. Not really. He expected maybe Hammond to get hit, or Suydam to be using the Mata boy as a shield or maybe even have a shotgun or an automatic weapon. He was wrong about all that.

There was a beat. Carter paused on the stairs and looked back the way they had come, but they weren't being ambushed. Suydam was running solo. Carter was debating whether to move forward or maybe not if it startled the suspect when Hammond fired.

Once. Just once.

Hammond was ex-military, and had enjoyed his time in the army. He loved his gun, and maybe his gun loved him back for all the attention he gave it. Everything he did that related to fire-arms he did *per doctrine*. He had told Carter enough times that when he had to fire, he would always fire at least twice.

Afterward, the single shot was another thing that would bother Carter.

Then Hammond was moving again, doctrine in place: gun braced in both hands, stop to fire, keep moving when not firing. Carter followed him up.

Suydam was down, sitting against the wall. They were on a broad landing that looked like it had once been another shop floor, a little smaller than the first since an area was walled off for offices and storage. Where the floor below had been abandoned even by its solitary tenant, however, it was plain that he spent a lot of time here.

And there it was. Right there. An actual psycho wall.

Chapter 2

THE DOOM THAT CAME TO SUYDAM

Suydam had done the thing real serial killers never do: he had mapped his madness onto the wall. In the experience of the police, serial killers were only marginally organized. They might have a reasonably detailed *modus operandi*, but then they'd erode it over time and repetition until it wasn't worth shit. They might prepare, but only as much as they would for any hunting trip. They might keep trophies, but they tended to be small and personal, such as jewelry or a lock of hair. They might express their nature, but only as a notebook, or sometimes as paintings.

None, as far as Carter knew, not a single fucking lunatic, would actually do the Hollywood thing and make a psycho wall. They turned up in movies and TV all the time—great, intricate tapestries of psychosis in tiny handwriting on a thousand notes pinned to a wall, or written directly onto the plaster. Random pictures, usually religious, would dot it, some things would be circled, and some things would be connected to others by hand-drawn lines or lengths of string. It all looked very good on the screen, some handsome actor examining the wall by flashlight (the psycho never has working lights), zeroing in on the single thing in the whole mass of details that would set them on the trail of the killer before he could claim his final victim: the martyrdom of Saint Anthony; the pharaonic curses; Tenniel's illustrations for the "Alice" books. Whatever.

In reality, serial killers were rarely as imaginative as screenwriters. They just wanted to kill people, and then masturbate themselves raw afterward. They had no handbook telling them that they had to be themed, had to leave clues, had to present a puzzle. In the police's experience, these people were only special in their own minds. "Well, fuck you, buttercup, and get over yourself" was the unofficial mind-set.

Hammond was not an imaginative man. The psycho wall did not distract him for a second. Instead, he moved to where Suydam sat, blood leaking out of him in lazy pulses, and kicked a gun away. It skittered across the bare floorboards and stopped near Carter as he reached the top of the stairs. He saw it was a strange little thing: a Taurus PLY, its barrel reaching no farther than the end of the trigger guard. CSU later identified it as the smaller caliber .22 model rather than the .25. It was another thing wrong with the day. Suydam's last line of defense was a tiny holdout pistol intended for concealed carry. It wouldn't even take hollow points. Carter's own backup pistol was a Ruger LCR-357, and he was content to bet his life on it. The Taurus was a dissuader, in his opinion, not a killer. It was a strange choice.

Of course, it turned out it didn't matter at all. CSU also discovered the Taurus wasn't even loaded.

Carter angled around the floor himself, since Hammond was staying by Suydam, but the area was obviously clear. The staircase opened into the middle of the floor, with a wooden railing guarding the well. There was nothing else in the room, no furniture, no crates, nothing. Just Carter, Hammond, Suydam, and the big end wall covered in crazy. Carter spared it a glance then.

The left end of the wall looked like the Hollywood version, all notes and pictures. The other three-quarters of the wall, however, was something else again. When Carter had been a kid, his mother had taken up a craft hobby. She would take corkboard and cover it with cloth, usually black, mount pins into it, and then spend hours running colored embroidery floss between the pins, back and forth, until the picture picked out by the pins became apparent. At the time, he'd called it lame, but that was just because of where he was in his life. He'd actually kind of liked watching the pattern form as she worked on her pin art, more than when it was finished.

The wall was the biggest piece of pin art he'd ever seen. Every pin was labeled with a small slip of paper that had been printed out, clipped, and glued up there. There was no pattern he could see in the labels. Some were locations, some were names, others were numbers, and others were even abstract nouns like "Desperation" and "Unawareness." While he could see no pattern in them, there was clearly one in the great loom of crisscrossing lines. It wasn't much of a pattern, to be sure. No inverted cross or pentacle for the forensic psychologists to get excited about. Just a thick, even field of colored strings, with a distinct thickening in the density of intersections running from the upper right down to about a third of the way along from the bottom-right corner on the lower edge.

"Where's the boy?" asked Hammond.

"This"—Suydam shifted where he sat, as if trying to make himself more comfortable, and flinched slightly—"hurts more than I thought it would." He raised the hand he'd been holding to the wound and examined it. A drop of blood fell from the dark red fingers and palm. His expression was as though he were considering an unpleasant thought rather than watching his life leak out of him.

"The *boy*, Suydam! What the fuck did you do to him?"

Suydam looked up at Hammond as if finding a wry humor in all this. "I pinched him. Quite hard. He squealed like a good 'un. Like a little pig. I knew he was the right one for the job, soon as I saw him on the street. Whining little crybaby. Perfect." He nodded at the closed door farther along the wall. "He's in there, Officer. I hope you have candy. Whining little shit that he is."

Hammond nodded to Carter, but Carter was already moving to the door. He took position on one side and tried the handle.

Suydam watched it all with amusement. "There's no one else here, Detective. I'm done. No more tricks. No more games."

Carter ignored him. He opened the door and followed through in a crouch.

A moment later, he called back, "He's here! Looks unharmed!"

"See?" said Suydam to Hammond. "I'm all done. The jig is up. The dance is over."

"Shut up," said Hammond. He called back to Carter, "Don't bring the kid in here. Call it in."

Suydam nodded. "Good idea. Coming in here might traumatize him, the poor baby."

Carter was already ahead of his partner, but was having trouble getting a signal for his cell. The building seemed to be steel framed, or maybe there was construction mesh in the walls. Either way, it was behaving like an unintentional Faraday cage as far as getting reception was concerned. He went to the window and finally got a one-bar signal.

In the other room, Suydam said weakly, "Hey, Detective. I think you killed me."

Hammond said nothing. He didn't say *good*, but he plainly thought it.

"Was planning on being dead already. Blizzard of bullets, you know. Suicide by cop." He coughed. "Seems to work out for everybody else who tries it. While we're waiting for me to go into shock, how's this? How about I tell you why I did it?"

"I don't care, Suydam."

"Oh. Okay. Okay. How about I tell you what all that's about?" He nodded at the psycho wall.

Hammond glanced at it. He really, *really* wanted to tear it down, but he knew it had to stay intact until it had been recorded. He envied the people who would finally get to cut every thread, pull out every nail, remove every label. He hated the look of the threads, like a thick layer of web. He hated how this expressed just what was so fucked up about Suydam, and how Suydam had created it like a work of art. He glared at it, following the threads with his eyes. He hardly noticed that Suydam was still speaking. Hammond didn't listen, but he heard.

Carter told Thiago Mata to stay where he was, that the bad man had been caught, and that Thiago would soon be back with his mom. He went back into the other room, the loom of madness on the wall.

Carter saw Hammond shoot himself through the mouth. He saw Suydam dead and smiling. He saw the caul of Suydam's insanity, his perception, his reason, and his reasons hung upon the wall. There must have been a breeze in the room, for it seemed to swell slowly outward before lapsing back.

Carter understood none of it, and that was just as well.

It was a difficult public relations pitch. The serial killer without a nickname, known as the "Child-Catcher," had been quickly and successfully run to ground before he could harm his most recent victim. The boy, Thiago Mata, had been rescued unharmed, and gentle questioning by child services had revealed he had suffered nothing at the hands of Martin Suydam but for being pinched, once and viciously, on his upper arm. He wanted to tell the child psychologist all about that at great length and repeatedly. He had a bruise, here, see? Thiago didn't care about the abduction, the ride in the pickup, the old building, or any of that. He really resented being pinched, however. The man had told him to cry out as if hurt, and he had tried, but it hadn't satisfied the man, who became angry and pinched Thiago hard here, see? On the upper arm. There's a bruise, see?

Two detectives, hearing a cry, had due cause to enter the premises. They had encountered Suydam, who, on being challenged, aimed a gun at one of the detectives. The detective, Charlie Hammond, fired upon Suydam once. He hit Suydam in the stomach with a 9mm round, which perforated the lower border of the spleen and the mesocolon, severing the splenic artery, before hitting and jamming into the spine. Suydam hemorrhaged massively, the body cavity filling with blood, and lapsed into shock within a few minutes before dying.

This was all to the good. Then the heroic cops narrative hit the rocks when the shooter stuck his pistol in his mouth and sucked on a 9mm himself. There was no reason for it.

Charlie Hammond was a fifteen-year veteran. His psych reports were clean, his home life was simple. He was once divorced, amicably and on the grounds of mutual incompatibility. She had moved to Chicago, and they still corresponded regularly by e-mail.

He drank in moderation, and got drunk maybe once a year, always in company. There was no secret drinking, judging by his apartment afterward. He was in a six-month relationship with a paramedic whom he'd met through the job. It was going well.

Charlie had no imagination, not the kind that makes people brood. When anyone who knew him was told he had killed himself, the first reaction was always disbelief. *Charlie? Charlie Hammond? Are we talking about the same guy?*

The department's PR people mulled it over for a while and settled on referring to the entire posse of police who were en route to the house in Red Hook when it all went down as "the arresting officers," Suydam dying when he aimed a gun at police, and one of the officers tragically dying due to an accidental weapon discharge. They'd worry about the fallout when it was all yesterday's news.

That was for public consumption. Internally, Charlie shot himself because "the balance of his mind was disturbed." It could happen to anyone.

Carter thought of the last time but one that he saw Charlie, angry with Suydam, but in complete control of himself. Then the last time, crying and laughing, tears on his face, the pistol between his teeth. He knew Charlie Hammond. For two years they'd been partners, day in, day out. He knew Hammond's moods, his enthusiasms, his pet hatreds. He knew Charlie Hammond as well as anyone else on earth, and he just could not draw a line between those two moments. Carter could not begin to imagine what had happened in the three or four minutes he was out of the room, checking on the boy and making the call.

Martin Suydam had wanted to die, that much was obvious. The blatant kidnap in broad daylight using a vehicle registered to him. Using the boy's cry to bring in the police he knew were out in the street. Provoking fire by waving an empty pistol at them. Suicide by cop, an unusually well-developed plan for it. Why he should want that was another thing.

Hammond's funeral came and went. His ex flew in from Chicago to attend, and she wept real tears at the graveside. His girlfriend was still in shock; she'd seen him just a few hours before when their paths had crossed. He'd been fine, talking about taking her out before the end of the week. Good times. His ex sat with her afterward, and they talked quietly.

Carter felt like an intruder. Every cop present knew he'd been right there when it happened, and couldn't say a word as to the "why" of it. Some of them seemed to resent him, as if it was his fault. Others pitied him, and Carter liked that less still.

He stuck it for barely six months after that. He got a new partner, but there was no empathy between them at all. The guy had come up from Miami and pretty obviously wasn't happy about it. Carter never did find out why he had transferred if he hated New York so much. There were rumors he'd been forced out of Miami, but

Carter didn't care about the gossip one way or another; he simply didn't want to be a cop anymore.

He handed in his resignation, astounding his lieutenant, who then spent an hour trying to talk him out of it. If he stayed on for another six or so years, the lieutenant argued, he could take early retirement instead. Why jump now when he'd covered half the distance? Carter couldn't give him a straight answer. He didn't have one even for himself. It was just time to go, that was all. He missed Charlie, and the job wasn't the same anymore. It was time to go.

He didn't mention the dreams he still had, of Charlie standing there with the gun in his mouth. Except, in his dreams, Suydam wasn't dead yet. He was sitting there, just like he had been, but he was looking at Carter. Carter could never quite read the expression on Suydam's face in the dreams. It wasn't a nightmare where things were arranged to scare him, it wasn't as if Suydam was grinning like Freddy Krueger or any shit like that. It was more like Suydam was in a bad situation, had made his best play to get out of it, and failed. He looked desperate. He looked scared. He looked hopeless.

Then the *clack* of gunmetal against teeth, and Carter's first thought was always, *Don't do that, you'll chip your enamel*, and then the gun went off.

Now Charlie was dead, and Suydam was dead. Suydam always went from being alive to dead at the shot, without actually dying. Suydam was alive, or he was dead. In the dreams, there was no transition.

The dream didn't end there. Carter would turn to go and get the boy, but he would stop because there was something behind him. He turned, and there was nothing there but two dead men, and the psycho wall. The threads billowed as if there was a wind blowing through the wall.

When he went to fetch Thiago Mata, sometimes he was alive, and sometimes he was dead, skull cracked open and amateur surgery carried out on his brain. Either way, he always complained about the bruise on his arm. Once, and once only, the dead version of Thiago Mata told Carter why Suydam had been killing boys, but Carter didn't understand the words—simple, English words—and awoke confused and frustrated.

Daniel Carter did nothing at all for a month after resigning from the NYPD. Then he printed off a DOS-0075-f-l-a from the Department of State's Division of Licensing Services site, and applied for a license. It took a while for him to think of five people to put down as character witnesses, mainly because he would need their signatures and he wanted the thing finished and ready to go as soon as possible. He ended up spending a full day finding the ones he'd chosen and having them sign. It made him feel like a bail enforcement agent, another license the DOS-0075-f-l-a covered. He had checked the first box, though.

APPLICATION AS (Check only ONE):
X *Private Investigator*

While Carter waited for the bureaucracy to sort that out for him, he downloaded another PDF, printed it out, and filled in as much as he could until he could find an office. He was going to need a business address; the home address he'd used on the private investigator's license application looked halfhearted to him. He wanted a real business address this time, something real to enter into the PD 643-041 Handgun License Application. He filled it out with particular attention to section one of the "Letter of Necessity," a detailed explanation as to why the applicant's "employment requires the carrying of a concealed handgun."

Chapter 3

FACTS CONCERNING THE LATE ALFRED HILL

The office was three blocks away from Suydam's house. At least Carter didn't have to go past there when driving to and from his apartment.

The Suydam house was sure to be demolished. The locals didn't like having a "murder house" in their neighborhood, and a developer had already stepped forward, offering to demolish and clear the site. They'd made a very small attempt to pass this off as civic altruism, but nobody thought they wanted anything but the real estate, and the developer gave up the pretense quickly.

The house had a cellar, and Carter was glad he hadn't seen it. Suydam had carried out his experiments in altered perception there, and the bodies of the remaining boys were found under fresh concrete in a subcellar. Suydam himself had consumed industrial quantities of hallucinogens—LSD, *Salvia divinorum*, psilocybin, and, his personal favorite, DMT—and painstakingly noted his experiences. These he had tabulated in a complex system that was identified as being largely based on the Aarne-Thompson classification system for folklorists. These sets and subsets were, in turn, weighted by an apparently arbitrary system of significances rendered as numbers to two decimal places. The system was sketched out in detail, though without anything but the most abstruse explanation, in the notebooks discovered in Suydam's bedroom. The system was mapped out more briefly on the left-hand side of the psycho wall.

The rest of the wall defied analysis. Several hundred pictures were taken to form a detailed mosaic, and a CSU tech undertook to create a database of the wall in her own time. The case was, after all, closed.

Carter was obliged to attend the inquiry into the shooting, and it was deemed justifiable, Suydam intent on being an asshole to the grave by provoking the police into shooting him. It got out that Hammond had shot himself, and one tabloid made a front cover story of it. By the next day somebody famous for being famous had suffered a wardrobe malfunction, and a random cop eating his gun was no way near as newsworthy as a celebrity nipple.

Now here Carter was, a gumshoe.

He hadn't been entirely sure what he was getting into, but it turned out that it was exactly what he had expected and nothing more. None of the additional work that he hoped would lift the job out of the mundane ever came along. Most of it was divorce work, some skip traces, background checks, and missing persons where the person obviously wanted to stay missing, but had left somebody behind who isn't so cool with that notion. Very occasionally he had to attend court as a witness. Far too often he spent his entire day on the Internet, accessing assorted databases—tax, voter registration, DMV. He'd only used such databases peripherally when he'd been a cop; usually somebody else was quite happy to do it. Now, however, he had a notebook full of passwords for privileged access databases that the public never got a sniff of, a notebook of the kind he had been told by his computer guy not to keep, as it was a bad security risk. *Fuck that*, thought Carter. How was he supposed to keep all those passwords straight otherwise?

That morning he had a client turn up in the office, which was something that didn't happen so much. Usually contact was made by phone or by e-mail. Perhaps only one in five clients, if that, actually wanted to sit in his office and talk to him, face-to-face.

None of the one in five was ever a smoky femme fatale, talking in one-liners and sitting provocatively on the corner of his desk. The desk was from IKEA, as was the single filing cabinet where he kept hard copies of contracts, and so were the chairs on either side of his desk. None of them would have suited a sultry femme fatale disporting herself upon them. She would have seemed out of place in the pine-toned office, with its pine-toned furniture and the sandy-haired man behind the desk with the face of a poetic boxer, as an ex-girlfriend of Carter's had once described him.

This time it had been a woman in the uniform of a diner waitress on her midmorning break. She said she had finally had enough of her husband's "fooling around," but Carter saw that what she really resented was his reluctance to pull his weight. It wasn't that her husband was fucking around, it was that he was doing it on her nickel. She wanted a divorce, and she wanted everything. Carter thought she had a good chance of getting it, too. He explained the legalities of what he did, and what sort of evidence would be necessary to get the day in court she wanted. He took her details and those of her husband, talked through what sort of plan he would use to gather evidence and how much it would come to. She didn't balk when he mentioned money, which was good. She'd made some inquiries of her own, and had made sure she had the money available for his services. He understood he was being paid in better than a year's tips; she had been planning this for a while.

He saw her out, and crossed to the window to watch her leave the small office block's side exit and walk to her car. He liked to do this; people skimmed his life at a tangent and then were gone again. It was easy to believe that they puffed into smoke when they walked out of his office. Watching them cross the parking lot kept them vital just a little bit longer.

He watched her drive away in an old white Honda, turned, and found Henry Weston sitting quietly in the chair on the "client" side of the desk.

He didn't know the man was Henry Weston at that point. He had no idea who Henry Weston was, nor had he ever heard of him. But now there was a man of about five feet six who couldn't have been an ounce over 120 pounds, with neat dark hair parted on the left side, wearing a three-piece suit that wasn't flashy, nor was it cheap.

Carter hadn't heard a thing. The spring in the door handle creaked when compressed. The upper hinge squeaked slightly. These were both noises to which he had grown very familiar over the last eighteen months.

The man who would presently turn out to be Henry Weston smiled at Carter. It was a very open, disarming smile. Nothing smug or supercilious about it; it was the smile of a man who'd heard a good joke and wished to share it.

"I'm sorry," said Carter. "I didn't hear you come in."

"I came in," said the man, as if to reassure him.

Carter didn't need reassurance on that point, but it was kind of the man to offer it, all the same.

"Can I help you, Mr. . . . ?" Carter held out his hand.

The man regarded it for a moment, then remembered his manners. He rose to his feet (the chair clicked a little when he rose, Carter thought. Why had it been silent when he sat?) and shook Carter's hand. It was a firm, dry handshake. Possibly too firm; he didn't try to crush Carter's bones, but the flesh itself was quite unyielding, more like shaking a neoprene hand than one of flesh and blood.

"My name is Henry Weston," said the man. "I have a card." This he carefully extracted from his jacket's breast pocket and passed to Carter for examination.

Carter took it and sat down, gesturing to Weston that he should retake his own seat. He did so, and it clicked as it took his weight.

Carter examined the card. *Henry Weston*, it read. *Lawyer*. There was the address of the law firm, Weston Edmunds, in Providence.

"Weston," said Carter. He tapped the card. "Of Weston Edmunds?"

"Yes," said Weston, still delighted with the world. "Yes, indeed. That is me."

"Joint owner."

"Sole owner. Mr. Edmunds is no longer with us, alas. But we'd just had the stationery printed, so it seemed a shame to change the name of the law firm."

Carter didn't find that funny, but Weston was amused enough for both of them. Carter opened the browser on his laptop and carried out a brief search. "Founded 1925," he said, keeping the surprise out of his voice.

"Indeed so. Mr. Edmunds died some considerable time ago. The firm has remained a family concern of the Westons ever since. And here I am."

And here he was. This wasn't sitting well with Carter; the Weston Edmunds website showed he was not some provincial lawyer sitting in his office and just handling small local business, like some sort of Jimmy Stewart character. Weston Edmunds handled complex litigations, intellectual property and communications rights, patents, and venture capital. It had a staff of more than a hundred, and they worked in a very nice office building, if the website was being honest. Weston must be a very rich man.

And here he was.

"Is this a . . . personal matter?" asked Carter.

"Yes!" Weston seemed even more delighted. "Yes, it is. There is good news!" His smile vanished and he looked aghast, as if he'd insulted Carter unintentionally. "Oh, but there is bad news, too. May I see some identification before we go any further?"

"You're in my office," said Carter. "You know who I am."

"I know I am in the right place, but it would be infelicitous if it turned out I was talking to the wrong man. It is a legal nicety, but I must insist on seeing some item of photographic identification."

Carter took out his wallet with ill grace, and passed Weston his investigator's license. He had already found a picture of Weston on his website, so didn't necessarily require some ID in reciprocation, although it was tempting to ask for it in retaliation. After all, the site could be bogus. But no, he didn't really believe that, and he himself was not the retaliatory type, in any case.

Weston looked at it for barely a moment before passing it back. "As I say, a nicety, but a necessity." His smile deepened, a man continually delighted with everything. Carter wondered how much of his vast fortune was going into medications. Few men are that pleased with the world and their fellow humans, and not one of that few is a lawyer.

Carter accepted his license back and returned it to his wallet. "You said there was bad news."

The smile fled again. "There is. I am so very sorry. I bring bad tidings. Alfred Hill is dead."

Carter shook his head. "I don't know any Alfred Hill."

Weston seemed curious rather than surprised by this. "You are sure?"

Carter racked his memory, but nothing emerged. "I don't think so."

"No family by that name?"

Here Carter was on firmer ground. "Definitely no Hills in my family. That, I would have remembered. No, I'm sorry, Mr. Weston, you've made a wasted trip."

"Splendid." The smile returned as if at the flick of a switch. "If you do not know Alfred Hill, then you will not feel any grief at his passing. That leaves only good news." He lifted a slim aged-leather briefcase from the floor beside his chair. Carter looked at the old-style satchel case with some envy for what it implied; that Weston was so rich, he could use things that were comfortable for him rather than having to project an image all the time.

Weston undid the case's clasp and removed a handful of documents, apparently its only contents. "You are the sole beneficiary of his estate. It does not comprise a great deal, but one is grateful to be remembered at all, hmmm?"

"I don't understand this. I've never heard of the man."

"He had heard of you, obviously. The identification in his last will and testament is quite specific." Weston did not stop smiling. "There is no mistake. Somehow, you have touched upon this man's life, and he decided to reward you for that at the time of his passing."

"There's nothing in the will to say why?"

"Nothing." Weston removed a piece of folded cream paper from an onionskin envelope and passed it over. "The will is brief, but exact."

Carter read it carefully, then again. "Can I make a copy of this?"

Weston spread his hands. "You may keep that copy, Mr. Carter."

"Isn't this the original?" It certainly seemed like it; the paper was heavy—at least thirty-two-pound bond, probably more—and felt expensive. The signatures seemed to have a different sheen from the printed text of the will when he angled them in the light, as if they were handwritten and not scanned and copied.

Weston was unconcerned. "I don't believe so, but even if it is, what of it? You are the sole beneficiary, after all."

Carter read the will through carefully, paying special attention to the details of Alfred Hill, and then to the nature of the bequest itself. The former told him nothing except Hill's home address, and the latter turned out to be the same thing.

"He's left me his house?"

Through the two or three minutes that Carter had been read-ing, Weston had simply sat there and watched him, the genial smile never leaving his face. "Indeed."

"I don't have any use for a house in Providence."

"Hardly my concern, Mr. Carter. I have executed Alfred Hill's last will and testament, and my role in this is complete. Do what you will with the Hill residence."

Carter skimmed through the document again. "How did he die?"

"How did Mr. Hill die? I thought you didn't know him?"

"I don't. I'm just interested."

"The cause of Mr. Hill's death is unknown. Indeed, even its occurrence is uncertain."

Carter looked at him. "You're saying there's no body?"

"Mr. Hill is missing, presumed dead. The court has ruled him so *in absentia*."

"He's been missing for seven years?"

"Seven years with sight of neither hide nor hair, Mr. Carter. Without communication with friends or family, without a trace at any and all of his known haunts, and our diligent inquiries have revealed no banking or tax activity. We hired private investiga-tors to find what they could, which was nothing. A tiny bit ironic that the trail ultimately ended in the office of another private in-vestigator, isn't it, Mr. Carter?" Weston was still smiling. Carter wondered if it would start to hurt after a while. "I enjoy irony. There's so little to surprise one in life anymore. Such coincidences are small delights."

Carter didn't care about just how much Weston gloried in the rich tapestry of life. "Then this property has been unoccupied for *seven years*? What condition is it in?"

"I'm sure that I have no idea, Mr. Carter. I am no Realtor, only a humble lawyer." Strangely, Carter didn't find the word "humble" coming from the mouth of the senior partner of a large law firm as disgusting as he might have. Weston was a rich man, of that there was no doubt, but the money truly seemed to be just a side effect of his job to him.

"So I might go there and find it ruined, or burned out, or gone altogether?"

"Well, I doubt that, as it was searched pursuant to the claim of death *in absentia*. It was still there then. Nothing untoward was drawn to my attention, so I suppose it still has its roof on, at the very least."

Carter considered; the drive up to Providence would take the best part of four hours. He couldn't start on the surveillance for the divorce job until the following week because the subject was currently out of town, and he only had a couple of searches left to do on a background check he'd taken on the previous day. Those could wait.

"Okay, I'll have a look at it," he said.

"Excellent," said Weston. "Even if it isn't a luxury condominium with gold-plated taps, Mr. Carter, I'm sure the simple pleasure of a windfall will go some way toward compensating you for your time." He gestured to the will. "You have the address there. Here"—he produced a pristine white envelope from those he had taken from the briefcase—"are the deeds, here is a local map with the location marked—"

"My car has GPS."

"Of course it does. And here are the keys." He produced a key ring holding two Yales and a mortise key. "My people tell me the latter is for the rear door, which was double bolted on the inside, so I shouldn't bother with that if I were you."

"Your people."

"My investigators." The thin wad of documents was now in Carter's possession, and Weston made a small spread of his hands, like a magician demonstrating that he had made them vanish. "I think that concludes our business." He stood, and Carter rose, too. "It has been a pleasure to meet you, and I hope your inheritance gives you cause for happiness. Enjoy it in good health, Mr. Carter."

They shook hands once again, and Carter accompanied Weston out into the hall. When the lawyer was out of sight on the stairs, Carter closed his door and walked to the window. More than usual, he wanted to watch the man out in the real world beyond his office. He had suffered a hard enough time believing in Weston while he had been in the same room as him, never mind now that he was out of sight.

Carter waited five minutes, but Weston did not appear in the parking lot. Carter went out into the hallway and looked over the banister, but there was no one down there at all. Finally, he descended the stairs himself and walked out the entrance. There was no sign of Weston.

Carter concluded there was no mystery; he had left by the rear service entrance. An eccentric choice, but Weston seemed to enjoy doing things differently. The world whirled on, and everything made sense.

Chapter 4

PROVIDENCE

Carter had been to Providence a handful of times in his life, and never by choice. It was always something to do with a case, or to help somebody out, but he had never willingly been to the place. He didn't like the city at all, but he couldn't have told you why. He knew the dislike was irrational; that didn't mitigate it in the slightest. The small flurry of optimism he had felt that this unexpected inheritance might be worth something was dampened long before the lawyer Weston had belittled it by implication; the discovery that it was in Providence, of all places, had already killed his buzz magnificently.

It was an old city, but he didn't feel that when he went there. It felt artificial to him, as if it was procedurally generated by some video game. There was never a sense of place he could feel comfortable with, just the nagging idea that they were constructing the city as he traveled into it, and struck it like a stage set when he left. He had once read a book by William S. Burroughs called *The Place of Dead Roads*. In it, there was an artificial town run by a conspiracy. It looked like any other place, but if you hung around long enough, you'd realize the old-timers were always having the same conversation in the same words, that the same things happened in the street again and again, that the existence of the town as a town was nothing more than a mechanical tableau, designed to encourage the casual visitor in the belief that all was normal, and that the casual visitor should move on.

Providence felt like that to Carter, except he could swear he could hear the clockwork whirring behind the bland facades of the buildings, the flutter of script pages when he turned away. He did not like Providence at all, and he didn't care what Providence thought of him in return.

The address was in an area to the northeast of the city he had not heard of before—Hastings. Carter's dislike of Providence grew calcified and unforgiving as he navigated the streets of Hastings. Everything seemed to be of white clapboard construction, every house looking like every other house. It was like driving through Stepford.

Carter felt a headache starting to nag. The GPS said he was close, so he pulled into the parking lot of a small strip mall next to a row of stores in older buildings. He bought himself some aspirin and a bottle of water, swallowed a couple of tablets, and went to find the golden castle he'd inherited.

He walked down the row of stores—hairdressers, sandwich shop, vacuum cleaner repairs, car parts, a couple boarded up—and was surprised to realize that the numbers were closer than he'd gauged to the address. He wasn't sure what to think when he reached 1117 Havilland Street, and found it was a store, too. To be exact, a bookstore. To be perfectly exact, a functioning bookstore.

Hill's Books he read on the sign. *Antiquarian & Secondhand*. The store window was lined with an amber-colored plastic film, to protect the books from sunlight, he guessed. Beyond it, he could see sets of encyclopedias, Dickens, Henry James, Shakespeare, and examples of prints like maps and stiffly engraved soldiers of the Continental Army. Everything looked yellowed and old, not entirely due to the colored light.

Inside, he could see electric lights were on, and the sign hanging in the door said *Open*. With misgivings, Carter entered.

A bell, an actual bell with a coiled brass striker mounted by it, struck a bright note as he swung the door open. The shop smelled just like every old bookshop he had ever been in. Not a huge number, but the smell was distinctive and not unpleasant. Everything other than the books seemed varnished and polished—the floorboards, the shelves, and the fancy paneling that rose up to hip height on the walls. It didn't look new. Nothing in the shop looked new.

No, that wasn't quite correct. Behind the counter, an African American woman was watching him, an open book on her lap. She was, he guessed, somewhere around her mid-twenties, not conventionally pretty, with broad cheekbones that would have given her the look of a lazy cat but for the very intelligent dark eyes that were currently looking at him. Not conventionally pretty, perhaps, but he found her attractive all the same. She wasn't simply looking at him, he realized; she was assessing him.

Seeing that he was studying her in return, she smiled. "Hi," she said, rising from her stool. She closed the book and put it on the counter by her. He unconsciously noted the title: *Diableries: Stereoscopic Adventures in Hell*. It took her a long time to get from "H" to the last "i" in "Hi." She had a voice that made Katharine Hepburn sound like Phyllis Diller. "Can I help you?"

Carter couldn't decide whether the smile was fake, flirtatious, or just patronizing.

"I guess so," he said. "This is 1117 Havilland, yeah?"

The smile faded. "Yes," she said. Her tone had become more cautious.

"I . . . Look, this is going to sound weird. Do you know an Alfred Hill?"

"He's my uncle." She had been leaning lightly on the counter with her fingertips, but now she straightened up.

Carter wasn't sure what to make of the present tense in that answer. Despite himself, his cop instincts were starting to nag.

"You've seen him recently?"

"What are you? An investigator? Debt collector?"

Carter looked around him. The shop was in pristine condition: the stock properly displayed, the interior neat, the exterior maintained. On a shelf behind the counter was a little cartoonish vinyl figure of some sort of monster, bright green, with tentacles dangling from its face and thin bat wings on its back.

Carter had been expecting a musty old house with maybe a few shingles missing and probably a few mice running around. A functioning bookstore with staff in it was nowhere in his plans.

"No. Well, yes, I *am* an investigator, but that's not why I'm here."

"No? Why all the questions, then?"

Carter knew this wasn't going to go down well, but bit the bullet and said it anyway. He pointed vaguely around him. "This place. It's mine."

The woman's face hardened. "What the actual *fuck* are you talking about?"

"You always talk to strangers like that?" She said nothing, but just glared at him. He figured she might throw a punch if he didn't explain things quickly. "Your uncle's been missing seven years, is that right? He's been declared legally dead. Didn't you know that?"

Her expression of surprise being quickly overwhelmed by anger indicated clearly that she had not known that at all. "This is the first I've heard about it. Who the hell . . . ? How could that happen without them telling me? I work here. He's my uncle, damn it! How is it . . . ? Who told you?"

"Your uncle's lawyer did."

"He did *what*? How could he do that without warning me? Wait . . . why was he talking to you?"

"I'm the beneficiary of your uncle's will."

"I haven't—"

"I'm the *sole* beneficiary."

The anger left her as suddenly as it had come. She looked at him as if he'd just come in to tell her he was very sorry, but he'd just run over her dog. She sat down heavily on the stool.

"This isn't right," she said finally.

"I'm sorry," said Carter, and he was. He knew there were plenty of people in the world who would be enjoying themselves in his situation. *Thanks very much for all your hard work. Now fuck off while I strip this place of whatever it's worth.* He wasn't one of them. "You've been working here for seven years without your uncle?"

"I dropped out of postgrad. He gave me the job." She looked hopelessly at him. "Not even a year later he didn't come down one day." She nodded at the ceiling, and Carter understood her to mean there was an apartment above. "I went to check on him, but he wasn't there. His car was still around the back, but no sign of him. He hadn't come back by the evening, so I called the police. Yeah, it must be seven years. Yeah . . ."

She reached under the counter and pulled out several ledgers. She checked the covers where accounting years were written in ballpoint until she found the one she wanted. She flicked through the pages. "Son of a bitch," she said, her finger on an entry. "Seven years ago today." She looked up angrily at him. "You didn't hang around, did you? Couldn't wait to grab the place."

"You've got me all wrong," said Carter. "The lawyer came to me. I hadn't even heard of your uncle before this morning. I don't know why he named me in his will at all. This is as weird to me as it is to you. I came up here thinking I'd inherited some run-down, abandoned house. A working bookstore . . . I wasn't expecting this at all."

She was looking at him suspiciously. "You didn't know Alfred?"

"Never even heard his name before."

"So who are you?"

"I'm Dan Carter."

There was a flicker in her face at that, but he couldn't exactly identify what it meant. It wasn't surprise or recognition nearly as much as it was realization, but the expression was gone in a moment.

The bell rang again, and the woman looked across at the entrance. This time she was startled. A man was making his way past the freestanding bookshelves to the counter. Carter sized him up very quickly. He knew a real Armani suit when he saw one, a pair of Salvatore Ferragamos that wouldn't have left much change from a grand, and a shirt and tie that he suspected could well be Kiton. He looked at the man's face—not movie star handsome, but self-assured and undeniably charismatic, blond and blue-eyed—and thought, *Politician*.

"Hi," said the man to the woman behind the counter, but his gaze slid over Carter. "Not interrupting business, am I?"

"Ken, I—" The woman seemed more flustered now than she had at the discovery that the bookstore belonged to Carter. "I wasn't expecting you for an hour. It's—" She shook her head hopelessly. Carter felt sorry for her. It wasn't a good day.

"What's going on?" said Ken, with the half smile of somebody whose instinct is to be friendly, but who will tear off your head if you turn out to be a problem. He looked curiously at Carter. "Is there a problem?"

"No. Yes. Yes, there's a problem. Alfred's been declared legally dead."

"Alfred . . ."

"My uncle, Ken! Hill's Books?" She ran her hand distractedly through her hair, black drizzled with red. "My uncle."

"I'm sorry, Emily. I know it must be a shock, but it can't be a complete one, surely? You've always known the day was going to come."

"Yes, but . . ." She looked at Ken and sagged with defeat. "I kinda thought I'd get this place."

Ken raised an eyebrow. "The will's been read so soon?" Emily nodded. "Then what's happening to it?"

There seemed no point in dragging it out. "I've inherited it," said Carter.

Ken squared up to him, no longer smiling at all. "And who are you?"

Dan decided he didn't like Ken. It wasn't a great revelation; he disliked people who wore suits worth more than his car. It wasn't envy so much as irritation with the sense of entitlement that came with such lifestyles. He could put up with most things, but arrogance—whether from some gangbanger or this Ivy League fuck—he had no time for.

"What's your interest?"

"Emily is my girlfriend," said Ken, indicating Emily with a backward jerk of his thumb. He didn't look at her as he did it. "I have an interest."

Carter looked at him, then her, and back to Ken. It wasn't an obvious pairing. In the movie, she would be played by Zoë Kravitz and he would be played by Aaron Eckhart. It wouldn't be perfect casting, but that was the gist of it.

"I'm Daniel Carter," said Carter, and extended his hand. It was a measured gesture. Ken could ignore it and look an asshole, or he could accept it and lose the wind from his sails. Carter knew he would go for the political option, and he did.

He took Carter's hand and shook it one of those firm, dry handshakes, delivering a squeezing pressure of a precise number of Newtons decided upon by focus groups that politicians practice. Carter still didn't like him, and couldn't see that changing anytime soon.

"Ken Rothwell."

The Rothwells. Of course. It would be.

"How are you related to Alfred?" asked Rothwell.

"As far as I know, I'm not. This is as big a surprise to me as it was to . . ." He looked to the woman. "Emily, was it? We never really got around to introducing ourselves properly."

She nodded.

"As big a surprise as it was to Emily," Carter continued. "Out of the blue."

"So, what are you going to do with the place?"

"I have no idea. I didn't know there was a store at the address, a going concern. I'll have to think about it." He looked past Rothwell to Emily. "Maybe I can just sell it to you. I don't know what to do with a bookstore."

She shook her head quickly. "I can't. I couldn't afford it. Some of the stock, it's worth a lot, never mind the building itself."

So get your rich boyfriend to buy it for you, thought Carter.

"Emily, we need to get moving," said Rothwell. "One of the donors can't stay for the fund-raiser, so I need to talk to her before it starts. That's why I'm here early."

"Okay. Okay. I'll lock up."

Carter had been intending to drive back to Red Hook the same evening, but the idea seemed less appealing now. "What time are you in tomorrow?" he asked Emily. "We can plan what to do with this place."

"Plan?"

"You're invested in this store, I'm not. You have to get a say in what happens to it; it's only right."

"Oh." The thought that the store wasn't just going to be taken away from her had clearly not crossed her mind. This small revelation seemed to put some heart back into her. "I'll be in by half past eight."

"Great, I'll see you then. Are there any good hotels around here?"

"Not really. You'd have to drive a ways." She considered. "There's a sports shop across the street. If you get yourself a sleeping bag, you could sleep here. In the apartment. There's a bed, so you wouldn't be on the floor, but the bedding's been in the cupboard all this time. Sleeping bag would be best. Yeah, I'd need to see your papers before I can let you do that, though."

Carter nodded. He wanted to look the place over anyway, and there was still some daylight. He couldn't imagine wanting to sleep in a musty apartment, but he was curious to see what was up there. If it was all spiders and Miss Havisham's wedding feast, he'd go to a hotel.

"*You* need to get ready," warned Rothwell. "You go, I'll check Mr. Carter's papers." Emily looked like she was going to protest, but he was having none of it. "C'mon! Grab your stuff and go. I'll pick you up in half an hour. Can you be ready by then?"

"My hair—"

"Looks great. Go!"

She allowed herself to be cajoled to the door, where he relieved her of the store's keys, kissed her, and shooed her out into the street.

The door closed, and she was gone.

Rothwell came back, and Carter made a guess from his body language that they were heading into *all guys together* territory.

"Okay," said Ken, smiling a smile he'd gotten out of a can, "let's get this cleared up. You've got the documentation on you, yeah?"

He leaned on the counter as he spoke and grazed Carter's personal space without intruding into it. It was the sort of trick they taught at half-assed "being a people person" workshops. Carter knew the next move would be to attempt to form intimacy by finding common ground. He wasn't sure why Rothwell cared so much about being in Carter's good books. He probably could have bought Carter a dozen times over without scratching his fortune.

At times like this, Carter felt a small and brutal comfort in the weight of his Glock 19 sitting in its Blackhawk paddle holster at his waist. It was a stupid source of confidence, he knew. He could hardly draw on somebody just for being a dick—the gun would hardly ever be holstered if that were the case—but just having the option kept him calm at times like this, because he *didn't* want to be the guy who drew on somebody just for being a dick.

Instead, he took the wad of documents from his inside pocket and spread them on the countertop. He even managed to smile while doing it.

Rothwell didn't spend very long going through them. He had already decided Carter's claim was probably legitimate, it was plain. He was just going through them for appearances, and to cull a few facts.

"Came up from Red Hook, huh? How were the roads?"

Carter considered saying he had no idea; he'd come in his personal Learjet. Instead he said the drive was uneventful.

"What do you do, Mr. Carter?"

"Private investigator" was one of those job titles people hesitate before saying. It carries baggage, and both sides of a conversation know it. The only thing the PI doesn't know is whether the other side is going to think Sam Spade or some low-life bail-tracer.

"I'm an investigator," said Carter. Leaving "private" out covered a multitude of sins, real and imaginary.

Rothwell gave him a curious glance. "Hard job, from what I've heard. Not great money."

"It's okay," said Carter, recognizing it as the standard euphemism for "barely okay" as soon as it was out of his mouth.

Rothwell finished gathering whatever bits of information he wanted from the papers. Proving Carter's bona fides seemed almost an afterthought. He didn't ask for anything that might actually prove that the "Daniel Carter" mentioned in them was the same person who was standing in front of him.

"You want to sell it?"

"Maybe. I'll work something out with Emily."

Rothwell laughed. "No. I mean to *me*. I'll take it off your hands."

Carter said nothing.

"I can give it to Emily."

Carter still said nothing.

"As a present."

Carter knew enough about the landed gentry of New York and New England not to show even a flicker of surprise. Kenneth Rothwell was, for example, a lawyer in the family white shoe firm or, at least, he had a law degree and a salary. How much actual legal work he did was moot. Sinecure or real job, he was where he was because it was the right place for him, for he was a Rothwell, and a kindly and entirely partisan God blessed his every step. Yeah, buying a little indie bookstore was not such a big deal for Ken Rothwell.

"That's sweet," said Carter. He meant, *That's sickening.* Just a few minutes earlier he'd thought of Rothwell doing exactly this, and discarded the thought as too cynical. Now here was Ken, living down to expectations. "Let me think about it. I'm still kind of surprised about how this is all shaking out."

"Sure, sure," said Rothwell. He was all smiles and nods, but his eyes were cold. He held out the keys and dropped them into Carter's hand. "I'll leave these with you, Dan."

"Thanks," said Carter. He was going to say, "Thanks, Ken," but remembered in time that he was no longer in grade school. He didn't bother to mention that he already had a set of the keys. Now he had both, and that suited him fine.

"I don't know the alarm code," said Rothwell. He walked to the door, paused with his hand on the handle. "If you're staying the night, I guess that's unimportant."

Carter nodded, and Rothwell left.

The bell over the door struck its plangent little note as the door opened and closed. The tone seemed to hang in the air for a long time. It seemed very quiet in the bookstore. *His* bookstore.

Chapter 5

THE OUTSIDER

That morning he hadn't owned a bookstore, and now he did. He picked up the abandoned documents from the counter, felt the paper between his fingers, reassuring himself that they were real. He refolded them and put them back in his jacket. It was time to survey his domain.

He flipped the sign on the door to *Closed* and released the bolts on the Yales. Satisfied that the door was secure, he walked back into the body of the shop and looked at the shelves. He would have to take Emily's word for it that some of the books were worth something; he could tell Dante from Dan Brown, but that was about his limit. There were shelves of old, *old* encyclopedias, books on theology, philosophy, mathematics, botany. Biographies of people he'd never heard of, autobiographies of people who were interesting in their own minds, books on gardening, boating, and all kinds of other stuff he didn't care about. He found the fiction shelves and a whole section of vintage detective stories.

He ran his eye over the Hammetts and Chandlers, the Latimers and Thompsons, tales of hardboiled dicks in naked cities. There was still a mild kick to it, being in the same trade, but it was fading. Maybe one day he wouldn't feel anything at all, or just irritation at how it wasn't like that, it was never like that.

Carter didn't read so much anymore. He wished he did, but he never had the time, or he could never find a book that really grabbed him. Owning a bookstore was not a good fit with him. Rothwell would give him a good price, he was sure. He wasn't so sure he wanted to go that way, though. Part of it was personal dislike, true, but he also wondered what would actually happen. Rothwell would just hand the place over to Emily like he said he would? Or maybe he'd just quietly dismantle it to take it away from Emily. Either way—a patronizing "little pastime for the little lady" or getting rid of it so he was her only focus—Carter didn't like it. The more he thought about it, the more it appealed to him to keep the place a going concern. Maybe give Emily a 10 percent stake in the place to keep her involved, a bonus on top of her wages. Yeah, she'd like that. Even better, it would irritate the fuck out of Ken.

Cool.

The stairs to the second floor were in a combined kitchen/storage area at the back of the store behind a door. Carter stood on the lowest step and inhaled. The air did not seem especially musty. He went up.

The staircase rose directly into Alfred Hill's apartment, performing a right-hand turn to come out into a notional line that separated the front bedroom end of things from the rear bathroom and kitchenette. It felt claustrophobic there, not least because the walls were as dense with bookshelves as the store below. Dark wood and a dull rainbow of book spines served to eat most of the light coming through the small front window. By it was a double bed, stripped of bedding and the mattress wrapped in plastic. The room smelled fresh. Carter realized that the building's only toilet was upstairs, so Emily must have had to come up here a few times a day. She had kept the place dusted and aired.

The mattress looked clean, and the idea of sleeping here no longer seemed so unreasonable. He made up his mind to go across the street and buy a sleeping bag. It probably wasn't very adult of him, but he liked the sense of this small adventure. He wouldn't eat there, but he would get some basic stuff while he was out.

He was just finalizing these plans when he heard the bell ring on the door below. His first reaction was his heart sinking as he thought a customer had come in and he would have to explain that the store was shut. Then he remembered he had turned the sign to *Closed*. He had locked the door and tested it. It must be Emily.

He took a step toward the top of the stairs.

But she had given her keys to Rothwell, and he had handed them on to Carter.

He walked down the stairs as quietly as the wooden steps would allow. The storeroom/coffee-making area was empty. He moved into the store proper and found it empty, too. The tone of the bell still hung in the air. He looked closely at it. It hung motionless.

The sports store was having a sale, and Carter got a good deal on a sleeping bag. On an impulse, he bought a cheap foam roll to lay over the mattress. He had no intention of sleeping on plastic and being disturbed by its crackling all night, but part of him maintained an irrational belief that the old but barely used mattress would harbor bedbugs. Exactly how they'd survived for seven years without feeding was part of the irrationality of it.

He hesitated before buying the bedroll. He knew he didn't really need it, just as he knew he hadn't really heard the door chime. Logically, he knew there was no way it had rung. The door was locked, the rear of the store was secure, and he was the only person in the building. There was, he admitted willingly, the possibility of something other than the door ringing it. Perhaps it rang in sympathy with other frequencies. A passing truck might have made the building shudder. Perhaps even the sunlight filtering through the tinted windows was enough to make the metal of the spring expand and shake the bell as the tension was released. These were all logical possibilities. Carter had never seen anything truly inexplicable other than what went on in some people's minds.

Like Martin Suydam.

Carter was eating in an Italian restaurant he had found a couple of blocks from the bookstore, a little family-run place. His fork paused, halfway between the dish of puttanesca and his mouth. He hadn't thought of Suydam for months. Hammond still troubled him almost daily, but Suydam had faded from his memory until now. He'd never seen a man so happy to be gutshot.

The restaurant owner saw the slowly lowering fork and bustled over with dismay to make sure everything was all right. Carter assured him that the food was fine, and the owner was content to refill Carter's wineglass and leave him alone with his thoughts once more.

So . . . Suydam. Carter still drank with some of the guys from the 76th and knew more than he should about how the clear-up of the case had gone. The man might have been dead, but missing child cases that had been suspected as his doing still had to be confirmed one way or another, and there was the chance that he was responsible for out-of-state abductions.

As it turned out, the educated guesses had been good: from the remains extracted from beneath the cellar floor and another body found dumped exactly where Suydam's exhaustive notes said it would be, all the disappearances ascribed to him were confirmed. His notes said nothing about taking any boys from outside the counties of the New York metropolitan area at all, and all but a couple were taken outside the five boroughs.

The notes were unusual in as far as they made sense. They were cogent and ordered, which came as a relief to the officers who'd had to read them. There was none of the cramped writing, over-writing, marginalia (relevant and not), random additions, and such that were usually the mark of a troubled mind. Suydam presented his thoughts as clearly as a scientist recording his experiments for posterity. But while reading the notes might have been straight-forward, their contents were still wearing on the psyche.

Suydam was obsessed with the limits of human perception, even the limits of machines. He wrote at length on something he called "The Twist," always capitalized. The detective who told Carter that detail didn't even bother making a joke about dancing. It was obvious they'd tried every variation of that in the precinct house and ground whatever few grains of humor they could find there out of it long ago.

"The Twist" itself was not explained. From his writings, Suydam took its nature as self-evident, and felt no impulse to explain it in notes that were always meant only for himself. He was not writing one of the ranting declarations of purpose so beloved of mass killers, after all. The psychiatrists and psychologists who studied the transcriptions and facsimiles could offer no explanation beyond the obvious, that Suydam absolutely believed in The Twist, and that all his efforts were bent on perceiving it more clearly.

To do so, he had attempted to hotwire the brains of young boys. He needed them young because their brains had not yet finished their maturation and were more "perceptive" than adult examples. More than once, he decried the "fossilized" and "pro-grammed" state of his own brain, its synapses long since in place, and "too much learning and experience" cluttering the halls of its architecture. The victims were all male because Suydam explicitly stated that women have enough violence visited upon them without him adding to it. It was comments like that, and parts of the procedure that were intended to be as humane as possible, that set Suydam aside from the body of serial killers. He had no psychosexual motivation. His notes even contained his worries that the abductions might be considered sexual in nature, and that people might think him a pedophile. Being a child killer was acceptable in Suydam's world. Being mistaken for a pedophile was not.

"The sickest thing?" Carter's friend had told him over beers. "Out of a whole shitload of sickness? The sickest thing was that the fuck was doing it for the good of humanity. This guy was a reg'lar altruist."

"Madness," said Carter, borrowing wisdom from elsewhere, "is when you keep doing the same thing and expect different results."

"Yeah!" The friend raised his bottle to this. His face clouded. "Yeah. The last three kids, he said he was getting there. The Mottram boy, he said he'd had a breakthrough. Estes he was real excited about, wrote that he knew what he'd been doing wrong. He'd get it right next time."

"That'd be the Watts kid?"

"Yeah . . ."

"And?"

The detective slung back his beer. "There weren't any more notes. Not after he took Georgie Watts. The notes just stop."

The notes just stop.

Carter thought about it while he walked back to Hill's Books with his purchases. Why would they just stop? Why would the assiduous note taker stop taking notes? He was still active, after all. He took one more victim. No, not really a victim. More like bait. He'd never intended to harm Thiago Mata, just to provoke the police into finding him quickly and to kill him. Hell of a thing. Suicide by cop. Suicide.

Why by cop? Why at all?

Carter shook his head slightly, an outward expression of inward exasperation. It wasn't his case. Suydam had claimed one last victim—somehow—in Charlie Hammond. That was it; Carter was done, done with all that.

The bookstore was as he had left it. He muffled the bell with his hand on entering, and found himself thinking of electronic alternatives. Specifically ones that could be turned off when they weren't needed. Then he realized he was thinking about the long-term operations of the store, and smiled to himself.

When he took his hand from the bell, it rang quietly and maybe even reproachfully. Carter was becoming fanciful, and he knew it. He put it down to the effect of the store upon him; being surrounded by all that fiction had to have some sort of effect on a man, didn't it? He was also beginning to like the place. Maybe he would keep it going as a concern, deal Emily in, and be a silent partner.

The ceiling above him creaked.

It was probably nothing, just an old building settling in the cool evening after a sunny day. Probably nothing, but Carter put down his shopping quietly, drew his pistol, and—having checked that the store front and rear were empty—made his way slowly up the stairs. This time he remembered the creaking step and made it to the top in near silence.

The studio apartment was unoccupied.

Carter swore under his breath. He was *trying* to like the place, but it kept putting him on his guard like this. He'd just have to get used to it.

There it was again, a definite belief that he would be involved in the store in the future. He thought of Ken Rothwell then, a man born with a mouthful of silver spoons, just saying he'd like to buy it, discussing it like it was a secondhand car. Fuck Rothwell and his money. Carter would give Emily a share in the store because she deserved it.

He went to his car to pick up the overnight bag he kept in the trunk for eventualities like this, and returned to prepare himself for the night. He stripped off the bed's plastic covering and checked the mattress closely, fully aware of how absurd it was. He found nothing, as he knew he would. He cut the navy blue foam bedroll out of its wrapping and ran it down the right-hand side of the bed, the side he found himself preferring even when sleeping alone. Then he laid the sleeping bag on it. Belatedly he realized he didn't have a pillow, but found one in a store cupboard. It was musty with age—the cupboards not having had Emily's regular eye upon them—so he stuffed it inside the cloth sack the sleeping bag had come in, shaped it with his hands, and laid it at the end of the bedroll. Not exactly five-star accommodations, but he'd slept in enough cars and even on a couple of concrete floors in his life to make him appreciate sleep anytime it involved lying down on a surface that conformed to the shape of the body.

It was already dark outside, and an Atlantic weather system had come ashore, bringing with it a steady, penetrating rain. Carter stood by the window and watched the cars go by through the blurred glass, traces of light against wet asphalt.

He should have felt alone, but he did not. There was an atmosphere in the apartment, as if it had risen up from the store below. Nothing malign, and nothing to stress his already oversensitive sense of self-preservation, but just the aura of a well-lived house. He gauged the place to have been built in the 1920s, maybe a decade or so earlier. There was something jaunty about it, even in its old age. If it had been a man, it would have worn a straw boater and sung in a barbershop quartet. Perhaps that wasn't the store's personality, though. Maybe that was Alfred Hill shining through.

Carter looked at the bookshelves for something to read while he wound down for sleep. These were Hill's personal books, he guessed. At least, none of the few he flicked through bore prices in soft black pencil on the flyleaves. He'd also noted that the stock downstairs contained—very old-school—a simple substitution cipher of the price the store had paid, a real hangover from decades before. He'd heard of such systems, but had never actually seen one used. It was strange to see the odd little characters there, refugees from a time before electronic points of sale, bar codes, and JIT management.

Hill's own collection was clear of any such markings, though.

There were a lot of them, but Carter started skimming the titles after only reading the first few as he began to realize that Hill's interests did not coincide with his own.

There were a lot of books of mythology, folklore, and the occult. None of them sported lurid covers. Instead, they were revealed by a riffle of the thumb to be dry, academic volumes. Carter hadn't realized it was possible to make satanic orgies boring, but one of the books he took down managed it.

Another shelf carried fiction, but it was all fiction involving mythology, folklore, the occult. He didn't recognize any of the writers—Arthur Machen, Lord Dunsany, H. P. Lovecraft, M. R. James, Frank Belknap Long—but the titles were as lurid as the academic books had been dry. He flicked through a volume of the Dunsany, nearly gagged on the violet prose, and put it back. No, there was nothing to read there, either.

Finally, and feeling a cliché for doing it, he went down into the store and picked a novel from the shelf of detective stories. He decided to at least not go for anything hardboiled, and picked up something British instead, *The Moving Toyshop* by Edmund Crispin. Carter liked impossible crime stories—he used to love reruns of *Ellery Queen* and *Banacek* when he was a kid—so a novel about a whole toy store vanishing looked like it might work for him.

He took the book upstairs, put it by the bedside, brushed his teeth, stripped to his underwear, and climbed into the sleeping bag.

The book . . . well. Quite quickly, Carter didn't know what to make of the book. He knew it was British, but he hadn't been expecting it to be quite *that* British. He read of Richard Cadogan, the famous but impoverished poet, who liked pistols but was a lousy shot. He read of Spode, Nutling, and Orlick, "publishers of high-class literature." But there was only a Mr. Spode, as Nutling and Orlick were fictional even within the novel. He read of a journey to Oxford, and realized he had no idea where most cities were in the United Kingdom. He could place London, and that was all. When Cadogan ended up marooned in Didcot, he could have been on the moon, for all Carter knew. Crispin threw in literary references, too, none of which meant a single damn thing to Carter.

Carter felt himself slowly being overwhelmed by the effects of a long day, travel, events, and now a book that was better than him, and knew it. He got as far as Cadogan's first sight of the eponymous toyshop and decided he'd buy the book in the morning and read it when he was more alert. He returned it to the nightstand, beat the makeshift pillow back into shape, and switched off the light.

Chapter 6

THE DREAMS IN THE BOOK HOUSE

Carter rarely dreamed, and when he did, he didn't enjoy it. Even as a child, he had avoided "I had the weirdest dream last night" conversations. His friends dreamed of catching buses that traveled so long that they forgot where they were supposed to be going and started living on the bus instead. They dreamed of it being their birthday, but every present was empty because friends and relatives had decided to wrap the boxes before going out and buying the gifts, because it was more efficient that way; look, here they are, in the garage the whole time. They dreamed of schtupping that girl in class who nobody liked because she had personality issues, but she was really nice in the dream.

Carter always said he never remembered his dreams. If pressed, he'd make something up. Late for school. Being locked out. Typical, boring anxiety stuff.

Carter didn't usually remember his dreams because, at an early age, he learned how to forget them. He didn't dwell on them. He didn't talk about them. The idea of a "dream diary" made him panicky. If he avoided every thought of them, derailed every train of thought that took him back to them, then they faded after a little while. It wasn't just the best thing to do. It was the only thing to do.

Over the years he had gotten very good at it, both the forgetting of his dreams and the lying about them.

Soon all that was left was the lingering dread of just how fucked up his unconscious mind was, and how much it wanted to destroy him. He managed to hide that, too. From the outside world, at least. As far as he knew, he'd aced every psych assessment, and he didn't take the skills of the department psychiatrist lightly.

That lingering dread, though, that was always there, and manifested in small ways. He disliked open spaces. Not real agoraphobia, but just a sense of vulnerability when he was outside in an open area. The sea, too, troubled him. He couldn't understand why anybody would want to go on it for shits and giggles. It was dangerous. He didn't panic if he had to go on the ferry, though. The idea of the ferry sinking while he was aboard didn't bother him any more than it would bother anyone else. That wasn't the nature of the dread—and it was an apprehension rather than a fear. It was something altogether bigger than just a morbid fear of drowning.

Until the deaths of Martin Suydam and Charlie Hammond, Carter had never had a dream he couldn't erase from his memory with a little mindful neglect, and Carter had *never* had a dream he had known was a dream as he dreamed it.

Tonight, he knew he was dreaming. He didn't know how, because nothing felt wrong or partially formed. He was in Union Street, actually standing in the middle of the street, right in front of the precinct house. Union Street wasn't wide, lined with redbrick tenements opposite the station all the way along but with gaps on the other side, like kicked-out teeth. One of the gaps was occupied by the precinct house itself, a brown brick building with a blue-tiled frontage.

Carter wasn't worried about standing in the street. There was no traffic, only parked cars. There were no people, either. He listened, but couldn't hear anything. No traffic sounds, no music, no aircraft, not even birdsong.

He went in because he was a cop, and why else would he be standing in front of the precinct house unless he meant to go in? He only remembered he wasn't a cop anymore much later. All the vehicles parked out front were patrol cars, which was odd. He'd never seen more than three or four out there before, but there was a shining row of twelve black-and-whites. They looked new. When Carter walked between two to get to the sidewalk, he was wary of touching them. It wasn't smearing their pristine wax jobs that worried him. It was that they were there at all, gleaming and reeking of newness. That wasn't the 76th Precinct he remembered.

He entered and the place was empty. No. Silent, he realized; not empty.

Lying by the public counter was a uniform cop. Carter saw the spray pattern on the wall, and knew before he even reached him that the man had been shot through the head. The face was untouched. Carter didn't know him and thought he must have started in the precinct after Carter left. That he still believed himself to be a police officer didn't glitch for him at all. The back of the skull was missing, a section of skull the diameter of a clenched fist blown out by the passage of a bullet. The dead man had his gun in his hand, so at least he hadn't died without trying to retaliate.

His gun was a S&W Model 5946. Carter knew it wasn't just any 5946; it was Charlie Hammond's. He didn't know how that was possible, or how he knew it from any other, but he was sure. He had a half thought that maybe the precinct reissued the handguns of dead cops. Now that its new owner was dead, too, would they reissue it again?

Carter went to the detectives' bullpen to find somebody to report the death to, but it was silent there. Every detective sat at their desk, every one of them was dead, every one of them had been shot through the mouth, every one of them held Charlie Hammond's gun.

Carter saw a flight of wooden stairs and climbed them, though no such stairs existed in the 76th Precinct house.

He was in the house of Martin Suydam. As he broached the top of the staircase, he walked through a length of crime scene tape that tore like gossamer.

Nobody else was there. Dark stains showed, soaked into the wooden boards and bare plaster by the wall where Suydam had died and in a wall spray where Charlie Hammond had emptied his skull. Now Carter felt he shouldn't be there, no longer convinced even within the warp of the dream that he was still a cop.

Suydam's psycho wall was still up. Carter thought that this was wrong, that somebody had specifically told him that everything had been taken away in preparation for the site to be razed, but he couldn't quite catch the memory slipping eel-like through his recollection. He went through into the side rooms from where he'd made the call, and stood by the window. Outside was a patch of woodland. Beyond it, he thought he could see the sea. Above him, the great sky. The wind sighed. He couldn't see a single building out there, just a green wilderness. As the wind blew, the sky seemed to bulge as if it were a diaphanous sail. The great blue arc of it seemed as insubstantial and flawed as a tangled cobweb, as deformed as Suydam's tracery of yarn on his psycho wall.

At the edge of the world, the sea rose to meet the sky, and it was coming closer. The sea rose, the sky fell, forming a shattered horizon that came toward Carter like an avalanche, a cave-in under the vault of heaven.

The house of Martin Suydam, the only building in the world, shuddered as everything failed. Carter watched it, truly terrified in a way he had never felt before. There was someone standing by him. He managed to look away from the awful sight through the window. It was Charlie Hammond, the exit wound in the back of his head obvious. He looked at Carter and smiled at him, kind, reassuring.

"That'll be The Twist," he said. He handed Carter his S&W Model 5946 and nodded, kind, reassuring.

Carter woke up. There was a man in the room, standing at the foot of the bed.

Carter woke up. He was alone.

He met Emily at the door at eight thirty sharp. "Let's get some breakfast," he told her.

She'd already eaten, she said, but coffee sounded good. He locked the two Yales on the door and handed her the keys.

She took him to a diner on the other side of the block. There was a police cruiser outside, the cop at the wheel reading a newspaper. His partner was in the diner getting coffees at the counter when they came in.

They took a window table and ordered. Emily could hardly help but notice Carter's distracted glances at the police car outside.

"On the run, are you?"

He looked at her, a little startled. "That obvious, is it? I tell you, I'm not going back to that chain gang." He glanced at the car again. "No, it just made me think of a dream I had last night."

"Guilty conscience?"

"I don't think so. Just reminded me of a bad time. I used to be a cop."

"And now you're an investigator? Ken told me. He didn't say what kind of investigator."

"I didn't tell him. I'm a private investigator these days."

"Sounds interesting."

"Sounds it, yeah."

Carter's plate of eggs arrived, and the conversation foundered for a while.

"You didn't sleep so well, then?" said Emily a couple of minutes later.

Carter shrugged. "Unfamiliar bed. That place creaks a lot at night."

"And you dreamed of your old job." Outside, the police cruiser had long gone, but Emily looked at the space where it had been. "Bad dream?"

"Just a dream." Carter didn't want to talk about it at all. If he talked about it, it might settle into his memory. He was already disturbed by how much detail he could recall: his reflection on the cars' windows as he passed them on Union Street; the feel of the police tape as it broke against him; the smell of blood when Hammond stood by him. He had never smelled anything in a dream before, of that he was sure. "Let's talk about the bookstore."

Emily drew a deep breath and let it out. "Sure."

She was looking at him warily. "First," he said, "let me put your mind at ease about the place's immediate future. I haven't seen the accounts, but it doesn't feel like it's on its last legs. What kind of turnover do you get?"

"Well, a little bit better now that Alfred's been declared dead." Carter frowned. Emily smiled wanly. "His pay's been going into his checking account for the last seven years. I guess that's yours now, too. Good luck proving it to the bank."

"Seven years of pay has just been collecting in it?"

"Sure. It was his business, so I just carried on giving him his cut from the profits, just as I did when he was around." She looked at him from under her bangs. "Gave myself a yearly raise, too, in line with inflation, and a Christmas and birthday bonus, just like I got when he was around. It's all in the books."

Carter finished his eggs and pushed the plate away. He signaled to the waitress to refill his cup. "That's fine. Doesn't sound like the store's in any kind of financial trouble. I thought times were tough for bookselling?"

"Generally, yeah. Hill's has always specialized, though. We hunt down stock you won't find anywhere else. We get collectors from all over the world. A lot of the real business is mail order. The stuff you see on the shelves in the store is for casual browsers. Most of my day is spent on the Net hunting editions and doing deals, keeping the web and social presence alive, parceling books up and phoning UPS." She leaned forward confidentially. "I can fill out a customs declaration in my sleep." She leaned back and smiled. It was a pleasant, lopsided smile. No, he concluded, more the grin of a practiced shit-kicker. He decided he liked her.

Her eyes narrowed, but she kept smiling. "You're looking at me weird."

"Just . . . don't take this the wrong way . . . Just you and a guy like Kenneth Rothwell. How did that happen?"

"Yeah, it's a weird one, and no offense taken. He just came in one day, asking about a book for a gift. We got talking. He bought a small fortune of stock, and I thought that was that. Didn't even know he was a Rothwell until he gave me his credit card and the delivery address. Then he came in the next week and asked me out. What's a girl to do? And he *does* look good in a suit."

Carter considered telling her Rothwell wanted to buy the store as a gift for her, decided it was impolitic, and told her anyway.

Emily was stunned. "As a gift?"

"Yeah." Carter couldn't tell if the news made her happy or angry. "I'm not selling it to him, though."

Her expression became guarded. Carter thought that Rothwell was used to getting what he wanted, and Emily knew it, too. Before she could spend too much effort coming up with ugly scenarios, he said, "I'm giving you half. Not as a gift, but because you deserve it. Hill's Books has been you for seven years, so I'm just making that more legal."

"You're kidding?" She was stunned all over again.

It was the idea he'd been playing around with the previous evening, and he still wasn't sure whether it was wise, but he had gone with impulse and it felt right.

"I don't kid much," he told her. "I'll be your silent partner."

She frowned. "And I still end up doing all the work?"

"If you don't like the deal—"

"No! Hell, no!" She put her hand reflexively on his, as if to stop him physically from withdrawing the deal across the table. "I love the deal! Equal partners?"

Carter nodded. He could see her running figures through her head. "Same work I've always been doing, but for more money. What's not to like? I accept, Mr. Carter." She took her hand from his and held it out to him. He took it and they shook.

"Glad to hear it, Ms. . . ."

She winced slightly. "Lovecraft."

"Ms. Lovecraft." He thought at first the wince had been because she had the same surname as Linda Lovecraft, and she must get shit for it all the time. Then he remembered that was Linda Love*lace*, but that he'd seen the name Lovecraft just recently. "Like the writer?"

"Yes," she said heavily. "Just like the writer."

"Any relation?"

She nodded reluctantly.

"You don't seem happy about it."

"The number of people I get coming to the store just to paw the books and talk to me. They never buy anything. Just turn up with Arkham House editions and ask me to sign them, like I wrote them or something."

Carter smiled disbelievingly. "Why you? Because you work in a bookstore? Don't the rest of your family get any hassle?"

"I don't have any family. Not now. I'm the last of the line. Once I'm gone, the name dies with me. Kind of. There are other Lovecrafts out there, but they're not blood."

"That's hard."

"Hard? Do you have any idea how many times I've wanted to change my name? Every time some nut comes in and tries to tell me that Cthulhu lives, or the Necronomicon really exists. Mr. Carter, I am sick of this name."

"Call me Dan, and I'll stick to calling you Emily, if that's okay?"

"That would be cool of you. Thanks."

"I was going to say maybe you'd like to rename the place after yourself since you'd be the one running it, but I guess 'Lovecraft's Books' isn't such a great idea after all. Bring in the wrong crowd."

"Don't get me wrong. It's great that people are reading, but it's the ones who treat it like gospel."

" 'It'?"

"H. P. L.'s 'canon,' his stories. Innsmouth and Arkham, all that garbage. His big idea was that there are super-powerful gods out there that are really aliens, and we're beneath their perception because we're nothing, or beneath their contempt if they even notice us. The big bad is Cthulhu, who's like a huge thing with an octopus for a head."

Carter remembered the green vinyl figure behind the counter in the bookstore and nodded. He guessed it had been a gift from someone poking gentle fun at her, someone she liked or she wouldn't have it on display. "What's an Arkham House edition?" he asked.

"Publishing house that popped up after he died, founded by a guy called August Derleth, one of H. P. L.'s friends. He thought H. P. L. deserved a bigger audience. But nobody would print his stuff, so Derleth helped create Arkham House to do it. I think it's still going. The name comes from one of a bunch of fictional towns H. P. L. came up with to set some of his stories in. Arkham's the main one, probably based on Salem." She looked hard and a little suspiciously at Carter, as if she supposed he was playing with her. "This stuff gets referenced all over the place. Games, T-shirts, movies, you name it. You really haven't ever read any?" Carter shook his head. Grudgingly, she accepted his ignorance. "H. P. L. couldn't write. Not well. Ever hear of M. R. James? No? English academic who wrote some ghost stories on the side. H. P. L. was really impressed by him and wrote an essay that said as much. A friend sent James a copy, and James wrote back to his friend tearing H. P. L.'s writing style to pieces. He was right to, as well." She looked in her coffee cup and sighed. "Just as well H. P. L. never heard that. It would have broken his heart. James was everything he wanted to be. Wealthy, educated, respected . . ." She snorted. ". . . English. If he'd ever found out what James thought of his work, it would have destroyed him.

"Actually, *this*"—she pinched the skin on the back of her hand—"would have killed him, too. H. P. L. was *all* about racial purity. If he only knew one of his descendants had fallen in love with a black girl. Truly, I would give serious money to see how he would've reacted. 'Why, what's all this spinning noise coming out of this coffin? Hi, Great-Great-Uncah Howard, I'm Emily. We're family. Yay!' 'Ohmagawd! A mulatto! A mongrel! My precious genes! Nooooo!'"

She had a sip of coffee while her malevolent giggles abated.

"So, anyway. I get all these guys—they're always guys—coming in and asking me if I've got the *Seven Cryptical Books of Hsan* in stock, so I do this smile"—she smiled a weak, reluctant version of her earlier grin—"and say, 'Oh, you're hilarious.' Or they tell me the president is really an intelligent fungus from Yuggoth, 'Not *that* intelligent, though, amiright?'" The grimace-smile again. "'Oh, you're hilarious. Now, are you going to buy anything, or are you going to get the fuck out of my shop? No, I will not sign your fucking Arkham House editions.'" She shook her head. "Sorry. I don't cuss much, but . . . Yeah, okay, I cuss a lot, but they just . . ." She made a muffled scream. Then, unexpectedly, she smiled at him. "*My shop.* I like the sound of that."

"*Our* shop. Maybe I should rename it Carter and Lovecraft so you remember your place."

"Hell, no. You realize there's a recurring character in H. P. L.'s stories called Randolph Carter? That name would just turn the store into an even bigger nerd magnet."

"There is? Okay, maybe not in that case. Okay, it stays Hill's Books as a memorial to your uncle, your former boss and my benefactor. I'll ask Weston to handle splitting the ownership. Him, or somebody cheaper."

"Weston?"

"Alfred's lawyer. He handled the will."

Lovecraft shook her head. "No, the store's lawyers are Harlow, Harlow, and Glenn. Local firm. I've never heard of Weston."

Carter frowned. "Maybe he was Alfred's personal lawyer. Kept the store separate. Henry Weston of Weston Edmunds. Know the name?"

"Weston Edmunds? Are you kidding me? They're huge. Big corporate lawyers."

"That's what I turned up. Maybe they were friends? I don't know." He took out his wallet to pay the check and flicked through the card pockets as he did. "He gave me his business card." He riffled back and forth in growing frustration for some seconds.

"Can't find it?"

He couldn't.

Chapter 7

DAN, THE DETECTIVE

Carter walked back with Lovecraft to pick up his things.

"You're not giving up the day job, then?" she asked.

"No. Not anytime soon, anyway. I've got a job starting on Monday, so I want to get up to speed on anything I can pull on the guy from the databases."

"Job. You're disillusioning me, Dan. I thought they were all 'cases.'"

"I just don't like sounding like Mike Hammer. When I was on the job, when I was still a cop, you saw some PIs who'd really bought into it. They were more Danny DeVito than Bogart, but they'd do everything short of talking out of the side of their mouth. Just playacting, pretending to be some gumshoe in a film noir. The guys used to make fun of them. *I* used to make fun. I don't want that to be me. I do the job and try to do it like a human, not some dick from central casting."

"A private dick," said Lovecraft. "No bottle of rye in your desk drawer?"

Carter laughed. "Jesus, no."

"You're a real disappointment, Dan. No overcoat, battered hat, nothing. Not even one 'Here's looking at you, kid' out of you. Detecting fail."

" 'Here's looking at you, kid' is from *Casablanca*. Bogart's not playing a detective in that."

There was a silence and Carter looked sideways at Lovecraft only to find her smirking. "Did I just step in a bear trap?" he said.

"Shure did, blue eyesh," said Lovecraft.

"Ah, come on. Knowing my movies doesn't make me a Phil Marlowe wannabe."

"I bet there's a gin joint with a flashing neon sign right next to your office. You stand by the window with a smoke hanging on your lip at night, looking out at the mean streets, talking to yourself in voice-over."

"It's not too late for me to hold on to the whole bookstore."

"Nah," said Lovecraft, unimpressed by the threat. "We shook on it."

"We didn't spit on our palms."

"Speak for yourself, Bogie."

Carter packed his overnight bag, but left the sleeping bag and foam roll behind. After all, the place was his now. Half his.

Lovecraft stood by the top of the stairs while he gathered his belongings. "You planning to move up here?"

"To Providence? No, not right now. I need to think about this."

"No, I mean this apartment. If I could move in, it'd save me rent."

Carter paused. "In all the time Alfred's been gone, it never crossed your mind to do that anyway?"

"No." She looked uncomfortable. "It was his, you know. Any minute, he could walk through the door."

"When did you stop believing that?"

She looked at the bed and the discarded plastic cover lying crumpled on the floor by it. "When you turned up. *Bing!* Reality check, please." She wasn't smiling.

Carter turned back to his packing. "Sure. We can work you living over the store in as part of the deal, I guess. But can you hold off for a while, just a few weeks until we've got everything legal with regard to the store? I'll be coming up maybe once a week while that's going on and I might as well crash here as anywhere."

They said good-bye at the door. He said he'd try to come up again soon, maybe in a week or a fortnight, and get the papers organized in the interim. They parted quite formally, with a "Good morning, Ms. Lovecraft" on one side, and "Drive safely, Mr. Carter" on the other.

Four hours and five minutes later, Carter was back at his office.

On Monday, Mrs. Leverson, she of four jobs and a shiftless husband, came in to say he hadn't been back all weekend and he'd called to tell her he would be away until Tuesday. "He says it's business," she said to Carter. Her tone was neutral.

"Do you believe him?"

"No," she said, her tone unaltered. She looked dispassionately at him across the desk. She reminded him a little of a snapping turtle.

"Then I'll start tomorrow. Have you written down his itinerary?"

"*Itinerary*," she said. It was the closest thing to a smile he'd seen from her, bitter thing though it was. "He doesn't have what you might call an *itinerary*, just the places he hangs around."

Carter took a handwritten list from her. The paper bore an orange cartoon of an attractive stereotypical housewife in the lower-right corner, her thought bubble bearing the words *Things to Do*. He glanced down the list. It was depressingly stereotypical itself—a menu of bars and bookies. At the bottom was a list of three names and addresses. "Who are these?"

"Girlfriends," she said. Her tone remained neutral.

"You know who they are and where they live? Why are you hiring me?"

"I know who they are, but I don't have no proof. You get the proof."

Carter nodded. He thought of Alfred Hill's untouched bank account. Seven years of income, eighty-four paychecks. It sounded like a lot. Why was he taking jobs to photograph men fucking women, again? He had no idea. He considered telling Mrs. Leverson that circumstances had changed and he regretted that he would no longer be able to take on her investigation. She looked so worn through, though. Like she didn't already have enough men letting her down in her life.

"Mrs. Leverson," he said instead, "you're in luck. I have a corporate client who has me over in that part of town anyway. I can cover both cases on their tab as far as expenses go. I won't need to invoice you as well."

She looked at him for several seconds as she digested his words. "I don't take charity."

"It isn't charity, ma'am, it's happenstance, a lucky accident. Serendipity."

He didn't think she knew what "serendipity" was, but then, why should she? In any case, the meaning was clear.

"That would be good," she said. "Thank you."

"Don't thank me, Mrs. Leverson. It's just how the cards fell." Her expenses would come to two or three hundred dollars, four hundred tops, he estimated. Paying for them would be Alfred Hill's gift from the grave to her. He had a feeling Hill would have approved.

He also wondered if Hill was even in a grave.

Distracted, his attention was drawn back to Mrs. Leverson by the solid sound of a gun in a plastic zip-top bag being placed on his desk. Carter winced; the sound was louder than it should have been, but not simply in terms of volume. It was just wrong, a misremembered noise. He had to narrow his eyes. The sun was suddenly shining in through the window to his left.

He looked at the gun thinking he must have missed something while he was distracted. It was a .45-caliber import, Czech, he thought. In a sandwich bag. He looked at her and frowned.

"I got the gun, like you asked," she said. She reached into her bag and took out a packet of cigarettes and a lighter. He said nothing, not quite trusting himself, while she took one from the pack and lit up. She took a long, grateful drag on it, blew out the smoke into the office air, and looked at Carter. "I did it just like you said. I took it from where he keeps it in his nightstand, never touched it with my bare fingers, and put it straight in a baggie." She nodded at the gun. "Unused one."

She looked at him. "He'll be back tomorrow night, around ten. I'm going to be out. That's when you should do it."

She flicked the tip of her cigarette clean in the ashtray on Carter's desk.

Carter didn't have an ashtray. He'd never had an ashtray. He hadn't smoked since his teens.

He started to breathe in to speak, but let the breath sigh out again, unused. Mrs. Leverson's hair seemed a few degrees darker red than earlier, and she wore it more loosely. He couldn't see how the sunlight would make something appear darker.

Mrs. Leverson dropped her cigarette into the ashtray. She looked suddenly at Carter with a panicked expression, placed both hands flat on the desktop. Her eyes were wide, and she tried to say something, but all that came out was a shuddering, incoherent noise. Carter shoved his chair back, feeling the legs scrape against the carpet. Afterward, he would remember that sensation and be unable to reconcile it to the fact that his chair was an office model on wheels.

Mrs. Leverson was convulsing as if electrocuted. Her eyes swung spastically in their sockets as her teeth chattered. Carter rose, trying to remember the EMT training he'd had. She seemed to be seizing, and he could just about recall how to deal with that. The first thing he *shouldn't* do was to put something in her mouth to bite on. Second, she might smash her face on the desk the way she was convulsing, so he should get her away from it. The floor was the safest place for her to ride it out while he called 911.

He reached the side of his desk, looked at Mrs. Leverson, and for a moment was unsure why he was thinking about fits. She was fine, the ashtray was gone, there was no smoke in the air, his chair had wheels, there was no gun in a baggie, God was in his Heaven, all was right with the world, except that Carter now entertained the possibility that he was becoming insane.

It worried him less than it ought, he found. He was still functional, after all, and he had heard so many times that a madman never knows that he's mad. He had just suffered some sort of episode, that was all. He was overtired, that was all. He needed a vacation, that was all.

Mrs. Leverson didn't seem to have noticed anything odd about his behavior. They concluded the meeting, he told her to carry on as usual, and he would do the rest.

After she had left the office, he went to the window and watched her walk across the parking lot. He couldn't remember her face anymore. When he tried to recall it, he saw her sitting opposite him, her palms slapping the desktop, teeth clattering, eyes rolling. She wasn't even human in his memory anymore. Her eyes clicked as they jerked this way and that. Her eyelids rose and fell mechanically. Her rictus grin was set into her face as an arrangement of hinge and armatures. In his mind's eye, Mrs. Leverson was a life-size ventriloquist puppet. Watching her walk to her car, even her hair looked like the fake hair of a doll. He hoped she wouldn't turn and look up at him.

She did not. She reached her car, unlocked the door, got in, and fussed over her bag for half a minute. Then she put on her seat belt, started the car, and drove away. Carter watched her until she was out of sight.

* * *

The following day found Carter watching Mr. Leverson spending his wife's earnings in a variety of venues, mainly bars. In two of them, Carter observed louche Mr. Leverson being overfriendly with women, none of whom was Mrs. Leverson. Carter took photographs with a Nikon DSLR, a high-resolution piece of equipment that had cost slightly more than his gun. Between its CCD and the long lens, he could be taking the pictures from Queens, if he could have gotten a clear line of sight. Maybe from orbit. The pictures would still be sharp.

While he watched, he played games of "What if . . . ?" In this case, what if he had access to spy satellites? Would it make his job any easier? He doubted it. Sifting through pictures of New Yorkers looking like dots, trying to find the right ones to zoom in on. Fine for looking at terrorist camps in the back of beyond, but not so much use when looking for one ant in the anthill of the city.

Thinking of people as ants made him think of Orson Welles in *The Third Man*. The people mere dots as seen from the Riesenrad, seen from on high. If one stopped moving, would anyone care so very much?

The camera made Carter feel a little Olympian. With every touch of the shutter switch, another nail was hammered into the coffin of Mr. Nat Leverson's comfortable future. It was very easy. Carter was glad he'd passed on taking expenses for this job. They were working out as well below his forecasts anyway.

The downside of surveillance was that it was boring, and that meant Carter's mind wandered. It kept wandering back to the meeting with Mrs. Leverson the day before. He tried to compartmentalize what he thought he had seen and heard in the same way he did his dreams, but—like them—the memory didn't want to be contained. There were too many things wrong with it. Oddly, the one that bothered him most was nothing to do with Mrs. Leverson, the gun in a baggie, or the implication that Carter had been hired to murder Mr. Leverson. The thing that bothered him most was the sun slanting into the office. The sun never had slanted in like that, and never could. A row of office buildings across the parking lot stopped any low sunbeams and, as far as he knew, always had.

Maybe the sun had caught an open window and reflected in, he thought, but no. The sun had been beyond the buildings at that time; how could it have reflected off anything? This was almost a reassuring thought; if he had just spaced out for a moment, then the gun and all the rest of it was all part of the same daydream. If the sun had been a possibility, though, it made it harder to deny the rest of it. Carter was intent on denying it. Nothing had changed in the room. He was overworked, and he had entered some sort of fugue for a few seconds. The human mind is a delicate thing, after all. You have to look after it. It needs rest, and pleasant distraction.

Emily Lovecraft appeared in his mind's eye. He'd enjoyed her company, even when talking turkey. Rothwell was a lucky man to be dating her. Fuck, he was a lucky man to be born a Rothwell. You didn't have to be addicted to the society pages to know who the Rothwells were; they had the footprint of the Kennedy or Bush families, the only difference was no scion of theirs had yet been president, and how long could that state of affairs last? The Rothwells were born for politics, or law, and often both.

Carter couldn't see how a guy like Ken Rothwell had settled on a book nerd like Emily. There must be any number of blue bloods who'd murder their own sisters to get on Rothwell's arm. Maybe it was to do with his political ambitions. Some spin doctor on his payroll had come up with the idea of him going out with somebody who knew how much a loaf of bread cost. Then again, to Rothwell's constituency a book nerd was a dangerous intellectual. No matter how he worked it, Carter couldn't quite see what Rothwell wanted from that relationship. Unless, Carter was forced to concede, Rothwell simply loved her, and that was all there was to it. Weirder things had happened.

Mr. Leverson was sitting near the window of his current bar with a woman who wasn't Mrs. Leverson. At one point, she dipped her finger in her drink and sucked it clean, taking her own sweet time over it, never breaking eye contact with her companion for a moment. For his part, he went a little slack-faced and started breathing through his mouth, watching her finger between her lips the whole time.

Yeah, thought Carter, taking more pictures with the polarized filter, *all completely innocent. Why don't you just blow him in public and then we can all go home?*

On Wednesday morning, Carter photographed Mr. Nat Leverson leaving an apartment that was not his. He seemed pretty pleased with himself, and Carter concluded he had probably gotten blown after all.

Carter doubted he would get anything better on Mr. Leverson than that, so he made a note of the address and decided to spend the rest of the day in the office, working from there.

On his return, he found an e-mail waiting for him from Emily Lovecraft. The tone was awkward with forced humor, and he wondered if she was worried that he was going to change his mind about the bookstore.

She also said she'd been wondering what the connection between her uncle and Carter was, and thought it must be family, even if the Hill name was unfamiliar to Carter. She asked him if he had a family tree. Perhaps they could find a common ancestor. The tone remained awkward even into this simple request, but somehow differently from the earlier greetings. Carter got the impression she was more interested in the family tree than she was letting on.

He wrote back immediately to say hello, to reassure her by treating the partnership as a done deal that there was nothing to worry about on that front, and to say he had never had much interest in the genealogy of his family, but he had an aunt who did it as a hobby, and he would ask her if she would send him a copy of the family tree as it currently stood.

Carter sent the e-mail, and looked at the dispatch confirmation on his screen for a long moment. He shook his head; he was reading too much into a short message. The tone was awkward simply because he was still all but a stranger to her, that was all.

He checked the address he'd seen Mr. Leverson leave against the list of suspected girlfriends Mrs. Leverson had given him. One of the addresses matched. He would check city records to confirm the name just for purposes of due diligence, but the case was all but closed. He brought his case notes up to date, and turned his attention to something more personal.

Henry Weston continued to bother him. He'd almost managed to put the man out of his mind when Emily Lovecraft told him that Weston was not the bookstore's lawyer and was unlikely to be Alfred Hill's, either. He had to agree with her. Why Hill would ask somebody like Weston to be his executor, and why somebody like Weston would agree, was an intractable mystery. All Carter could think was that maybe they had history, maybe old college buddies or something.

There was no return in any of this, Carter knew, and it was a waste of time and effort, but at least it might stop the question nagging at him. So he fired up the databases, and prepared to research Alfred Hill, and then Henry Weston.

At the end of three hours, he had everything he would usually expect when doing a background check of an upstanding citizen like Alfred Hill. School, college, some tax data, a few general Internet hits, and then the trail stopped abruptly seven years before, as he knew it would.

By his laptop, Carter had a scratch pad he used to list the kinds of searches he would make, and to tick off as he made them, storing the gathered information on the computer itself. The sheet for Alfred Hill was largely checked.

The sheet for Henry Weston was hardly touched. He found Weston on institutional sites, sure enough—here was his name at Cornell, here were his company papers for Weston Edmunds, here was his membership in the American Bar Association (a small surprise to Carter, the ABA being more a teaching and ethics organization than vocational)—but there was almost nothing else. No professional gatherings, no blue plate dinners, no functions at all. It was as if Henry Weston lived in his office and only rarely left it.

If Carter didn't know it was impossible, he would have suspected "Henry Weston" to be a synthetic identity, put together for witness protection or something similar. It *was* impossible. Weston was a family member of a distinguished legal dynasty with a pedigree of ninety years. It was inconceivable that he could be anyone else but Henry Weston.

Maybe, Carter concluded, he just really liked his privacy.

Chapter 8

THE HORROR IN THE PARKING LOT

It was a clear afternoon, and a clear walk across an uncrowded parking lot. There was nobody else within a hundred yards. Professor James Belasco had no reason to believe he was in the last minutes of his life. He was healthy and had, as far as he knew, no enemies who hated him enough to cause him harm.

In this latter point, he was incorrect. Soon he would die in unnecessary terror and confusion purely because he had an enemy who hated him greatly, yet had never shown him that hatred. Like Fortunato, he would die an ugly death because he did not realize there was a Montresor in his life.

All that was in his mind that afternoon was getting home, grading some papers, then carrying out a swift pass of the academic publications that had been stacking up in his e-mail. His personal interests in topology would garner most of his attention, but he would keep a pastoral eye out for anything that might impact the theses of his students.

He reached his five-year-old Ford Focus and unlocked the door. There was nothing, not a hackle rising or a sense of discomfort, to tell him he was being watched, nothing at all to tell him this was the last time he would unlock the door, climb in behind the wheel, and carelessly throw his briefcase onto the passenger seat.

Belasco leaned back in his seat, drew a deep breath, and sighed it out. He worked his head from one side to the other to relieve the tension he felt in his neck, tapped the steering wheel lightly with his fingertips. Finally, he drew on his seat belt, and reached for the key where it waited, unturned, in the ignition.

As he lifted his shoe from the rubber mat in the footwell, there was the distinct sound of water stirred by the movement. Belasco's fingers hesitated on the key, and he looked down. The mat was dry, his feet were dry.

He frowned, put it from his mind, and went to turn the key again. As he did so, his foot shifted toward the gas pedal and, once again, there was the sound of water being disturbed.

Belasco looked down. There was no water in the footwell, although . . .

His frown became curious. There *was* something down there after all. In the air, he caught a glimpse of a fine white wisp that vanished as soon as he saw it. Then more appeared. It took him a moment to understand what he was seeing. It was like looking at light reflected from the surface of a lake, the crests of the waves and ripples showing more strongly than the troughs. He watched the layer of waterless ripples, visible only by the light coming through the car windows.

He was having some sort of perceptual event, he knew. Perhaps some sort of stroke. There was no water there, yet there was water there. Experimentally, he lowered his hand into the surface of the rippling plain and wafted it back and forth. The ripples broke against his hand, and he could distinctly hear the sound of water being splashed. He could even feel a sense of resistance to his fingers, and perhaps coolness. Yet when he lifted his fingers clear, the sensation immediately vanished. His fingers were not wet. There was no water.

With a shock, he realized that the water was rising. It was already at his knees and the ripple layer was appearing across the top of the front passenger seat. He watched as a loose paper lying there gently rose from the bone-dry seat cover, floating on phantom waters.

Belasco looked out the side window, fully expecting the glittering layer to be covering the whole parking lot. After all, such an effect could hardly be localized, whether or not it existed only in his own mind. He was surprised and alarmed to see it was not. Outside looked perfectly normal; the water that was not water was confined to his car, and it was still rising. When it reached his waist, he decided it was past time to put scientific observation aside and vacate himself from the experiment in progress.

The door wouldn't open. It didn't feel locked; there was no give in the handle at all. It might as well have been cast directly as part of the door. He undid his seat belt easily enough, the non-water splashing with his movements, and he tried the handle again. It refused to move even slightly. He turned the key to switch on the electrical systems, and the dashboard illuminated as normal. He'd feared they might short, but apparently the non-water was non-conductive.

Belasco pushed the toggle to lower his window. Nothing happened. He could hear the motor laboring, but the window wouldn't move at all.

The water was up to his chest.

He was still not panicking, but worry was becoming fear. He tried the door handle again, but it still resisted even when he put his weight behind it, moving not a millimeter. He reached across to the passenger door and, as he did so, his face dipped beneath the surface of the glittering nothing.

He couldn't breathe. Nothing filled his mouth, nothing at all. Certainly not air.

He sat up, eyes wide, gasping. It was as if the car was filling with a heavy, unbreathable gas. He found himself thinking in those terms because it was easier to rationalize than the concept of ghost water. He ignored how the light glittered across a liquid that was itself invisible and almost intangible. He ignored how it splashed and how he felt drops of nothing strike his skin, to leave it dry but for his sweat.

Keeping his head above the layer, he tried the passenger door, but it would not open, as intractably sealed as the other.

Finally, fear blossomed into panic. Belasco lay across the seat and kicked at the passenger window. He felt the water resist his movements, saw the surface surge in reaction to his movements, held his breath as his mouth dipped below the glittering reflections. The window might as well have been made of steel. His kicks did not even make the glass vibrate under the blows. He turned and braced himself with his back against the seat and his feet against the windshield, then tried to force it out. The glass did not bow even the tiniest fraction to all his frantic strength.

James Belasco was observed as he died. The increasingly desperate responses to his deteriorating situation were mentally noted as the experiment approached its conclusion. How the car slowly lowered on its suspension as it filled with water that wasn't there. How the shell of the car, its body, doors, and glass, all behaved anomalously. How Belasco clung on to the very end, pushing his face into the diminishing layer of breathable air in the compartment.

When even that layer had gone, Belasco writhed and convulsed, drowning on dry land. It lasted almost a minute. Then he hung there in the roof space, floating facedown.

The body slowly sank to lie sprawled across both front seats as the car simultaneously rose on its suspension. Less than two minutes later, all was normal once more, but for the small detail of the corpse of a man who had died as no man had ever died before.

* * *

Carter's cell phone rang. He checked the display before accepting the call. The number wasn't withheld, but neither he nor his phone's directory recognized it.

"Hello?"

"Mr. Carter?" said a voice. He didn't know it. The ambience on the line sounded as if the caller was outdoors. "The private investigator?"

"Speaking."

"Mr. Carter, my name is James Belasco. I'm a professor of mathematics at Clave College. I . . ."

There was a pause of several seconds. Carter was about to speak when Belasco continued, "I believe I'm in danger. Would it be possible for you to come to the math department as soon as possible?"

Carter wasn't even sure where Clave College was. It only rang a few distant bells. Before he could ask for directions, Belasco said, "No, that might not be safe. Meet me in the east parking lot. I drive a silver Ford Focus."

"If you're in danger, Professor, you should call the—"

Belasco hung up.

Carter looked at the phone, nonplussed. He called the number back, but after ringing for thirty seconds, it was put through to voice mail.

Carter was in his office, so he did a fast search. Clave College, it transpired, was in Providence.

Carter pushed his chair back, a chair still blissfully on casters, and rubbed his mouth as he thought. He'd been intending to go back to Providence for the weekend anyway, and the Leverson case, such as it was, had tied itself up in a gift bow; he'd already had his last meeting with Mrs. Leverson. She'd nodded a few times, said very little as he laid out what he had learned, paid him in cash, and left very quickly. He got the feeling she'd somehow been hoping to be proved wrong, despite everything.

His schedule was clear. Fine, he would head up to Rhode Island a couple of days earlier than planned.

There were police vehicles in the parking lot, and an ambulance pulling away as Carter approached. The lot was taped off and so Carter had to go around the block to find a parking place. He walked back and joined the crowd of students and gawkers who were just starting to dissipate.

"Hey," said Carter to a group of three who were talking about getting a drink, "what happened here?"

"They found a dead guy in that car," said one, and pointed to the silver Ford Focus that was the center of CSU attention.

"Suicide," said another.

"Dude, you don't know that," said the first.

Carter thanked them, and they headed off to find a bar. The CSUs were taking away a cell phone in an evidence bag. Carter guessed that meant they'd found it in the car rather than on the body. On impulse, he took out his own cell, selected the call he'd had from Belasco, and returned it.

The crime scene tech carrying the bag stopped as the phone in it illuminated and vibrated.

Carter stepped over the line and approached the nearest cop, holding up his wallet to show the PI license in the window. He nodded at the tech who was passing the ringing phone to a colleague, and held up his own phone.

"That's me," said Carter. "I need to speak to the detective in charge."

The senior detective's name was Harrelson. Carter had never heard of him, but Harrelson knew Carter.

"I know that name," he said when he examined Carter's license.

"It's not an uncommon one," said Carter, knowing what was coming.

"You used to be a cop?"

Carter nodded.

"The Child-Catcher? That was your pinch?"

Carter nodded again. He knew there was more to come.

Harrelson, a raw, broad man with razor rash on the folds in his neck, handed Carter's license back to him. "That was rough about your partner, man. I'm sorry."

Carter smiled the tight little smile he kept for these times. He said the words automatically, a reflex he had conditioned so his mind could be elsewhere as the words rolled out. "Thanks. It just happened. There was no warning, no hint. Never really know why he did it."

The syllables slid out of Carter's mouth, less an explanation than a catechism. As always, they worked, because the listener never really wanted to hear them anyway.

"So," said Harrelson, the "brotherhood of cops" business out of the way to his satisfaction, "you knew the deceased?"

"No. Not at all. I just got a call from him at"—he checked the call log of his phone—"13:06. I'd never heard of him before. Said his name was James Belasco, he was a math professor here, and he thought he was in danger. Asked me to meet him at the college, then changed his mind and said the lot. Told me he was in a silver Ford Focus."

Harrelson looked across the asphalt at the car. "You get many calls like that in your work?"

"None," said Carter. "Never before. I was coming up to Providence anyway, so I thought I'd check it out. Work's work."

"You didn't call him back."

"I did, twice. Went to voice mail both times. Your techs will find my messages when they go through his cell."

Harrelson nodded, still looking at the car rather than at Carter. He seemed distracted.

"What happened to him?" asked Carter. He wasn't expecting a straight answer, if he got one at all.

"Don't know. The ME's gonna love this one." He rubbed his neck where the shirt collar chafed the skin.

Carter hid his surprise. Harrelson actually wanted to tell him. "Oh?" he said, priming the pump. "Why's that?"

"Only time I ever seen a body with foam on its lips like that, it wasn't drugs. It was drowning."

"In a parking lot?"

"In a dry parking lot, yeah." Harrelson laughed. "It'll be some kind of poisoning. Maybe his lungs filled. Breathing in chlorine gas can do that."

"Maybe." Chlorine gas was fractionally more likely than a man drowning in his car, Carter guessed. "This place have a chemistry department?"

"Yeah, but not a big one. Chlorine's easy to make, though. They used it in World War One, didn't they?" Carter shrugged. "Yeah, they did. Must be pretty easy to make." Harrelson finally looked at Carter. "We'll take a statement now, while you're here. Take a look at your phone to check the call timings, too. Okay?"

Carter reached Hill's Books just as Lovecraft was closing the place. "Well, hello," she said, opening the door to his wave through the window. She smiled and frowned at the same time. "I wasn't expecting you back so soon."

"Work brought me up to Providence, so I thought I might as well stay over," he said. "How's business, partner?"

"Not so bad, partner," she replied, letting him in. Her body language was tense, but happily so. She was having a hard time hiding a grin.

"What's going on?" Carter asked slowly.

The grin broke out. "A coup," she said, "an absolute solid gold coup. I've been hugging myself for the last twenty-four hours. Get this: two days ago I had an inquiry after a pretty obscure book, *The Defeat of the Spanish Armada* by William Cecil, the Baron Burghley. Burghley was a big deal in the court of Elizabeth the

First." Carter looked at her blankly. She shook her head. "Doesn't matter. Anyway, the client wants it in a first edition. A *first edition*." Carter still wasn't showing the requisite excitement. "That's 1588, Dan! So I check it out, and all I find is that a copy came up for auction a year or two ago, and went for over thirty K. That's too rich for this business. We've never dealt with anything that rare. So I put the inquiry to one side with half a plan to put it the way of some of the bigger fish and maybe wrangle a commission out of it *if* it happens.

"This morning I'm going through my e-mails and find a sales list from an English country house. They're not going to auction. They want the money fast, so they got in somebody to price the books and just put them straight on sale, first come, first served." She raised her eyebrows, encouraging him to speak.

He obliged her. "And they had this Armada book?"

"And they had the Armada book! First edition, not excellent condition, reboarded last century, good but not great binding, and going for . . . five thousand! That's pounds, so about eight and half thousand dollars. The list was sent in the late evening there, so I'm guessing not many of the Brits are awake, and not many collectors outside the UK will be as interested as them. But time's ticking. I didn't have time to get in touch with the potential buyer, so I made an executive decision and bought it. Sale confirmed first thing next morning, UK time. Few hours later, the buyer agrees it's the best copy they'll realistically get, and pays out . . ." She could hardly stop herself from laughing. "Eighteen thousand! About nine and half thousand dollars gross profit for a few hours' work. How awesome is that?"

"Especially since you never even saw the book."

"I will *never* see the book. Got a colleague in the UK who'll handle the exchange for me for a commission. Nothing big, three hundred and change, plus the courier expenses. Even then, we're still nine thousand ahead." She shook her head, excited by the retelling. "Weird never even seeing the book. I feel like a speculator. 'Hey, stuff! Go from here to there, and make me some money.'"

"You look like you'd have burst if you hadn't had someone to tell that story to," said Carter, laughing with her.

"Ah, I told Ken, but he doesn't get it. Difficult for him to think down to a level where nine thousand is a big deal. That's not a criticism. It's just the way it is." Talking about it reduced her excitement a little and the words no longer flowed, but broke against the rocks as the torrent of her enthusiasm subsided.

"I haven't eaten," said Carter. "Have you?"

"No. No chance this afternoon." She brightened. "I am going to buy you dinner, to celebrate my business acumen and all-around genius."

"No," said Carter, "the *business* is going to buy us dinner to celebrate your business acumen and all-around genius."

"That's kind of the business."

"It's the least it can do."

Chapter 9

THE CRIME OF THE CENTURY

Carter took a brusque phone call from the Providence Police Department the next morning, asking him to come in as soon as possible.

He had suffered a bad night's sleep again, and was beginning to think he and the little studio over the shop would never get along very well. This time the dreams had been chaotic and so metamorphic that he could barely remember any of the cavalcade of faces and events he had been dragged through by his unconscious mind. All through them, he had a feeling of being observed. It was nothing to start with, no worse than the sense of being under the eyes of the proctors during a school exam. As the dreams, the many, many twisting and interconnected dreams, writhed on with him as an unwilling passenger, however, the observation became first critical, then antagonistic, and finally fully malevolent. He'd awoken—he'd *dreamed* he'd awoken—to find the figure from his first dream in the building sitting on the end of his bed, face turned away. Then he'd awoken again, alone. He did not remember ever suffering from such double awakenings before.

He arrived at the station house, identified himself, was badged as a visitor, and taken to an office. When he was shown in, his stomach sank. Harrelson was there, looking uncomfortable, and so were two other men, one white, one black, both in their forties. Carter made a mental bet with himself that the white guy with the silver foxing at the temples was Harrelson's lieutenant, and the slim black guy in the nice gray suit was his captain.

"Mr. Carter," said Detective Harrelson, "I'd like to introduce you to Lieutenant Piers—" The white guy with the silver foxing extended his hand. Carter shook it. "And Captain Aspinall." The slim black guy in the nice gray suit extended his hand. Carter shook it.

"You've been on the job, Mr. Carter, so we'll skip to the chase," said Aspinall. He took some report sheet from the desk against which he was leaning. "In your statement, you said you had never heard of the deceased, James Belasco?"

"That's correct," said Carter.

"Never met him? You're sure?"

Carter was beginning to regret the good food and wine of the previous evening. He'd gone straight to bed when he got back. Maybe an hour's research on Belasco would have stood him in better stead.

"I'm sure. Or, if I have met him, it would've been casually and his name never came up."

Piers said nothing, but watched Carter steadily. Carter had a feeling this had all gotten the captain's attention too early in the investigation for Piers's comfort, and there was something too mild to be real resentment there as a result.

Harrelson handed Carter a photograph, a blowup of a license picture. "Recognize him?"

Belasco didn't look comfortable in the picture. He was in his fifties, and probably used hair coloring. The immediacy of the

DMV photo had robbed him of the opportunity to organize his hair properly, and the parting looked a lot like a comb-over. Belasco must have hated that picture.

Carter shook his head. "No. He's pretty distinctive. I think I'd have remembered him." He handed the picture back. "And I have no idea what the danger he was worried about was, or even why he called me when there must be a hundred PI offices between Providence and Red Hook."

This caused a pause, and the exchange of significant glances between the police officers. Carter knew better than to ask why; they'd get around to it any minute.

"We pulled the camera feed from the parking lot," said Harrelson. "It's not great quality, and Belasco's car was in the corner of the frame. We got some usable images, though."

He opened the file and produced prints of time-coded images. "Here's Belasco getting into his car." The code read 12:57.

"The camera angle's too high to see him in there. Take a look at this."

It was simply a picture of the silver Ford Focus sitting there, timed at 13:01. There was something wrong about the picture. Carter looked hard at it.

Harrelson passed him the next. It was identical to the last, but the code was 13:04. No, not identical. The shadow was different. It took Carter a moment to understand why that should be. "What's going on with the suspension? Why is it higher on this one?"

"That's a good question, ain't it?" said Harrelson.

"Nobody gets in or out after Belasco," said Piers, "but it bellies down on its shocks, and then rises up again. CSU estimate you'd have to put at least three other adults in there to do that."

Carter handed the pictures back, confused by what he'd just seen, and by why they were showing them to him. "I can't explain that."

"It gets better," said Aspinall and nodded to Harrelson.

The next picture showed the car's passenger door open. A man in a dark overcoat and a hat was leaning in. There was something shiny on the passenger seat. It took Carter a moment to realize it was a shoe, one of Belasco's shod feet. "That's how we found Belasco, lying across the seats," said Harrelson. The time code read 13:06.

So did the code on the next one, taken some thirty seconds later from the video. The man standing by the car, Belasco lying still in the car, presumably dead. The man had a phone to his ear.

13:06.

"Holy shit," said Carter.

The officers thought he was reacting to the realization that Belasco was not the one who had called him. True, that was part of it, but what concerned Carter most was he recognized the man in the hat and coat.

He had been sitting on Carter's bed that morning.

After he left the Providence PD precinct building, far more confused than when he entered, Carter went for a long, meandering walk to clear his head.

He wanted to think he was reading something into nothing. All he had of the man he had dreamed of was two momentary glimpses, once in silhouette, and once turned away. One man in an overcoat and hat looked pretty much like another. There was just something about it, though. There wasn't a single view of the man's face, and—despite it looking like he had bare hands in the recording—there were no unaccounted-for fingerprints on the door handle, glass, or the phone itself. He must have been wearing latex gloves, or even painted out his fingerprints with latex solution.

The timing was irrefutable, however. Whoever the stranger was, he had undeniably watched Belasco die (die *somehow*—the ME was taking her time over it), walked over, calmly taken Belasco's phone from his corpse in broad daylight, called Carter to bring him to the scene, and walked away. Whoever he was, he knew full well where every camera in the vicinity was. He was only on the parking lot camera, and he'd kept his back to that. Every other camera in the vicinity had been checked, and he wasn't on any of them. There were gaps in the coverage so it certainly wasn't impossible to walk away undetected, but it was unlikely, unless those gaps had already been discovered and a safe path plotted.

All of which meant that whatever had happened (Carter couldn't quite bring himself to accept that it was a homicide, not while the cause of death remained unsettled) had been exhaustively planned and the area reconnoitered. Carter was sure he had never met or heard of Belasco, and the evidence was that the ignorance was mutual. Carter's number was only found in the call log of Belasco's phone, not the contact list. In the recording, the man plainly tapped in the number with the thumb of his right hand, his left hanging empty by his side. There was no notebook, card, or scrap of paper to consult. So, the man in the overcoat and hat had entered Carter's number from memory. It was a small, unusual detail in what was becoming a large, unusual case.

The biggest question in Carter's mind was not why Belasco had died, how Belasco had died, or who had been complicit in that death. It was, why Carter? Why drag him into it? If the timing had been very different, he could have believed it was an attempt to frame him, but the timing almost seemed to go out of its way to exonerate him from collusion immediately. Harrelson didn't strike Carter as the sharpest detective he'd ever met, but he was no chump, either. It was simple and quick to eliminate Carter as a suspect, and so it had proved.

Carter entertained paranoid ideas of it being an unnecessarily complicated double plot to frame him for murder after having first framed him for coming up with a perfect alibi, the second stage of the plan not yet having gone into operation. His paranoia never persisted for long, however; there was enough shit happening in the world already without having to imagine more.

Specifically, there was somebody out there who would want to bring him right into the middle of a police investigation, and knew just how to do it. That much was indisputable, and demonstrated that he really didn't need to be paranoid. Somebody clever was out to get him, although what "get" meant in this case was beyond Carter. In his experience, motives were simple. There was greed, there was jealousy, he'd seen plenty of revenge played out in gang-related crimes, there was even sadism, and sometimes there was flat-out stupidity, which was a pretty powerful motivator in itself.

For the first time in his careers as a cop and as an investigator, he could see opportunity, and the shadow of a method, but the motive was just missing. No, he admitted to himself, there was one other case in which he could find no motive he could understand. Martin Suydam.

Carter phoned Detective Harrelson.

"Mr. Carter," said Harrelson. He sounded surprised. "How can I help you? Have you remembered something?"

"Can you talk?"

There was silence on the line. Carter had the distinct impression he was making Harrelson nervous.

"How d'you mean?"

"I mean," said Carter carefully, "the Belasco thing is freaking me out a little. I want to talk to you about it without your lieutenant and captain standing there."

"Look, Carter." Carter noted the drop of the honorific and was glad of it. "This is police business now. I know you're going to feel involved—"

"I *am* involved."

"—but you're just going to get in the way. You know how this works. We don't need you playing Sam Spade in the middle."

"What kind of resources are they giving you?" There was silence on the line. "Yeah, that was what I thought. The ME will come back with an inconclusive report, maybe even try and farm it out for a second opinion, because he doesn't—"

"She."

"—because she doesn't want a mystery death on her record, especially not somebody middle class and maybe notable in his field. Your lieutenant will decide that, yes, the man who made the phone call was a little weird, but there's no actual evidence of wrongdoing. It'll sit as an open case for a while, then go cold and slide out of sight. Maybe it will be closed because somebody decides there's no case at all. Maybe not." Carter looked up at the sign on the bar behind him. "There's a bar around the corner from you called McLaren's."

"Christ, no," said Harrelson, "that's a cop bar. Find the Dantzic Brew Vault. It's a couple of blocks from McLaren's. I'll see you there in twenty minutes."

He hung up.

It was closer to thirty when Harrelson turned up, looking harassed. Carter had chosen a beer for him. Harrelson struck him as a dark brew sort of man. Harrelson looked at the glass when Carter slid it toward him, muttered, "I'm on duty," and drank from it anyway.

"You've got me as a resource," said Carter.

"I've got the whole fucking department."

"No, you don't. I know how this goes, Harrelson. The Child-Catcher thing went weird, too. You never met a man less likely to eat his gun than Charlie Hammond."

Harrelson was looking at him warily, as if suspecting some sort of entrapment.

"I'm not talking about a whitewash or anything like that. People just stopped talking about it, pretended it had never happened." He shook his head. "It's a strange fucking thing to see the biggest case in the city just fade away out of people's minds like that. It's going to happen to the Belasco death, too. It already is. It's like seeing the world rewritten before your very eyes until it's just a fading memory for most." He tapped the tabletop. "If you're directly affected, you can't do that, though. I can't because hat-and-coat dragged me into it. You can't because it's your case."

"Maybe there's no case."

Carter winced. "Bullshit. It's a homicide."

There was silence for a minute.

Then Carter said, "The ME's report's already in, isn't it?"

Harrelson said nothing.

"What's in it? What killed Belasco?"

"The report is provisional," said Harrelson. He took a quick drink from his glass. "It's inconclusive."

"Wow." Carter nodded slowly, impressed. "That much of a career threat, huh? Your ME must be regretting ever opening that body bag."

"I saw her. Asked about the foam on his lips. Said I'd seen something similar in drownings." He shook his head, reliving disbelief. "She looked like I'd just asked her to go down on me. Couldn't get me out of there fast enough. I think . . ." He said it reluctantly. "I think they're going to put it down to some kind of seizure and close the case."

"So, you've got the 'whole fucking department as a resource,' huh?"

"I got fuck all." He glared at Carter. "I got a guy who looks like he drowned in a dry car, an ME who ain't answering her e-mails, a lieutenant who is *real* keen to unload a gangbanger case on me, and I got you." He took another quick drink. "And you're an asshole."

"How long before you get closed down?"

"As soon as the ME gets the balls to sign off on a final report. That'll be early next week now. She's gonna spend the weekend agonizing over it."

"What will it say?"

Harreslon barked a humorless laugh. "What's it gonna say? What *can* it say? Natural causes. She'll find some Latin name for a whole family of conditions, and say that did him. He fitted and he died. What else *can* it say?" He looked in his glass, but it was empty now. "That Voldemort offed him? That it's an X-*Files* episode? Call the fucking Scooby Gang? Jesus."

"Okay." Carter finished his own drink. "Okay. I'm going to ask around. If I find anything out, I tell you. If you find anything out, you tell me. We keep it off the Net."

"I ain't got time for a new hobby."

"I know. This is mainly going to be on me. I got questions. I just want you to hear the answers."

"They're gonna be toxic."

"I know."

"This is going to bite me, I know it." Harrelson got to his feet. "Okay, Carter. Keep me in the loop."

"Two-way street, man."

Harrelson was walking away. "You're still an asshole."

The first firing range Carter found insisted on his joining the NRA as a condition of membership. He passed on that, and found a gun store with an indoor range. He showed his ID and his concealed carry, and bought an hour on a twenty-five-yard lane, a box of ammunition, a pair of eye protectors for $2.99, and disposable earplugs for 50 cents.

He hadn't held his gun for any reason other than to clean it since the day Hammond died. He used to be fastidious about booking time on the range until then. After, it hadn't seemed so important.

The Glock didn't feel good in his hands anymore. It was awkward, and he spent a minute experimenting with his grip to get it to rest snuggled into the web of his thumb. Even then it felt heavy and alien.

One of the store workers was overseeing the range and stopped by Carter's lane. Carter didn't notice him until he said, "You've fired before, yeah?"

He sounded unconvinced by his own question. Carter had carried out a safety test to the worker's satisfaction before he was allowed on the lane, and had done so easily and intuitively.

"Out of practice," said Carter. "I've let myself get out of practice." He forced a comradely smile. He wished the man would go. The man didn't.

"Try letting off a clip. Don't worry about your grouping. Just get the feel of it."

"Thanks," said Carter. His smile was feeling painful. The store worker still didn't go.

Cursing inwardly, Carter turned his attention back to the lane. At least the target was a simple silhouette body mass sheet, and not one of the bullshit novelty targets he'd seen sometimes. Generic "Taliban," zombies, clowns, dinosaurs, zombie clowns. They pissed him off bad. It wasn't a fucking game.

Almost unbidden, he released the safety, and his index finger slid inside the guard.

The first shot surprised him, but old reflexes were shaking off the rust. He fired rapidly in a series of controlled double taps, just like Charlie swore by, just like Charlie didn't use on the day of his death.

Five, six, seven duos of slugs went out from the Glock, grouping well in the innermost body mass zone.

Then there was just one bullet left in the gun and, as he fired it without hesitation, he saw Suydam standing there, the stunted shape of the Taurus PLY in his hand. He was smiling as Carter gutshot him.

Carter lowered his pistol quickly, unconsciously reengaging the safety and moving his index to lie against the frame. He puffed out a breath in shock, but it was just a card target. It had never been anything but a card target.

The store worker had mistaken the sharp exhalation for exhilaration. "There you go! Good shooting, my man! Like riding a bike, right? Last one's a mite low, but it would have done the job okay." He laughed. "Just not quick."

Chapter 10

THE SORCERY OF STATISTICS

"You look like shit," said Lovecraft.

"It's been a problematical kind of day," he admitted.

He'd arrived at the store an hour before closing, feeling wrung out and reeking of propellant fumes. He'd ended up emptying the box of ammo at the range and buying another. He'd left behind several bullet-riddled card targets and an impressed gun store employee. Lovecraft had greeted him by telling him he stank like Custer's Last Stand.

There was nothing wrong with his marksmanship, but he had discovered that he no longer enjoyed shooting. The lack of pleasure in it depressed him. He'd never subscribed to the whole Second Amendment fetish, and the NRA could go fuck themselves, but he'd always enjoyed shooting in and of itself, even when it became a necessary part of his job. Even that hadn't taken the joy out of it. He'd never, ever fired in anger, though, and now he wondered if he could. The pistol in the paddle holster at his waist, the gun he could feel weighing there right that minute, had stopped being a tool and become a liability in the balance sheet of his sensibilities. Watching Charlie snuff himself had done that.

"Have you eaten?"

Carter perked up at the question. He'd enjoyed eating with her the previous evening. "No. Haven't felt hungry until now."

"Well, eat." Belatedly she realized he'd misunderstood her. "Sorry. I'm seeing Ken tonight. Look, use the kitchen upstairs. Make yourself something, watch some reruns." Before he could respond, she slapped him gently in the chest. "You're adorable. Just like a lost puppy. Go and get some groceries while I close up the shop, and I'll cook for you."

"I can cook," said Carter, unsure whether to be grateful or irritated by the offer.

"Nobody said you couldn't. Get the groceries, and take your damn gun smoke with you. You're upsetting the books."

She was as good as her word, if underwhelmed by the choice of ingredients he brought back. She made him a Spanish omelet while they talked.

"I guess you can't talk about your cases," she said. "Client confidentiality, and all."

"No. Not usually. I'm kind of my own client on this one, though, so I'm giving myself permission to talk about it."

"What an understanding client you have."

"Maybe," said Carter, "but he pays badly."

Carter spent the remaining cooking time and about half the eating telling her about the Belasco investigation while Lovecraft listened, eating an apple. He noticed she lost interest in the apple as the story progressed.

When he finished, her first question surprised him.

"What was Belasco a professor of?"

"I said. Math."

She gave him an *I'm talking to an idiot* look. "There's math and there's math. Which particular discipline?"

Sighing vexedly, Carter fetched his jacket and checked the notebook he kept in the breast pocket. "Topology. What is that, anyway? Maps?"

"Surfaces. The math of surfaces."

"I was kind of right, then."

"And kind of very wrong." She went to take a bite from her apple, and changed her mind. "Clave has a good academic reputation. Small college, but high-powered. If Belasco had tenure there, he must have been quite something."

"You think somebody at the college engineered his death?"

"Okay, two things. First, yeah. If he was murdered, however it was done has baffled an experienced medical examiner. Takes either really obscure knowledge or a really clever head to do a thing like that. Second"—she looked seriously at Carter—"I think you should walk away from this."

The forkful of omelet halted at his mouth.

"Seriously. This has nothing to do with you. You said yourself, you're not getting paid for this and you hate your client."

"I can't do that."

"You're not a cop anymore, Dan. Yes, you can do that. If only from a position of self-preservation. If there is a killer behind all this, it's someone who killed Belasco for reasons that are probably beyond normal human comprehension. Belasco scoffed at one of the perp's equations—"

Perp? mouthed Carter, raising his eyebrows at her.

"—or crossed his sevens and somebody hated that, or stole somebody's favorite pencil. If they've killed once and got away with it, they might want to try again if somebody pisses them off even slightly. Investigations piss people off. You start doing the gumshoe in the wrong venue, and you might end up the one with foam on your lips."

Carter finished the last scraps of his omelet in silence.

"I never knew you cared," he said. He let his fork fall with a clatter on the plate.

"I don't. You haven't signed the legal papers yet. Hand me half the store and then you can go off and get yourself killed with my blessing." She checked her watch. "Ah, crap. I always cut these things too close. Got to run."

She gathered her belongings and swept out with a muffled wish that he might have a good evening, sweet dreams, and not be killed by a mad scientist.

The door closed, and he heard her lock it after her.

Albert Einstein said that the only way to win at roulette is to steal from the table while the croupier isn't looking. That was an unlikely thing to happen in Einstein's day, and even less so today. In the modern casinos of Atlantic City, more eyes than just the croupier's are on every table.

Roulette is a simple enough game, and anyone with the most basic grounding in statistics can work out the odds on a standard American double zero wheel easily enough. The presence of the zero and double zero slots means that the house edge never drops below 5.26 percent. In short, roulette is a game played for fun, a lottery, and not one from which any professional gambler would seriously try to make a living.

The weekend had passed, and the pits were relatively quiet in the day. The pit managers, however, remain vigilant. While some con artists and cheats prefer to operate when the casino is busy, hiding their activities amid the crush, others assiduously groom themselves to look incompetent, put on a cheap rayon shirt, and visit when things are slow, to be as baffled as anyone when they have a run of "luck."

One such guest was currently sitting at the roulette table, under the camera-moderated eye of the manager for that pit, Bernie Hayesman. The roulette table scams, what few of them there were, tended toward childish simplicity, primarily stealing back chips from failed numbers or sliding them surreptitiously into a winning neighbor. They were transparent and embarrassing, and some idiot tried them all the time. The croupiers and the floormen (a third of Hayesman's floormen were women, but the title had become traditional—besides, "floorperson" sounded ridiculous) were long since inured to such pathetic ploys, and Hayesman was rarely troubled by calls from the roulette table.

Today was different. Hayesman had taken a call from Alia Rand, his floorman covering the double zero table, asking him to put the camera on the guy in the blue shirt. Hayesman did so.

The guy looked like a geek, one of the genii they got now and then who couldn't tell the difference between statistics and numerology. Even when they got cleared out because their infallible system sucked dick, they'd go away to improve it to new heights of uselessness, come back in a few months, and lose it all again. You had to love these people.

The math is simple; the house *has* to win. So when it doesn't, either somebody's cheating, or they just got a run of luck. Casino people know there's no such thing as luck, just the odds. It all evens out in the end, and the house 5.26-percent-plus edge continues to cut. Any bursts of luck at the wheel soon fall away, and the gambler loses.

This guy wasn't losing. He had a small heap of chips by him. He didn't gamble on every spin, but once every three or four, he would shove everything onto red with a weird little spasm. And then red would come up.

He never bet on black, and he didn't bet every time red came up, but when he did it was always on red, and he always won. Every time he did, his stack doubled.

Hayesman hailed Rand on her Bluetooth earpiece. "How many times has he won, now?"

"Including the times you've seen, seven. He started on twenty-five bucks, now he's got thirty-two hundred. I got a bad feeling about him the third time it happened. Once is normal, twice is coincidence, three times was starting to feel like voodoo."

Hayesman knew what she meant. Three consecutive wins on

the colors wasn't statistically staggering—it was odds of about twenty to one—but the way the guest placed the bet with such certainty . . . well, it meant nothing objectively. Subjectively, it felt wrong. The guest knew something that was giving him wins. That was just a gut feeling. After seven consecutive wins, a chance of about a quarter of 1 percent, the gut feeling was becoming a certainty.

The guy won again. Hayesman took the desk calculator out of the drawer and stabbed in some numbers. That was a win at odds of 833 to 1, rounding the decimals. If the guest kept this up even a few more times, it would hurt the house's bottom line badly; Hayesman knew enough about geometrical progressions not to want one on his watch. He looked up from ruminating over the number on the calculator's display to see another win. The man was gathering a crowd, and looked to be enjoying the attention. He had almost thirteen grand of the casino's money in front of him. It wasn't a huge amount in the casino's dealings, but two more wins would take it over fifty grand, and that just wasn't going to happen.

"Close the table, and check it," he told Rand. "If the guest makes a move toward another table, bring him up here. I'll talk to him."

The table was closed amid expressions of dismay from the onlookers. The guest himself seemed unfazed by events, tipped the croupier fifty bucks when he changed the pile of $25 and $100 chips for a more convenient fistful of 5G grays and 1G oranges, and wandered off. As soon as the table was unattended and the guests were elsewhere, the duty mechanic arrived to look it over. The wait until no one was around was diplomatic—it didn't do to imply that a guest had been cheating without proof. It was doubly important not to imply such a method of cheating was even possible, because unsupported paths to wealth prosper in greedy minds, and such minds are not uncommon among casino guests. Hayesman had seen enough crops of idiots coming in with half-baked *Mission: Impossible* gadgets not to want to encourage them.

Hayesman returned to the plate of ribs he had ordered and that had just been delivered when the geek on the wheel started to do so suspiciously well. He enjoyed it in quiet solitude for a little over five minutes before there was a knock at the door. Rand put her head around to ask if he was free. Hayesman looked regretfully at the cooling ribs and said yes.

The geek looked about as prepossessing as he had on the closed-circuit TV. He dressed like his mother had sent him out, and Hayesman hoped he'd spend some of his money on some new clothes. It wasn't *The Big Bang Theory* or *Napoleon Dynamite* levels of poor choices, but the wardrobe still looked oddly standardized. Maybe all the geek's clothes were the same so he never had to think about what to wear in the morning. Hayesman remembered reading that was how Albert Einstein bought his clothes. He rubbed his brow; that was the second time he'd thought about Einstein that day, he was sure, but he couldn't remember what it had been about the first time.

"Enjoying your lunch?" asked the geek. Hayesman knew right that second that he would never like the guest.

"That was quite a run of luck you had just now," he said, wiping sauce away from his mouth with the edge of his napkin. He suddenly realized he was looking like a B movie gangster, took the napkin from his collar, and dropped it on his plate. "You have a system?"

"Not really," said the guest. "I just decide when I want to double my money, and then bet. It was working pretty well."

"There's a little thing called 'The Rules of Probability' that say that's not such a good system, sir."

"Rules." The man wrinkled his nose. "There's always a higher authority to appeal."

Hayesman leaned back in his chair. He was coming to the conclusion that the guy was probably just honestly lucky for those few spins, and could easily have lost on the next spin. "You talking about God?"

The man seemed slightly pained by the suggestion. He shook his head.

"You know how likely that little winning streak of yours was?"

The man looked up, his eyes flickering a little from side to side as if he were reckoning it up in his head. "One in seventeen hundred and fifty-seven," he said after two seconds.

"And do—"

"Point," interrupted the guest, "seven eight six six. The decimals go on for a while, but you get the gist."

"And do you see why we might take an interest in those kinds of figures? Sir, our whole business is built on understanding those Rules of Probability, and nothing makes us more wary than when we see what we call *unusual patterns of betting* that keep somebody winning."

"This is all fascinating," said the guest.

Hayesman couldn't get a handle on him at all. Most people have seen enough films and TV to know—or to think they know—that being taken off to an office in a casino is a bad thing. In reality, being beaten, shot, and buried in the desert for Vegas or given concrete boots in Atlantic City was utterly out of character for modern casinos. The wise guys had been superseded by entities bigger, just as ruthless, and way smarter. Smart enough to stay within the law, and where the law wasn't suitable to their needs, rich enough to lobby and get it changed.

Most people would be looking pretty panicky by now, but the guest just looked bored. Hayesman decided to skip the lecture about how *unusual patterns of betting* clued in observant floormen and their pit managers. He would just cut to the chase.

"Your pattern of betting was very unusual, sir, and your results were off the chart."

"But I haven't done anything wrong."

"Nothing we can prove. But this isn't a court of law, sir. It is a private business, and we can choose who we deal with. We choose not to deal with you."

"You mean, *you* choose not to."

"I represent the company in this matter. If you disagree with the ruling, you may communicate your grievance to the company by writing to this address"—he took a card from a box on his desk and held it out—"marking it to the attention of Guest Relations."

The guest made no move to take the card. Hayesman lowered his hand and dropped the card to the desktop. "The address is also available on our website."

There was near silence. The guest had gone from smug to pettishly angry. He kept exhaling heavily through his nose.

"But it was your decision," said the guest. He didn't say it as if he were arguing. He simply wished to be clear on the facts, no more, no less.

"There's not a manager in the country wouldn't have made the same call, sir. I'm sorry, but there it is. I'm afraid you are no longer welcome at the Oceanic."

"I keep the money, though? Yes?"

Hayesman was positive that very second that the man had cheated. He had no idea how, but now he was sure. Without an understanding of the method, however, he was on thin ice if he withheld the guest's winnings. "How much have you got in chips, sir?"

"Twelve thousand seven hundred and fifty dollars," said the man. He said it without hesitation and without looking at his chips. Hayesman had a feeling he could tell you exactly what change he had in his pocket and the mix of coins that made it up. The guy was either eidetic or had a trained memory. Hayesman had seen his like before.

He took a cashbox from the deep drawer in his desk, unlocked it, and counted out $12,750. Rand took the money and offered it to the guest, her hand held out for the chips. The man regarded her for a moment, then gave in. He put the bills in his wallet and looked at Hayesman.

"Are we done?"

"We're done. Have a nice day, sir, and—please—don't come back."

The man smiled. "*Bon appétit*," he said. Rand led him out.

Rand was joined by three other floor staff outside the office, and they formed up around the guest as he was walked off the premises. It seemed to amuse him.

"I'm flattered that you think it would take four of you to subdue me," he said to Rand as she led the group through the old-school coin slots to a side exit.

"SOP," she said. "There's nothing personal in this, sir." She could hardly wait to get him out of the building. They'd had to deal with real sharpers, drunks, and people who couldn't tell the difference between the house's edge and actual fraud. It could get messy sometimes. In comparison, this guy was quiet and cooperative. The bad, *bad* feeling she was getting from him was not something she could rationalize or justify, but it bothered her more than if he had been fighting drunk and cussing her.

"Okay, okay," he said, suddenly speeding up and getting ahead of his escort before they knew what he was doing. There were no other guests in that corner, and ahead of them was the fire door they were taking him to. Despite the sense that all was not well, Rand couldn't see any good reason to feel worried. Yet she was, profoundly and certainly.

"The house always wins. I get it. I truly do. You, ma'am, gentlemen, are just doing your jobs. Let me tip you." He had some coins in his hands, and for a bemused moment, Rand thought he was going to give them his spare change. But instead, he fed the coins into four slot machines, two on either side of the aisle, triggering each before going on to the next. When he was done, he went to the door by himself.

"Three point two four five two times ten to the twenty-seventh." He smiled, a cold thing. "Enjoy."

The first machine leaped into noisy life as the last reel clicked home. Rand was distracted from the closing door by a harsh electronic fanfare. She glanced at the machine, and did a double-take as she saw it had hit its maximum jackpot.

Another fanfare from the opposite side of the aisle, and another jackpot, and another, and another. The four machines played their triumphant tunes as lights flashed and coins vomited from four prize chutes.

The door closed.

Chapter 11

THE TERRIBLE YOUNG MAN

Questioning was a different skill now.

When he was still a cop, you flashed the badge and people started talking. Even if they were lying, or evasive, at least their lips were moving and you could get something out of them. Of course, there were always the idiots who got their cues from TV and the movies, echoing, "You won't get nuthin' from me, copper," since Jimmy Cagney first sneered into a camera, or its modern counterpart, "I want a lawyer." They always said, "I know my rights," but usually they didn't. They panicked and gabbled, or they shut up about the wrong things and talked more than they realized. The last generation of gang members he'd had to deal with before resigning, the "fuck the po-po" people, they were so focused on posing for their mug shot that it occupied most of their attention budget for the day and then they'd talk without even re-alizing it. It's a truism that the vast majority of criminals are not too bright. For every Moriarty, there's an army of guys who use Velcro shoes because laces are too challenging.

As for civilians, getting them to shut up once they know they're talking to a cop is the hard part.

That all changed when Carter became a private investigator. People regard PIs as in pretty much the same compartment of stereotypes as reporters: bottom-feeding scum they don't want to talk to.

It had taken some ingenuity and psychology to find a way around it, but Carter had found a pretty good solution. He disassociated himself from the actual act of investigation, putting the focus—and any associated onus—on the client. If he simply introduced himself as a PI, things turned cold. If, however, he could identify or at least hint to them (whether it was true or not) that he was simply a hireling, then he became just an employee, another working stiff.

He'd rapidly discovered that, in any case where a particular family was involved, he just had to say, "I've been retained by the family to check on the details," and people became helpful, or even sympathetic depending on what the case was about. If somebody's gone missing or been assaulted and the police don't have the time or people to throw at it, who wouldn't want to help the family? Carter had learned there didn't even have to be a family directly involved for the magic of the phrase to work.

If that failed or didn't work in context, he would try to imply he was an outsourced insurance investigator. It was weird how many people were more in awe of insurance investigators than they were of the police. Carter guessed the police could only arrest you. Insurance investigators could fuck up your premiums.

On this occasion, a passing reference to "family" was enough to do the trick. James Belasco was well regarded by the small cabal of academics tenured at Clave College, but they didn't know much about his personal life. He had been married, but his wife had died some three years before from sepsis. There had been no children. His colleagues said that he had worked longer hours after that, and produced a greater number of papers. Of all the professors at Clave, he was considered safest in tenure, and would probably have stayed there until retirement.

"I didn't know he had family," said Pauline Watson, Belasco's assistant.

"A brother in Cleveland," lied Carter. "I think there was an argument a few years ago and they didn't talk. A few months ago they started speaking again, looked like reconciliation was in the cards, then this happened. The brother just wants to know everything was done."

They were in Belasco's office. Already one shelf of books had been boxed, but the move had been put on pause then.

Watson caught the direction of Carter's glance. She shrugged. "It's a nice office. There was an attempt to land grab it. I know it seems cold, but . . . well, some of the other staff, their social skills could use work. The dean herself had to send around an e-mail telling people the office was to be left alone until she said otherwise." She smiled, more a social construction than an expression. "I'll be honest, Mr. Carter, I don't really understand why you're here. The professor died because of some sort of lung infection, didn't he?"

Carter had seen the postmortem report, and it wasn't helpful. Belasco's corpse showed every sign of having drowned, except there was no water in his lungs. The ME had vaguely hand-waved at the idea of a lung irritation creating a similar effect, but without much enthusiasm. All that could be said with any certainty was that Belasco had asphyxiated, and it looked more likely to have been due to a natural cause than not.

Providence PD was not keen to make more work for itself, and was happy to accept that. Detective Harrelson was not nearly so happy about it when he tipped Carter off about the findings. The whole business with the phone call had fallen between the cracks—no, it had been *dropped* between the cracks—and his lieutenant and captain seemed to regard it as a freakish detail with no real bearing. It bothered Harrelson a great deal and, he told Carter, he was going to keep an eye out for anything else about the Belasco case that might cross his desk or the desks of any of his colleagues.

"Yes," said Carter. "It was just some sort of lung infection, but the brother . . . he's broken up about it. You know how it is when you decide to do something after meaning to deal with it for years, and then something stops you? I guess that's what's happening with the professor's brother. He's upset and seeing a pattern where there isn't one. Just lousy luck. But . . . I'm being paid to ask around. I have to ask some pretty paranoid questions. Gets embarrassing, to be frank, Ms. Watson."

"What sort of paranoid questions?"

"Nothing too crazy, just the usual. Did Professor Belasco have any enemies? Did he move in any suspicious circles? Did he have any dangerous habits? Usual things."

"The professor?" Watson almost laughed. "He wouldn't mind me saying this, used to joke about it himself, but he was a very boring man. Pleasant, but his work was his life. After Gemma died, it really was all that there was to his life. He was here most of the time. I don't think he had an opportunity for some sort of clandestine life."

"No other women?"

"None. Unless they could talk pure math, he didn't have much interest."

"No enemies?"

Here, Watson grew quiet and looked uncomfortable. "Nobody who hated him enough to kill him, if that's what you mean?" she said finally.

"Anybody who disliked him at all," said Carter, at pains to be casual. It was no big deal. He wasn't going to make a song and dance about it. She should just tell him to get it out of the way.

"Scientists don't usually get on well with *everyone*," said Watson. "You have to understand, Mr. Carter. There are some powerful egos out there. If they get even a little bit bruised, they can hold a grudge for life."

"Any example?"

"Nobody that would kill, put it that way."

"I didn't think they would." Carter took out his notepad and warmed up his most charismatic smile. "If you could give me who-ever had the professor on their shit list, I can ask them a few questions, prove they didn't have anything to do with it, and tell my client there's no story here other than what the police have already reported." Watson seemed loath to name names, but keen to spill gossip all the same. "There must be *somebody*?" he said gently, nudging her toward that gossip.

"There was one," she said reluctantly. It was a reluctance that faded quickly as she told Carter the story.

His name was William Colt. It was a good name for a cowboy, but Colt was about as far from a cowpuncher as it was possible to be. Looking like a suitable candidate for a David Byrne biopic set around the time of *More Songs About Buildings and Food*, Colt was not a popular man around campus. Carter found himself adjusting his approach to suggest (without stating as much) to interviewees that he had been hired by the academic administration to investigate William Colt with an eye to either defunding or even expelling him. Once whoever he was interviewing understood by Carter's double-talk that Colt might be deep in the shit, they could hardly wait to help pour more on his head.

"Arrogant asshole" and variations was a common epithet, along with an admission that he was undoubtedly brilliant and any institution would be happy to have him, and indeed could take him with Clave College's blessings, just so long as it was understood that Clave wouldn't take him back when his new college discovered what an arrogant asshole he was.

Nor was he quite the genius he had been when he first joined the college. His work was produced as and when he felt like doing so, and he was failing to maintain the tutorial levels that were expected of him as a postgraduate. He seemed to have raised the hackles of just about every lecturer he had ever encountered, but he did have one special bête noire.

James Belasco.

Normally their paths would hardly have crossed, Colt's field of study being combinatorics as opposed to Belasco's topology.

"That all changed about a year ago," Professor Delaine told Carter as he walked with her across the campus toward the commissary building. "I think Will was getting restless, and the idea of specializing in one branch of math was frightening him a little. We talked about career options, but he kept talking about how limiting he found it, and how if everything was mathematics, then mathematics was everything."

"What did he mean by that?"

"Every branch of science likes to think it's important, and of course, they all are. But they're specializations. Much of biology, for example, is biochemistry, which is a specialization of organic chemistry, which is a specialization of chemistry, which is a specialization of physics, and physics is practical mathematics. No matter which set of *matryoshka* dolls you open in science, the innermost is always math." She winced slightly at a memory. "Will thinks there might be another doll inside that."

"Something underlying math? Such as?"

"The purest form of it. The mother of everything. He's not the first to think that way, and he's not the first to be disappointed. The truth of it, Mr. Carter, is that we're already there. The different branches of mathematics are simply different aspects of the same discipline. The innermost doll looks like calculus from one direction, number theory from another, and so on. The next doll outward takes those views and begins to interface them to the real world. Information theory, game theory, statistics, modeling reality from the purity of numbers.

"It's probably blasphemous of me to say it, but God is right there in that act. From the 'Let there be light' of pure math through the five subsequent days of creation embodied in applied mathematics. I'm an atheist because I don't need a god to explain the universe. I have seen the truth of the numbers, and they should be enough for anyone."

"But not Colt?"

"No. Young and restless. Which is good, don't get me wrong. Restless minds are questioning minds, and curiosity makes us what we are. William's didn't take him into the broader world, though, not when he had it here on campus in microcosm. He made a nuisance of himself in some of the other departments. He was the subject of debate for some weeks in the collegiate corridors of power, such as they are. Then he lost interest, and turns up when he feels like it. His work is still good, on the occasions he produces it, but not as sharp as it used to be. He's lost some of his fire. Coming into money was probably what did it."

Carter's cop instincts were not about to let a mention of sudden wealth go by, and he asked about it.

"He won a decently sized prize on the state lottery, some tens of thousands." Professor Delaine grimaced. "A startling event. The faculty was appalled. A mathematician, somebody who actually understands numbers, buying a lottery ticket. It beggars belief."

Delaine was hardly the only member of staff to be more or less candid about William Colt, but none of them could offer any concrete suggestions as to why there was enmity between him and James Belasco, other than Colt not taking the work seriously. It was left to Carter to do a little detective work to find somebody who would give him details.

A very little detective work, as it turned out. Outside Belasco's office was a notice board bearing a schedule for tutorial groups and this Carter had photographed in passing. Now he checked the names of those in the groups against the society lists in the student union building, and found a couple of likely candidates. Having made friendly contact with campus security, and after a few more inquiries, Carter was able to locate one of the names having lunch in the cafeteria.

Jason Xu smiled when Carter introduced himself and started spinning a line about a potential disciplinary action against William Colt.

"Bullshit," said Xu good-naturedly. "This is about Professor Belasco. Everyone knows it."

"Okay," said Carter, "that's cool. I prefer being up-front in any case. Colt and Belasco. I keep hearing about bad blood, but no details."

"You think Colt killed the prof?" Xu was eating a Caesar salad in a plastic container. He speared a piece of anchovy with his fork and chewed it while he waited for an answer.

"It's not a murder inquiry. This place would be dense with homicide cops if it were. I'm just trying to find out what went on in the professor's life. It's a pretty broad brief, but it's what his family wants me to do." Carter didn't mind not being *entirely* up-front. "I keep hearing the name William Colt. What was going on there?"

"Colt's a dick," said Xu without hesitation. "He's smart. No one is saying he isn't, but he knows it and thinks it's a superpower. He's like . . . what's that kind of autism? The mild kind?"

"Asperger's?"

"Asperger's syndrome, yeah. He just doesn't deal so well with reality. Goes around like he's the lead character in a movie and everything has to be about him."

"Playing a role, huh?" Carter had found Xu's name on the Roleplaying Society notice board.

Xu laughed. "Man, don't get all *Dark Dungeons* on me. I know what reality looks like. A game's a game. When we put the dice away, we're done for the evening. Colt's not playing a game. He honestly thinks the world's a big story and it's all about him."

"Okay. And how did that play into his relationship with Professor Belasco?"

"He suggested . . . nah, he flat out *said* that Belasco had a poor intellect. That's fighting talk in these halls. It's not even true. Belasco was a prodigy back in the day. You find his name all over. Not such a bright star these days, but that's math for you. Almost every big name you can think of did all their best work before they were thirty. Newton developed calculus when he was, like, twenty-six. You know that? Colt got off on saying Belasco's best work wasn't that great, and he was burned out."

"He said this to Belasco's face?"

"Pretty much. He was snide about it. Really got into Belasco's grill. A guy can only have so much patience with that kind of shit. Colt was saying he was warming to topology as a field—"

"That was Professor Belasco's specialty, right?"

"Yeah, and Colt was saying he was going to rewrite the book on topology and everyone who went before him would be forgotten."

"Like Belasco."

"Yeah. Like Belasco. Belasco didn't take it lying down. Colt is, as mentioned previously, a dick, and has pissed off just about everybody on campus at one time or another. Belasco had been sitting on some shit that Colt pulled over in archaeology, but then Colt pissed him off so Belasco was going to put together a formal complaint."

"Which you know how?"

Xu laughed. "Because he said it right in front of us in the tutorial group. Kicked Colt out, and said he wouldn't be happy until Colt was expelled." Xu shook his head, smiling ruefully. "The prof's standing went up with us all that day. Nobody can fucking stand Colt, man. But now . . . Belasco's dead." He looked appraisingly at Carter. "You *sure* this isn't about a homicide?"

Chapter 12

"Such a thrilling life you lead."

Lovecraft was packaging books while Carter told her about the day.

"I don't see what this Colt kid has to do with anything," she continued as she neatly sliced squares of Bubble Wrap with a pair of open scissors. "He's an asshole. So what?"

"He's the only one I could find with anything like a motive," said Carter. "'So what?' is a good question. I don't know. I just don't know."

"Go back to New York. Haven't you got any cases there?"

"Not now. I closed an investigation just this week and that's all I had. I can't leave this one. Somebody wanted me involved. Well, I'm involved. I want to know why I was dragged into the Belasco death."

Lovecraft finished cocooning a first color edition of *Alice's*

Adventures in Wonderland, and began sealing it with tabs of tape already cut and arranged in a row along the edge of the counter. "Yeah, that was weird. I can see why that bothers you. So, what did you find out in archaeology?"

"What?"

"You said he had caused trouble in the archaeology department. What was that about?" She regarded his blank expression, and grinned. "You forgot to ask."

"It's on my list."

"You have a list? Wow. Mr. Organized."

"Colt's been missing for a few days. His car's gone, too. The timing's suspicious."

"A few days? So he wasn't here when Belasco died?"

"He hadn't been seen. Told someone he'd had a breakthrough in number theory and was going to break the bank at some casino." Carter checked his notes. "He won a lot of money on the lottery, too. Or at least he said he did."

"Gambling problem?"

"Only the kind where you wonder what to spend all the winnings on. The lottery thing seems to be true. Maybe he really does have a system?"

Lovecraft snorted with derision. "Get real. A lottery is just random numbers. Every one of those things is scoured by statisticians to spot patterns. Maybe the balls aren't perfectly uniform in some way. Maybe one of the machines is a little eccentric. Waste of time. The whole point of a lottery is that it's a lottery. You can't come up with a system that gives you a magic set of numbers. Only time I've ever heard of a lottery being scammed statistically was in Ireland, I think. It was possible to buy enough tickets to give a better than fifty-fifty chance they'd win the jackpot, and that week's jackpot was big enough to pay off the investment. They had to buy hundreds of thousands of tickets, though, and there was always a gamble it wouldn't work. Plus, they had to hire a small army of shills to buy the tickets without arousing suspicion that the probabilities were being gamed."

"Did it work?"

"Yeah, but it'll never work again. The lottery people detected irregularities in the betting patterns and are wise to it now. Plus, it was *still* a gamble; they could have lost everything but for smaller prizes. *Plus*, it cost a fortune in seed money. I don't think your lone postgrad has that sort of backing or organization."

"He just got lucky."

"Maybe he thinks he's lucky now. Going to break the bank at Monte Carlo."

"Don't think the freeway goes to Monte Carlo. Maybe Atlantic City's more his speed."

"Does anyone still go to Atlantic City? I'll stick with imagining him playing baccarat against Le Chiffre like James Bond."

"I saw that movie. It was Texas Hold'em."

"Philistine. Saying such things in a house of books. Shame on you."

Carter's phone buzzed. It was Jason Xu.

"Hey, you said I should call if I remembered anything? Well, I haven't, but I thought you'd like to know—Colt's back on campus."

Carter was back at Clave College within the hour. He already had the details of Colt's car, and prowled the college parking lots first, but didn't see it. Debating the possibility that Colt had already been and gone, Carter parked in the same lot as the Belasco death site and went looking for Xu.

The route took him past the mathematics building and, as he walked by the side entrance, he saw a man who looked a lot like a young David Byrne walk out carrying a black duffel bag slung across his shoulders.

Carter walked on without hesitation, got to the corner, and checked his phone as if he'd just received a text. He wasn't sure why he was being so circumspect; there was no good reason why he shouldn't have just approached Colt, confirmed his identification, and then asked him a few questions. He could only put it down to a hunch, although the more he analyzed his feelings, the more he realized that he had already marked Colt down as—if not Belasco's murderer—certainly involved. There was too much circumstantial detritus floating around the man. Colt *felt* guilty, although Carter could not be sure of exactly what.

He also wondered if there was some fear there. Belasco had died in a way that seemed to have baffled scientific theory. Maybe he had just had a fit, or maybe the fit was induced, and maybe the fit was induced by Colt. Carter had no desire to join Belasco as a footnote in a forensic journal. He would observe William Colt, and see if the bad feeling he had about Colt had any reality to it. Maybe he was just what everyone thought he was, an egotistical cocksucker of a genius. Just that and no more, as if that wasn't enough.

A sideways glance showed the playacting with his phone had been unnecessary; Colt was walking away from him. Carter quickly consulted his mental map of the area and decided to risk losing Colt in favor of getting his own car. He started at a brisk walk until Colt was hidden behind the mathematics building, and then broke into a run.

He reached his car and drove out onto the street, turning left to see if he could spot Colt. He had barely started looking when a red Mazda3 went by with Colt at the wheel. He must have parked on the street rather than using a college parking lot. The car looked new; maybe he hadn't wanted anyone to see it.

Carter drove down an access road to the rear of the chemical engineering building, made a three-point turn, and headed back out in pursuit of the red Mazda3.

Colt was easy to follow. His car was distinctive even at a distance, and he was in no hurry. Carter was able to hang back far enough to let a couple of cars between him and his quarry, and to avoid ever being directly on Colt's rear fender.

Carter had carried out enough mobile surveillance to keep much of his attention not on Colt, but on the traffic ahead of the

Mazda. Seeing changing traffic conditions ahead allowed him plenty of time to make decisions as to how he should proceed. The only even slightly problematical moment was when a slow driver pulled out in front of Carter and proceeded at a determined five miles per hour below the limit. It was a rookie mistake to hope the slow driver would get out of the way or suddenly discover the gas pedal, so Carter carried out a resolute overtaking maneuver the first chance he got. It brought him a little closer to Colt than he would have liked, but he tucked in behind a twenty-year-old Lincoln and hid there for the next few minutes before progressing back to his former tailing position.

Colt was heading roughly southeast, taking him away from his apartment, which was only a couple of blocks south of the campus. From Carter's inquiries, little was known about Colt's extracurricular activities. Wherever he was heading might very well turn out to be interesting, or at least illuminating.

They were now deep into suburbia. There were very few nonresidential buildings to be seen, and soon there were none, only streets of white houses weatherproofed to bear the rigors of the neighboring Atlantic. Carter checked his GPS and discovered that if Colt didn't reach his destination soon, he'd be in the bay.

Then Colt swung south, and headed down a road leading onto a small peninsula. The road onto the isthmus was narrow, and Colt's car was the only one going down it. While heavily treed, it would only take a glimpse for him to realize he was being followed. Carter fell back still farther, giving Colt plenty of lead. According to the GPS display, the peninsula was something around three hundred yards long with two rows of houses backing upon one another served by parallel roads that split from the access route as soon as it cleared the confining isthmus.

Carter considered his options. He could drive over there, but the chances of being spotted were good. If he walked over, however, that would seem suspicious in itself. He decided he would risk taking the car in, playing the role of a lost stranger who had made a wrong turn.

He took his car in slowly in case of meeting oncoming traffic. As the houses of the prim Providence street behind him vanished beyond the looming English and red oaks that lined the peninsula road, Carter felt a cold sense of isolation settle upon him. "Road" was an overstatement; his car shuddered its way along a rutted and ill-kept track. It had been surfaced once, but was now pitted, and Carter had to watch for potholes.

Any relief he felt at breaking out of the oppressive green tunnel was instantly quashed by the sight of what was, according to the map, Waite Road.

It certainly wasn't much to look at; before him the road ran straight ahead along one row of houses, then arced to the right to form a shape that looked overall like an asymmetric tuning fork or the mirror image of an "h." The houses were all of the same form, built in the 1930s by the look of them, and all were occupied and maintained. That said, they weren't maintained with much emphasis on appearance. The roads Carter had navigated to reach there had been lined with houses that were clearly the owners' pride and joys, or—at least—the product of stringent local laws and possibly residents' associations.

Waite Road didn't care, or at least the arm he could see, the row facing eastward toward the river, didn't. The lawns were not overgrown, but looked more like they were kept in check by the grazing of goats rather than mowers. The paintwork was white, but patches of moss showed here and there under the eaves. About half the houses had cars in their drives, and all of them were pickups, none of them new. None of the houses had any swing sets or outdoor toys visible. None of the houses had any view of the bay, the east side of the road bearing a dense stand of trees. More oaks, Carter saw.

Carter had been in bad neighborhoods before, ones where being an unfamiliar face had gotten people shot in the past, but he had never been in one that felt so *wrong* before. Waite Road was an appendix to Providence, both in the sense of being something added that was not absolutely necessary, and as an organ whose function was obscure. The last thing he had expected in the city was a place that felt like a failed *Deliverance* theme park.

There was a rough track off to the left where a path worn by generations of vehicles turning had been given a patina of permanence with a grudging few sacks of gravel thrown onto the rutted earth. Carter drove by it and then backed down along the track as far as he dared, which at least served to make his car partially hidden by the oaks and not quite so obvious from the road itself. His initial plan had been to stay there until Colt came out again, but he quickly decided he would need to be more proactive if he wanted to find anything out. This second plan ran into problems when he felt a powerful reluctance to open the door and get out.

He wasn't scared, he told himself, it was just that the place had put him on edge. It was idiotic, he knew. The citizens along Waite Road would just be normal folk, and it was only the strange isolation of the place that was working upon his nerves. Even so, it took a swift check of his Glock before he felt secure enough to step out of his vehicle.

Outside, he felt foolish. There was nothing odd about the place; it was just run-down. Probably some historical quirk of the city's zoning laws meant this place was overlooked. Still, he thought as he broke out of the tree line on the bay side, it seemed odd that such prime Rhode Island real estate was being underused like that. The view across the water was excellent, though he could understand why the stand of trees was necessary as a windbreak.

He walked southward along the shoreline until he gauged he was about level with the farthermost house, and reentered the trees. He walked cautiously through the leaf mold and frail grass until he could get a good look at the house without being seen in turn. The plan was to make his way northward through the trees, examining each house in turn until he found Colt's car, although as he hadn't been able to see it from the neck of the road, he thought it must be down the other arm. This supposition was disproved immediately.

The farthest house on the bay-side arm of Waite Road was

half as wide again as its neighbors, but that was the limit of its grandness. It was no mansion; only the same as the other houses around it, but more so. In fact, Carter wasn't convinced it was a residence at all, or not purely so. There was a sense that it was some sort of communal building, a community center, in as much as one street bearing maybe a dozen houses can be a community.

And there was Colt's red Mazda3, parked down the far side of the building. Of Colt himself there was no sign. Carter looked quickly around to make sure he was unobserved and, as there didn't seem to be a soul anywhere around, took a few pictures of the house. The lower windows showed nothing but darkness within, whereas even the shutters were closed on the second floor. Carter guessed that, with some of the winds that blew in off the Atlantic, the shutters weren't just there for show. Then again, he thought, none of the residents gave the impression they did anything for show, if their homes were any evidence.

He waited for half an hour, then an hour, but saw no activity whatsoever. Deciding he might be in for a long haul, he went back to his car to get some bottled water, an MRE heater, and a pouch of coffee. Maybe a ration pouch, too; he was just beginning to feel the absence of the meal he'd missed by responding to Xu's phone call. The coffee wouldn't taste much like coffee, but sometimes you just want something hot, and he'd drunk enough of the coffee pouches to have acquired the taste. With a small frisson of perverse pleasure, he remembered he had a cappuccino pouch in his map pocket.

He was still smiling at the thought of committing a crime against coffee connoisseurs the world over when he cleared the trees and saw that somebody had discovered his car.

A man was standing ten feet from it, his back to Carter. He wasn't moving, just looking at the car like a man might stand motionless near a horse or a cow, for fear of spooking it. Carter was quiet on his feet, but the man heard his approach all the same and turned to face him.

He wasn't very old, early to mid-twenties, Carter guessed, and he surely wasn't very handsome. He stood about five feet ten, and must have been carrying around 240 pounds. He looked at Carter through heavy-lidded eyes with the attitude of a corpulent child.

"You shouldn't park here," he said. Then, belatedly, "This your car?"

Carter smiled a friendly smile, although battling banjos had suddenly appeared on his internal sound track. The man was wearing faded jeans, a pair of battered blue and white sneakers failing at the toe caps, and a lumberjack short-sleeved shirt over a gray tee.

"Yes. I got lost. I couldn't see the through road. Could you tell me where I am, please?"

"This is Waite's Bill," said the man. His slow speech worked with the half-closed eyes to give the effect that he was sleepwalking. "This is private property."

"I'm sorry," said Carter. "I got lost. I didn't realize I was trespassing."

At least that explained the sudden change in civic ambience, he thought. Waite Road was essentially a gated community, water providing its fences and sheer antisocial weirdness acting as its gate. He wondered how anybody got on the housing list here. Then he wondered why anyone would want to get on the housing list in the first place.

The man had lost interest in him, but was looking out into the bay. A handsome motor yacht was passing by, heading out to sea.

"Nice yacht," said Carter. "Okay for some, huh?"

He noticed the man look up a little; he hadn't been looking at the yacht at all, but only the water.

"Don't want a boat," said the man. "I want to go swim."

Carter frowned. It didn't seem very warm out there, and the undertows would be fierce. "I'm not sure that's such a good place to go swimming. Maybe the other side of the bill . . . ?"

"I'm good at swimming," said the man.

Carter doubted that, but said nothing. The man seemed tractable, though, so perhaps he could get some local background out of him. He walked over to stand by him, mapping out a conversational strategy to befriend him on the way. The guy was obviously very into swimming, so that would be his "in." Fine.

He stood by the man, looked out over the dark waters of the Providence River as they wound out into the ocean, drew a breath to speak, and then everything went to shit.

Chapter 13

THE NAMELESS CITY

At some point, everyone suffers small physiological glitches. The human body is, after all, a complex entity, and tiny perturbations in its structure and chemistry can have notable, frightening effects. From a sudden-onset migraine to the random, racing heartbeats of atrial fibrillation, down to smaller effects such as a nervous tic or a brief period of blurred vision in one eye. The body usually compensates, and the troublesome effect passes.

For several long seconds, this is what Carter believed. His primary concern was that the changes in his perception meant that he could not safely drive until the small glitch in his metabolism passed. He would be glad when it did; a sour yellowness had settled upon his vision and it made him feel soul sick. It was like looking at the world in old photographs—not with the warmth of sepia, but damaged pictures found in an old box, a transparent cellophane-like layer separating from the image like an insect's wing.

No sooner had the thought crossed his mind, when he realized the underlying truth of it; he felt he was seeing the world through someone else's perception. His own, but not him.

Carter's sight blurred with double images, multiple images, and they were not the same. He was breathing heavily, becoming aware of the sound of his breath rasping in and out of his throat, the coldness in his lungs. What a shambolic scarecrow a human is. How full of paradox and obsolescence. Life quivered fitfully inside him, a flickering light in a stormy universe. He felt small and inconsequential. He felt the truth pressing in upon him, up from the ancient Earth beneath him, down from the still more ancient stars above, a pressure of reality that would crush him like a louse between fingernails.

He was vaguely aware that he had fallen to his knees, one hand on the cold grass of the riverside. He was too far from normal sensation to even feel panic at what he was experiencing. He was beyond fear, beyond wonder, beyond reason on a spectrum that tended into a darkness he could not fathom.

He knew he could no longer trust his perceptions, that he was suffering some sort of fit, some sort of fugue state. It didn't matter how real the waves of motion beneath his fingers felt, as if the ground were nothing more than a thin sheet beneath which a billion, billion worms and roots writhed; it wasn't real. It didn't matter that he saw across the bay clumsily superimposed upon itself, again and again, juddering images of the built-up land he knew, along with banks of primal woodland that had never seen humans, and strange tall buildings constructed of some smooth, red-orange stone that glowed in the rays of a sun that was behind the clouds; it wasn't real. He saw the water and the sky join in a flickering, jagged line and the line, a synthetic horizon, travel toward him emitting a crackling roar as all creation flexed in ontological agony.

It was real. As real as anything else. As real as anything had ever been.

Carter wanted it to stop, would do anything for it to stop. Nothing existed except for the torment of the moment. There was no past and no memories, there was no future and no hope. There was only the now, and the anguish of that thin slice of existence. He could bear it no longer. He had already suffered a second, or a minute, or a year, or forever, and it had to stop, and he knew where the stop switch was.

He fumbled for his pistol.

He felt the front sight tap against his incisors.

He worried momentarily about chipping the enamel, even though the frame was polymer, not steel.

He thought of Charlie Hammond's S&W Model 5946.

He thought of Charlie Hammond.

He didn't fire.

In Atlantic City, Bernie Hayesman looked at the plate of ribs, and he was not happy. He had asked for an omelet, a simple omelet to be sent up to his office, and they had sent ribs. He couldn't understand it. He'd spoken to the chef personally. They'd discussed eggs, if briefly. There was no earthly way "omelet" could have been misconstrued as "ribs." He looked at the plate of ribs, and the ribs looked back. Neither he nor they were overjoyed at the situation.

The runner who'd brought in the food was hanging around the door, looking nervous. Hayesman was generally considered a good guy, but woe betide anyone who screwed up, because then he would come down upon them like the wrath of Jove. The runner couldn't see how he could be blamed for this particular screwup, but he was nevertheless wary of the possibility. "I could get it changed," he said. "Should I ask them to do an omelet, boss?"

Hayesman waved a hand dismissively. "It's cool. I'll eat these. You can go."

The runner left, and Hayesman was left alone with the ribs.

He ate them slowly and unwillingly. The last time he'd had them, he'd ended up eating most of them cold because of that ass-hole kid and his roulette "system."

Then Rand and her team had come back after kicking the guy out, and they'd looked kind of freaked-out. Rand had kept herself on an even keel until she'd sent her people back on the floor. Then she'd sat down without permission. She was ex-services, and she *never* sat down in the presence of a superior without permission. She'd told Hayesman about the slots, and how she'd taken the ones that had hit near-as-dammit simultaneous jackpots out of service and called in the engineer. She said she didn't expect him to find anything, but she was really keen for a rational explanation.

The engineer didn't find anything. The slots showed no signs of having been interfered with in any way, and the probabilities set on the reels were absolutely in line with house rules.

"He figured out what the chances of all four machines jackpotting at the same time were," she'd said. Hayesman had never seen the usually unflappable Rand so shaken. "That kid said some numbers when we threw him out. I can't swear to it, but I think he said what the odds were. They were massive, boss. Astronomical."

Hayesman had told her that it was nothing. Just a conjuring trick, just some dick trying to make himself look good. That she shouldn't worry about it.

Hayesman worried about it. If the kid had been smarter about how he used whatever shtick he had come up with—and the thing with the slots had convinced him that there *was* some shtick—he could have taken the casino for a lot more than he had. He'd been so barefaced about it, though. Like he didn't care.

Hayesman belched. Great. Now the ribs he hadn't ordered and didn't want were giving him gas.

He decided he was going to start an investigation in the morning. Casino laws in some other countries were sticklers about gamblers identifying themselves beforehand, but he didn't have a clear idea who the kid had been. There was surveillance footage, though. Maybe if they could find him going to his car, they could get a license plate and go from there.

He didn't feel so good. He pushed the plate away from him. No more of those. He'd eaten enough. He felt his gut moil slowly within him like a languorous sea creature.

He didn't like the thought of bringing in upper management on this. They'd want to know why he didn't get the guy's name at the time, and he had no good answer to that because, simply put, he'd underestimated him. He hadn't taken the guy seriously and, by the time he pulled that Harry Potter shit with the slots, it was too late. Better late than never, though, and at least the Oceanic could earn some brownie points with the community by putting the shout-out on somebody who might break banks if he wasn't spotted early enough.

Hayesman grimaced. That omelet was looking really good about now. He didn't usually have an acid digestion, but he had a bottle of Pepto-Bismol in the bathroom for the rare times it troubled him.

He made to stand, and sat down again immediately. Something was definitely wrong with his guts. Maybe flu. He really needed to get to the bathroom in case it was something violent. He'd had sudden-onset flu once in his life, and had not enjoyed the moment when he lost control of his bowels.

He didn't dare move from his seat, however. The internal pressure in his bowels was becoming painful. He felt bloated, and . . . no, he could feel *bloating*, could feel his guts swelling inside him. This was bad, he could tell. Not just inconveniently bad. This was really, health-threateningly bad.

He decided he had to risk the short walk to his office's en suite bathroom. He would have to do it doubled over and with his ass clenched, but whatever was wrong with him was getting worse, and out was definitely better than in.

When he tried to rise, though, he couldn't. He tried again, but his legs and arms were too enfeebled to lift his body. His first thought was, again, flu, and that it had weakened him. But he dismissed that almost immediately. He didn't *feel* weak. He had suffered the enervating effects of illness enough in his life to know how that sapping of strength felt, and this wasn't it. His muscles felt normal, with none of the aches that flu would have caused. It took him several seconds to realize the truth, and he immediately disregarded it as impossible. Then the chair groaned beneath him and he had to accept it.

He was growing heavier, putting on weight literally by the second. His clothes felt tight. He watched with too much disbelief to be horrified as the legs of his pants grew taut with the expanding flesh within. Then he was distracted by the sight of his stomach visibly expanding. A shirt button popped off.

It wasn't possible. It just couldn't be happening. He shoved the half-finished plate of ribs away from him, looking for reasons no matter how absurd and settling upon some incredible form of poisoning. Even as the plate skidded away from him across the surface of the desk, he knew it wasn't the cause. He fumbled with the handset for the casino's secure communications and for a terrified moment almost dropped it. If it ended up on the floor, he doubted he could reach it. Already the arms of his chair were digging into his sides, pinning him in it.

"Rand!" he blurted as soon as he opened the "red" channel for emergencies. "Help me! For Christ's sake, help me!"

There was no reply for a moment, the longest moment. Then Rand said, "Boss? What's happening? What's wrong?"

"I'm sick, I think. Something's wrong with me. I'm in trouble, Alia. Help me . . ."

The last word turned into a groan as the chair arms dug deep into the sides of his growing torso.

Hayesman never, ever used first names with staff. He was old-school. Rand didn't have a problem with it; it kept things military and she was fine with that. Hearing him call her "Alia" shocked her more than if he'd been screaming. She set off for his office at a sprint, palms flat, arms pumping, shouting an order at a hospitality greeter as she went by him to call 911, medical emergency in Hayesman's office.

He couldn't even look down anymore. His neck had swollen and might as well have been in a cervical collar for all the movement he could manage. The underside of his desk was digging into the upper thighs, and he could feel and hear seams giving way in his clothes. His feet were in agony; he wore good shoes and they were refusing to split.

He was going to die. He knew that. There were so many things left to do, some bridges to rebuild, some things to attend to. He regretted that the chances to attend to them were now gone for good, and he would die with so much unfinished business. He'd worked too much, he realized. That old work-life balance. He'd fucked it up and now he was going to die unfulfilled, and all the hours and concentration he'd given to the casino were nothing to him.

His last thought was his wonderment at just where all this fucking meat was coming from, anyway?

Twenty feet from Hayesman's office door, Rand stopped at the sound of a dull explosion. It was more a rumble than a concussion, a heavy blow that shuddered through the floor. She couldn't imagine what it might mean. She reached the door, and remembered in great detail afterward how the handle felt in her hand, and how it looked as she turned it and opened the door.

She wasn't sick, which later struck her as remarkable, but she was leaning against the outside wall of the office in shock when one of her fellow floormen caught up with her and looked in. *He* threw up.

Carter woke to find almost an hour had passed, he was lying by a pool of his own vomit, and the man had gone. He had his pistol in his hand.

He dropped the weapon and rolled onto his feet, where he stood unsteadily, staring at the pistol as if he had awoken holding a scorpion. He shook his head, clearing it of the wisps of memory of the experience that had felled him. He breathed deeply and slowly, recovering composure and reveling in the pleasure of breathing, putting away that feeling of dismay and even disgust at how jury-rigged and inadequate the human body was at doing the simplest things. He had felt it before in a curious anticipatory state, as if a curtain was about to be pulled back and the utter pathetic failure of humanity revealed by comparison to something greater. Something else. Something . . .

The vomit was thin and watery; at least he could now be grateful that he had missed a meal. It was growing dark. He looked up and down the spit of woodland between the houses and the water, but there was no sign of the man. Carter couldn't even bring himself to be angry. The man had not been the most focused individual, and it was not too much to presume he had psychological issues. When Carter had suffered his . . . episode, the guy had either been frightened and run away, or understood nothing untoward was happening and just wandered off. Carter favored the second theory. Either way, the man was gone, and Carter was *really* hungry now.

Across the water, the streetlights were already on. He didn't remember seeing any on Waite's Bill, and decided to leave before it got darker and the chainsaw cannibals who surely occupied the weirdly isolated little road came out to play. He turned to walk away, and kicked something. It was a battered blue and white sneaker, failing at the toe cap.

Behind him, Providence River lapped at the bank.

Colt's car had gone, which didn't surprise Carter in the slightest. After a brief reconnoiter to confirm it, he returned to his own car and drove out of the trees and off the spit of land. He felt an undeniable leavening of his spirits as he traveled through the oaken tunnel and back into the real world, such as it was. It was foolish, and he would have chided himself for it in the normal run of things, but his experiences on Waite's Bill had been unusual and unpleasant, and he put it down simply to being glad to be out of there. He would research the fuck out of Waite Road in general and the last house on the eastern arm in particular. Even if he had come across solid evidence that Colt had just gone there selling cookies, he would not have given a damn. The place had more than bothered him. He now understood that it had scared him, even before his fit or whatever the hell it had been. He would see his doctor to get a clean bill of health, and then he was going to tear the roof off every house on that absurd little street and find what secrets lurked within. Carter did not like to be scared; being scared made him angry.

Back off the peninsula, he saw the lit streets and houses that had irritated him with their small-town conformity before, yet he now appreciated them as markers that he was back in a world he understood.

In the driveway of a house on the corner, a man was washing the windshield of his car clean of gull shit in the illumination of his garage and porch lights. He paused to watch Carter drive by with open curiosity and, on an impulse, Carter pulled up.

He walked back to the man, assuming the mien of a confused out-of-towner as he approached.

"Hi! I was wondering if you could help me? My GPS is screwing up or something, and I can't find Dalton Road."

"Dalton Road? I don't know any Dalton Road around here," said the man.

"Maybe I got the name wrong," said Carter as if to himself. He knew there was no street of that name in the city. He nodded at the isthmus road. "So that's not it? I couldn't see a sign."

The man laughed. "Man, soon as I saw you coming out of there, I *knew* you were lost. *Nobody* goes on Waite's Bill unless they're a Waite."

"What?" Carter didn't have to work hard to portray consternation. "There must be a dozen houses down there. They all belong to one family?"

"The whole spit does. That's private land."

"I didn't see a sign."

"There isn't one. Isn't really needed. People who go down there, they come out again pretty quickly." He leaned closer. "Not real friendly, the Waites. That's if you even see them. When we first moved here—must be . . . yeah, fifteen years ago—the wife and me went down there just to say hi, being new neighbors and all. Got to the end of the road that gets you over the land bridge and, man, we just stood there. You've seen those houses. Doesn't feel right down there, you know? Gave it a minute, turned around, and we walked out again. Never been over there again in all the years since. You see a Waite, they're in a pickup, they drive out, they drive in, never look left or right."

"They are literally all Waites?"

The man nodded his head from side to side indecisively. "I got to say, I don't know that for sure. In the neighborhood, we just call them *the Waites* because of the name of the bill and the little road in there. Some of them are Waites for sure, because they own the land, have for as long as anyone knows. And they all look kind of related."

"I saw one guy while I was over there." Now Carter leaned closer, making the man a co-conspirator, at least in his own mind. Men, Carter knew full well, could be the most amazing gossips with the right handling. "I got to admit, 'inbred' was the first thing I thought."

"Yeah," said the man, drawn into enjoyable small talk, "the men are all *ugly*. Real ugly."

"The women, too, I guess."

"Yeah, well, yes and no. They're not going to be getting on *Project Runway* anytime soon, if you know what I mean. They got those big Waite eyes, for one thing. Kind of too big. But . . ." He didn't speak for several seconds, staring at the dark tunnel of trees that led to Waite's Bill. He flinched as he realized how long he'd been silent. "They're not so bad. The younger ones, anyway."

Carter looked down the road, too, mainly to avoid eye contact. He didn't know what the man meant by "younger" and didn't need to know. He didn't want to know.

"Well, I'd better get on my way. It's getting darker and I still have to find Dalton Road. I think I must have got the name wrong. I'll call and check."

They shook hands, and Carter left.

Chapter 14

AD OBLIVIONE

Carter decided not to go see the doctor after all. When he ran through in his imagination how he would describe his symptoms, especially the hallucinations and the sudden desire to eat a bullet, he realized that it could work out very badly for him further down the line. Besides, he felt fine now, and the feeling had not come back.

The vividness of it was taking its time dimming, however. More than once he would find himself doodling tall towers with a few odd asymmetric windows on his notepad while talking on his office phone. He was pretty sure he'd never seen their like in anything historical or even any movies he could think of. They had come from his imagination, that was all. He hadn't realized he had such a strong imagination. Now that he knew he did, he kind of wished he didn't.

The research had proved troublesome. Waite's Bill was off the grid in a variety of ways. He could get basic information, and things like census data, but otherwise it was as if the peninsula existed as something the city did not deign to acknowledge, the civic equivalent of an anal wart.

Finally admitting defeat, at least as far as online resources would permit, he girded himself to do things the old-school way and look at physical files.

The drive from New York to Providence was beginning to become routine to him, and he wondered if he should check out the opportunities for a PI there. New York was proving disappointingly repetitive in terms of work, the big agencies garnering all the interesting cases. He was very aware that he was dining on crumbs from their table, and he did not enjoy it at all. He could always get work with them, and had already been offered some outsourcing from one agency purely because they had more clients than they knew what to do with. But no; he wanted to be his own boss.

Inquiries at Providence City Hall took him around three departments where they looked at him with rising disgruntlement before he was sent to the archives. There he made the acquaintance of an intern, whose enthusiasm was thankfully matched by some local knowledge.

"Waite's Bill?" said the young man, who introduced himself as Luis Blanco. "There's a name you don't hear too often." He led Carter through a file storage area into a room that looked like it belonged in an academic library. He seated Carter at a worn deal table and gave him some white cotton gloves to wear. "Some of these papers are *old*," he explained.

"This is the earliest document we have on Waite's Bill and Waite Road." He carefully opened out an antique, discolored sheet of parchment.

"How old is this?" asked Carter. He was being polite; the document was clearly too old to have any relevance to the current state of affairs on the little peninsula, but he needed Blanco's enthusiasm if the search for anything useful turned into an extended trawl. So he would indulge this little history lesson, as long as Blanco kept it brief.

Blanco grinned. "Sixteen thirty-six. That's the year the city was formally founded. But get this . . . the deed makes reference to a house already having been on the bill for sixteen years. So, that's around 1620."

Carter was having trouble reading the curling copperplate, partially obscured by stains and marbling of the parchment. "Who owned it then?"

"Jonas Waite, it says here," said Blanco, pointing. "Married to . . . what is that? Tamar? Is that a biblical name?"

"A Waite? The *same* Waites as are there now?"

"I guess, though I'd have to check to be sure. That's quite something, isn't it? The land's belonged to the same family for almost four hundred years now, and they still live there, assuming it *is* the same Waites. Got to be, hasn't it? It's not that common a name. It's got to be."

Blanco was able to give Carter two hours of his time, and in that period, judicious samples of documentation covering the intervening generations showed beyond reasonable doubt that the descendants of Jonas and Tamar Waite had held the tiny spit of land without interruption for the entire time, and were still to be found there to the present day. The papers showed that they had built a fortune through ships, primarily a fishing fleet until the late nineteenth century, but some mercantile shipping, too, including bringing in slaves to sell or to work on their farms, a trade they maintained until the very minute of the emancipation. The minutes of a council meeting showed the Waite patriarch of the time, one Newton Waite, had argued vehemently in favor of slavery, referring to the Africans in terms of bestial idiocy, a servitor race that should not and must not be given self-determination.

"Nice guy," said Carter.

"Meh." Blanco shrugged. "He gets a pass because it was a

different time, different world. There's so much stuff like that in the records. People talked like that then, that's history. It's people who talk like that now—no pass for them."

After Carter finished up, he swung by Hill's Books to get some food and, if he was being honest with himself, to see Emily again. Over a sandwich, he told her about the investigation, of the mysterious Mr. Colt, and the even more mysterious Waite's Bill. He didn't mean to talk about the strange fit he'd suffered, but did so anyway, even if he played down its intensity.

"That ever happen to you before?" asked Lovecraft, her expression unreadable.

He'd answered, "No," before he remembered the glimpses of people who were not, could not be there, of the increasingly unforgettable dreams that troubled him, or of events he had experienced that never truly occurred. He lied and told her his doctor had given him a clean bill of health.

Then he'd told her of Waite Road and what he had learned about it.

"Sixteen twenty? Seriously?"

"They're an old family."

"No, I mean, 1620? I'm not sure that makes sense. Sixteen years before the founding of the city, there just weren't any Europeans around here. They weren't far away—up in Boston or down in New York . . . hell, it wouldn't even have been New Amsterdam back then. Just some fur trappers. I'm not even sure Boston was 'Boston' that far back."

"I don't understand what you're getting at."

"I'm getting at the fact that there was no settlement here in 1620. The natives weren't necessarily all that friendly, Dan. Contact with Europeans can do that. A lone family out on their own, maybe days away from help? It's crazy. The date must be wrong."

"It looked pretty clear to me. The document wasn't in great condition, but even I could make out the reference to sixteen years."

"Then I don't get it. The Pokanoket were pretty friendly to the settlers, but an isolated group in Pokanoket territory without permission, that would be provocative."

"They made a deal?"

Lovecraft nodded, but didn't seem entirely convinced. "Must be, I guess. It's not like a handful of settlers could have scared the Pokanoket into leaving them be, now, is it?"

Carter took a call from Detective Harrelson, and they arranged to meet in the same not-a-cop-bar where they had met last time. Harrelson sounded distracted, perhaps even worried on the phone, so Carter decided not to ask for details beyond what the cop was prepared to give without prompting, "More weird shit happened."

Harrelson was already nursing a beer when Carter arrived. Carter got one for himself at the bar and sat down in the booth with him.

"The way Belasco died was off, right?" said Harrelson.

Carter didn't know why Harrelson might need reassurance on this point, but offered it anyway. "You know it. Whatever happened to him, somebody made it happen. I don't know how, but he was murdered."

Harrelson took a long drink from his glass, and Carter saw that he wasn't just distracted, or even worried. Harrelson actually seemed afraid.

"There's been a death in New Jersey. Atlantic City. Every cop on the eastern seaboard has already heard about it, and it'll be all over the media soon. The brass will spin it, try to make it seem weird, but not *weird*, if you understand me."

Carter shook his head. "Slow down, man. I'm not following you? Who died?"

"Pit boss at the Oceanic." Harrelson opened a battered satchel on the upholstered bench beside him and took out a scene photograph. "He was alone having his dinner. Calls for help, they get there and find this." He slid the picture across the table.

Even before Carter tried to interpret the image, his first impression was that there was a lot of red in it. He looked at it in silence for almost a minute as he tried to understand what he was looking at. There was a desk, covered in what he had to assume was blood, and ragged organic shapes. It was what was behind the desk that confused him. Rationally he knew that people sit behind desks, but this wasn't a person. It was organic and malformed, lots of blood, and massive. It was like a beached whale. He tried to work out what exactly it was, like teasing the correct image out of a puzzle picture. Even when he understood, it took several more seconds to accept the conclusion as anything other than a random, ridiculous passing thought.

"What," he said slowly, "the actual fuck?" He looked up at Harrelson. "This is a man? He's huge!" He was too aghast that anything that massive could be human to even start to think about how the man had died. "I've seen some fat fuckers in my time, but . . . And he was a pit boss?" His understanding of the workings of a casino had taken a knock. While the bosses might spend more time looking at camera banks than they might once have, they would still have to walk the floor pretty frequently. The corpulent body in the picture looked like mere human legs could never hope to lift it.

"Bernie Hayesman, pit manager. That's what they call them now."

"And what the hell happened to him? Looks like somebody went in his ribs with a chainsaw."

Harrelson shook his head. "No. No one else was there. Floorman got the call that Hayesman was in trouble and started running to get to him. She was there inside a minute. Just before she reached the office, Hayesman"—he tapped the picture for emphasis—"*blew up.*"

Carter raised his eyebrows. "There was a bomb?"

"No. Maybe. If there was, it was inside him. He exploded."

"Jesus," said Carter. He'd heard of cows farting so much methane that a stray spark could blow up the barn, but he'd never heard of anything like this. He looked at Harrelson suspiciously. "Why did you think I'd be interested in this? I mean, yeah, it's got gawk value, Christ knows, but what does this have to do with Belasco?"

Harrelson took another picture from a folder in his satchel. It was a driver's license record. Carter read the name—*Hayesman, Bernard*—and then looked at the picture. Hayesman was in his early fifties, hair well receded, tired eyes, and looked at worst a little fat in the face.

"How did he get from this to that?" asked Carter, indicating the file picture in his hand and then the death scene.

"Yeah, well, there's the thing. How did he get from that to that in half an hour? Because somehow he managed to put on maybe seven hundred pounds in that time. His clothes were torn, the chair was pretty much grown into him. I don't *know* what this has to do with Belasco, but two guys die in really strange ways—really, *really* fucking strange ways, you understand me?—within a week of each other, my ears go up. So"—he leaned back—"now you scratch my back. Have you got anything to go on with Belasco?"

Carter considered being evasive, and decided against it. Nobody was paying him for the Belasco investigation, so anything that could kick it into police hands was in his interest. Maybe if there was anything in all this and Harrelson came out smelling of roses, it could only help Carter's standing with him. Having a friendly cop was a good situation to be in for a PI, after all.

"Maybe. There's a student at Clave, a postgraduate. Had some kind of disagreement with Belasco. I don't have anything solid, though. Just some loose ends and strange behaviors I don't like the look of. I'll e-mail you what I've got, but there's not much there."

Harrelson gathered up the pictures and put them away.

"There's not much of anything in this. Not so far. Just two dead guys who shouldn't be dead, and no good explanation of what happened to them. Took two trucks to get all the meat from this poor fucker to the morgue. It's like Belasco all over again; the examiner's taking a long time to submit his report because, well, holy shit, what can you say about a thing like that?"

"This hasn't just happened?"

"Nah. They kept a lid on it for as long as they could, and to be honest, I'm impressed they even managed to keep it quiet for four days."

"Four days?" Carter thought of Waite's Bill and the world unwinding around him. "What time?"

"The poor son of a bitch was having ribs for his dinner, so . . . dinnertime. Sometime around dusk, I guess. It'll say in the report." He looked curiously at Carter. "Does that mean something to you?"

"Not really. Just a coincidence. Oh, and it means the guy I've got eyes on wasn't in Atlantic City when Hayesman died. I know *exactly* where he was at the time."

Later that day he sent Harrelson a few scraps of information: Colt's name, a couple of photographs, and a little about how Belasco had lost his temper with Colt.

An hour later Harrelson e-mailed back to say mention of a guy who did too well at roulette and had been expelled from the Oceanic had come up in the Hayesman investigation. The description sounded like Colt. The security cameras on the parking lot hadn't gotten a clear view of the man's license plate as he drove off after being kicked out, though.

"Does he drive a red Mazda?" wrote Harrelson.

"Fuck," said Carter when he read that.

Chapter 15

A REMINISCENCE OF BERTRAND RUSSELL

Lovecraft seemed quite subdued by her standards when Carter told her what he was working on the next day, and the way it was working out. He didn't mind giving her details—client confidentiality wasn't a problem when he was his own client, as had been pointed out—and he needed someone smart to act as a sounding board. Sometimes just talking to somebody about things could help him see them in a different way, even if they didn't say a word. Just accessing that little part of the brain that wonders how somebody is interpreting what you say can be enough to give a new perspective. In this case, however, he was too distracted by Lovecraft's silence to gain much by it.

"I can't see what you're getting out of this," she said after some prompting. "Maybe you should walk away from it."

"You're kidding? Two men are dead, and I'm involved. I don't know how I'm involved, but that call from Belasco's phone means I am."

"You're only involved because somebody involved you. That's not the same thing at all. You haven't found anything to connect you and Belasco, or with this guy in Atlantic City, *or* with that mathematician. There's nothing, Dan. Not a damn thing."

"Nothing I can see yet."

"Maybe there's nothing to see. You need to look at this in terms of profit and debit. On the downside, this is occupying your time, wasting your resources, and might just get you killed in some gross and eldritch fashion. On the plus side"—she shrugged—"what? I can't think of anything." She noticed him looking at her. "What?"

"'Eldritch'? Like the guy out of The Sisters of Mercy?"

"I don't even know what you're talking about. 'Eldritch' means 'weird.' Old man H. P. L. was fond of the word. Read much of his stuff and you find yourself using it."

"What's it like having somebody famous as an ancestor?"

"Underwhelming. Hey, you said you'd get me a copy of your family tree. Have you got it yet?"

"Oh, right. Yeah." He took a flash drive from his pocket and handed it over. "Can I have that back when you're finished with it? It's a nice one."

"Sure." She plugged into the laptop she had behind the counter and waited while the anti-virus software automatically scanned it. "You could have just sent it in an e-mail, you know."

"I could've, but that's how my aunt sent it to me and as I was coming here anyway, it seemed pointless to."

Lovecraft looked at him over the top of the monitor, her skin underlit by its glow. She looked smart, bookish, and, Carter realized with a small shock of revelation, attractive.

In his teens, he'd gone through a brief stage of what he had thought of at the time as sensible concerns about race, but which he now saw to be the bigotry of a boy who was frightened about the future, and not sure what about it frightened him so much.

The subsequent career at the pointed end of society in the police force puts a man under pressure, and he can either let his prejudices sink in deep, or he can look at society as a pretty flaky machine that is, nevertheless, all we have to be getting on with. In that with machines, the color of the cogs has less to do with things than where they are. He'd taken a step back, and he was glad he did.

He still got a momentary spark of something stupid in its reflexiveness sometimes when he read a news story where some black kid had done some kind of stereotypically black thing that gave a certain strata of white folk a hard-on of righteousness, a spasm of old prejudices. The thing was he knew it, and recognized it as an ugly artifact and not a sincere impulse. It was like having an aging Nazi living in the attic of the mansion of his mind. Occasionally he would hear the thudding of a walking stick on bare floorboards from that part, and a croaking rant about the superiority of the white race. He ignored it every time, and slowly the voice grew weaker and more infrequent.

A small but appreciated bonus of his determined walk away from instinctive racism was that the world had so many more women to appreciate. Once he would have had trouble getting past Lovecraft's skin. Now, in the glow of the laptop's screen . . .

"Why are you staring at me?" Lovecraft's eyes were visible over the screen top, and they were narrowed.

"I wasn't. I was just thinking, and my eyes had to be pointed in some direction. Sorry, didn't mean to stare." He nodded at the computer. "Find anything to link me with Alfred Hill?"

She didn't answer for several seconds, concentrating on the genealogical chart. Her eyes weren't scanning, only fixed on one part of the screen. "No," she said suddenly. A click of the track pad and the file was closed. "No Hills at all."

She seemed relieved when the door clicked open and the bell rang. For no reason he could fathom then or later, Carter found the sound of the bell threatening, reminding him specifically of the time when it had rung despite the door being locked. That time, and not the many other times he'd heard it ring normally. There was something mocking in its note, which he knew was subjective but nonetheless caused his hackles to rise.

Lovecraft ignored him, smiling at the customer and tacitly dropping Carter from her attention. Nodding a little ruefully to acknowledge his dismissal, he turned to leave.

William Colt was standing in front of him.

Colt ignored Carter, and it took a massive effort for Carter to reciprocate, allowing his gaze to swing past Colt and onto the bookshelves. His heart was abruptly hammering with the adrenaline of surprise. Already he could feel a cold, breathless hollowness inside him. Colt had made him somehow, that much was clear. At first Carter thought that was impossible, but then pulled events together and came up with a feasible scenario: Colt had seen his car when it was parked off Waite Road, probably when Carter was unconscious, Colt had noted the license number and then had a PI check it out. It was likely this hypothetical investigator would have turned up anything recent with Carter's name on it, which would have included Alfred Hill's will when it was registered for probate, and the will led to the bookstore.

Carter found himself staring at a shelf of books on art history without seeing them at all. There were three shelves of political memoirs at head height, which seemed out of place, but he wasn't much interested in the vagaries of Lovecraft's shelving organization right that moment. His full attention was on listening to anything Colt had to say to Lovecraft. If he had read Colt's character at all correctly from what he had learned of him from others, whatever he had to say was going to be arch and superior. Carter was not to be disappointed with this analysis.

"Hi," said Colt, smiling broadly at Lovecraft. "I'm looking for a book."

Lovecraft sensibly eschewed any variation of "Well, you've come to the right place," and instead asked did he have any particular book in mind?

"Yes. It's by Carl Jung. *Synchronicity: An Acausal Connecting*

Principle. Earliest edition you have, please. It was published originally in 1960, I think."

He continued to smile the whole time as if citing a book was mildly flirtatious. Carter could only see the side of his face, but he could see Lovecraft fully, and her responding smile was not in any form sincere. Colt made her nervous.

"The one hundreds section is over here," she said, easing past Colt to get to the shelves. He made little effort to step aside, falling in behind her as she led the way.

"You use the Dewey system."

"Got to have a system," she replied. There was a tautness in her voice Carter hadn't heard before. She wasn't just nervous. She was afraid.

She knew Carter was in the store with her, she knew he carried a gun, she had no reason to think that her customer was anything out of the ordinary and certainly not that he was the subject of Carter's investigation. All of this, yet she was afraid. Carter was aware of the weight of his Glock 19, but it failed to reassure him. He had a sense, a strange tangential awareness, that whatever threat Colt represented was not something a gun could deal with without bad consequences. This was a chess match, not a potential firefight. He couldn't see why a chess match seemed to put the fear of God into Lovecraft, but it had, and that made him worried, too.

"I'm all about systems," said Colt.

They were passing the "000" section, the outcasts of Dewey Decimal Classification, amid the things that were new or unknown when Melvil Dewey devised it in the 1870s, along with the things he wasn't sure what to do with, all salted away under the handwaving of "Generalities." Collections, journalism, parapsychology, philosophy, computing, books about books, books about the Dewey Decimal Classification system and libraries in general.

Carter couldn't see them clearly. He found something interesting to gain his attention in a book about mezzotinting. He had no idea what "mezzotinting" was before he took it down from the shelf, but apparently it was some way of making pictures. He opened it and pretended to peruse it, his attention on Lovecraft and Colt from his new vantage point.

"Jung . . . Jung . . . Jung . . ." Lovecraft chanted as her finger swept along the shelves. Carter half expected Jung to appear, having been summoned.

"Here you go," she said with relief that must have been obvious to Colt, all the sooner to get him out of her store. She took down a book and showed it to Colt. He took it from her and flipped to the copyright page.

"It's the 1973 edition," he said. "I was kind of hoping for a first edition."

"That's the only copy we have in stock. We . . . I could look around other dealers for a 1960 copy, if you'd like?"

Colt looked at her. He was no longer smiling. Then suddenly he was. "No. This will do fine. It's in good condition for a softcover over forty years old, isn't it? Yes, I'll have this. Oh, and this." He took down another book from the same shelf. "I've been looking for this one, too. From the same series. Some crossover, but never mind." He was holding the book up to show Lovecraft the cover, speaking to her like a child. He looked back over his shoulder at Carter, but Carter had already buried his nose in his book, pretending to find himself fascinated by an example of the mezzotinters's art (*Artist: Arthur Francis. An interesting view of Anningley Hall manor-house in Essex, circa 1800. 15 by 10 inches*).

Colt was talking to Lovecraft again. "*Psychology and the Occult.* Jung was fascinated by the supernatural. He was pretty skeptical in his early career, but became more open-minded as he grew older. The usual thing to say is 'Oh, he got more credulous because he was losing his edge.' Wouldn't it be more interesting if he was actually getting closer to the truth after a lifetime's work?" He laughed. "Wouldn't that be something?"

They walked back to the counter, Lovecraft more eagerly than Colt, who dithered by the triple zeroes. Lovecraft realized she was alone and turned to find him studying the spines of the books. "Is there anything else you wanted?" she asked.

"Oh, I want lots of things," he said. Then he pointed at the shelf. "I was just looking at these books on librarianship. You have a couple of copies of *AACR2* here, the cataloguing rules. There's a mathematical dimension to that, you know? I'm a mathematician myself. You love books? I love numbers, and the two of them collide right there." He tapped the copy of *AACR2*. "I used to think math was pure. Icy pure and the most beautiful thing it was possible to be. Everything you call 'beauty' bleeds out of math. Symmetry, the golden section, nature itself is a mass of fractals.

"Then I read about Bertrand Russell. You probably just think of him as a philosopher, but he was a mathematician first. Let me tell you about Russell, the absolute purity of math, and library catalogues."

So, Russell is in his late twenties. He's already written some interesting papers on the foundations of mathematics, including some work on geometry. Non-Euclidean geometry.

Colt smirked as he said it.

He has a bright idea. He looks at those foundations of math, and he sees something wrong. It's pretty easy to understand the paradox he saw if you think of it being about books, and catalogues.

Imagine there's a country where every town and village has a public library, and in the capital is a central library. One day, the chief librarian realizes he doesn't know what books all the local libraries have, so he sends out a directive. He tells them to catalogue all their books, and send a copy to the central library so there'll be a record of all the library books in the country in one central location. As good as gold, all the local librarians catalogue their collections, and send copies of the catalogue to the central library.

Now the chief librarian has a stack of the catalogues, hundreds of them, and decides another level of reference is necessary for people to be able to find the right catalogues easily. So, he sits down to create a catalogue of all the catalogues.

Are you following this? Good.

But he finds a problem. The local librarians haven't all catalogued their collections in the same way. No AACR2 to guide them, see? All the local libraries have put their copies of the new catalogue they just drew up out for the use of their patrons, but some of them have decided that the catalogue itself is therefore part of their collection, and must therefore list itself. The other librarians haven't. So you've got catalogues that catalogue themselves, and catalogues that don't.

The chief librarian decides—for no good reason apart from it makes the example work—that he's going to put the two types of catalogues into two separate catalogues. One lists catalogues that list themselves, the other lists the catalogues that don't.

All this is completely representable in mathematical form.

But now . . . do you see the problem? The paradox? When the chief librarian has finished, then for consistency these two catalogues must also be catalogued as they're part of the central collection. The catalogue of catalogues that do catalogue themselves can safely be listed in its own pages. But what about the other? If it's added to the catalogue of auto-catalogues, it's inaccurate because it's not listed in itself. If it's added to the catalogue of catalogues that don't list themselves, then it's just listed itself and so it's in the wrong place.

"There was a seismic shock in math. Set theory had a hole you could drive a truck through." He shrugged. "They patched the hole, but that's all it is. A change in semantics. The hole's still there, but now it has a bunch of mathematicians in front of it telling you to move on, nothing to see here. Makes you wonder, doesn't it? What else is broken in the 'purity' in math."

Colt had stopped smiling quite early on in his flight into didactics. Now he seemed very serious indeed, almost angry. He realized he was still standing there with Lovecraft with two books in his hands, and smiled again. It was just a crease in his face.

"How much are these?"

* * *

Carter kept a bookshelf between himself and Colt while the mathematician paid for the books and left with "Have a nice day." Lovecraft said nothing in response. The bell rang, and Colt was gone.

Carter found Lovecraft backed up against the wall behind the counter, the back of her hand to her mouth, and her eyes wide. She looked like she'd just witnessed a serious accident, not sold a couple of books to a mathematician. She was staring in the direction of the door where Colt had left a moment before. The last reverberations of the bell still hummed, the last high vibration leaving the metal.

"Are you okay?" he asked. She ignored him until he stepped behind the counter and gently touched her upper arm. She cried out then, and looked at him with horror.

"Oh, Jesus," she said. "Oh, Jesus fuck! Did you see him? Where were you?"

"I was right over there the whole time. Calm . . . calm down, Emily. I was right there, watching. If he'd pulled anything, I would've shot him."

"Pulled anything? Jesus Christ. Didn't you hear what he . . . ? Don't you . . . ?" She looked at him as if seeing him for the first time. "No. Of course you d— Look. It's nothing. I just got a bad vibe from him. I . . . thought you'd gone. Some guys, you don't want to be in the store alone with them."

She was lying. Carter didn't need to draw on his police experience to know that Lovecraft had known he hadn't left the store. Colt had represented a threat to her that even the presence of Carter with a gun at his hip did nothing to ameliorate.

"How do you know him?"

She frowned, and looked at Carter. This confusion, at least, was sincere. "What are you talking about? I've never seen him before."

"You don't know who that was?"

She was starting to look worried again. "Should I?"

Carter frowned, too, now, looking at Lovecraft as if he didn't know what to make of her at all.

"Don't look at me like that," she said. She was becoming angry, reacting against her earlier fear. "I'm not lying. Why the hell would I know who some random guy coming in off the street is?"

Carter didn't know whether he should tell her. But he had a feeling he was going to need allies, and that meant going from a position of trust. She might have just lied to him, but she had her reasons. That much was very evident.

"That was Colt. William Colt." He'd never mentioned the name to her before, and it was plain that it meant nothing to her now. "The man I'm investigating for the Belasco and Atlantic City deaths. Him. He's the guy."

"Him?" Lovecraft looked at the door. She seemed to be finally understanding something. "It was him," she said under her breath.

Chapter 16

COOL AIR

Lovecraft didn't want to talk, and began mentioning that she was going out with Rothwell soon and had to go. Carter didn't like the way the air had soured between them. There seemed no reason for it. She clung to the lie that she thought she'd been alone with Colt in the shop, and he could see that challenging her on it would cause things to deteriorate between them still further, so he let her be.

William Colt, on the other hand, he was not about to leave be. No fucking way.

Hill's Books was nowhere near the university campus. It wasn't impossible that he'd decided to hunt around local bookstores to see if he could find those Jung books, but the timing made it unlikely. "Synchronicity." Carter knew that was the idea that there might be something behind coincidences, but he didn't buy that, just like he didn't buy that Colt had just decided to wander into that store right then on a whim. He'd come in knowing damn well that Carter was there, and he'd intimidated Lovecraft somehow. That, Carter admitted to himself, was something that confused him. His experiences of threats were legal, financial, or physical. He couldn't see how you could scare the shit out of somebody with math, but it seemed you could. Well, okay. Just because he didn't understand the threat didn't mean it wasn't one, and he wasn't going to stand by and watch a self-satisfied fucker like Colt walk away from having laid it on Carter's business partner. That wasn't happening.

Carter realized he was getting almost unreasonably angry over something he didn't understand. He was pacing up and down in the apartment over the bookstore, leaving Lovecraft to close up.

He heard the bell, and the sound of the door being locked, and realized she'd gone without even saying good-bye, and that just made him angrier still. He went to the window and watched Lovecraft cross the road. She waited on the corner for about a minute, before Rothwell, punctual as ever, arrived in a blue Buick Verano Turbo. Carter watched disconsolately as they drove away; the Buick was one of three different and expensive cars he'd observed Rothwell driving or, sometimes, being driven in on the four occasions he'd seen him pick up Lovecraft. The man's garage must look like a luxury dealership.

He was watching it disappear into the distance when he saw a red Mazda3 swing out of a parking lot down the way and head in the same direction.

Carter was past believing in coincidences.

"Mother*fucker*," he swore as he went down the stairs three at a time. Unlocking and relocking the door behind him took too long, and by the time he reached his car—a two-year-old white Toyota Camry, chosen specifically because they were a common sight on the roads—both vehicles were long gone.

Undeterred, Carter followed the road in the hope that he might regain sight of the distinctive Mazda. Ten minutes of frustration and too many sets of red lights later, he gave up. The chance of them staying on the same road fell every minute and the pursuit was already becoming a fool's errand. Instead he pulled over and called Lovecraft to warn her. He was shunted to voice mail twice before he gave up in frustration. He sent her a text message in a last attempt, but doubted she'd bother to check her phone until it was irrelevant.

He tapped his fingers on the steering wheel and tried to think what to do next. The first thought that came to mind was a bad, idiotic, dangerous one. In the normal run of things, he would probably have disregarded it for exactly those reasons, but he was angry and frustrated, the encounter in the bookstore had left him feeling marginalized and stupid, and any distance he felt in the Colt investigation had just gone out the window. Colt had decided to make it personal, to beard the lion in his den.

Fine, thought Carter. *Let's see how you like it, fucker.*

Carter had learned Colt's home address when he did the follow-up research after his investigations at Clave College, but had had neither the opportunity nor the necessity to check it out first-hand. He'd been expecting a small apartment in a block or even a shared house, but what he found surprised him. Colt had a good, three-bedroom house all to himself on a residential street. It sat alone, the lawn out front well tended, the boards of the house pristine white. Not for the first time, Carter wondered how it was that Colt just seemed to blunder into money. It didn't seem to matter enormously to him—the choice of the practical, unostentatious home and car showed that—but the stuff just stuck to him. Carter had seen his credit ratings and at least gotten an idea of his bank balance, and the man was making math look lucrative.

The business in Atlantic City was perhaps an insight; Colt was very good at squeezing cash out of coincidence. Carter had a feeling Colt could be a millionaire or more easily enough by playing the markets, but that would be time-consuming and time was more precious to him than money. He made enough so he didn't have to think about it, and that was enough.

Carter had to admit the world would be a saner place if people shared Colt's cool view toward the pursuit of money, but that left another question to be answered. If money wasn't Colt's primary motivation, what was?

If Belasco and Hayesman were any indication, and if Colt was actually involved in their deaths, then revenge seemed pretty important to him. He certainly seemed to be on a hair trigger when it came to taking offense. Belasco had slapped his wrist for not focusing on his thesis and general jackassery, and Hayesman had barred him from the Oceanic for suspected cheating. He'd even let Colt keep his winnings, but that hadn't saved him from a grotesque death. It was all pretty thin for killing, but Colt had done it anyway.

Seemed to have done it anyway, Carter had to remind himself. There still wasn't a scrap of real evidence. Just coincidence and intuition. *Synchronicity* and intuition.

There was nobody around, and Colt hadn't troubled to put an alarm on the place. Two minutes' work with lockpicks at the rear door and Carter was in.

Carter's first impression was that he'd wandered into a show home. The place was unnervingly clean and tidy. A note from Colt's cleaner and the hum of a Roomba making the rounds of the den showed he was very keen on keeping his home fastidiously dust-free.

Carter wondered if he was bacteriophobic or just thoroughly anal-retentive, as room after room showed the same sterility. Books shelved in perfect order suggested the latter.

There were some oddities. Everything was in its place except for a boxed set of Blu-rays lying by the TV, the individual discs left carelessly on top of the box. Carter didn't examine them closely, but just read *The Meaning of Life* from the uppermost.

In another room, he found a shelf of board games that, upon closer examination, were all playable solo. He could draw two con-

clusions from that, both equally likely and probably both correct: that Colt had no friends, and that he was more interested in
the idea of playing against blind chance than against other people.
If he could beat a randomly shuffled deck of cards or the roll of a
die, then that was enough.

More than enough, to judge by the room of discarded technology Carter found. A utility shelving unit was half filled with
cardboard storage boxes, each containing superannuated or broken laptops, tablets, phones, and desktop computer components,
mainly hard drives, although he also found one with RAM strips
and CPUs. Each was in an antistatic bag, labeled with exactly what
it was and the reason for its abandonment. The vast majority said
Obsolete, even if only a year old, sometimes even less.

Carter reluctantly put a perfectly operational third-generation
iPad back into its box. According to the dates on the label, Colt
had bought it on its first day of release, then wiped and stored it
the very day the fourth-gen version came out six months later.
Carter didn't have a tablet at all, useful as it might be. He stepped
back from the shelves and regarded them with truculent envy. It
just wasn't right, a man sitting on a treasure trove of usable gear
like that. He hoped a burglar would come along and rip the whole
lot off one of these days. He even knew a few who'd be glad of
the tip.

Clearing his mind of pettiness, Carter continued the search for
anything useful. It went quickly; the lack of clutter meant he could
clear a room rapidly. He'd been involved in detailed searches of
suspects' apartments in the past, and wished they'd been even half
as Spartan and organized as Colt's. Everything was in its place and
there was a place for everything. The very formality of the house
meant that anything out of the ordinary would have advertised
itself. There was nothing. If Colt had anything to hide, it would
either require a structural search of the house that Carter simply
didn't have the time for, or he had it stowed somewhere else. A
mental image of the house at the end of Waite Road appeared

sharply in Carter's mind, and he shoved it to one side. He didn't even want to think of his experiences on Waite's Bill, never mind contemplate breaking into one of the houses.

He finally found one single oddity amid the tidy files, folders, boxes, and drawers. A bill from the college's Material Sciences unit for materials, workshop time, and staff help in a project that involved "rapid prototyping" puzzled Carter. What did a mathematician want that needed something called "DMLS" and four kilos of aluminum? He took a picture of the bill and put it back where he found it.

Carter checked his watch. He'd been in Colt's home for almost half an hour, and that was probably too long. He carried out a last sweep of the house to ensure he'd left no traces before leaving.

He was in Colt's bedroom at the front of the second story, staying back from the window but still with a view of the street, when he saw the red Mazda3. It was parked directly across the street, not in the house's driveway.

Colt was leaning against it, arms crossed casually, watching his own house. He saw Carter and waved. He was smiling.

Carter froze.

Colt's smile grew into a grin. He blew out his cheeks and held his nose, a pantomime of somebody holding his breath. He dropped his hand and started laughing. Carter watched as Colt got back into his car. For a moment he thought Colt was going to park on his own property, but no. He drove off.

Carter got the bad feeling to end all bad feelings. He'd walked into a trap, but exactly what kind of trap, he couldn't tell. Whatever Colt had arranged, standing around in his house was not going to improve Carter's situation. He would get out immediately, downstairs, back to the kitchen, out of the door—and fuck relocking it—over the backyard fence, and away.

Carter headed for the stairs. He was only a few steps down when he wondered if he was suffering a migraine. He hadn't suffered one since his teen years, but he couldn't think of any other way to account for the flickering light he could see in the stairwell, dashes and motes. As he descended, they seemed to grow larger, and he found it more difficult to move. The carpet on the stair seemed sodden, sluggish with extra mass in among the strands, yet when he looked at it, it was perfectly dry.

Belasco.

He remembered Belasco, how he had died, drowning on dry land with no water closer than his car's radiator.

Colt was going to drown Carter in exactly the same way, while he was elsewhere. Then he'd come back in a few hours, probably with a witness, and—*Oh, my. Criminy, whatever has happened here?*—discover Carter's corpse.

Why, no, officer. I can't imagine what happened here. I've never met this man before.

Carter waded through dense air. He could feel the pressure of nothing in particular making his pant legs cling close to the skin, but only a ghost of a sensation of cool wetness anywhere around him.

He had a sudden memory of one of his teachers at school inviting questions about anything, and some smart-ass trying to stump him with "Why is water wet?" The teacher's answer seemed just sophistry at the time, like he was dodging the fact that he didn't know, but in later years when Carter remembered that afternoon, he realized his teacher had been dead right. "Wetness, not in the technical sense of viscosity but as a sensory perception, is not inherent in water. Rather, it's our perception of water, and how we react to its physical properties. You're talking in a subjective rather than a scientifically objective sense. You want to know why water's wet? Because we sense it as wet. We *make* it wet."

The water that was up to Carter's chest in the stairwell didn't come close to ticking all the boxes that made him define it as "wet." He couldn't see it, except for the ripples of a nonexistent liquid surface catching light he wasn't convinced came from anywhere in the world he'd been pretty sure was the only Earth up until that minute. It didn't move against his skin in any way he could feel except for a sense of resistance, more like a steady wind blowing when he tried to move rather than a liquid. It didn't make his skin cool when it was exposed to air. If anything, there was just a distant impression of coolness below the surface.

Experimentally, he lowered his head below the "surface" and opened his mouth. There was an oppressive pressure against his tongue as something with the mass but not the substance of water rolled in. Carter knew he didn't want to try to breathe it in. He'd seen Belasco's postmortem report. The non-water might not make good drinking, but it would drown him as certainly as a lake of the real thing.

He could feel himself growing buoyant the farther he moved into the layer. He could also see that the layer was rising rapidly up the stairwell; it wouldn't be long before it reached the ceiling of the upper floor, and then it would be all over for him. Carter took a deep breath, and dived.

If his life hadn't been in immediate danger, Carter might have taken a moment to enjoy the sensation of flying. It was not as effortless or as swift as the average superhero made it look, but there was still wonder to be had in making steady progress through the air of the front room and back toward the kitchen using a breaststroke. The time limit imposed by his lungs took almost all the pleasure from it, though.

He reached the kitchen doorway, grabbed the frame, and drew himself through, driving himself to the rear door. He grabbed the handle, wondering if the non-water would surge out in an invisible flood when he opened it. Then he remembered that the door would, of course, open inward. If this was normal water, the weight of it would be too much for him to pull against. He had made a mistake going forward; he should have tried to escape from the first story. It was too late to berate himself for the error. If he got out alive, there would be time then.

The handle wouldn't move at all. It wasn't that it was locked—he knew he'd left it unlocked—but that it simply wouldn't move at all, as if the handle had been welded to the mounting plate. There was no sense that it was made up of separate parts, only that the handle, lock, and bolt had become a single immovable unit.

Carter didn't know how that was possible, but he didn't know how the non-water was possible, either, and that didn't stop him from floating in it. He could see clearly in it; there was no sense of pressure on his eyeballs, or the prickling of an alien medium against the cornea. The water wasn't wet. Cool. That meant it wouldn't fuck up his pistol.

He drew his Glock, sighted on the glass panel making up the top half of the door, and fired.

The gun fired perfectly, the sound of the detonation only slightly muffled by the strange environment. The good news stopped there. The shot ricocheted off the glass to lodge somewhere in the kitchen wall. There wasn't even a mark to show where the bullet had struck it.

Carter fired again, but more as an experiment than in any real hope of shattering the glass. Again the bullet struck the target and again it ricocheted off, causing no apparent damage. Carter knew that even bullet-resistant glass would have shown a mark. Whatever Colt had done to seal the glass belonged to the same school of fucked-up physics as the non-water. Carter suspected he could empty the magazine and there'd be nothing to show for it except a few random holes in cereal boxes and the walls.

He reholstered his pistol and turned to go. As he did, he noticed the spent brass from the shots lying on the floor and, on an impulse, gathered them up. There was nothing he could do about the slugs, but he was damned if he was going to leave evidence of his last frantic attempts to escape for Colt to gloat over.

His lungs were starting to labor as he made the bottom of the stairwell and pushed himself up it. The layer had completely flooded the stairs, and he didn't find breathable air until he broke the glittering surface a foot above the floor of the upper hallway. He hungrily dragged in deep breaths as he waded through the deepening flood, heading for the rear bedroom where Colt kept his old technology. In the corner was a steel-framed chair. Carter picked it up and without hesitation swung it at the rear window.

It was like hitting a concrete wall. There was no reverberation in the glass, no sound beyond the metallic tone of the tubular steel form striking something at least as strong as itself.

Carter went back out onto the landing, taking the chair with him. There was a hatchway into the roof space in the ceiling, the hinged trapdoor bearing a simple ring at one end to allow it to be pulled down with a hook. He used the chair as a step stool, standing on it to reach the hatch. He hooked his finger through the ring and pulled. The trapdoor refused to move an inch, or even a millimeter. It was as solid as if it were just a detail carved from a single great sheet of marble.

Carter stood on the chair, considering his options, the glittering surface of the water that wasn't there already rising rapidly up his thighs. Colt had created a killing cube within his house, marked out as an area circumscribed by the outer walls, and becoming a greater volume as its height increased toward the first-story ceiling.

It was at his waist now, rising. He forced himself not to panic, not to feel fear. He drew his gun again, and fired at the ceiling. The walls in the kitchen had proved not to be bulletproof; if he could make a hole here, he might be able to use it to breathe through until whatever the non-water was abated and vanished, as it had apparently done in Belasco's case.

The bullet ricocheted off the ceiling, and there wasn't even a smudge on the magnolia paint to mark the impact. Colt had thought ahead. Carter had to hand it to him; the man knew how to construct a solid death trap.

The falling brass from the pistol slowed in the air, or whatever was there instead of air. Carter caught it easily. It wasn't even hot anymore.

The layer was at his chest. Carter wondered what else he could do. The trap was closed, and he couldn't find a way out. The water that wasn't water would soon reach the ceiling, and he would survive no more than a few minutes without breathable air. He could feel his chest tightening with panic, but he held it there. Panic would kill him. He might die, but he wouldn't die like that.

The layer was at his throat.

He thought back, trying to find anything in his recent experiences that might make a difference, some flaw in Colt's method, some error. He found himself thinking about Colt's story about Bertrand Russell and the impossible catalogue. An error in the purity of math. Finally, as the layer lapped at his chin, he understood. He understood that Colt had worried at that little hole in math, and torn it wide. Mathematics was everything, and Colt had found the cheat codes of creation.

Colt deliberately hyperventilated, flooding his blood with oxygen to give himself a precious few seconds more. Random thoughts buzzed around his awareness. He recalled reading some list of last words on the Net. Queen Elizabeth the First of England was supposed to have said, "All my possessions for a moment of time." Being queen hadn't bought her so much as a second of extra life. What did he have that might do it?

Nothing.

Nothing at all.

The layer closed over his face.

Chapter 17

THE PISTOL IN THE HOUSE

Carter had heard there were worse ways to die than drowning, and that was self-evidently true. You could be eaten by army ants, or cook slowly, or dissolve in acid, or explode like that poor son of a bitch in the casino. Even setting aside the really nasty end of ways to die, though, drowning was supposed to be not so bad. Some understandable panic, and then dreams and game over. It sounded okay when it was put like that. On the other hand, not one of the people who had told him this over the years had actually experienced being drowned themselves, so what the fuck did they know?

Carter knew he didn't want to die right then. He had too many balls in the air, too much unfinished business, and he especially didn't want to be killed by William Colt. Carter had his standards, and if he was going to die with his boots on, it wouldn't be because of some smug motherfucker in a button-down shirt killing him with math.

He tried to find an air pocket in the recess where the trapdoor was, huffing in what little was there. Then he felt a closeness trickle in at the corner of his lips, and he clamped his mouth shut.

Now there was nothing to do but wait. Either the layer would drop again before he drowned, or he would drown before the layer dropped. Those were the possible outcomes, and he didn't see any others. He concentrated on staying calm, on avoiding burning through the oxygen in his lungs and in his blood for as long as he could. He thought of nothing, clearing his mind, trying to stretch that moment of his being long enough that whatever timer Colt had put on this fish tank of his would finish first.

The seconds passed. The minutes accumulated. The oxygen burned. The layer did not drop.

Carter could hear his heart beating. It was beating faster as his body started to realize that there was insufficient oxygen in his blood to keep him alive. So, it beat faster to get the oxygen from his lungs around his body, because there's always oxygen to be had in the lungs. Yeah, that's the ticket. Beat faster, and faster, and faster. At the same time, the amount of carbon dioxide was building in his lungs as his blood dumped the stuff there, the exhaust from his metabolism. His lungs weren't keen on high levels of carbon dioxide, and started autonomic actions to clear the stuff out. That's it, buddy—breathe. You need to breathe. You really, really, *really* need to breathe.

Carter fought it until he was beyond thought, in an agony of burning lungs and terror of dying. Then his mouth opened, dead air burbled out into non-water, and he drew in the breath that would kill him.

He thought of Lovecraft and what she would think when he didn't come back. Of what would happen to the store. He thought of Colt winning. He thought of vague aspects of his childhood, trees, sunlight, the smell of grass and hot concrete. His dog, dead all these years. He thought of Charlie Hammond. And he heard Charlie say, right in Carter's ear, cheerful and clear . . .

That'll be The Twist.

Carter convulsed, drowning in midair.

There was a light, and Carter was not going to it, or even going away from it. It was all around, and he had a sense of motion, as if he was sliding somewhere. Faster and faster. At first it felt like he was on a water slide, then what he imagined it was like being on a luge, and finally he was traveling so quickly, he might as well have been falling. He had vague memories that he had been murdered, drowned, and that if this was what being drowned was like, then it really wasn't so bad.

The light bent around him, and what lay beyond was brilliantly lit beneath a stark sun, but distorted as by imperfect glass or a thin veil of water. It seemed a shame to him that he couldn't see more. There were buildings out there, vast, with asymmetric windows and interesting in a way that the skyscrapers of Manhattan weren't. He really wanted to see them. He *really* wanted to see them.

He reached out, and his hand broke the veil. He saw the buildings, saw that they were not constructed to any pattern of human usage, that they were inhabited. He snatched his hand back for fear that the denizens of those colossal spires might see him pathetically cringing behind the veil like a child hiding behind a lace curtain.

Yet there was an impression he could not shake off, though it writhed in the muscles in his neck, an apprehension that those intelligences that dwelled in the towers were utterly unconcerned with him, even though they did perceive him now. He was unimportant to them at even the level of fleeting curiosity. The dwindling perspective of their neglect crushed him inwardly.

He was sure he should be dead by now. Did dying really take so long? Were these the last perceptions of a dying mind, crushed into the last moment? Or was this what passed for Heaven and

Hell? The afterlife was a fever dream, and his mind would fail long before it could become paradise or torment. That wouldn't be so bad, he thought. Not so bad at all.

Then death spat him out.

He awoke to the sound of the wind in the trees, water lapping, and the drone of distant aircraft. Carter rolled over and realized he was lying on grass, not carpet. Somehow he had escaped Colt's house and ended up on the lawn outside. Even as he was sitting up, part of his mind was telling him that his conclusions were wrong. There was nothing neat and trimmed about the grass he was lying on; it was wild growth. Nor were there any trees much bigger than saplings around Colt's house. He sat up, looked around, and knew exactly where he was. How he had gotten there, however, was a different question.

The abandoned sneaker from a few days before was still there, and he could even make out the tire tracks of his car. Not much had changed on Waite's Bill.

Looking around to make sure there was nobody to see, he drew his pistol and quickly checked its load. Three rounds were gone. Three shell cases were in his jacket pocket.

Reholstering his pistol, he next looked at his phone. It worked perfectly, which he knew from bitter experience was not something it would do if immersed in water. In *real* water. The photo of the bill he had found in Colt's files was there, just like it should be.

So. All the physical evidence pointed to his recollection being accurate. It was a shame the stuff about physics being broken and how he had spontaneously traveled five miles was also part of the narrative. He decided not to think about it. Thinking about it felt like a mistake. It was tempting not to think about anything. It was tempting to walk into the water and never think about anything again.

There seemed little point in standing there like an idiot in the hope that a solution to an impossible escape from an impossible trap might simply present itself, so Carter walked out onto the road with his hands in his pockets and his head down. He felt he was being watched as he entered the leafed tunnel that led off the spit of land, but he didn't look back. He felt stupid and inconsequential, and kept thinking of the buildings in his vision. He didn't want to look back because he didn't want to give whoever was watching—if anyone was watching—the satisfaction of seeing him look around for them. He didn't want to look back to see who was watching—if anyone was watching—because he didn't want to see them. Because he didn't know what he would see.

The house on the corner where he had spoken to the owner loomed into view, alone and not overlooked by its neighbors, like a solitary guard placed upon Waite Road by the unconscious wariness of civic planners. There was no one outside today, and Carter was glad of that. He would have looked suspicious coming out of the connecting road on foot, and the owner would surely have recognized him. His life was already complicated enough.

Carter, not dead and bemused for it, walked up the rise, phoning for a cab as he went.

Ken Rothwell had not enjoyed his evening. Emily had been distracted the whole time, even eventually offering a rain check. He'd dropped her off at her apartment, and her good-night kiss had been perfunctory and, once again, distracted. Rothwell smiled and accepted her apologies, assured her it wasn't a problem, said, "Good night," and seethed all the way home.

He was no fool, and it hardly took a genius to see that she'd been becoming more distant and preoccupied ever since that PI had turned up and claimed ownership of Hill's Books. He'd heard nothing from Carter after offering to take the business off his hands. Instead Carter had offered joint ownership to Emily. Rothwell was still trying to decide if that was a nice gesture to her or a considered insult to him. Maybe it was both; on the couple of occasions he'd found them shooting the breeze in the store, they'd seemed as thick as thieves. The chatter dried up pretty quickly when they saw him, too.

Rothwell didn't think of himself as a jealous man. He was deluding himself.

He arrived back at his town house at two in the morning, having gone around the bars after leaving Emily. His license would have been in danger if he'd been stopped, but he was past giving a fuck. Besides, he had a stash of magic that made a lot of problems like that go away, a stash that came in a variety of denominations.

The only staff he maintained was a housekeeper, Amara, and she had been long gone when he entered and disarmed the alarm. He hadn't especially been paying attention, but just as the alarm zone indicators all showed green, he could have sworn one zone was showing the alarm was already deactivated there anyway. No, he had imagined it.

He kicked off his shoes and left them lying haphazardly in the hall before going upstairs in his stockinged feet to have at least one more nightcap and maybe decide what he was going to do about the Emily situation. More specifically the Carter situation. Everything had been fine until that guy showed up.

He entered his study and found the lights were already on. He blinked in mild surprise; Amara must be getting slack.

Then he noticed the man.

The man was sitting in an easy chair in the corner, regarding Rothwell with amusement. Rothwell had seen enough movies to know this was about when the man would say some pithy one-liner and shoot Rothwell with a silenced pistol that made a sound like a cat sneezing. Admittedly, in the movies the assassins always dressed a little classier than this man. The button-down collar didn't work in context at all.

"Hello, Mr. Rothwell," said the man. He was still smiling.

"How did you get in here?" asked Rothwell. He cursed himself inwardly; this was playing out just like a movie. He was just bringing the sneezing gun moment closer talking like that.

"Ways and means," said the man. "Actually, they're why I'm here. I'd like to talk to you about a . . . mutually advantageous proposal."

"Why couldn't you come through my office?"

The smile lessened. "Because I'm an impatient man. I have something of enormous significance and only one lifetime to take advantage of it. It makes me inclined to cut corners. If you're not interested, I don't much care. I'll find somebody else who won't waste my time. Politicians breed like rats. I'll find somebody sooner than later."

"No, no, no," said Rothwell, chiding the man like a child, "you're going nowhere until you answer my question. How did you get in here?"

"Honestly?" The man seemed pained. "Okay, but just quickly. I went to a locksmith and had him cut a key randomly. I told him it was for a college film project and would end up being destroyed so we didn't want to use a real one. I used it to get through your front door."

"How?"

"How?" The man looked at Rothwell like he was an idiot. "By putting it in the lock and turning it. How do keys usually work? Maybe you have a flunky to do that for you. Anyway, that got me inside. Then I entered a code into the alarm that I'd randomized with a decahedral die." He took a ten-sided die from his pocket and rolled it on the desk by his side. "Seven . . . nine . . . five . . . three. That's your code, isn't it?"

Rothwell had watched the die rattle out the numbers with each roll with an expression of deepening disbelief. "How the hell did you do that? Are you a conjuror?"

The man smirked. "I'm a magician, if that's what you mean. Oh—" He took a key from his pocket and tossed it onto the desk, picking up the die and returning it to the pocket. "Here's the key I used to get in. You can have it. Useful to have a spare, isn't it?"

Rothwell picked it up and compared it with his own. He could see no differences in the milling. "This is bullshit. You did not get this cut randomly."

The man gave up any pretense of friendliness. "You are such a fucking waste of skin, Rothwell. You happen to be born into money and you think it makes you special. No. It means you were lucky. Once. I'm lucky *all* the time. *That's* special. What's funny is that you think your one-shot little bit of luck is going to get you into the Senate. No . . . fucking . . . way. This is a blue state these days, 'Ken.'"

"For now."

"How long were you planning on waiting? You can piss your money up a wall trying, but you will never get into government running here. Unless"—the man raised an admonitory finger—"you get *real* lucky. The kind of luck I deal in. Onetime offer. Say yes right now, or I find somebody with some balls who *really* wants that ol' brass ring."

Rothwell looked at him steadily. "Let me make sure I understand you. The key, the alarm code . . . you say you can influence chance?"

"I say it because it's true."

"Fine. Let's see you put your ass on the line over that." Rothwell went to the heavy maple-wood desk, felt under the edge of it, and released a catch. A concealed drawer slid out. From it, he removed a revolver with an unusually long cylinder. "This," he said to his visitor, "is a Taurus Judge. It fires 410-gauge shotgun shells. Not a nice thing to be shot by." He smiled at the man. "Let's up the game a little, huh?" He broke the pistol and removed the load it was carrying. He took out a new box of ammunition and showed it to the man. "Critical Defense cartridges. Fires a bullet followed by two .35-caliber ball bearings. Really, *really* not a nice thing to be shot with. Bought these the other day. Haven't had a chance to try them out yet." He broke the seal on the box, removed a cartridge, and slid it into one of the cylinder's five chambers.

"What is this?" asked the man, curious rather than worried. "Are you seriously suggesting that we play Russian roulette?"

"Fuck, no." Rothwell grinned at him. "I'm suggesting we mathematically model my chances of making it to the Senate. You like probabilities, don't you? Tell me . . . what's your name, by the way?"

"Colt. William Colt." Colt's eyes never left the pistol in Rothwell's hands.

"Colt. I like that. That's a good name. Bill Colt. You sound like a hero of the Old West there."

"Nobody calls me 'Bill.' "

"Why not? It's a good, manly name. So, anyway. My Senate chances. What do you reckon, Bill? Eighty percent?" He showed Colt the one filled and four empty chambers. Colt said nothing. "No. I'm a realist. I can't see it being any better than sixty." He slid in another cartridge. "But the pundits are saying even that's delusional. They say I'd be lucky to make forty." Another cartridge. Rothwell was grinning and could feel himself sweating. He was glad he was a little drunk. "And then there's you. What was your nuanced political view of my chances? Oh, yeah. 'No fucking way.' Let's round that down a little to a nice pitiful twenty percent." He slid in a fourth cartridge. He regarded the one empty chamber philosophically. Then he laughed, spun the cylinder while looking at Colt, and closed the pistol. "Like the man said, I guess that makes me shit out of luck. Stand up, Bill."

Colt slowly got to his feet.

"Okay," said Rothwell, "here's the deal. I'm going to point this pistol at you now, and I'm going to squeeze the trigger. We'll see how lucky you are. If you're not lucky, then I shot an intruder in my home. If you are, I guess we can talk. How's that?"

Colt surprised him by laughing, just once. "You have a very muscular approach to experimentation. I approve. Fire away."

Rothwell decided he'd had enough of Colt. He'd never killed before, but now it came to it, it felt like it might be pretty easy. He wouldn't even have to dispose of the body. Just call 911 and put on his best shocked voice. Maybe it might give him some kudos with Emily. Poor traumatized Ken. Yes. That would work.

Rothwell steadied the pistol in both hands, worked back the hammer, and squeezed the trigger.

The pistol clicked.

Now it was Rothwell's turn to laugh. "You really are a lucky son of a bitch, Bill. Okay. We'll talk."

He broke the pistol to empty it. And froze.

It wasn't an empty chamber under the hammer. The cartridge had misfired.

"Well," said Colt, smiling the slightest ghost of a smile, "I wonder what the odds against *that* happening are?"

Chapter 18

THE SHADOW OVER PROVIDENCE

It took Carter a long time to fall asleep that night, despite a deep exhaustion that ached through his every fiber. At least he did not dream, or did not remember his dreams—a small mercy. He awoke late, and came down into the store after showering to find it long open and Lovecraft behind the counter. She was uncommunicative, almost surly, and Carter left her to get some breakfast and to decide what he was going to do.

"Nothing at all" felt very tempting, he realized over his bacon, eggs, and black coffee. Colt was staggeringly dangerous, and yet there was nothing that could realistically be put at his door. Carter could keep after him, but whatever had gone wrong with Colt's previous attempt on Carter's life was not certain to save him next time. Maybe he was only alive because Colt had planned it that way. It was difficult to have an opinion when his antagonist kept breaking the rules of reality.

Carter looked around the diner and felt very isolated. There was nobody he could talk to about this. Harrelson had misgivings about what was happening, but Carter doubted he thought there was anything more than some deep cleverness in the methods used to kill Belasco and Hayesman. There was a rational explanation behind it all, just something more ingenious than shooting them.

Harrelson hadn't seen a building fill with phantom water, though.

Carter could take his near-death experience as a warning and step back from the investigation, he guessed. Never finding out who called him on Belasco's phone would grate against his curiosity for the rest of his life, but at least he would *have* a life.

It was a fool's paradise, and it wouldn't last long. Colt wasn't your average underachieving serial killer, but that was still where he was headed, and he would follow the usual progression. He would get messier, less attentive to details as his MO evolved. More would die, nothing was more certain. More miserable, terrifying deaths brought on because they accidentally shoved by Colt on the sidewalk, or they talked with their mouths full, or he just didn't like their faces.

Usual police procedure would founder. Building a case depended on demonstrating cause and effect. Colt had set fire to causality just for the pleasure of pissing on it to put it out. They'd have to reactivate witchcraft statutes to find laws vague enough to convict him.

Reluctantly, Carter saw he had no real choice. William Colt had to go down.

Carter studied the photo of the Material Sciences Department bill he had on his phone. What had they manufactured for him on their "rapid prototyping" equipment? The date was two weeks before Belasco's death. Maybe they'd built him a wand out of four kilos of powdered aluminum. That seemed as likely as anything.

Right now, however, it was a Sunday, so that would have to wait for tomorrow. In the meantime he would go back, make himself a pot of coffee, and sit down to read the ever-loving fuck out of *The Moving Toyshop*. No book was going to make him feel like a detecting reject.

"DMLS stands for 'direct metal laser sintering.'"

Carter couldn't help but notice that everybody was prepared to think the worst of Colt. He just had to show his license, explain that he was conducting an investigation into the activities of William Colt, and that was all he had to say. People just accepted that Colt had done something bad and that they'd be happy to see him suffer for it. "Arrogant" was mentioned more than once. Colt seemed to have mislaid his copy of *How to Win Friends and Influence People*.

Stacy Winters of the engineering department was a postgrad working toward her doctorate, and had responsibility for the fast prototyping equipment. Carter was talking to her in her office, and discovering that she remembered Colt very well.

"It's a way of building an object from a 3-D CAD file. Three-dimensional printing except with metal instead of plastic, so you're dealing with much higher temperatures. Our setup uses a two-hundred-watt laser to melt and fuse metallic powder with a good level of precision. We build a lot of components for engineering projects, and one-offs for stuff other departments need for experimental rigs."

"What did Colt want you to make?"

"To be honest, I don't really know what it was. It was an imperfect cube. When he came to us, it sounded like an interesting project and he was prepared to pay, so I said, yes, why not? We hadn't done anything like it before, and experience is always good, especially when somebody else is picking up the tab."

"A cube? Just a cube?"

"An *imperfect* cube. The angles were off. The archaeology department had gotten their hands on something kind of out of the ordinary, and Colt wanted to carry out a mathematical analysis of the ratios of it, lengths of the sides, the angles, and so forth."

The mention of the archaeology department reminded Carter that talking to them was on his to-do list anyway. He mentally shifted them to a higher priority.

"The archaeologists wouldn't let him take it, obviously, but he suggested a nonintrusive way of making a copy by laser scanning it," said Winters. "No plaster casts or that kind of thing. They liked the idea, just like we liked the idea of producing a physical facsimile, so we did it. It would have been a great piece of interdisciplinary cooperation if Colt wasn't such an asshole.

"He didn't seem to understand that we weren't going to produce a solid block of aluminum for him, even if he was paying for it. We wanted to structure it as hollow, and that meant being clever in how the CAD file was used. Colt didn't want that, he wanted it identical. I pointed out that the original was made from stone, so he should choose his battles better. He backed down pretty quickly, but he still rode my team every step of the way. *Such* a dick. I was glad to hand the thing over at the end of the process."

She opened a pictures file on her desktop. "Here. This is what we made him."

The images were of a polished aluminum cube about six inches along an edge. It was an imperfect cube, just as Winters had said; the corners were obviously not neatly 90 degrees. It sat on a workbench, gaps showing under it where it refused to lie flat. The sides were marred with hundreds of grooves running more or less but not entirely parallel to one another.

"This is a copy of something the archaeological department is looking at, is that right?" asked Carter to confirm. The cube was intriguing, but he couldn't see Colt's interest in it.

"Yep. Speak to Professor Hubbard; he was our liaison during the scanning part of the project."

Professor Hubbard was of a similar mind to Winters when it came to the subject of William Colt. He also made the same unsubstantiated assumption that Carter was carrying out an investigation into Colt on behalf of the college regents, presumably with the intention of expelling him. Carter got the impression that both Winters and Hubbard knew they were making assumptions, but their natural optimism that, whatever the outcome, it would put Colt in the shit with *someone* meant they didn't care.

"It was an interesting idea for a project, and I allowed my enthusiasm for the newness of the idea—at least to me—to get the better of me. As it is, it would seem to have been little more than a vanity project for Mr. Colt. He promised to keep me abreast of his analysis of the artifact, and has not done so. I haven't heard a word from him since the laser scanning part of the procedure was completed. In fact, I thought they'd run into practical problems and canceled it until you told me differently."

"What was Colt's interest in the cube?" asked Carter.

"Academic. Entirely academic. The thing has no convincing attributions to origin, or date. It's inorganic, made of porphyry." He noted Carter's raised eyebrow. "That's a form of hard, igneous rock, purplish in color. Anyway, it's inorganic, so radiocarbon dating is a nonstarter. It's also in no recognized style, so it could have been made last year as easily as a thousand years ago, for all we know."

"Where was it found? Surely that would give you some context?"

"In the net of a bottom trawler. Deep-sea fishing isn't well regarded around here, Mr. Carter. It's hugely damaging to the seabed both ecologically and archaeologically. When they turned up the artifact, they handed it over as a sop to local feeling. I'm still not convinced it isn't a bit of failed sculpture that a disappointed artist threw over the side of a boat in disgust."

"There seems to be a lot of interest in it, all the same."

"*Seemed.* A nine-day wonder, to air a useful old phrase. These days the appetite for such ephemeral sensations is greater than ever. The Internet feeds on such stories. Would you like to see it? It doesn't get many visitors now that its novelty has worn off."

Hubbard took Carter into his office and opened the bottom

drawer of a battered gray filing cabinet. He removed an object covered in a soft cloth and placed it on his desk. "Behold, the mystery," he said dryly.

The cube was, Carter had to admit, an underwhelming experience in the flesh. It was just as had been described, and simply the stone original of the aluminum copy. If anything, the copy was more impressive.

"May I touch it?"

"Go ahead," said Hubbard. "We carried out trace tests when the thing was first handed in and found nothing you wouldn't expect from a chunk of stone pulled up from the bed of the Atlantic."

Carter picked it up. It felt heavy, and nothing more. He'd almost expected to be momentarily tormented with one of his strange visions, but there was nothing except the experience of holding a cube of stone. It felt very smooth, even the striations having no sharp edges.

"Nothing at all to date it by?" he asked. "No way of telling where it came from?"

Hubbard shook his head. "No. As I said, carbon-fourteen dating is useless in its case. We tried thermoluminescence and briefly investigated the possibility of oxygen isotope chronostratigraphy being of any utility, more in hope than expectation. Both just weren't suitable. The thing lying in water for heaven only knows how long removed a lot of options. We did use electron microscopy to study the striations. We were looking for tool marks.

"Nothing, which is suspicious in itself. It implies the striations were thermally cut. We consulted some friendly geologists to see if there was any possibility the thing was entirely natural and not a wrought artifact at all. They assured us that there was no record of porphyry forming anything like this. So, either the striations were smoothed by, well, I can't imagine . . . acid, perhaps? Or they were incised with something like a plasma cutter. Neither possibility speaks of great antiquity."

"Atlantis?" said Carter. He was sure to smile when he said it.

Hubbard didn't smile back. "If I had a dime for every person who'd . . . What's the matter, Mr. Carter?"

Carter's smile had vanished abruptly as he idly turned the cube in his hands, and happened to look down at it. The face upon which it had been resting when he first saw it was now uppermost. It, too, displayed the dense pattern of apparently semirandom striations cut into the otherwise smooth stone. Running across the striations was a ridge, as high as the striations were deep. Where it crossed them, the striations bent to join it, or perhaps branched from it to head off for themselves. He turned the cube until the beginning of the ridge was in the upper right corner. From there it ran in a straight line of slightly varying thickness down to about a third of the way along from the bottom-right corner on the lower edge as he looked at it.

In the eye of Carter's mind, the striations looked a lot like threads.

His voice was a whisper. He spoke slowly. "When exactly was this thing handed in?" he asked. He put the cube down on its cloth.

Hubbard looked curiously at him. "It would be four . . . no, just five months ago now. Why do you ask?"

That was long after Suydam died. It was impossible. Carter wanted to think it was a coincidence, but that was impossible, too. The ridge, the striations, the bunching of the lines. He would never forget that pattern.

"I've seen something like this before," he said. It was a partial lie. He had seen something *exactly* like it before.

"Really?" Hubbard looked at the cube again, his curiosity reignited. "In a museum? A book? Where?"

"At a crime scene," said Carter. "I'd put it back in that bottom drawer again if I were you, Professor, and forget about it. Better still, drop it back in the Atlantic. Atlantis can choke on it."

The position of Owen Worley's house meant that he and his family saw much of the comings and goings of Waite Road. Generally it was uninspirational viewing; the residents of the street all tended to drive cheap pickups, and once you'd seen one, there was little to differentiate them from one another. What passed as excitement was what happened every few weeks; somebody would turn down there on the assumption that it would be a shortcut to one of the roads to the west. Then they would find that the road led onto an isolated spit of land, and they'd have to turn and come out, feeling shameful for trying to rat run through and being caught out. Owen never failed to smile and wave at the impatient assholes if he was outside when they drove by.

Yeah, there'd been that guy the other day who'd stopped and actually talked to Worley. He'd been okay, hadn't taken offense. Most just drove by with their tails between their legs. Once or twice they'd stopped and gotten in his grill, which kind of proved his point. Only an asshole wouldn't be able to take such a mild piece of hazing as that.

Recently, he'd noticed an outsider visiting pretty frequently. He drove a red Mazda, and looked a mite like that guy who used to be on MTV a lot, singing a song about running along a road that didn't go anywhere. He wasn't a resident, and—apart from service vehicles like the mail—about the only regular visitor. Maybe he was the boyfriend of one of the Waite girls. That kind of made Worley envious.

The Waite men he'd seen were a real bunch of sad sacks. They looked stupid, with heavy stupid faces and dim stupid eyes. The women, however, were something else again. He'd started telling the guy who stopped the other day, but he'd given Worley a look that made Worley shut up. Well, more fool you, buddy.

The Waite women weren't beautiful in that brilliant-toothed, immaculate-hair, movie-and-TV way. They weren't plain, either, but Worley found it hard to apply words like "pretty" to them. They were something else. "Striking," maybe. "Attractive," definitely.

They didn't dress up, they didn't wear much makeup, if any, but Worley would have nailed any one of them if he thought he could get away with it. The oldest looked like she was in her forties, but he'd thought that when he and his wife had moved in opposite Waite's Bill fifteen years before, so he guessed he just wasn't very good at gauging how old people were. The youngest he'd seen was maybe sixteen. Maybe. Normally he wasn't much into jailbait, but holy fuck.

A couple of weeks before he'd been out front mowing the lawn on a Sunday morning. One of the interchangeable pickups had swung out of the bill's approach and headed up the slight rise leading west into town. It had stopped more or less in front of him while the driver, a typical Waite man with dead eyes, got out to make sure the load of boxes and junk in the back was properly secured. While he fussed with ropes, his passenger—one of the girls—slouched with her arm out of the window.

Worley would swear he wasn't staring. He'd just stopped to wipe his brow. That was all. Just stopped for a minute, and happened to be facing that way. He wasn't staring.

The Waite girl looked at him suddenly and it was just as he happened to be looking at her, at her naked arm, at her hair, her profile. It just happened that way. He wasn't staring.

She looked him dead in the eye, and she smiled. No. She *grinned*. It wasn't a happy, joy-of-life grin, but the grin of somebody who's just won. A grin of victory. It looked good on her.

He'd blushed. Big guy like him, and he'd blushed. It was just because of the mowing, though. It had made him hot. He'd turned away as he became aware of a forming semiboner, and walked into the house to get himself a drink.

He had heard her laughing as the door closed behind him.

He'd hated it, feeling horny because of her. Jesus, was she even legal? It made him feel like a pervert. Even more so when he beat off thinking of her. Even more so when he imagined her under him as he fucked his wife. Waite's Bill, just down the little isthmus road. Waite Road, just there at the end. Its proximity itched. He scratched hard.

But the guy in the red Mazda, no, he couldn't be the boyfriend of any of them. Worley had seen him drive in alone and, after a few hours, or even overnight, he'd drive out again, still alone. He entertained the idea that maybe one or another of the women was a whore, but that didn't make sense. Why would they have only one client? Still, the thought of going over there with a fistful of bills and buying a few hours with a Waite woman occupied him for a while.

Worley was alone today. His wife and daughter were away for the week seeing family in Maryland, so he had the run of the house to himself. He'd taken a few days off to get some work done on the place without falling over his family, and had rapidly sunk into a routine of treating every day like a Sunday. So, there he was on the porch to pick up the mail in underwear and a robe when the red Mazda drove out of Waite's Bill. He saw it slow at the corner and drive past his house still in first.

For the first time ever, the driver wasn't alone. There was another guy in there. He looked disheveled and kind of shocked to Worley's eye, so out of the norm that it took Worley a second to realize he was looking at Kenneth Rothwell.

His jaw dropped. That was just weird. What had a guy as rich as God been doing on Waite Road?

Rothwell didn't look up—he just carried on looking shellshocked. The driver, though, Worley had a momentary glimpse of the driver looking across and seeing him there on his porch. Then the Mazda was gone, off up the rise and out of sight. Worley went back inside, shaking his head.

It nagged at him for the rest of the morning, distracting him from his chores and his work. He drove his car onto the drive to wash it, and then decided he'd rather have lunch first even though it was early.

He came out to find one of the Waite women half sitting on his car's hood. No, not one of the women. It was the girl. The one who'd laughed at him. She wore jeans and scuffed blue shoes and a T-shirt. She wasn't wearing a bra, Worley saw that straightaway. She was dark haired and pale, and her pupils were as black as obsidian. She smiled, and it was a close cousin to that grin that had confused him so much. She slid off the car and walked to him, and he could only stand there foolishly as she did so, his heart speeding, his blood beginning to burn him.

He felt now, though he didn't truly apprehend it, what it was that was so attractive about the Waite women, so irresistible to him, at least. They were feral creatures, with the lamina of civilization so thin upon them that they tore it with ease. There was something of an ancient incomprehensible wisdom about them, or knowledge at least, that reeked of the land before the Europeans came, or even before the first Americans came across the land bridge from Asia. A power of ages combined with a vulpine vivacity. The Waite family were animals, just like us all, but unlike the rest of us, the Waite women knew it.

She stood close by him, and touched him on the forearm, her light fingers stroking his skin, now dense with gooseflesh, as she spoke quietly to him, and he heard no words. Then she led him indoors and he followed dumbly.

They didn't spend the afternoon together, no more than a vivisectionist spends an afternoon with a subject upon the operating table. The Waite girl operated upon Worley methodically and without mercy, taking him places darker than the perverse commonalities of a century that thinks it has seen it all. It was pleasure of a virulent kind, with each orgasm a precipice to which she dragged him more reluctantly, again and again until he was broken, and then went quietly afterward.

She left him at dusk without even telling him her name. She left him dead-eyed and alone with the new vistas she had placed in his mind. He had little coherent memory of seeing a red Mazda leave Waite Road. The day would be nothing but a blur by tomorrow. Soon he wouldn't even be sure if he'd just gotten very drunk and daydreamed the whole thing. The one thing that would stay with him would be that he had no interest in Waite's Bill. Why would he care who came and went? It didn't matter. So little that he'd once been concerned with actually mattered. He would just carry on being Owen Worley, reliable worker, loving husband and father. It had all been revealed as an act to him, and he was good at it, so he would just carry on.

Reliable.

Loving.

He could still hear her laughter.

Chapter 19

"I need some money," Carter told Lovecraft. "I still don't have any control over the accounts yet, and I need some ready cash for the investigation."

Lovecraft knew Carter was aware of what she thought of the investigation and didn't bother reiterating it. Instead she said, "How much?"

Carter slid a printout across the counter.

She read it, then she frowned and read it again. Then she picked it up, so she could look at it more closely and express her incredulity in its fullest form.

"You have got to be kidding. What is this thing?"

"Colt had one made. It's a copy of an artifact that has the college archaeological faculty stumped, and Colt has an exact copy. Whatever he's doing, that cube's got something to do with it. I need one to study."

"You don't think you're getting a little . . . paranoid about all this stuff, Dan?" she asked with evident reluctance.

Carter didn't have the time or the patience for that right then. "He tried to kill me. I still don't know how he failed."

"What now? He did what?"

Carter was going to lie about how he'd gotten into Colt's house and then decided, *Fuck it.*

"I broke into his house to search. Found some odd shit, including the twin of this invoice, but nothing out-and-out incriminating. On my way out, I saw Colt from the window. Emily, he *knew* I was there. I think he'd been planning it. He mimed drowning at me, and then drove off."

"That's not trying to kill . . ."

"I couldn't get out. The place was tight as a drum. No, tighter. Way tighter. The doors were sealed, the windows wouldn't open. Then the place started to flood."

"He flooded his own house?"

"Yeah. No. He flooded it, but I'm not sure it was water. Or, at least, not water from around here." Lovecraft was already looking at him like he was a lunatic. *What the hell*, he thought. *In for a penny.* "And by 'around here,' I don't mean this state. I mean this universe. I know, I *know* how this sounds, but I am not a fanciful man. I work on the basis of human behavior and solid forensic evidence. I count being able to swim through somebody's house without the use of water as pretty compelling evidence that somebody is fucking around with the laws of physics."

He looked at her closely. "I don't even know why I'm worried about you believing this stuff. You already believe it."

Lovecraft looked away, finding distraction in the invoice and the clutter of the counter.

"That's why Colt freaked you out when he came in here. You had a bad feeling about him, and then he as much as told you that he knew how to buttfuck causality. You were scared because you knew it was true. Well, it is. He almost killed me with that party trick."

"How did you get out?"

Carter felt very tired. It had taken a while, but he was finally running out of adrenaline and reaction was setting in. "I don't know." His voice was weary. "I have no idea how I got out of there. I woke up over an hour's walk away. I don't know how I got there."

Lovecraft's brow furrowed heavily, and she ran her finger back and forth along one section of the counter. Then she spoke with great reluctance, as if letting out a secret that could never be recalled.

"Waite's Bill?" asked Lovecraft.

Carter admitted to being surprised several times in his life, perhaps even stunned on a very few occasions, but he doubted he had ever been honestly astounded, even by recent events. They had happened, and he had dealt with them to the best of his ability. Lovecraft had astounded him. He looked at her as if he'd never seen her before for several seconds. Then he went to the door, locked it, flipped the sign to *Closed*, and said, "Tell me everything you know."

Lovecraft was sitting at the small kitchen table in the apartment above the store. Carter couldn't settle himself enough to sit while she spoke. Instead he stood, and sometimes he paced.

"Everything . . . is kind of fucked up," said Lovecraft. "And by 'everything,' I mean *everything*. Nothing is right, nothing is as it appears. I don't just mean in some nihilistic, conspiratorial, paranoid kind of way. I mean fundamentally. And the joke is, it used to be worse.

"Then, back in the twenties, a group of guys figured out what was wrong, and how they could fix it."

"Hold on," said Carter. "You keep saying things were wrong. What do you mean by that?"

"I mean, things were out of kilter. What you've experienced, but a lot worse."

"No," said Carter. "No, I don't buy that. That kind of shit would be all over the history books and old accounts."

"A lot of it is," said Lovecraft quietly. "The 'Age of Superstition.' But most of it was hidden or dismissed and, afterward, it got hard to remember it in any case. You want to hear about these guys or not?

"So, there was already a high level of background weirdness. These people, they were already sensitive to it, and then Charles Fort had published *The Book of the Damned* just after the First World War, which just made concrete a lot of their fears. They corresponded with Fort, met with him secretly."

She paused. Carter's brow had furrowed at the first mention of Charles Fort, and the furrowing had deepened at the second.

"If you have no idea who Charles Fort was, just say so," said Lovecraft.

"I have no idea who Charles Fort was."

"Fine. He wrote a bunch of books that suggested that science wasn't all that, and that it—and we—might be missing a few tricks. That there might be more things in Heaven and Earth than you can see through a telescope or a microscope or in a particle accelerator."

"Religion?"

"Not really."

"Magic? He believed in magic?"

"Not necessarily, but he didn't disbelieve it, either. That's the important thing. Fort was all about keeping an open mind.

"Anyway, they discovered there was a way to wind things back, to cover up the holes in reality where it had worn thin. You have to bear in mind that quantum theory was a new thing back then. A lot of mathematicians and physicists hated it, because it damaged the solidity of Newtonian physics. Einstein didn't like it, Schrödinger hated it. The thing about Schrödinger's cat was an argument *against* quantum theory, not to show how cool it was. He was another one who got pulled into the little circle of guys who could see things were already bad, and that something had to be done."

Carter looked at Lovecraft, coldly appraising her. The enthusiastic bibliophile and businesswoman was absent. Now her whole demeanor was of somebody carefully explaining how they had accidentally killed your mother, and trying to make you understand it was out of her control. Every fact had to be defined, annotated, restated to avoid ambiguity.

"Who are these 'guys' you keep talking about?" asked Carter.

Lovecraft said nothing for a long moment. Then, very reluctantly, "One was Howard Phillips Lovecraft. The writer. My ancestor. The other was his friend. Randolph Carter." She looked sideways at Carter. "Your great-great-great-uncle. He's there in your family tree, if you want to look. You wanted a connection between you and this bookstore. There it is."

"You said Randolph Carter was fictional."

"I half thought he was. H. P. L. made some reference to him in his private journals that were inferred to mean he was using the name as a pseudonym for somebody he didn't want to name, borrowing the name from his fiction. Turns out, no, he meant what he said.

"Between them they did something. There are no surviving notes to explain what, but they did it on Waite's Bill, and it changed everything. Not in a rhetorical sense. They changed *everything*.

"When it was explained to me by my uncle Alfred, he called it a 'perceptual twist.' A different perspective that works for everything, and is entirely objective. They imposed a new paradigm."

"Just like that? They changed reality in their lunch hour?"

Lovecraft glared at him. "You just don't understand how fucked up it was. It took years to prepare, but only a few hours to do. Believe me, The Twist was waiting to happen. They just shoved it a little way down Entropy Hill, and it settled there really happily."

Carter heard "The Twist," and didn't think of a dance craze. He thought of Hammond. "So explain Colt."

Lovecraft shrugged. "Maybe *really happily* was an exaggeration. H. P. L. and Randolph, they were doing what nobody had ever tried before. What nobody had even attempted. There'd been a few people down the centuries who had misgivings about things, but they usually lived in times where saying it would be the same as saying, 'Hey, everyone! God fucked up!' Not real clever.

"It wasn't perfect. Maybe it's possible to push back here and there if you can see the flaws in the original Twist. I think that's what Colt's doing. Everything rests pretty much on probability, and probability is his main thing, from what you've told me."

"Why Waite's Bill? Why is it so important?"

"I don't know. I only know it gets a lot of mentions in H. P. L.'s notes. He never says why it's important. He knew why it was, and didn't bother noting it. I wish he had. When you said you'd followed Colt there, I knew where it was all going."

Carter walked up and down once more. He was trying to control his anger, but it was difficult because he didn't know where the anger was coming from. Maybe it was because Lovecraft had deliberately kept him in the dark. Maybe it was because he believed what she was saying and really didn't want to. Either way, the anger got away from him.

"This is such bullshit," he said. "I'm out of this. You want the store? It's yours. I'll give you a good price for my half, and then I am done."

Lovecraft looked at him as if he were an imbecile child. "Yeah. Right. This is absolutely something you can walk away from."

"I have nothing to do with this, and I didn't even know my 'fictional' great-great-great-uncle did until you just told me. I don't have a dog in this fight, Emily. I *am* walking away."

"Tell me how that works out for you when you get dragged back into it again. Dan, don't be a fucking idiot. There's somebody out there who wants you involved. They won't let you walk.

They pulled you into the Belasco investigation. They'll do it again the very next time Colt does his numbers voodoo." She laughed bitterly. "Or maybe they won't have to. What do you think Colt's doing right now? He set out to kill you, and you escaped. That makes you a double threat. You were enough of a problem for him to want to kill you already, but now you wiggled out of it in a weird way, and he's going to be wondering how the actual fuck you did that."

"I don't know how . . ."

"I know! He doesn't. No Scottish giant is going to walk in here and tell you you're a wizard, Dan, but Colt's going to be pretty worried that's exactly what you are."

"A wizard. Fuck's sake, Emily . . ."

"Colt breaks basic physical laws to do what he does. If that isn't magic, what is it? And if it is—for want of a better term—magic, what does that make him? It's not about pointed hats and Gandalf, man. It's about lifting some heavy math and somehow being able to see through The Twist. He doesn't see things as they appear. He sees them as they really are—profoundly fucked and held together with one Band-Aid.

"Look, H. P. L. was a romantic. He *wanted* there to be magic in the world. He hated how science had overwhelmed it. Wait a minute." She went to the bookshelves in the apartment and took down a black volume. "This is a fragment of a novel he *really* wanted to write, but he never did. Wrote less than five hundred words of it, and never any more. Listen to this." She found the page, and started to read.

"*When age fell upon the world, and wonder went out of the minds of men; when grey cities reared to smoky skies tall towers grim and ugly, in whose shadow none might dream of the sun or of Spring's flowering meads; when learning stripped Earth of her mantle of beauty, and poets sang no more save of twisted phantoms seen with bleared and inward-looking eyes; when these things had come to pass, and childish hopes had gone away for ever, there was a man who traveled out of life on a quest into the spaces whither the world's dreams had fled.*"

She closed the book and looked at Carter. "You get that? That's the opening to *Azathoth*. That's a love letter to magic. He wrote it in the early twenties. And he went off to find real magic with his pal Randolph Carter. They found it. And—what do you know?— then they spent years trying to destroy it again. They saw stuff, Dan, and it made them decide that science was boring, but better."

Carter stopped pacing. He pulled up a chair and sank into it, defeated. "Fuck. Why couldn't I have inherited a bar instead?"

"So," said Lovecraft. She watched his face carefully. "What are you going to do?"

"Do? Same as I was before. I'm going to close Colt down before he hurts anyone else. None of this changes that. I don't care if he is offing people with pixie dust instead of a gun like a good American; he tried to kill me, and he came into the store to threaten you with math and philosophy. The motherfucker's going down."

"My hero."

"Yeah."

Lovecraft was counting out bills from the cashbox in the store while Carter looked on with interest.

"That's a lot of money to hold in petty cash," he said. By his guess, there had to be somewhere around ten thousand dollars in the box.

"It isn't petty cash. It's for buying books off the books, if you follow. Some dealers want cash in hand. They can be kind of secretive." She looked at the amount on the invoice again, swore under her breath, and carried on counting. "What do you want this thing for, anyway? Colt's a dick, but he's also a very smart, very talented mathematician. I don't think you'd be able to just say, 'Abracadabra,' and do the shit he does."

"I've got a theory about the pattern on it, but I'm going to need a copy as a reference."

"Just the pattern? Did you really have to have your copy in aluminum, too?"

"The file was already set up for the metal sintering process. Redoing it for plastic would have been a false economy. Besides, this way it's good and solid and won't deform. Plus, if push comes to shove, I can beat him to death with it."

"I didn't hear that," said Lovecraft. She snapped an elastic band around a roll of bills and handed it to him. "This is coming out of your side of the business." She took a small pad from the cashbox, arranged a sheet of carbon paper in it, and started writing heavily with a ballpoint.

"Here's a thing," said Carter, pocketing the money, "unless he had a secret hiding place somewhere, I didn't see Colt's cube in his house."

"You think he carries it with him? Maybe in his car?" She finished writing and slid the pad and pen across the counter to Carter. "Receipt. Sign right there."

"Maybe." Carter took up the pen and signed. "But I don't think so. I think he does his heavy-grade juju somewhere safe, and the cube's there."

Lovecraft nodded. She didn't need it spelled out for her. "That's not a plot of land with a wholesome history. Maybe you can fix Colt without having to do it on his home turf?"

"That's the way I was thinking. I don't plan to go back there," said Carter, but it was a lie.

He couldn't see any way of finally concluding matters *without* going back there. Colt was the immediate problem, but Waite's Bill was one going back decades, generations, maybe centuries, maybe even longer. Mathematical genii come and go, but the land lives on. There was something wrong about that place. The "Perceptual Twist" had occurred there, and it seemed it could be at least partially twisted back there. It was where parallel lines met, and circles meekly allowed themselves to be squared. It was the dark heart of esoteric fuckery, and Carter would bring his judgment down upon it.

Chapter 20

THE PURPLE KEY

The cube was ready a week later. Carter returned to Providence after spending the last few days working in New York, picked the cube up from the Material Sciences laboratory, and took it back to show Lovecraft. They studied it over lunch at the Italian restaurant a two-block walk from the bookstore.

"It's . . . heavy" was Lovecraft's first comment.

"It's about nine pounds of aluminum."

"Make a good paperweight." She put it on the tabletop, and gently pushed down on one corner. It rocked. Lovecraft tried it on every face, but it wouldn't sit stably on any of them. "Maybe not such a good paperweight. What the hell is wrong with the angles in this thing?"

"Weird, isn't it? Not a good idea to look at it for too long, either. Or think about it too much."

Lovecraft looked at him suspiciously, then pushed away the

cube as if it were a cup of coffee she'd just discovered was poisoned. "You're saying it's part of The Twist?"

"I think it's pre-Twist. That's the way the world used to be before our folks changed things. That wasn't affected somehow." He looked at it closely, and ran a finger along a grooved edge. "*Why* it wasn't affected is another question."

"I have a theory," said Lovecraft, "if you want to hear it? It's got a long line of coincidence in it, but coincidences just ain't as rare as they used to be around here. Okay, try this. How about the original of this cube, the thing that's sitting in a filing cabinet at Clave, was in the hands of H. P. L. and Randolph way back when. How about it was the key to causing The Twist in the first place. In the stories, Randolph has some weird psychic talents. Specifically, he can Dream, with a capital 'D.' There's a place called the Dreamlands, and only special people can get there. Randolph's one of them. He also has a thing called the 'Silver Key' that allows him to go to the Dreamlands in his physical body."

"What are these 'Dreamlands' like?"

"In H. P. L.'s writing, they're kind of high fantasy, but more like *The Thousand and One Nights* of Scheherazade than *Conan the Barbarian*. Thing is, maybe that's all projection on H. P. L.'s part. He was desperate to write some *Arabian Nights* kind of stuff. Remember that opening to *Azathoth* I read you? That's the kind of story it was leading into. He was a huge fan of a writer called Dunsany, a British lord no less, who wrote these pseudo-ancient tales with a synthetic mythology. H. P. L. wrote a few stories set in these Dreamlands, but they were very Dunsany in style. I wonder if he used the experiences of his friend as a framework to write the kind of fiction he wanted to."

"I don't understand what you're trying to get at. The Dreamlands never existed?"

"Oh, I think they did, and do. But they're not like H. P. L. portrayed them. And the Silver Key?" She nodded at the cube.

Carter laughed. "This is only silver because the copy's made from aluminum. The original's a kind of purple color."

"Yeah, because H. P. L. would surely have called it the 'Purple Key,' he being such a stickler for accuracy. He wasn't much of a literary stylist, but give him some credit, Dan. The point is, it's a key—maybe . . . probably—and Colt has figured out how to use it." She glanced at the cube and snorted humorlessly. "Time was, if the forces of evil wanted an artifact, they had to do it the old-fashioned way, with hooded cultists breaking in during the night, killing at least one guard with a ritual dagger that they leave behind for no reason, and then stealing the original. These days, you just laser scan the fucker and build a copy in a 3-D printer. Yay, twenty-first century."

Carter stirred his cooling *cannelloni* with his fork. "So, your theory is a literary one? I was hoping for something practical."

"No, the literary thing was just me not staying on the subject. The theory isn't too practical, either, but it might explain what happened. I think H. P. L. and Randolph got their hands on the original."

Carter shook his head. "It was recovered from the seabed."

"So? Doesn't mean it was down there eighty or ninety years ago. Work with me on this. Look, they get their hands on the Silver Key—which is purple, but what the hey?—and they create the Perceptual Twist, stabilizing the world. But they have a problem. Anyone with the Key can twist it back, or worse, use it for evil ends, yes? So, they got rid of it. Took a boat out and heaved it over the side. Problem solved, they thought."

"Why didn't they destroy it?"

Lovecraft grimaced; she was well into guessing territory now. "Two reasons. One is porphyry is hard. That's not such a reason, though. I'm sure a cold chisel and a mallet would still have broken it up just fine. The main reason is that it's ancient. These guys, they were romantics. H. P. L. especially was in love with the past. They couldn't destroy a thing like that any more than they could take a pickax to the Rosetta Stone.

"What they had no way of knowing was that, in a few years' time, deep-sea drag trawling would be a thing, and the cube's final resting place wouldn't be looking so final anymore. That is my theory . . . it is mine, and it belongs to me, and I own it, and what it is, too."

Carter looked at her, stunned.

"Sorry, that was kind of abstruse of me," said Lovecraft. "You're not a fan, huh?"

"Son of a bitch," he said finally. "It was right there. Right in front of me. Everything was perfect in Colt's house, not a thing out of place, except for a Blu-ray. *Monty Python's The Meaning of Life.* Have you seen it?"

Lovecraft shook her head. "I don't know Python that well. Not much of a fan, but I always liked that dinosaur sketch. It stuck with me." She shrugged. "So, go on, tell me about *The Meaning of Life.* What's it got to do with anything?"

"It's a set of sketches, really, but there's one with this fat guy, beyond obese, gets conned into eating just a tiny bit too much by a waiter who hates him."

"He throws up?"

"He's spent the whole meal throwing up. That's why the waiter hates him. No, he *explodes.*"

Lovecraft's jaw dropped. "Oh, shit. You are kidding me? That's what he did to the guy in Atlantic City? Death by Monty Python?" She shook her head in disbelief. "Colt's broken in the head."

"He's definitely sociopathic."

"A sociopath with the key to creation." She looked at her *penne all'arrabbiata* "I don't feel so hungry anymore."

"We have a copy of the key, too."

"You figure out how to use it, Dan, and I'll start cheering then. Meantime, this is like one of those old *Star Trek* episodes where some kid or somebody has godlike powers, but the kid's an asshole."

"How do those stories finish?"

"Far as I remember, something else godlike turns up to sort them out. *Deus ex typewriter,* because the writer has come up with an unbeatable bad guy and written himself into a corner. Kirk and his crew, they're all about damage reduction for a TV hour before another godlike being shows up and says, 'Hey, dude. Not cool.' Kind of lame, really."

"I don't think a godlike being is going to show up and sort Colt out for us."

"Maybe it's you, Dan. Maybe it's me. Maybe we'll figure out how to use the cube. Maybe we just beat him to death with it like you said. That'd work for me."

As they walked back, Lovecraft nodded at the messenger bag slung over Carter's shoulder that contained the cube. "So what are you planning to do with that, anyway? Spend a few days meditating over it until you get superpowers?"

"Yeah, I doubt it's going to be as convenient as that. Nice thought, though. No, there's something about the pattern on it that reminds me of something. I'm going to ask around, see what I can turn up."

Lovecraft snorted. "Dan, don't be an asshole. If you have a lead, spit it out. I'm on Colt's radar as much as you."

"True. That's true. Okay. You've heard of the Child-Catcher?"

Lovecraft stopped dead in the street. "You are fucking *kidding* me?"

Carter stopped a couple of paces farther on and looked back at her. "You've heard of him, then?"

"Don't dick with me. He was news all over the country. That man was evil. What's he got to do with anything?"

Carter nodded to suggest they carry on walking, and Lovecraft did so, though shocked and unhappy. "I thought he was evil, too. Then I started to think maybe he was mad more than bad. I'm starting to think maybe he was neither."

"Meaning what?"

"I'm wondering if he was . . . I don't know what to call it. Differently sane?"

"He cut up little boys while they were alive, Dan."

"He vivisected them. Every case like this I've worked or heard of, the motive was invariably—*invariably*—psychosexual. Suydam, the Child-Catcher, he was different. No sexual motivation was ever proved, and we had his house, his notes, everything. We had the man's mind all mapped out. It wasn't about sex. It was about science. Fucked-up science, and he was no scientist, but he thought he was onto something. Whatever he found, or thought he found, he tabulated the thing. Made a big-ass diagram of it."

"How does that tie him to Colt?"

"I've been working hard to forget what I saw in Suydam's house, but his diagram, his findings . . . they looked a lot like the markings on the cube."

Lovecraft said nothing, but her body language was taut.

"I could be wrong," continued Carter. "I didn't look at the wall with Suydam's big theory on it for longer than I had to. I don't think I'm wrong, though. I'll call in some favors, see if I can get an accurate copy or photos of it. Then we can compare it and maybe get an idea what Colt sees. Suydam's notes never made much sense, but combined with what we know now, maybe we can shake some out."

"Dan," said Lovecraft, "have you ever thought of just shooting Colt?" Carter started to laugh, but then he looked at her. She was quiet and serious.

"I don't know if I can do that," he said.

He didn't say no.

Carter called New York CSU the next morning from his office in Red Hook, and asked for Peter Hurwitz.

"Hi, Dan!" said Hurwitz, pleasurable surprise evident in his voice. "Good to hear from you. How are things down among the gumshoes?"

"Not so bad, providing you like divorce work."

"And do you?"

"Not as much as I thought I might. Look, Pete, I was wondering if you could help me out with something. It's okay—I don't want to borrow a mass spectrometer or anything like that."

"You can always ask," said Hurwitz. "Just don't take it to heart if I have to say no, that's all."

"It's about the Suydam investigation. I'm . . . having a few problems putting it in the past. The way things went down, I know it sounds stupid, but I kind of need some closure from it all, you know?"

There was silence for a few seconds. "I never got to say how sorry I was about Charlie," said Hurwitz.

"Yeah. Charlie's part of why I'm having trouble with it. We lucked out and then he ended up dead for no good reason. Wasn't the way it was supposed to work out. I've been going through the notes I still have, and it's helping. Seeing how we could have found Suydam through police work. It helps."

"Dan, I'm not sure that sounds healthy."

"Maybe not, but I'm sleeping better for it. At the time, I never tried to understand Suydam. He was just a son of a bitch and that was the long and the short of it. I think I'm ready to do that now."

"What are you asking for?"

"The psycho wall. One of your team mapped it, didn't they?" There was no reply, just the sound of Hurwitz breathing. "I'd like to see the notes, if I could. I have pictures, but they're not detailed enough to see the labels, or even the whole wall at once."

"Maggie," said Hurwitz. "Maggie Chun. She mapped it. We had the photos, and didn't need any greater detail than that, but she wanted to build it as a computer model. Thought it would be a useful side project, exploring how to store spatial data like that. I think she had an eye on maybe writing a book about CSU work, too."

"Is she there, Pete? I'd like to speak to her."

Several seconds of silence. When Hurwitz finally spoke, it was with great reluctance. "Dan, she's on medical leave. She had . . . an episode. Overwork. She's not here."

"Oh. I'm sorry to hear that about her. I don't know her, but she sounds bright."

"We're all bright here, Dan, you should know that. But, yeah, she's really sharp. It was a blow to lose her."

"Could I . . . ?"

"The overwork was because of the damn psycho wall. She was doing a full shift, going home, and doing another shift working on it. She never needs to think of that thing again, Dan. You should do the same. Suydam had sticky insanity. It stuck to Maggie and she had . . . she"—he lowered his voice—"she had a fucking *breakdown*, man. You won't find any closure staring at that wall."

Carter knew then that Hurwitz would never hand over Chun's phone number or address. He had always been protective of his people, and letting Carter loose to rake over the work that had put Chun on medical leave would definitely not qualify as "protective."

"Okay," said Carter. "It's okay. I'm really sorry to hear about your CSU. I hope she's better soon."

"She's resilient. Just . . . it was just overwork. She never knows when to take a breath. If I'd known she was digging herself a pit like that on her own time, I'd have said something to her."

They talked of other things for a time, and then said good-bye.

Carter looked at the phone for a long time. He'd already made up his mind what to do, and was trying unsuccessfully to talk himself out of it. Then he opened his laptop and started a persons search for "CHUN, Maggie."

Lovecraft insisted on coming to the interview. Her rationale was quite simple. "The girl's fucked up. You're more fucked up than you realize. I am the only handily available person concerned who has so far avoided being fucked up, long may that continue. You need me there to steer you away from foil hat territory."

Carter had called ahead and decided to be candid. It was hardly necessary; as soon as he identified himself, Chun had said, "This is about Suydam, isn't it?"

She needed no convincing to see them. To the contrary, she was eager to meet, almost needy.

Maggie Chun was living in Queens, in a well-preserved Crafts-man bungalow painted in sky blue and white. She arrived there as Lovecraft and Carter did after the drive down from Providence, and let them in.

She made them black coffee. "I'm staying at my mom's until I go back to work," she said, excusing the lack of food or milk in the refrigerator. "She would be really mad if she knew why I'd come out today. She doesn't want me even thinking about Suy-dam. I'm trying not to, but . . ." She made a hopeless gesture.

"Look, Maggie, if talking about it is going to mess you up, that's really not what we want," said Lovecraft. "Your health comes first."

"No!" Chun said it so forcefully she even startled herself. "I . . . It needs to be worked out. The department has got me see-ing the psychologist, and that helps, but he doesn't get it, either. I can't talk to him about it honestly, because it sounds psychotic. You were there, Carter. You saw it. You know."

Carter looked into the blackness of his cup. "What do I know, Maggie?"

She leaned forward, craning sideways a little to look at his downturned face. "That he wasn't completely wrong. Suydam saw something, thought something. I don't think he was wrong." She straightened as Carter looked at her. "How he did it was wrong, I'm not defending him or excusing him. But he saw *something*."

She sat back, and looked at her hands as she fussed with a thumb ring. "There's something there."

Lovecraft exchanged a glance with Carter, and said, "Like things have been twisted a little out of true?"

Chun looked at her sharply. "Twisted. Several of the notations on Suydam's wall talk about a perceptual twist. That's one way of looking at it, I guess. It's not how I read it.

"I have an uncle who's into photography. Lifelong hobby, ever since he was a kid. He used to have a 35mm SLR with motor drive. I loved the sound of that thing. It was like the beginning of 'Girls

On Film.' Y'know, the Duran Duran song? It's an exciting sound. Anyhow, he dropped it once, and something went wrong with the camera. It would only wind once every other exposure.

"You'd think that he'd have junked it or got it fixed, but he loved it all the more afterward, because it took two pictures to every frame. A fast double exposure, two almost identical pictures overlaid on each other with only fast-moving things in obviously different places. Once he got the exposure setting adjusted, he'd shoot whole canisters with that camera. He used to say it was like looking at our world and the one next door at the same time, pretty much the same but just out of sync.

"That's what I think Suydam was getting at. Worlds out of sync. Close enough to touch, but we can never quite reach it. That's what he was trying to do with those kids. To see our next-door neighbor clearly."

"Have you ever heard of a guy called William Colt?" asked Lovecraft, as much to break the uncomfortable silence as anything.

"No. Who's he?"

"Just a name that got mentioned," said Carter. He didn't want Chun going off and researching Colt herself. That might not end well. "An outlier. Suydam's theory. How far do you think he was from proving or disproving it?"

Chun seemed surprised. "It's all there, right on the wall. All of it. He'd finished. He'd seen it. Mr. Carter, you were right there. Why do you think Suydam went to so much trouble to die?"

"I still don't understand why he didn't just shoot himself. He had a gun in his hand when we went in, and we found another two in the house."

"He was a lapsed Catholic," said Chun. "And self-destruction is a sin."

Chapter 21

WHAT THE MOON BRINGS

Black lines, red line, blue, and green in white space. Carter rotated the model, re-zeroed it, zoomed in, read annotations, zoomed out.

Carter was looking at the patterns in his office, after dropping Lovecraft off at the station to go back to Providence. Maggie Chun had done a remarkable job building a virtual model of Martin Suydam's wall. Suydam himself would probably have been ecstatic to have seen it, magnificent in all its deranged glory.

Carter zoomed out once more and looked at it as a whole, a dark network of interactions marked by positions, lines, and definitions. The nomenclature of the labels were nested, and marked further iterations of relationship between the irregularly placed points. Carter could switch off the original wall's appearance and replace it with patterns wrought by these subordinate connections. At first glance, they were a mess of lines, more or less parallel, but not quite. There were five such subordinate sets. As he clicked through them, he held up the aluminum cube, turning it in one hand.

One, two, three, four, five . . . they matched the patterns of striations on the cube's sides perfectly, as far as he could see.

But the star was the sixth side, the side Suydam had fashioned with colored threads on his wall. The side with the thickened line from the upper right down to about a third of the way along from the bottom-right corner on the lower edge when aligned in the same manner. What was that, and why did Suydam regard it as so important that, of the six data sets, this was the one he laid at the front of his pattern?

Carter ran his thumb back and forth along the crease. "Here comes The Twist!" Hammond said in his dreams, and that was probably what Suydam had called it. Lovecraft had called it a "perceptual twist." Chun said it was the next iteration of reality printing through. Carter eased a growing tension across his shoulders, driving the fingers of his free hand into the muscles. Why did he think they were all wrong? Why did he think the truth was more dangerous still?

He mentally shook himself. These were dangerous thoughts. When you start to believe that only you know the truth, it doesn't bode well. When the alternatives are all enough to put you into a psychiatric wing, you realize you're just putting yourself forward as King of the Mad.

Perhaps, he thought, he should get drunk. Maybe it was all just conspiracy bullshit and he was working himself into the same sort of state of frothing belief in coincidences being significant usually occupied by the flat earthers, the hollow earthers, the moonshot and Kennedy conspiracy theorists, the birthers and the truthers, the reptilian ruler nuts, nukes-in-a-volcano idiots, and the whole fucking flock of resolute mouth-breathers.

Alcohol looked like a rational act. A lot of alcohol. It might help him forget, at least for a while, about almost drowning on dry land. No amount of skepticism would get him past that. He had either suffered an incredibly disciplined psychotic break, or he was just looking to get drunk so he could ignore the big picture for a little while.

That seemed a fair trade, so he got his jacket and headed for his favorite bar.

Emily Lovecraft always knew her relationship with Ken Rothwell was a mayfly sort of affair. They liked each other well enough, and enjoyed the novelty of their different lifestyles, but Lovecraft knew that as soon as his political ambitions got out of neutral and he really started reaching for the prize, she would be jettisoned as unsuitable. She wasn't rich, her politics were liberal, she was a dangerous intellectual, and she said "fuck" too much.

Still, she was expecting him to be up-front about it. One evening there would be an "I want to talk about us" kind of conversation leading up to "It just isn't working," and she'd promised herself a spa weekend if he resorted to "It's not you, it's me." What she definitely had not been expecting was for him to go emo on her.

Rothwell had always been a politician, right from birth. It's what he had been raised to do. He lacked intellectual heft, but, God, could he ever do a firm, dry handshake, look you full in the face with those blue eyes, smile like he almost meant it, nod while you talked, and seem to take an interest. Jumping Jehoshaphat, you *would* buy a secondhand car from this man, and be glad to have done so.

When he dumped her, it would play out like he was selling her an insurance policy. What she actually got was sullen silences, distraction, and dropping her off at her house three times in a row without even hinting he wanted to stay over. She truly didn't mind if he did, and for a good while neither did he, but now all of a sudden he was giving her the kind of perfunctory kiss you give an elderly relative, and scuttling back to his car. It was sad; her projected scenario for the breakup had included one last farewell fuck, and now that seemed unlikely to happen. He wasn't great in bed, but he had a good body, and that was distracting enough for a busy girl.

"Ken, is everything okay? You've been kind of distant recently."

They were on her doorstep. She'd had enough of him being weird with her and had decided that this was going to be the make or break evening. She'd given him every chance during the meal, then they'd gone to see a production of *Richard III*, and now here they were, on her doorstep and still with no definite resolution.

He seemed honestly surprised at the question. "Have I? I'm sorry. Not been sleeping too well. I'm not feeling myself."

"Have you seen a doctor? Could be a low-level virus or something. Hangs around making you miserable, then either goes away or turns bad. You should get yourself checked out."

"Yeah." He gave his car a longing glance that Lovecraft did not miss. "Yeah, that might be it."

"Want to stay over? I'll dust off the waffle iron for you. Waffles . . ."

It was a strange thing to see. He looked at the car and his need to leave was palpable. Then he looked down for a few breaths, and then he looked at Lovecraft. He smiled and it was like he was selling her aluminum siding.

"Sure," he said. That smile frightened her a little. "Sure. I've been neglecting you, and I'm sorry. Yes, I'd like to stay. Thanks."

Just under an hour later, Lovecraft was obliged to beat the putative senator repeatedly on the side of the head with her clock radio.

When he had come in, he looked around like he'd never seen the place before, and he never stopped smiling. Lovecraft began to wish she'd just made do with the dry little kiss at the door and seen him on his way then, but now she was stuck with him. They'd sat around, talking awkwardly like characters in a movie made by somebody who will never be John Cassavetes. Then they went to bed, Lovecraft trying to work up some enthusiasm for what was shaping up to be a swift mercy fuck, all the quicker to get Rothwell out of the house and on his way home.

Rothwell was never very freaky in bed. Lovecraft got the impression that he thought pretty much anything other than missionary was an assault on his masculinity, probably unconstitutional, and downright un-American in any case. Tonight, however, he was different. Unnervingly different. He wanted to kiss, a *lot*, and got a little bit bitey in the process. He got close to drawing blood a couple of times and she had to tell him to stop. Then he rolled her over and covered her with his body. He was strongly built, played sports in college and had kept up with some track sports long after. Alongside the racquetball and squash, he had kept himself strong and athletic. Lovecraft liked his body, but she wasn't very happy about what he was doing with it at that exact moment. She'd momentarily thought he was going to try something utterly alien to his normal lovemaking and go doggie-style, but then she felt him part her buttocks.

"No," she said, and half laughed to show she wasn't offended by the sentiment, but wasn't up for that.

Rothwell ignored her. He was so strong. Lovecraft started to feel worried.

"Ken, no. I don't wanna . . ."

She could feel him bringing pressure to bear. His hands were on her wrists.

"Ken . . . no!"

She struggled. He was breathing heavily. It was as if he'd lost the ability to speak, he was so stupid with lust.

"Fuck's sake, Ken! Get off me!"

He paused, and she thought she'd gotten through to him. Then he said in a dreamy, thick voice, "I love it when you talk dirty." He started to penetrate her.

Lovecraft felt fear, but it was as nothing to her sudden blazing anger. She brought her wrist to her mouth and—in not trying to break his grip—Rothwell permitted the movement, bringing his own wrist within range of her teeth. Then she bit him, hard, and if she had gotten down to the bone it would have suited her just fine.

He cried out and snatched his hand away, and in the moment when her hand was free, she snatched the clock radio—a nice piece of equipment in a wooden box—and twisted far enough to get a clear shot at Rothwell's head. She slammed it hard upside his head, but he only grunted, so she angled it for the next blow so that the corner struck first.

He cried out, and his weight lifted enough for her to push her shoulders back and wriggle out from under him. She ran to the side of the room and stood, glaring at him, naked and furious. He looked at her uncomprehendingly, holding the side of his head. Even in the gloom of the bedroom, she could see his ear was bleeding.

"You wanna do that," she shouted at him, "you use lube, you go slow, and you better *ask fucking nicely first!*" He was looking at his hand, seeing the blood there. "And when I say no, I mean *no!* Saying no and struggling is not playing hard to get, Ken! What the fuck were you thinking?"

"Emily." He said her name slowly, as if remembering it, as if it were something alien on his tongue. "I'm sorry."

"Sorry? You just tried to *rape* me, Ken!"

The word stung him, made him flinch as if she'd spat in his face. "No." He shook his head. "No."

Lovecraft didn't know what to think of him. He seemed stunned, not just by a couple of solid blows to the head, but stunned at his actions. All in all, though, she would be happier with him out of the house.

"You'd better go," she said. "We'll talk about this, but in broad daylight." *And in a public place.*

"I'm sorry," he said again. This time it sounded a little more sincere, or at least human. "I don't know . . . that wasn't like me. I'm sorry. It's the strain."

Lovecraft wanted to ask "What strain?" but didn't want a conversation.

Rothwell looked at her. She'd never seen him looking confused before. Not just puzzled, but confused all the way down to the metal.

"I'm going to win the election." It wasn't political bravado, or the sureness of a rhetorical flourish. He said it as if he was telling her he had been diagnosed with an inoperable malignant cancer and was still in denial about it himself.

"I'm not talking, Ken. Not now. Get dressed, get out, call me in a couple of days, and then we'll talk." She took her robe from the hook on the back of the door and shrugged into it. "I'm going to the kitchen. You don't go in there. You go straight out the front door when you're ready."

She left him there. She made herself tea and drank it slowly, still furious with Rothwell, yet simultaneously concerned for him. Maybe he really was under more stress than she knew, and was falling to pieces. It was no excuse, but it was a reason. Even that made her angry, but this time with herself. She'd lost count of the number of times she'd been exasperated with women in abusive relationships who just wouldn't leave the bastard. *C'mon, sister, you've got to cut those ties. He's never going to get any better.* Was that what she was doing? Rationalizing a mitigation for him so she didn't kick him to the curb like she ought to? She'd always thought of herself as strong, never the willing victim.

She glared at her cup of tea as if it were to blame. Late at night was not a good time to be trying to think things through. She remembered a Russian proverb she'd happened across in her reading: "The morning is wiser than the evening." She'd sleep on it. Maybe ask . . . she wasn't sure who to talk to. Carter, maybe. He was an ex-cop. Cops have seen it all. Fuck. She heard the front door quietly open and close. After a minute, she heard his car pull away. She looked at the tea and realized she hadn't used the decaf. Fuck.

Carter had driven up again to speak with the bank directly about Alfred Hill's account, and dropped by at the store afterward. It started with general morning greetings and then, by means and diversions, Lovecraft turned the conversation as she wanted it to go and Carter fulfilled her hopes by—without explicitly being told—suddenly raising a cautioning hand to stop the talk, and said, "Am I understanding you properly? Are you telling me Kenneth Rothwell forced himself on you last night?"

Lovecraft liked the olde worlde charm of "forced himself." It was a phrase alive with the sound of ripping bodices.

"*Tried* to," she corrected him.

Carter was stuck for the next adumbration. Giving up on diplomacy, he leaned closer over the counter and mouthed, *Anally?*

She contented herself with just looking at him. Certain questions may be answered not by an affirmative, but by the absence of a negative.

"The fuck," said Carter with quiet venom.

"So, I don't know what to think. He's never done anything like that. Always been the gentleman. Do I put this down to a one-off moment of freakiness that will never be repeated, or do I drop the bar on him right now before he gets out the gimp suit and tells me to put the lotion in the basket?"

"When did I get to be your gay friend who helps you with your relationship problems?"

She raised an eyebrow. "You're gay?"

"No, but it's usually part of the job description. You're asking the wrong man, Emily. I didn't like him on sight. I don't like him, or his silver spoon, or his sense of entitlement. I'm bound to say you should dump him, because I think he's the sort of man who deserves to die alone, hugging his money."

"Wow. Thank you, Dear Prudence."

Carter shrugged. "But if you want to know my professional opinion, it's that there's a fifty-fifty chance he'll do it again. If it's in him to do that once, then sometime he's going to be drunk, angry, or both, and he'll take it out on you. There you go. That's my view."

Lovecraft was only half listening. "You know what? Him suddenly getting heavy like that wasn't even the weirdest thing about his behavior. He was all kind of distracted and *off* and then, pretty much the last thing he said was 'I'm going to win the election.' He said it like a death sentence."

"It would be for Rhode Island if he got in." Carter was still not in the mood for kindness. "He's delusional. He's not winning this election. It's hardly a week away and he's dying in the polls. Surprised his minders are letting him out of their sight, it being so close."

"He's gotten good at shaking them off. I'm kind of surprised I'm still on his arm, to be honest. I know his people have been telling him to dump me since the campaign started. I always kind of thought this was a dry run for him anyway, just to put his face about. Like he needs to. Then he'd dump me, get some blond girl with nice teeth whose ancestors came over on the *Mayflower*, and do it for real the next time. Now he's saying he's going to win. Dan, I've got to tell you, that's really out of character for him. He's been going around in public saying he's going to be a senator, but in private he's never said a thing about what he'll do when that happens. He's just been talking as if he won't win, and he expects not to win. What the hell changed?"

Carter realized, way too late in the day for it to be any use, that perhaps he should have mentioned earlier that Colt had followed them that day when Rothwell came to pick her up. But now he told her, and she was predictably pissed with him.

"Colt *followed* us?"

"I tried to call you to warn you. I texted you."

"The fuck you did!" But she got out her phone and checked it. "There's nothing here."

Carter checked his own phone. "Look at my call log. And . . ." He showed her the text telling her to watch her back because Colt was following them.

She read the display, and looked at Carter. She seemed scared. "How can that happen?"

"Just a glitch in the cell network. That kind of thing happens all the time."

"No, it doesn't." She shook her head. Her phone lay in her hand, a small traitor. "No, it doesn't."

Chapter 22

IN THE VAULT

The next day Carter spent almost two hours aimlessly walking the streets, thinking through the possible consequences of what he was about to do. Finally convincing himself that it was impossible to predict and that he should brace himself for some bitter hindsight, he made the call.

It rang three times before he was answered. "Hello," said the male voice at the other end. "Who is this?"

"This has to stop."

There was a pause. Carter couldn't tell if it was surprise, shock, realization, but there was a pause. Then the voice on the phone said, "Hello, Dan." If he was surprised, he hid it well. "This is big of you to call me. Is this a man-to-man chat? Are you telling me to stop or you'll stop me with your bare hands, or something?"

"You're in danger. We all are. Every time you do what you do, things get broken a little bit more."

The voice laughed. "That's it? You're calling because of your personal concern for me? That's sweet. Thanks. Let me ask you something. It's for my mental health, so you'll be helping me if you tell me the answer. I know you're all about helping people, Dan. I'm just a hotbed of anxiety over this, you'll really be helping. Just tell me. How did you get out of my house?"

Carter said nothing.

Perhaps provoked by the silence, the voice said, "The place was as tight as a drum. Tighter. Not a fly could get out, not a microbe, not a molecule of air. You're bigger than all of those, Dan. How did you do it?"

"You can't expect me to tell you," said Carter, avoiding the truth of his own ignorance.

"No. No, I can't. I must admit, it's nice to have an archenemy. You're the hero, of course. I'm Moriarty. No Reichenbach Falls this time, though. The villain wins."

"You think of yourself as the villain?"

"Yes. Oh, Dan, the things I have done, none of which I'll discuss on an open phone line. The . . . options I have. I don't think you'll be able to pull a stunt next time like you did in my house. I won't give you the opportunity."

"If I'm such a pain in your ass, why did you pull me into this?"

Another pause. "Are you fishing, Dan? I'm not sure what you're fishing for if you are."

"The call I got from Belasco's phone. Don't pretend you don't know what I'm talking about."

"I don't need to pretend. I was nowhere near."

"You arranged it."

"You're delusional."

Carter laughed, a harsh, derisive bark. "*I'm* delusional? I'm not the one who thinks he's some sort of criminal mastermind."

"Just a mastermind. The criminality is collateral, and soon to be moot."

"*Moot.* Listen to you, like the bad guy in a cheap James Bond knockoff. I'll say it again. You have to stop. You're not as in control as you think you are. You're not even the first to be doing what you're doing."

Abrupt, guardedly curious: "What do you mean?"

"I'm saying what you're doing—The Twist, the Perceptual Twist, is that what you call it?—has been done before, and not so long ago. It didn't end well."

"You're flailing, Dan. That's pretty weak tea."

"Martin Suydam. You hear of him? The Child-Catcher, yeah? I saw it there on his wall, the same pattern mapped out."

"Suydam?"

"He saw what you saw, and committed suicide by cop to get away from it."

"Suydam." The voice turned the name over. "Impossible."

"Oh, I'm sorry. Is your uniqueness fraying? Yes, you and a child killer have a lot in common. That must make you feel really good in yourself."

"I don't know what you saw, but it has nothing to do with what I'm doing."

"Denial. That's sweet. Tell you what, why don't you tell me where you are, and I'll arrange to have some cop friends of mine come around and help you with *your* suicide, because that's where this is all heading."

"How's your little friend in the bookstore?"

"She's fine. She's also irrelevant to you and me. Keep her out of things."

"Oh, you're a protective one, Dan. And her with such a big important boyfriend, too. Is he treating her well? I hope so. He seemed okay when I spoke to him. A very sensible guy. Typical politician. Cunning rather than intelligent."

Carter's face tightened, but he kept any new emotion from his voice. "You spoke to him?"

"Oh, yes. You'll be shocked to hear this, Dan, but when I showed him what I could do for his campaign, he was very, very impressed. He thinks I'm working for him now, but he's got that the wrong way around, hasn't he? Who would have thought it? A corruptible politician? I don't think that can ever have happened before in the long history of American politics, do you, Dan?"

Noise on the line.

"What?" said Carter.

"I said, there's corruption, and then there's *corruption*, of course."

A click, and the call ended.

Harrelson entered the not-cop bar, went to the rear, and paused when he saw Carter was not alone. He sat down beside Lovecraft, regarding her with open suspicion.

"You didn't say anything about any third parties," he said to Carter.

"Detective Harrelson, this is Emily Lovecraft, my business partner."

Harrelson frowned. "What? Like the writer guy?"

Lovecraft nodded. "Just like the writer guy. You didn't get me mixed up with Linda Lovelace, so kudos to you, Detective."

"I saw that *Re-Animator* movie. That was crazy."

"I didn't write it."

"But you've seen it?"

"Yes."

Harrelson nodded judgmentally. "That was crazy."

Carter had had enough of the impromptu film critics' evening. "We know who killed Belasco."

"Yeah, the guy you told me about, William Colt. I know. The name kept turning up when I was interviewing. I checked his bank records and he was in Atlantic City not long before the pit boss died. What's his name? Hayesman. Had a run-in with a guy who sounds a lot like Colt. So, yeah, if Belasco and Hayesman had been shot or poisoned or something a judge might recognize as murder, I'd be all over Colt like a rash. But they died like something out of a story a tabloid editor would blue pencil. Hard to make a case when no law's been broken."

"The law's been broken, Harrelson, believe me," said Carter. "Just in new ways. And it's going to get worse. Colt's making a move into politics."

Harrelson looked askance at Carter. "He's what?"

"He has a Senate hopeful in his pocket."

"Ken Rothwell," said Lovecraft with some reluctance.

Harrelson laughed. "You got to be kidding? Rothwell won't get within a mile of the Senate. 'Hopeful' is all he's ever going to be."

"Yeah, I'd have agreed, until Colt got involved," said Carter. "But him, I wouldn't bet against anything Colt wants to influence. He has a way of rigging the game."

Harrelson grunted, thinking about what one of the floor staff at the Oceanic had said about the slot machines in their statement. "Holy fuck. Yeah, I see what you mean."

"There's no point in using any phrase that includes the words 'there's no chance' where Colt is involved. This is a man who, pretty much the first thing he did when he got this . . ."

"Power?" offered Harrelson.

"Ability. Pretty much the first thing he did was kill his professor for pissing him off a bit. He's already raising his sights. I don't want to know what the upper limit of what he will do is. I don't even want to give him the chance to find out. I think . . ." He looked at Lovecraft, then Harrelson. ". . . we're going to have to deal with this ourselves."

"Whoa." Harrelson raised his hands as if to shield himself from the implication. "No, no, no. I ain't going off the reservation for something like this."

"For something like this?" Carter was incredulous. "Then what—"

"No, the man has a point," said Lovecraft. She was looking unhappily at her empty glass. "It's just a guy who can do real magic, and he wants to control the country, and he kills people for next to no reason. It's not like it's a big deal. Can I get a drink? That went too quickly."

"No such thing as magic," said Harrelson.

"Like fuck, there isn't. The guy's breaking mathematical laws, the very laws that govern creation. If that isn't magic . . . Well, it is. It's magic. That's what magic is. And Voldemort in a button-down collar is going to get his way unless we stop him now, while he's still an amateur."

Harrelson looked at her coldly. "You say 'stop,' but that ain't what you mean."

"He's killed twice, he tried to kill Dan—"

"He *what?*"

"—he isn't suddenly going to grow some morals. Yeah, so by 'stop,' I mean 'kill.'"

"Maybe not," Carter said quietly.

"Dan," said Lovecraft, "there's no alternative. The man's a sociopath. There's something wrong in his head. You can't fix him."

"I'm not talking about fixing him. I'm taking about stopping him without killing him. There's a common factor here in everything he's done. Maybe that's his weakness."

Lovecraft frowned, then understood. "Waite Road."

"Waite Road?" said Harrelson. "The place out on that spit of land? What do you know about Waite Road?"

Carter briefly described Colt's visits, but didn't mention his own experiences there, or how he had woken up on Waite's Bill when he should have been dying in Colt's house. He wasn't even close to understanding that himself; he didn't want to put it out there so others could scratch their heads and treat it as a curiosity.

Harrelson sighed and said "Fuck" under his breath. He ordered more drinks and, when the bartender had gone, said, "Waite Road doesn't have a great rep. When I was a rookie, the precinct used to haze us by sending us on a fool's errand out there, just to freak us out. The Waites . . . Jesus, have you *met* any of them?"

"One of the men," said Carter. "I think there was something wrong with him."

"There's something wrong with *all* of them, and not necessarily the same thing, either. The men are kind of dead behind the eyes, and the women . . . they're way too *alive* behind the eyes. Few years ago I was passing the courthouse and one of the Waites was getting married. I recognized the groom, too. Petty crook, bad guy. There he was in a cheap suit looking like he was brain-damaged. Not smiling, hardly looking around, like he was dreaming it all. He falls clean off the radar after that. Rap sheet that kicked off in juvie, couldn't keep out of trouble if it meant his life. And then, boom, he's a solid citizen. Wish I could say it was the love of a good woman, but the bride scared me more than he did, and he's six-three. She's some little thing, maybe five-four, hardly more than a teenager. Good-looking, too. But, Jesus, I finish shaking the guy's hand, trying to give him some bullshit speech about having responsibilities now, and he's just looking at me like he doesn't understand English anymore, and I turn around and *she's* there, grinning at me, and it's like a great white shark has snuck up on me, because, man, there was something scary about her. I forget all about how good-looking she was at a distance because, close up? My balls pretty much sucked up into my body."

"I like your friend, Dan," said Lovecraft. "He's graphic."

Harrelson ignored her. "You know how some guys just sweat trouble? You know they like hurting people, because you smell violence on them? Like, they stink of it? She did that, too, in spades. I walked away. Straightaway, and I could hear her and the other Waite women laughing. The men? Not a peep. They just stood around like zombies." He flinched at an unpleasant thought. "Hey . . . you don't think—"

"No," said Carter. "Just because Colt and probably the Waites deal in weird shit doesn't mean we start treating *Famous Monsters of Filmland* as a mug book. The Waite men are, I don't know, *wrong* somehow, but they're alive."

"Okay. Brass tacks. What exactly are we talking about doing? What is this hypothetical lawbreaking that I am absolutely not going to be involved in?"

"We just need to know what it is about Waite Road that's so important to whatever Colt's doing." Carter looked at Lovecraft. "Is it just because Randolph and H. P. L. did whatever they did there? Is that why it's important?" Even as he said it, he knew he was being optimistic. That would have meant the site was reproducible, and they might be able to do whatever the fuck needed to be done wherever. But life rarely makes things easier.

Lovecraft shook her head. "No. The place was important. The Waites owned it then, too, remember. It's been their land before there was even a Providence to speak of. The record's patchy. If H. P. L. wrote about it in detail—and if he didn't, that's not like him—whatever he wrote is long lost. Whatever Randolph did there, he did because it *had* to be done there. There's something off about that spit of land. Probably why the Waite family claimed it in the first place."

"Okay. Back to Plan A, then."

Harrelson frowned. "I musta missed something. What Plan A? Hypothetical Plan A."

"The one where we go in like gangbusters and generally fuck the Waites up. Find whatever's so important to Colt and take it or wreck it."

"That's not a plan. That's a bunch of serious felonies."

"Plan B is the one where we sit on our asses watching Colt put a puppet into the Oval Office in a series of incredibly unlikely landslide victories."

"I prefer Plan A," said Lovecraft.

"Only 'cause Plan B sucks so bad," said Harrelson.

"Seriously, man, are you in?" Carter asked Harrelson. "It's fun pretending to be the Scooby Gang while there's beer on the table, but we're going to have to ante up on this, and soon. Colt's pissed off with me, and he will have another try at offing me. Nothing is more certain. I'm not going to give him the chance."

"Slow down, cowboy." Harrelson leaned back in his seat. "When are we talking about?"

Carter and Lovecraft exchanged glances. "Tomorrow," she said.

"In broad daylight?"

"Night sure as hell won't work to our advantage. Them, I'm pretty sure it will."

"'*Our*'?" Harrelson gave her a hard look. "Ma'am, there's a chance it's going to get messy."

Lovecraft returned the hard look with a few percent interest. "And?"

Harrelson shot Carter a glance, but he was staying out of this one. Harrelson tried to find a way to put it delicately. "There may be trouble. Anybody goes in there needs to know how to handle a gun. Do you?"

Lovecraft angled her head back until she was looking at Harrelson down her nose. "I trained as a librarian, and I run a bookstore. Fucking right I can use a gun."

"Seriously?" asked Carter, surprised despite himself.

"There's a Mossberg 930 with a folding stock under the store counter. Never had to use it in anger, but I trained to use it five years ago after a guy came in and got . . . fresh. Mace got me out of trouble that time, but it was close. So, yeah, a shotgun. I retrain every year. I know my way around it. I even reorganized the shelving, so if I have to engage somebody between the counter and the door, only the political autobiographies are in danger and who gives a fuck about those?"

Harrelson nodded, impressed. "Library school sounds a bunch more two-fisted than I'd thought."

Carter thought back to when he'd been listening in on Colt's conversation with her, while pretending to browse the shelves. He'd actually noticed the block of political memoirs and thought at the time that they seemed out of place. That they had been placed like that so they could be sacrificed if necessary while Lovecraft was laying down 12-gauge fire from behind the counter was a sobering realization.

"Holy shit," he said quietly.

"Looking pale there," said Lovecraft. "Better get in some more drinks."

Chapter 23

THE WHISPERER IN DARKNESS

They were back at the apartment over the bookstore, and they were looking at guns. Lots of guns.

"Holy shit," Carter said quietly, for the second time that evening.

"Thinking of opening a gun store, Detective?" asked Lovecraft. She was sitting with the Mossberg across her lap, cleaning it. By her legs was a bag containing its cleaning kit and some accessories. Carter could see a sling strap; then Harrelson craned over to look in the bag and said, "Is that a tactical sight? Sweet."

Lovecraft fished in the bag and produced a short length of steel tube. "And a two-shell magazine extension. Never needed it for anything but training." She started fitting it.

Carter returned his attention to the odd collection of weapons Harrelson had brought in a large black duffel. He knew it wasn't uncommon for cops to occasionally misappropriate weapons found on the job, but this was altogether too wholesale an array for that. "Where did these come from?"

"Some half-assed 'Kill the President to Protect the Constitution' bunch of morons. This is nowhere near the amount of firepower they had. We did a combined operation with the FBI and cleaned them out pretty quickly. They were no real threat; just a shitload of weapons and jerking off to a fuckwit manifesto they'd written on Big Chief writing tablets. There was so much evidence we ended up just sticking it into any car with an empty trunk. I didn't put any in mine, but somebody did and didn't tell me. A week later, I pop my trunk and there's this survivalist's party favor sitting there looking at me.

"I shoulda handed it in, obviously. But I didn't, and nobody said anything."

"Are they on record?" Carter picked up a Beretta, thought better of it, and put it back down.

"Nope. All brand-new. Still grease on a lot of it, and the serials aren't in the system. They're clean."

The weapons certainly looked new. The Beretta Carter had examined was a Pico .380, a relatively recent release. He took it up again, and nodded. It was time he accepted that they were well outside the law with what they were planning, and that he should just get on with it. "Okay. Okay," he said to himself. He offered the pistol to Lovecraft. "How are you with pistols?"

"I've fired on a range with one, but that was a long time ago." She regarded the pistol with suspicion. "Kind of small, isn't it? I'm happy with my shotgun."

"You'll need a backup weapon. The Mossberg takes, what? Seven in the tube and one in the chamber?"

"*Nine* in the tube," said Lovecraft, tapping the magazine extension under the barrel.

"So ten shells, but it's a semiauto. You can get through ten faster than you might think in combat. You run dry and there's still trouble in the offing, you might not have time to reload." He offered her the pistol again. "Take it. It's a good gun."

She accepted it pragmatically rather than gracefully. "It's so *thin*."

"Compared to that bazooka of yours, everything looks thin," said Harrelson. "There's a couple of spare mags in the bag and a box of Fiocchi Extrema hollow points. They're good rounds. You can fuck somebody up really good with those things."

She examined the resin frame below the metal slide. "It says here I should read the manual before use." She looked meaningfully at Harrelson.

"Gee, I'm sorry," he said with no sincerity whatsoever. "The bag of illegal firearms came without documentation. Whatever was I thinking?"

She smiled and put the pistol to one side. "I'm going to need a holster."

"We'll pick one up in the morning."

In the morning. In the morning, they would go to a gun store, chat up the guy behind the counter, discuss the practicalities of holsters, joke, make some purchases, say good-bye to the guy behind the counter, and then later that same day, chances were that they would use those purchases in the commission of multiple homicides.

It was a sobering thought. Carter found a bottle of wine and some beer in his fridge to reverse the thought's effect.

Colt was awoken at two in the morning by a phone call. He fumbled for his phone in the darkness of his bedroom, despite a small voice of remembrance saying, *But didn't you turn it off?* But it was ringing, so obviously he hadn't.

He checked the display and saw the number was withheld. The last call he'd had like that was from Carter. This one surely was, too. Colt hesitated, thinking, the phone thrumming in his fingers. He wasn't sure what to do about Carter. He was certainly a nuisance, and maybe even a threat, but the way he'd escaped at least made him an interesting threat. Colt was beginning to treasure interesting things. Since the cube had shown him that so much he had previously regarded in life as interesting was instead merely flawed, he had found that his pleasures in life were decreasing as his powers increased. He had been faced with the specter of an all-consuming *ennui* if he had carried on as he had been doing, with only an eye to simple temporal pleasures.

Carter had inadvertently helped him away from that path. He had traced Carter to the bookstore, and there he had met Emily Lovecraft. An actual Lovecraft! He'd thought that bloodline had died with the writer. That was nice, but Carter's protectiveness toward her was even better. Such a white knight, such a platonic *cicisbeo*, while her boyfriend fucked her regardless.

And what a boyfriend. The serendipity of a putative senator falling into Colt's path at the exact moment he was wondering how to proceed. It was perfect; why scrabble for every yard of growing power when you can have boring people do it for you? Colt was confident he would have had Rothwell in the Senate soon enough. Then a run for the White House backed with some astonishing good luck.

That had been the plan, anyway. Taking Rothwell to Waite's Bill had been a mistake, though. Oh, well. Plenty more politicians where he came from. Colt would just have to find a new one to puppeteer.

William Colt, the *éminence grise*. He liked the sound of that. He'd do a better job of being the president's brain than Karl Rove ever had for George W. Bush. A moron backed by an idiot. Colt was going to be the best power behind the throne since the days of Richelieu. And nobody would ever suspect him of being more than . . . oh, whatever. Oh! The guy who predigests the data and serves it up like pap for the president every morning. Didn't Reagan used to have his briefings delivered as cartoon drawings?

The phone was still ringing. Colt took the call.

"Good morning, William," said a voice. "I hope I am not disturbing you?"

It wasn't Carter. The voice was male, middle-aged, educated, and slightly amused. Probably New England? Not a strong Bostonian accent, but there was a hint of it.

"Who is this?"

"I *would* say, 'a friend,' William, but that would probably raise your hackles. So I shall just say, 'a concerned party.' I wanted to warn you. All your plans are about to take a knock."

"What are you talking about?"

"Your plans. I'm sure you have some, a clever fellow like you. Well, somebody is about to stick an unwanted spoke in your wheel. After they're done, you'll just be a socially inept mathematician that nobody likes again."

Colt didn't trust himself to speak.

"A clever fellow, but perhaps not a *wise* one. Would that be fair to say, William? I think you must know the truth of it yourself. I'll just tell you, shall I? Daniel Carter. He's far more dangerous than you've given him credit for. Dangerous in ways I don't think you entirely understand."

"I'm going to hang up."

"How kind of you to warn me. But you're still going to listen, because you're wondering how I can know these things, which is really the big question. Who I am is small potatoes compared to that. Anyway, here's the important thing that you need to know. You know Carter already knows about Waite Road, of course. What you *don't* know is that he intends to do something about it."

"Do? Do what?"

"Well, he has a very hands-on approach to problem solving, so I'm sure you can figure that out yourself. By this time tomorrow, the Perceptual Twist will be fixed permanently, and you won't be able to play with it any longer. Bye-bye, dreams of glory."

"Will you answer even one question?" Colt was trying to think of ways The Twist could help him find who the caller was. Currently, sorting through Scrabble tiles to form a name was the only thing he could think of, but it was so close to casting lots that it repelled him aesthetically, and aesthetics had a lot to do with using The Twist. If it felt wrong, it didn't work.

"Yes, just the one. And that was the one. If only you'd asked, 'Why are you telling me this?' instead. Get some sleep, William. You have a destiny to save in the morning."

The line went dead.

This was a bad game. A good game was where you knew all the rules, could work out a viable strategy and the tactics needed to achieve it. A good game was a game where new players didn't keep appearing in a puff of smoke and fucking everything up.

William Colt sat up in his bed in semidarkness, looking at the phone as if it were going to give him any answers. He was beginning to regret his early moves in the game. He'd told himself that Belasco was just a useful guinea pig and that there was nothing personal in what had happened, but that was bullshit. He could have just chosen somebody at random and there would have been no trail to follow. But no. He'd been an asshole and killed a man with whom he was known to be at loggerheads. Then he went to Atlantic City and showed off. The money hadn't been enough to make up for exposing himself like that. He should have gone with his first idea of influencing the state lottery; millions of dollars just sitting there for the taking, and nobody would have thought anything of his winning because it would have appeared to be blind luck. Stupid, stupid, stupid. He'd done it for another lottery for a smaller prize, after all.

He'd been drugged with the power of it, though. The discovery that there really is no such thing as "random" was too much to be taken soberly. It meant everyone was wrong about everything, and he was the first man to truly be right. Maybe not the first. Maybe the stories of Simon Magus, Merlin, possibly even Muhammad were about guys just like him, who'd seen how things weren't like how other people saw them. He'd briefly considered starting a religion. It had made L. Ron Hubbard a rich man, after all, and unlike that old fraud, Colt could actually perform miracles. The trouble was that starting a religion pretty much also meant writing a holy book, and that looked like hard, boring work.

If he couldn't get rich and powerful through organized religion—a path whose institutionalized mendaciousness didn't appeal in any case—there was always politics. Still plenty of lying, but at least he wouldn't have to pretend that he was behoven to some god or another.

Despite which, sometimes he still had little power fantasies about going to Mecca, proclaiming himself the new prophet, and doing all the Muhammad stuff like flying around on a horse. Even if they didn't buy it, it would be worth it just to see the look on their faces. They wouldn't buy it, no, but only because he was a pasty white guy. So fucking racist.

Then along came Carter. Colt still wasn't being smart when he set up the trap in his own house, and provoked Carter by going to the bookstore. Yes, Carter had fallen for it, but then . . .

But then he'd escaped. Colt couldn't understand that. He hadn't slept a full night after he got back, all set to "Oh, *gasp*, Officer! There's some dead guy in my house! He must have broken in and then had some sort of fit!" but somehow the son of a bitch had gotten out.

How? That question had robbed him of his sleep. The trap was perfect. He'd worked hard to make sure Carter wouldn't get out. It was impossible, but the trap itself was impossible, and that gave Colt pause. Maybe Carter understood the cube, too? Maybe not completely, but enough to get him out of a bad situation like that. *Impossible* plus *cube* equaled *possible*, as Colt understood all too well.

This wasn't part of the game. Only Colt was supposed to understand the cube. It was supposed to be a game for one. Everybody else, *everybody* else was supposed to be just a pawn. If Carter was another player, Colt didn't feel so secure anymore. Carter was an ex-cop. He knew how to beat the shit out of somebody. Colt's only advantage was the cube, and if Carter had it, too, the playing field tipped in his favor. Colt didn't want to have the shit beaten out of him.

Carter's phone call had unnerved him further. Colt had played it cool throughout, but he'd been sweating. The mention of Martin Suydam had been the worst, though. Colt had heard of Suydam—of course he had, he didn't live in a cave—but he'd just been a serial killer, not something the country was short of.

The media had shut up about the Child-Catcher pretty quickly after he'd died, now that Colt thought about it. He hadn't been much interested, so he hadn't cared at the time. After he'd finished talking to Carter, however, he'd gone straight online and searched for whatever he could find.

There wasn't much. Much less than he would have expected. The arrest had gone wrong, a cop had died, and the surviving cop was one Detective Daniel Carter. That shook Colt. He'd been inclined to blow Carter's story off as a lie, but that changed his attitude toward it. The reports didn't have much to say about what Suydam was doing with the stolen kids, but it wasn't pedophilia, which might have been why they lost interest so rapidly. One news site said he was carrying out occult experiments "akin to those of the Nazis," which seemed to Colt to be assuming a lot. A conspiracy site specifically said Suydam was carrying out experiments in perception, and even referenced some old Jeffrey Combs horror movie like that was a clinching argument.

Maybe that reference was coincidence, but as a man who could manipulate coincidences, Colt felt very sensitive to those he hadn't manufactured.

Then Carter had thrown in another hand grenade. Somebody had gone out of their way to get him involved.

Colt would bet serious money that exact "somebody" had just gotten off the phone with him. Which meant his situation was even worse than he'd previously thought. Not only was he not the only player in the game, but he was being played himself. He hesitated before thinking he was a pawn like everyone else, but he knew, despite finding the keys of destiny, he was not entirely in control of his own.

This sucked. It sucked so fucking hard. He had to start steering again, get himself out of this. The voice on the phone had said Carter was going to hit Waite Road. Colt couldn't countenance that; he was sure there were other viable sites in the world, but he didn't know where any were and he would be vulnerable while he looked. Again he cursed himself for going too fast when the cube's power was new to him. Why did he kill those people? Just stupid showing off. Everything was going too fast and it was his own fault.

He had no choice. He had to defend Waite Road, despite knowing he was dancing to the voice's tune. It was an unavoidable bottleneck in his options, though. If his political plan was going to go anywhere, Colt needed Waite Road untouched. Once Carter was no longer a problem, Colt would have breathing space to broaden those options so he never got cornered like this again. Find the voice and deal with the voice; that was next.

Good. Good. He was planning. It was all good.

Colt controlled his breathing, and lay back down. Sleep took some time to come.

Chapter 24

ALIENATION

Lovecraft didn't like going to Rothwell's home, largely because it felt like she was leaving Earth to get there. The house was almost stereotypically 1 percenter; a house too big for one man so he filled it with next to nothing at all. The lack of books in the place made her wince inwardly every single time she visited. She had trouble trusting anyone who failed to feed their inner self properly. She'd gently ragged him about it once, and had been wise to do so gently, for he became very defensive on the subject, did the "dead trees" speech, and said he kept his library on his iPad. She later had an opportunity to check out this voluminous virtual library and discovered it consisted of several financial journal subscriptions and an unread *Fifty Shades of Grey*. She *was* sure she was glad he hadn't read it, though, and surreptitiously deleted it from the device so he didn't get any ideas about using it as a manual for how rich, handsome guys should act.

After their last meeting, she'd momentarily harbored suspicions he might have gotten himself a new copy after all. There'd been silence between them and it seemed likely that their relationship had hit the buffers and that was that. A little earlier than Lovecraft had been anticipating, but not something that surprised her unduly. The call had been a small surprise. That it had come from Rothwell's mother was a much larger one.

Elise Rothwell was not of the usual *Steel Magnolias* school of matriarchy. She was a small, quiet woman, but she knew her mind and she was smart. It had been her suggestion that had put the idea of the Senate into her son's mind in the first place, not because she had any great interest in politics herself but simply because she saw it as an obvious career for a good-looking man with charisma, money, and connections. Besides, politics was the family business. It simply wasn't normal to go into politics because one held strong political views, in Elise's opinion. That would be setting a dangerous precedent.

Elise had never warmed to Lovecraft, and the feeling was mutual. Lovecraft wondered if race played into the mild animosity she felt from Rothwell's mother, but finally decided no, it was because she was politically wrong for Elise's only child. Lovecraft had watched with a strange mix of amusement and dismay as Elise had fought to stop her eyes from rolling when she heard Lovecraft ran a bookstore. That mild animosity made Elise reaching out to her all the more surprising, and distinctly worrying.

There wasn't much foreplay after Lovecraft got to the house. Elise met her, greeted her stiffly, took her to the kitchen, made her a coffee *herself* (Lovecraft noted the housekeeper was missing, and the sense of disturbance in the working of the household deepened), and then said, "Kenneth isn't well."

Lovecraft remained silent.

"Have you noticed anything out of the normal recently, dear? You see him quite frequently. Anything out of the normal?" She said it with a sudden false smile and a spastic gesture to flick away a wisp of hair at her temple.

Lovecraft realized with a small shock and a tiny, unbidden thrill of *schadenfreude* that Elise, glacial Elise whose every sentence to Lovecraft had always carried the subtext "You are not good enough for my son, and I live for the day he throws you aside," was frightened. Honestly, soul-deep frightened. Then Lovecraft thought what it would take to provoke that, and her pleasure in Elise's fear faded away.

"What's happened to Ken, Mrs. Rothwell?" Sometimes she liked to provoke *la grande femme de la société* by calling her "Elise," enjoying the flicker of that false smile raised to hide irritation. Now instead that smile was deployed to conceal panic, and it was doing a poor job of it.

"He isn't well," Elise repeated. Her tone was pettish—*Didn't you hear me the first time?* "I think it may be overwork. He's been spending so much time working on his campaign."

Lovecraft had been kept assiduously away from the campaign; she didn't have much sense that he'd been slaving over it, though. This was just supposed to be a trial run, after all.

At least, it was as far as Elise knew. She didn't know about Colt. She didn't know that unless Carter's plan worked, her little boy was on a jet-propelled toboggan all the way to the White House, and wouldn't that be nice? No, Elise did not have the first idea how much and what sort of stress her son was under.

Or perhaps she did. She turned her face toward Lovecraft, that fake smile writhing like a snake on a griddle, and Lovecraft saw the torment lying beneath it. "The thing is, dear," said Elise, the forced lightness in her voice killing both herself and Lovecraft, "I think Kenneth has had a breakdown." She angled her head to the other side. It was so mannered, she looked like an automaton. "A *mental* breakdown."

The specificity of the description was the most polite scream of grief Lovecraft had ever heard.

"Mrs. Rothwell," she said, "Ken *has* been acting a little . . . unlike himself recently." She didn't think it was necessary to mention "a little unlike himself" meant attempted anal rape. "I think you're right. The campaign has been more stressful for him than I think either of us realized. I hate to be the one to suggest . . ."

Elise wasn't listening. "He attacked Amara."

"I'm sorry?"

"Amara. The housekeeper. So much trouble. Apparently we're going to have to ship her whole wretched clan over because of this."

Lovecraft spoke slowly. "When you say 'attacked' . . ."

"Sexually. He . . ." Elise looked at Lovecraft, utterly bewildered. "She's so *homely*. Why would he do that? I imagine his love life is quite busy"—which Lovecraft parsed as *You black people do sex a lot, don't you?* but let it go—"so why does he take it into his head to lay hands on Amara?" She touched her own top lip. "She's quite hairy," she whispered.

Lovecraft could see that Elise wasn't going to provide any indications of her son's state of mind, only her own. "May I see him?"

"Yes. Yes, of course. It's why I called you, after all. He's in his study. You know where that is, don't you? Perhaps you can find out what's wrong with him."

Lovecraft got up and went to the door. "The election . . . ?"

"I don't see how he can go ahead. I've already told Marcus to wiggle him out of it. It means giving the Democrats a clear run, but Kenneth was never going to win this time. We'll put around something about illness or an emotional upset." She looked appraisingly at Lovecraft, seeing two birds that single stone could deal with. She shook herself out of the momentary reverie. "In any case, it's important we clear this mess up and make sure Kenneth is fit and ready next time."

"Yes," said Lovecraft. "That's the important thing."

Elise nodded and smiled, impervious to the ironic sentiment.

Lovecraft found Rothwell in his study, just as his mother had said. He was not, however, at his desk. He was sitting on the floor, his back against the wall, his legs splayed. He wasn't looking unkempt, as she had been expecting. He was washed and shaved, and his clothes were fresh.

In his hand, he held a revolver that he played with lazily. Love-craft's heart started at the sight of it, but she breathed again when she saw the cylinder was out, and—even from where she was standing at the entrance—she could see the chambers were all empty. Between his legs she could make out what looked like thick crayons on the carpet.

"Hi, Ken," she said quietly.

He looked up at her and smiled. He seemed sad, philosophi-cally so. It was not a mien she was used to seeing from him. "Hello, Emily. I suppose Mother called you?"

She nodded and walked closer. As she did, she saw the cray-ons were not crayons at all, but cartridges. "She's concerned about you."

"Hmmm . . ." He put down the gun and picked up one of the cartridges. "Yes. I'd be concerned about me, too. Look at this." He waved her closer. "Here's a funny thing." When she kneeled down beside him, he showed her the rear of what she could now see was an empty .410 cartridge. "See that?" He held the brass closer so she could inspect it.

There was little to see, but for two small dimples in the metal of the center fire cap. "Hammer's fallen on that one twice," she said, unsure what he wanted from her.

"Beautiful. Observant. Clever. I really like you, Emily. It's a shame you're going to leave me. Mind you, I was going to leave you, so that's fair. Nothing personal. You're just too left-wing. Sorry." He looked her in the eye. She'd never seen him so guileless, so open and undefended. "You were going to leave me, weren't you?"

She nodded. "I'm sorry."

He shook his head, absolving her. "No, that's good. That's the right thing to do. I tried to fuck you in the ass when you didn't want to. Hard to get by a thing like that. I'm sorry about that, by the way. Did I say that at the time? I'm sorry. I keep having mo-ments. Had one last night."

"I heard. The housekeeper?"

He nodded. "There's something not quite right with me, isn't there?" He held up the spent cartridge. "Hammer fell on it twice. The first time was a misfire, but it fired perfectly the second time. I fired all four in the cellar." Lovecraft knew the house had a single-lane firing range in the cellar; they'd had impromptu shooting matches down there when they'd first started going out together. She'd caught on quickly that he could just about stand losing as long as it was only by a small margin. It had still been fun, though. With a pang, she realized those matches had stopped at about the time she'd come to understand the true dimensions of their relationship. "Bang. Bang. Bang." He looked at the cartridge, ran his thumb across the dimpled metal. "Bang. Why didn't it fire the first time, Emily? If I could understand that, maybe I could understand what's wrong with me. There's something not quite right with me."

"Kenneth." She said his name gently, as if to a child. "Does this have to do with William Colt?"

He smiled at her. A big, open smile. "Beautiful. Observant. Clever. I'm not as clever as I thought I was. I don't think I'm clever at all. Yes." He toyed with the cartridge. "It's everything to do with William Colt. He's very clever." He looked at Lovecraft again and the smile faltered. "I'm sorry, Emily. There's something not quite right with me."

She held him as he wept.

Elise Rothwell looked up from her third untouched coffee of the morning to see Lovecraft enter the kitchen. She saw the young woman's eyes were red, but said nothing. She shied away a little when Lovecraft placed a revolver—silver and black, its cylinder out and empty—on the counter.

"I don't think he's suicidal," she said, "but I'd keep that away from him, all the same."

"What did he say?"

"Not much. I think he's had a small breakdown. He's not lost to us, Mrs. Rothwell, or at least, that's the impression I get. He's had some sort of shock."

Elise looked at her uncomprehendingly. "A shock? What kind of shock? When could that have happened?"

"I don't know. It could have been as simple as him thinking something he didn't want to think, and it shook him. Only he knows what did it. But I think with help, kindness, and a little time, he'll be okay. He'll be better. I'm no psychiatrist, though. I think he's going to need one. And, please, don't put him somewhere. It might be better if he stays in familiar surroundings."

"He can stay with me for a while," said Elise Rothwell. "He grew up in that house. It might make him feel safer."

"That sounds good."

"Somebody discreet to help him. I think I know who to ask." Elise shook herself as if awakening from a dream and arose, all bustle and intent. She picked up the cooling coffee cup and tossed its contents into the sink, placing the cup and saucer in the dishwasher. "I shall get that organized at once." She looked at Lovecraft as if she were the help, the vulnerability gone, her briefly annealed armor hardening once more. "Thank you for coming, dear. I'm sure you have things to be getting on with."

Carter and Harrelson were waiting for her in the apartment above the bookstore when she got back. It was quickly obvious to them that she did not especially want to talk about where she'd been. Harrelson passed her a plastic shopping bag. "We got you a holster for the Beretta," he said. "Hip holster. Figured being able to draw fast would be more use to you than concealment. And I brought along my old Blackhawk ankle rig if you want to try that instead." He shook his head. "This had better be all we think it is. I'm pissing away my career here if we're caught, and there's probably jail time coming, too."

"If we're wrong, then it's a hell of a shared delusion," said Carter. "We deserve to be in an institution. Not a penal one, either."

Lovecraft looped the hip holster on and tried the Beretta in it. Under her jacket, it was all but invisible. "Looks like I get a fast draw *and* concealment," she said. She hoisted the Mossberg with its strap, extended magazine, and extra cartridges stored on the folding butt. "This thing weighs a damn ton with all the extra shit on it." She shrugged. "Rather have it than not, though." She put it in the duffel bag, now emptied but for the gear they were taking, and dropped in Harrelson's ankle holster next to it.

"Okay." Harrelson sat on the sofa, rubbing a smear of gun oil from the palm of one hand with the thumb of the other. "What's the plan?"

Carter looked at Lovecraft, who shrugged.

"Yeah," said Harrelson, "that's what I figured. We just swoop in and . . . ?"

"Mess things up," said Lovecraft. "We don't know what's so important about Waite Road, but something is. We find out what it is, and break it."

"In the end house," added Carter, "the one like a meeting house. That's where Colt went."

Harrelson smiled, albeit ruefully. "It'll do. It's not even the weakest due cause I've ever seen a warrant issued for. So when are we doing this?"

"Now?" said Carter. "Good a time as any."

"No," said Lovecraft.

"No?"

"Lunch," said Lovecraft.

Chapter 25

THE THING AND THE DOORSTEP

They took Lovecraft's car, an aging Ford station wagon that would not have looked badly out of place in an episode of *The Rockford Files.*

"This is . . . characterful," said Harrelson. "Metallic brown. Nice."

"Get in and shut up," said Lovecraft. "No. Better. Shut up and get in."

"Don't argue with an armed librarian, Detective. Oh, and I call shotgun."

"Fuck's sake," Harrelson muttered, "like a picnic."

Lovecraft's admonition to Harrelson to be quiet proved unnecessary. As they drove, the gravity of what they were about to do grew on them oppressively, and conversation did not come easily, nor did the prospect of imminent action improve the atmosphere as they approached the landward end of the isthmus leading onto Waite's Bill.

Lovecraft slowed the car, coming to a halt some twenty yards from the entry road. "Okay. Anyone wants to back out, here's your last chance. I won't hold it against you if either or both of you want out."

Carter was looking at the house overlooking the entrance. It was looking just on the edge of being unkempt. The grass was untended, and the car sat in the drive with mud over its rims like it had been driving in a field. It seemed at odds with the character of the man he'd spoken to there not so very long before.

"What about you?" said Harrelson. "None of us have to do this. That includes you."

Lovecraft shook her head. "They hurt a friend of mine. If they can hurt him, they can hurt anyone. I can't let that go."

"Colt tried to kill me," said Carter. "He'll try again. Big picture aside, it's self-preservation." He looked at Harrelson. "You're the only one without a dog in this. If we fuck up, this could go very badly for you."

"I'm not letting you down."

"We could do with a reserve," said Lovecraft suddenly. "You know? Like in battles? You could be our reserve, Detective. Hang back here, and we'll call you if we need you. Then you'd be responding to a call for help."

"Plausible deniability," added Carter. "Stand you in good stead if IAB get involved."

Harrelson considered it. "I'd need my own car."

"Walk up to the main street and hail a taxi. You could be back here in half an hour."

"Yeah." He wavered, a man in dilemma. "Yeah, you're right." He got out of the car, leaned by Lovecraft's window, and said, "Thanks. Don't get killed while I'm gone."

They watched Harrelson climb the incline toward the main street in the mirror.

"That was good of you," said Lovecraft.

Carter didn't argue the point. "It's not his war. And he's right—we don't have a plan. All we have is a shitload of weapons and some personal animosity. What are we supposed to do? Kick down the door and shoot everyone?"

"I thought that was SOP for cops? Sure I read that somewhere."

"Heh. Okay, how about this? There's a stand of trees along the riverward side of the street. You take station there with the shotgun. I'll go to the house, knock, introduce myself, go in, and . . ." He slowed to a halt.

"Why do you go to the door?"

"Because you're the one with the shotgun, and it's not concealable. Also, I've had combat training."

"Cool. Have the woman without the combat training cover your back. What could go wrong? Okay . . . hypothetical: you go in. I wait, and I wait, and I wait, and meanwhile they're cutting you to pieces inside in sacrifice to their dark god, and I'm outside. Waiting. I don't see how that's a win for us."

"I'll be on my guard. Push comes to shove, I'll fire a shot as a signal. Then you can come in. No, better yet, call Harrelson to tell him you're going in. If he's only a minute or two away, wait for him."

"This sucks. This is the worst plan ever. Kicking down the door and shooting everyone is beginning to look pretty sophisticated in comparison to that." She sighed. "Unless we can talk the FBI into believing what's been happening, it'll have to do. Okay. Let's . . . just get it over with."

She drove slowly onto the isthmus road, and slowed still further as the trees closed around them. "Jesus," she muttered under her breath as the daylight, poor enough as it was beneath an overcast sky, attenuated still further and felt dank and unhealthy. Emerging from the tunnel hardly helped things. Waite Road stood before them, and felt almost hyper-real, as if Providence was a studio set and now they had emerged from the backlot. Carter and Lovecraft felt actual and extant in a way they never had before, fictions rising from the page.

At Carter's direction, Lovecraft turned left and along the short dirt track to the lick of open land between the river's edge and the wooded windbreak. "Turn it around and park here," he told her. "The car can't be seen from the houses or the road, and we can get here quickly enough if need be."

If need be. The possibilities to fulfill *If need be* were too multitudinous to consider. They both had a strong sense that the expedition would finish with them leaving Waite's Bill in a hurry and then pretending nothing had ever happened.

They got out of the Ford and opened the bag of weapons. Lovecraft took out her Mossberg, put the sling over her head and right arm. She took a loose cartridge from the bag and slid it through the port. "And one in the chamber. Okay. I would say, 'Locked and loaded,' about now, but I already feel like a big enough asshole."

"Got your pistol?"

"Never took it off. Spare mags in my jacket pocket. Left-hand side. Yeah, I'm that organized. You?"

Carter ran through a mental checklist, tapping holster and pockets as he went. He hesitated once, wondering if he'd done the right thing leaving the cube behind, but it was a brief hesitation. "I'm good." He and Lovecraft looked at each other. "Right. Here we go."

They moved farther down the riverside in the direction of the estuary until they were close to the end, where Carter judged the end house would be. They entered the stand of trees crouched, and moved from cover to cover. Neither felt at all like soldiers, but only like kids playing soldiers. They felt ridiculous. Only the heft of the weapons reminded them that it was an unusually serious game they were playing. As the trees started to clear and they caught glimpses of the narrow road with the houses on the other side, they paused.

"You can get a little closer than this," said Carter, "but do it on your belly. I'll go back, go around, and approach down the road like a normal person. Got your earpiece?"

Lovecraft took a Bluetooth earpiece from her pocket, the blue LED covered with a small tab of tape to hide it, and put it on.

"Cool. I'll call as I approach the house, and leave my phone open. You should be able to hear any conversation. You good?"

Lovecraft nodded. She wasn't feeling good at all, but they both knew that. "I'm good." She adopted a Western twang. "Go get 'em, Floyd."

Carter nodded and disappeared back the way they had come. Lovecraft waited until he was out of sight, took a deep breath, and went on her belly, the shotgun held in one hand. It was strange seeing it there, smooth, black, metallic against the dirt and leaf mold. She crawled forward four or five yards and took station behind one of the many oaks on the spit of land.

Carter moved within the trees as much as possible, angling his return so that he estimated that he would emerge somewhere near Lovecraft's Ford. While he wanted to be exposed as little as possible, the price was staying within the tree line and, like much else on Waite's Bill, that was inherently unpleasant. Anywhere else, the predominantly oaken stand would have been pleasant and natural. Here, even the trees felt wrong. There was a sense of moving through growth rather than life, like negotiating the strands of a cancer or a parasitic fungus rather than a small wood of honest trees.

He was pleased when he was finally able to leave the trees and emerge into the open. He was more pleased still that he had judged it to a nicety and was opposite the Ford. He was less pleased that he was no longer alone. He wasn't pleased at all that the figure standing by Lovecraft's car and studying it with mild curiosity did not appear to be human.

Carter stopped dead. The creature turned its head slowly to regard him. It was the color of a dead fish, and its eyes were large and cloudy. It stood much taller than a man, perhaps almost eight feet or so, and it was hairless and naked. Water still beaded on its smooth, batrachian skin, still dripped onto the unhealthy grass. Carter could see the trail it had left on the turf from the river's edge where it had surely emerged.

Man and monstrosity regarded each other for half a minute, more. Carter quite forgot he had a gun. He was barely aware that he had legs and that running was an option. That seemed too trivial a response. He was standing before something that could not be. Running or shouting or shooting were the actions of a character in a TV show or an urban myth. The correct action, the only reaction, was to let the moment last like the keening, perfect note of a tuning fork.

But even such a note must eventually fade.

"Hi," said the monster. It had many teeth in its mouth, small piercing cones of bone or perhaps cartilage.

Carter didn't trust himself to say anything. He only nodded.

"I know you," said the monster. "I met you before."

"I . . . don't remember that."

"Sure you do." The monster's voice was strange, grating and liquid, an inhuman larynx forcing out human sounds and crushing them slightly in the process. "Sure you do. It was right here." The monster looked around and Carter saw a flexible crest like a fin running down the rear of its head and onto its spine. There was something so organic and natural in it, any last lingering hope that he was just looking at somebody in an incredibly sophisticated rubber suit faded in that observation.

The monster looked down and Carter saw there was an abandoned battered blue and white sneaker there, failing at the toe cap.

"Sure you do," said the monster again, and it was right.

"You wanted to go swimming," said Carter.

"I can now. I'd wanted to for so long, but the women wouldn't let me. Said I'd drown. Said I wasn't ready. But there was a change and I could swim, so I did. If I don't eat now, I don't get hungry, but I get small." It looked out at the river. "There's lots to eat out there. I got really big, didn't I?"

Carter saw the massive muscles sliding under the anuran skin. In the obtuse light he saw for the first time the thin gills at its neck that throbbed with every beat of a cold, inhuman heart. "Yes," he said, "you got really big."

The monster regarded him with distant, alien curiosity. Sometimes nictitating lids swept across the cloudy eyes, but rarely. "I met you before," it said again, and then, "You're that Carter guy, aren't you?"

"What?"

"The women talk about you. I forget what they say. It wasn't interesting." It swung its head toward the river and gazed at it with yearning for a long moment. "Sometimes I think I hear others calling, others not from Waite Road. It's not real. There aren't any others, only us, and there ain't many of us. Only, like . . ." It looked at its hands as if to count. "Not many." It turned back to Carter. "I'm gonna go swim now. Bye."

It fell to all fours, and Carter had a momentary impression of great webbed fingers splaying out as it half hopped, half ran like a dog to the water's edge. There it did not hesitate, but lowered its head and launched itself in a powerful jump, driving itself through the surface of the Providence River. It barely left a ripple despite its great bulk, only a sudden swell beneath the surface as it swam away, its great legs pushing back the water as it shot down into the dark depths that were so much more fascinating to it than the world of man had ever been.

Carter took some awkward staggering steps until he could lean on the Ford, where he stood and hyperventilated for a few seconds until he could bring it under control.

He had a choice. He could either conclude that he had hallucinated and that he was, to a greater or lesser extent, insane. Or he could accept that he had actually just seen a real, intelligent creature that might be described as a "monster."

He wasn't sure why this was so much more difficult to accept than swimming through thin air in Colt's house. He could only think that he had accepted that phenomena as being caused by science, even if it was a broken piece of science of which Colt had taken advantage. He didn't understand all of science. Hell, no single scientist understood all of science. He didn't really understand how electronics worked, he didn't entirely understand how a flat-screen TV worked, he didn't have the faintest idea what quantum theory was about. YouTube was full of amazing demonstrations of science, of which Coke and Mentos were the very least. It didn't take such a great leap of faith from there to Colt's drowning-in-air trick.

So, that was one thing. A chat with a hulking amphibian humanoid was something far, far different. It didn't make sense. There was no background to it beyond the *Creature Double Features* of the past and febrile tabloid stories. Earth was a small world. There was no space for another sentient species, and the monster was part of a species, not some mutation, not some freak. How was that possible? It wasn't, yet he had seen it with his own eyes. The paradox whirled in Carter's mind like a broken escapement. He could feel it spinning eccentrically, chipping away the certainties and sureties around it that he needed to function. Carter could feel himself becoming insane.

He was saved by the sound of a small and irritating electronic tune playing in his ear. He accepted the call without thinking.

"Where the hell are you?" said Lovecraft in his earpiece. "How long does it take to walk around? I can't even see you on the street from here."

"I . . . thought I saw something." He watched the flow of the river and allowed it to calm him, working hard not to think what was beneath the surface. "It was nothing, though. I'm okay." He took a second to swallow, and asked with a lameness that was evident even to himself, "Are you okay?"

"I'm fine." She said it with flat suspicion. "Can we get on with the intricate master plan now?"

"Yeah." Carter took a deep breath, feeling his heart rate settle. "Yeah, let's do that. I'll be out front in a minute or so."

He checked his Glock once again, more from a sense of

needing routine than concern. Then he walked down the short curving dirt track and emerged where the access road joined with Waite Road. A moment more brought him out of the shade of the trees, and the street lay before him. He stood for a moment and looked at the nondescript houses. The lack of any sign of children had struck him as a mild curiosity the first time he'd been here. Now it seemed significant and sinister.

Carter steeled himself, and walked toward the end house on the left-hand fork of the street. He could see no one, but there was again a strong sense of being watched. No signs of life anywhere, no movement and no sound but for the swaying of the tree branches and the sighing of the breeze, but the black windows seemed to gaze upon him with infinite calculation and threat.

He knew Lovecraft likely had eyes on him by this time, but the thought of the extra gun did not settle his nerves at all. He felt like only he and she were on that whole spit of land, and yet he felt that other life crowded around them, too. Different life. The image of cancerous growth grew in his imagination again, of parasites, and forms alien to human perception and experience.

He stood at the end of the driveway leading to the last house, resisted the very powerful urge to glance back at Lovecraft, and walked up to the front door. The driveway was entirely empty of vehicles, he noted. Now at last he felt certain of what to do. He rapped smartly on the door and waited.

There was a silence, although Carter had the impression of a dull concussion more than a sound, as if something heavy had fallen inside. The seconds passed and the temptation to turn, shrug at Lovecraft, and go home where things made marginally more sense washed over him. He resisted this, too. He was just raising his hand to knock again when he heard movement on the other side of the door, and then the click of the lock being disengaged. He lowered his hand and prepared to deliver his rehearsed line about a moment of their time and an ongoing investigation.

The door opened, and there was William Colt, smiling at him.

Carter started to speak, but surprise prevented him from getting further than his lips forming the necessary shape for him to utter the first phoneme of "What the fuck?"

"Hi, Dan," said Colt, and shot him.

Chapter 26

THE SHUNNED HOUSE

Carter tasted blood. He was confused and disoriented, and he took the taste to be a sign that all was far from well, although he had trouble remembering why. The left side of his forehead out toward the temple hurt, too. There was cheap carpet against the right side of his face, and there was a bad smell: something dank and unclean, like rotting vegetables or a faulty drain, but neither of those.

As he recovered awareness, he struggled fitfully and thereby lost any chance of pretending to still be unconscious. His hands and ankles were bound. Not handcuffs; something broader and more giving than steel bracelets. Leather restraints?

"Oh, here you are," he heard somebody say. "At last. You banged your head as you fell, Dan. Sorry about that. Wasn't part of the plan. You okay?"

Colt, Carter realized. It was William Colt's voice.

He tried to speak, but his mouth was entirely dry, and he had to work his tongue to try to make saliva.

"I Tasered you," said Colt, sincerely apologetic. "Sorry about that, too, but you'd have made trouble. I wasn't sure what I expected to happen. Haven't done it before. Something nice and convenient like you going, 'Oh!' and folding up conveniently. But you didn't. You kind of spasmed and your whole body arched over sharply, like"—there was a rustle of clothing and Carter guessed Colt was demonstrating—"and you banged your head on the doorframe. You bit your tongue, too. I'm really sorry about that, Dan. I didn't want to hurt you. I still don't."

Carter opened his eyes slowly, the light sliding in as pain. It hurt too much and he closed his eyes again. He heard a ruffling of cloth, and the click of thin plastic regaining its shape. The mouth of a bottle was put to his lips.

"Here," said Colt, "it's water. Drink."

It was warm, but it was water. Carter thought of poison or drugs, but Colt could have killed him at any point, so he drank.

When he had swallowed a couple of mouthfuls, Colt took the bottle away. "You shouldn't have too much, not after taking a knock on the head like that. You might throw it up again. How are you feeling?"

"Like shit."

"Yeah. I imagine so." Colt exhaled heavily. "I had everything figured out until you turned up, Dan. Sorry, but I thought you were just another idiot trying to get in my way. I was wrong about that. That's okay. It was a learning experience. I've learned humility. I'm not God. Hey, if God had gotten a lesson like that and learned humility, it would be a better world, wouldn't it?"

"You believe in God?" Carter couldn't keep the surprise out of his voice.

"No." Colt half laughed. "No. I'm no theist. Especially not now. If there is a God, or gods, they're as flawed as all get-out. Not sure you can really think of anything that error-prone as any sort of gods you'd want to worship. But there are things powerful enough to be gods. I'm pretty sure about that. I've seen their fingerprints." The sound of the bottle's cap being screwed back on. "I just haven't seen *them*." Another half laugh. "Maybe just as well, huh?"

Carter risked opening his eyes again. Colt was right about the nausea; he was glad he'd only had a light lunch or he would be choking it up by now, and that would be a shame on such lovely carpet.

The sofa Colt was sitting on was no great improvement; a twee overstuffed thing in a floral print. The wallpaper on the wall behind him was a delicate shade of yellow. On a casual table by the side of the sofa lay a familiar, slightly irregular cube. Carter wasn't surprised to see it there; it only confirmed that whatever Colt did, he did here.

Carter tried his wrists again. Definitely broad leather straps, the kind of thing you see in classier sex boutiques. "You always stun visitors?" he asked.

"No, not usually. But I knew you were coming."

Carter's mind flew through possibilities. Only Lovecraft and Harrelson had known about this, but neither made much sense. Unless Colt had gotten to Harrelson, in which case Harrelson made a better actor than cop to have carried it off. Would Harrelson have offered a bag full of firearms in that case? No, Carter couldn't see either Lovecraft or Harrelson selling him out. Colt seemed in a talkative mood; maybe Carter could just ask him.

"How did you know that?"

Colt was wearing a check shirt, Hush Puppies, and pale chinos, sitting with his hands clasped between his knees. "Would you be surprised if I said I don't really know? I got a phone call. A *mysterious* phone call. I'd love to know who it was from. Especially since you tell me that you only got involved because of a mysterious phone call. Was that true? I can't see why you'd lie, but I have to be sure. Was that true?"

"Yeah. On Belasco's phone right after you killed him. Some

guy in an overcoat and wearing a hat. That's all the parking lot's cameras turned up. Ring any bells with you?"

He was hoping to rattle Colt with that, or at least build up a little trust between them so, if he had to lie later, he stood a better chance of getting away with it. Colt shook his head, interested but unperturbed. "That could be anyone, couldn't it? That's why people wear overcoats and hats in situations like that. They could be anyone. Well, fuck. I was hoping for something more useful."

Colt leaned closer. "Dan. I have a strong sense that I'm being played. I don't know why anyone would do that. Why would you go out of your way to give somebody the kind of power I've got, hmmm?"

"I wouldn't."

"Not you. I meant in the sense of 'Why would one go out of one's way . . . ?' And why drag you into it? Dan, why didn't you die in the house? That's really bugging me. Why aren't you dead?"

"I don't know, Colt." Carter was wondering how long he'd been stunned. It can't have been so very long or Harrelson would be back by now, and he didn't strike Carter as the kind of guy who would wait for long before going on the offensive. He slowly rolled himself a few degrees over, ostensibly to look at Colt more squarely, but really hoping to feel his phone in his pocket. It had gone. Unless radio silence was enough to alert Lovecraft or Harrelson, then it looked like the cavalry wouldn't necessarily be riding in anytime soon.

"I don't think you know, either, Dan. But I have to be sure."

Carter didn't like the way this was going and, with an intention to distract, said, "You just happened to have restraints lying around the place?"

Colt smiled. "Well, it's not *my* place anyway, Dan. And, yes, they did. The Waite family isn't much like any other family I've ever come across. You might have, being an ex-cop and everything, but I don't think so. There are Waites in every single one of these houses, Dan. Waite Road really is the street of Waites."

"I wasn't expecting inbred hillbillies in Providence."

"That's not kind and it isn't accurate. They're not inbred. Every one of the Waite men comes from elsewhere. The family name is maintained by the women. They wanted you, you know. I had to talk them out of it."

"I'm not marrying a redneck anytime soon. Not on my bucket list."

Colt's smile returned. "Like you'd have a choice. They're very persuasive. Not with me, of course. That's not my relationship with them at all." His smile faded and his brow clouded. "Very much a business relationship. Anyway, that's neither here nor there. I need to know how you got out of the house. It's important, Dan."

"I don't know how I did it."

"Yes, well, can't really take your word for it. Sorry. Wish I could, but the Waites are insistent, and I can understand their concern. They've been living with The Twist for a long time and it's important to them. Of course it is. Somebody starts just, kind of . . . shrugging it off . . . You know we were talking about gods a minute ago? Well, what you did is kind of heretical to them. Blasphemous, even. They're not happy with you, Dan. Can you understand that?"

Carter looked at Colt. "Colt, you're in as much danger as I am. Can *you* understand that?"

Colt broke eye contact to look off and up into the middle distance, thinking. "I know I am, but not from the Waites. I'm too important to them. Y'know, I thought they were just riding on my coattails at first, but now I'm not so sure. I might be riding on theirs. The Twist is tied into their destiny, Dan. That's how they see it, and I guess they're right."

Carter scrabbled around for anything he could use for ammunition, anything he could use to undermine Colt, and settled on recent events. "You screwed up with Ken Rothwell."

Carter was disappointed when Colt barely reacted. "Yes, I know. That was a mistake. I saw your friend go off with him and thought, *synchronicity*. I recognized him immediately. I read the papers, you see? I thought, *Well, here's how I leverage one form of power into another. It's meant to be.* But it wasn't. There's perceived destiny, something tangible but just out of reach, like the Waites' destiny. And there's just seeing a pattern in coincidence. With everything that's been happening, I thought I'd know the difference without trying, but I was wrong. Rothwell's whole worldview was so rigid. I guess that's why he wants to be a politician. Showed him he was wrong about the way things work and that the reality has the most amazing opportunities. I thought he'd like that, thought it would excite him, but no. *Crack!*" Colt almost shouted it. "More than he could bear. And there go my political ambitions for the time being. Have to be more *circumspect* about it next time. People like you and me are different, Dan. Special. More than I realized. Turns out there's a knack to dealing with all this stuff."

"There's no trick to how you do it," said Carter. "You're a sociopath."

"Yes," said Colt, nodding philosophically, "there's that. I do have a certain degree of dissociative behavior. You don't though, Dan. You're a reg'lar guy, a straight-up guy, a pillar-of-the-community kind of guy. Why aren't you as broken as Ken? What's so special about you? Good idea to tell me before the Waites lose patience."

The door opened. Carter couldn't see who was there, but Colt looked up, nodded, and then said to him, "Oops. Time's up, Dan."

Carter was lifted by his elbows by two men who brought him to his feet, and then off them, dangling so that his toes barely brushed the floor. They turned him to the door. One of the women was leaning by it, watching events proceed with interest. She was wearing a red tee washed to a patchy pink, the transfer on it flaked and indecipherable, jeans that ended at her shins, and sandals, dark brown hair in a scrunchie. She looked to be in her late twenties, all but her eyes, and there was no dating them.

She was smiling; Carter doubted it was because she was being polite.

"Hey, remember what they used to say in old Westerns, Dan?" Carter heard Colt say behind him. He put on an accent. *"Don't let them give you to the squaws, boy."*

"Who was that meant to be?"

"Walter Brennan," said Colt, offended.

"Nothing like him," said Carter. He was carried out.

In the hallway was a cheap, lurid rug. The men held him still while the woman lifted the rug and exposed a long trapdoor. Carter looked around, looking for anything that might provide an advantage. He couldn't feel the weight of his pistol at his hip, nor of his backup on his ankle; they could hardly have missed it while securing his feet.

Thinking of the ankle restraints, he looked down and saw that they were indeed made of broad brown leather, but looked more like historical artifacts from some abandoned asylum rather than an upmarket sex shop. They were certainly old, and had seen heavy use to judge from the cracked leather and aged stains on them. The stains looked like they might be old blood.

The woman hooked her finger into the recessed ring and lifted the trapdoor, six feet long by three feet wide easily. From the underside it was plain that the trapdoor was reinforced wood and must weigh a great deal. The effortless way the woman had raised it was something else to worry about. Carter raised the bar of "necessary force" still higher; as far as he could see, the only way to be sure of dealing with the Waites was through the use of lethal force. Part of him was starting to worry that still wouldn't be enough.

The men started to move forward to what looked like simply a dark pit, but as they drew up to it, Carter saw the top of a set of utilitarian wooden steps descending.

"Wait, you idiots," said the woman. She said it without vigor or rancor, as if "idiots" was a standard and accepted term for the men of the street. Carter remembered Harrelson's story about the man who'd married into the Waites. Looking at the two holding him, they looked similar enough to be brothers, and much like the man he'd spoken to on the riverside that time. Yet if what he'd learned was true, the men weren't related by blood at all. A thought about the lack of children on the street started to form, but he withdrew his attention from it, throttling it before he came to any conclusions he didn't want to know.

The woman descended the steps until she could reach under the lip and flick a switch. The harsh fluorescent glare of strip lighting flickered into life with the clacking of initiators. The woman walked down, turned, and waited, watching the men as one released Carter's elbow and gathered up his feet, leading down the steps, his fellow holding Carter under the armpits. The procedure felt very practiced. Carter never stopped looking for opportunities, and he never stopped failing to spot anything at all. It would have been too easy to accept that there was no way out, to slip into despair, to go to his death—for they surely meant to finish him—without hope. Daniel Carter did not intend to do that. He would choose his moment, and he would fight. All noble enough but, as he reminded himself, pointless if the moment never arrived. The bindings were secure and the Waites were watchful. He concluded his best chance would come from an external distraction. If Lovecraft should want to kick in the door and start firing, this would be an ideal moment.

In the meantime, he would keep gathering data in the hope that some fragment of it might prove useful. The steps were not professionally made, but sturdy enough. The cellar floor was earthen, but an underbed of smoothly rolling stone was visible beneath it. The woman wore a knife in a brown leather scabbard on her belt, about a six-inch blade, he guessed. The lighting was a pair of cheap tube lights mounted on a wooden lattice across the ceiling, and again was not a professional job. The walls were irregular and continuous stone was visible in many places; it seemed the cellar had been crudely excavated down into the surface of a large boulder. Lovecraft was sitting in the corner, her hands tied with cord.

Well, shit.

"If you were depending on her," said the woman, "you made a bad choice."

Chapter 27

THE VERY ODD FOLK

"So, let's go back to the top and start again, huh, Dan?" Colt was descending the stairs behind Carter. Carter was still looking for options. There was an exit from the cellar; a crudely cut hole in one wall opened into darkness. Carter distinctly felt a breeze blow from it. Not a dead end, then. Or, possibly a dead end with ventilation. He'd take that chance if he could get an even break here.

"We don't want to hurt you—"

"So you say," interrupted Carter.

"It's true," said the woman. "You're interesting, Mr. Carter. We want to know all about you."

"And I'm telling you nothing. So I guess that's a stalemate."

"No," said the woman, "not while we have your friend. *She* we have no use for."

Lovecraft was watching him and must have heard the words, but she didn't flinch or react. Carter guessed she'd already heard enough threats to desensitize her to them. She looked disheveled, but not beaten up. He wondered what had happened. Then he decided to ask, largely because it was putting off the inevitable.

"How did you catch her? How did you even know where she was?"

"We sent a couple of the men to go around the long way and sneak up on her, Mr. Carter," said the woman. "As to where she was, the trees told us." Carter glared at her, but she only smiled lazily. "They whisper all the time. Easy to unnerstan' them if you only listen."

"Okay, Dan," said Colt. He was sitting halfway down the steps. "Crunch time. Tell us what we want to know, or Keturah will start playing with Ms. Lovecraft there. It'll get messy."

"Keturah?" scoffed Carter, but he was just playing for time, and everyone in that cellar knew it.

Then Lovecraft spoke. "It's Hebrew. The second wife of Abraham. Old Puritan name."

"Well, now, ain't you educated?" said Keturah Waite, crouching by Lovecraft. "Shame that it's not really what we wanna know. But Mr. Carter could take a lesson from that for sure. Be a little more forthcoming"—she drew her knife and held it against Lovecraft's cheek—"afore I start peeling."

"'Afore'?" said Carter, clutching at straws. "You people really are inbred."

"Okay," said Keturah. She looked unimpressed, even bored. "I'm tired of this shilly-shallyin'. I'm going to cut Ms. Lovecraft's right ear off now, an' maybe that'll concentrate your attention, Mr. Carter."

"Don't!" snapped Carter. "Don't hurt her! There's no need!"

"You ain't takin' me serious, Mr. Carter. There's a need."

"I am taking you very seriously! I—"

Keturah looked at one of the men and nodded toward Carter. The man punched Carter in the stomach without hesitation. The surprise caught him as much as the pain, and he tried to double up, his bound feet scrabbling on the floor for purchase as the two men held him up. When he finally stopped writhing and they hoisted him up straight, his eyes were streaming.

"I just want to say . . ." Lovecraft was speaking, her voice small and frightened. "I just want to say something. Can I say something?"

"Go ahead, sweetheart," said Keturah. "Talk some sense into your gentleman friend."

"No," said Lovecraft. She was at the edge of tears herself. Carter felt desperately useless. It wasn't right she was suffering. He should have ignored her badass act and told her to stay in the store, handled this with Harrelson. He wanted to apologize to her, but he could hardly breathe. "No, I want to talk to you, Keturah. I want to say something to you."

"Me?" Keturah Waite smiled, very mildly surprised. "And what have you got to say to me, Miss Lovecraft?"

"I just want to say, you had better let us go."

Keturah's smile faded with disappointment. "That's it?" She raised the knife again. "Okay . . . fair warning, darlin', this is goin' to hurt."

"You'd better let us go, or you are going to die."

The knife halted in its movement. "Did you jus' threaten me, girl?" There was menace in Keturah's tone now. Not her usual bored feline sadism, but something more atavistic and brutal. "Did you just fuckin' *threaten* me?"

"I warned you. Not a threat. I warned you. I'm warning you."

"Fuck the ear. I'm cutting your nose off." The knife shifted, changed angle, and—at the sound of a shot—stopped.

Keturah dropped the knife and it rang on a surface of exposed stone. She fell sideways and crawled away from Lovecraft, clutching at her side. When she drew her hand away, it was dark with blood.

The shot had stunned them all. Despite the closeness of Keturah's body first concealing the sight of the Beretta Pico and then muffling its report, the sound had resonated strongly in the small cellar, bouncing from the rock walls. The man on Carter's right made no effort to dodge, but only made an incoherent lowing as Lovecraft raised the pistol gripped firmly in her bound hands, her hands shaking and her face creased with fear, and fired again, and again.

Colt was already on his feet and out of there, his shoes clattering on the wooden steps, and the second Waite man followed him at a clumsy lope, shying from the pistol as Lovecraft tried to get a clear shot at him as he ducked behind and around Carter. He ran up the steps on all fours.

Lovecraft fired again, but the bullet struck a step and stuck in the wood.

Keturah was thrashing on the floor, screaming in an endless keening note that never seemed to break for her to draw breath. Her blood splashed and sprayed as she rolled and convulsed. Carter had seen people shot on more than one occasion in his life, but never anything like this. Lovecraft was staring at the shot woman, the Beretta gripped in her bound hands. Lines of blood spatter lay across her clothes and skin. Carter looked down at the shot man. He wasn't dead, but he was only lying there, his head casting from side to side, as confused as someone shaken from a deep sleep.

"Emily!" he snapped at her. He had to almost shout it before she suddenly looked up at him, startled. "Get me loose! Quick!" He hopped around on the spot until his back was to her and waggled his fingers urgently.

She got up and came to him. "I can't do it with the gun in my hand!"

"Put it down, then! For Christ's sake, Emily, please? Hurry! They'll be getting more men and guns!"

He heard the clatter of the gun being half placed, half dropped to the rocky floor and felt a small relief that the thing didn't go off.

Emily fumbled at the restraint buckles, made clumsy by her own bonds and her terror. "Why is she making that noise?" she asked as she worked. "Why won't she stop?"

Carter looked down. The corner of the room where the woman was still thrashing like a landed marlin was dense with blood. A human body carried more blood than most people liked to think about, and God knew a little of the stuff could make a fuck of a mess, but this was extraordinary. "I don't know," he said. "She should be in shock by now."

His hand were free. He had never been restrained like that in anything other than bedroom games, and would have loved to have rubbed his wrists and generally felt the Indiana Jones "and in a single bound, he was free" vibe. There was no time. As soon as the wrist restraints grew loose, he shook them off, got down on the floor, and released the ankle restraints, too. Once they were off, he grabbed the Beretta and Keturah's dropped knife from the floor.

Keturah was still screaming, still thrashing in a pool of her own blood. Carter looked away; maybe it was just the way the cheap tube lights lit the cellar, but the blood just didn't look right. It was too dark, even for venous blood, and where it lay on the pale dirt between the exposed rock, it seemed too bluish, more a purple than a crimson. He thought of what he had seen by Lovecraft's car earlier, and then drove the obvious corollary from his mind. This was no time for that. Now was the time for simple, visceral intent and action. If he stopped to think about what was really happening there, what the true nature of their situation was, he might never start again.

"They didn't search you?" he asked Lovecraft. He made her spread her hands apart like an opening orchid so he could reach the cords with the knife's blade. The edge cut the cord very easily. It wouldn't have taken much effort for Keturah to cut off Lovecraft's nose with it, especially given how strong she had seemed.

"It was sticking into me, the way I was lying, so I put on the ankle rig instead. They didn't search me at all. Just took my shotgun, and my bag, and my phone."

As Lovecraft spoke, her eyes kept flicking sideways to Keturah, and then immediately back to Carter. They had to speak loudly because she was *still* screaming. They looked down at her. Coated in her own blood, her white eyes wide and glaring at them. Carter shook his head, shook it at her vitality and the small sea of blood she had lost yet barely seemed to need. He shook his head and denied the possibility of her. "Not possible," he said. "Not possible." He shot her between the eyes, and the screaming stopped as if by the flick of a switch.

Lovecraft flinched and made an incoherent sound that might have been a gasp or may have been a half word to stop Carter, uttered too late.

"Look at it," he said, and it was not plain whether he meant the scene or the body. "Look at the blood. Look at it all. The color. I didn't kill anyone. Not anything human."

Now in the silence, they heard the heavy footfalls above as the Waite men, implacable and entirely expendable, came to avenge their kin.

The Beretta had two rounds left in it. Lovecraft had felt nervous about having one in the chamber, but Harrelson had talked her into it. It was as well that he had, as it broadened their narrow chances from hopeless to almost hopeless. Still, the thought *We have a bullet each* came sliding into Carter's mind like a snake. It wouldn't come to that, he chastised himself, but then he thought of stolid, solid, reliable, last-man-who-would-ever-put-a-gun-in-his-mouth Charlie Hammond doing *exactly* that.

"Any more ammo?" He could see they'd taken her jacket, which he knew she'd stored the two spare magazines in, but he was hopeful she might have moved them to elsewhere on her person as she'd done with the pistol.

"No. And they took my bag," Lovecraft reminded him.

"Okay." Two bullets and a knife. He was beginning to regret delivering the coup de grâce to Keturah Waite on purely logistical grounds. They could hear that the rumbling of steps above them had quieted.

Colt's voice upstairs was just about discernible. He sounded hysterical and muffled by at least one closed door between him and the hallway where the trapdoor stood open. Then, very clearly, somebody racked a shotgun. A live shell clattered onto the floor; there was scrabbling to recover it, and a sharply whispered admonition not to rack a shotgun when it already has a live shell in the chamber.

Carter's face tightened. A shotgun in the confined space did not seem like a survivable scenario. Lovecraft was ahead of him.

"We have to get out of here," she said, and she was looking at the hole in the wall as she said it.

"Take this," he said, handing her the knife, "and go. I'll cover us."

She stuck the knife through her belt and clambered through the jagged hole into darkness. "Does she have a phone on her?" she called back. "Or him? It's pitch-dark back here, we're going to need light."

"Fuck," muttered Carter, and quickly searched the man. He was still alive, and watched Carter's face with a strange, childish obsessiveness. He had no phone, but he did have a sheath knife and a battered old Zippo gas lighter. As he moved to check Keturah's body, the man gently caught his wrist. Carter started, and gripped the knife hard, ready to strike. But the man just looked up at him and said quietly, "Thanks . . . thanks . . ." Then he seemed to lose interest, and looked away.

Unused to being thanked by somebody who had been involved in his kidnapping, Carter turned to Keturah. It was impossible not to end up with her blood on him. The pool around her was bigger than she was by a couple of feet all around her, and better than an inch deep where the depression in the imperfect floor had caused it to collect. He felt it soaking through the knees of his pants as he kneeled by her, saw it smear and color his hands as he went through her pockets. It didn't feel warm, and Carter guessed the rock floor was draining the heat from it rapidly. But it didn't feel like blood, either. He'd had the misfortune to get the stuff on him too many times in the past, and this blood was not what he was used to. It felt thin and oily, and the distinct and foul smell of normal blood wasn't there at all. Instead, there was a faint acidic tang to it, like vinegar.

He pushed these observations from his mind and concentrated on the task at hand. She did have a phone, but it was an old-style handset with a gray LCD screen and a dim backlight. It would be no use as a flashlight.

As he started to get to his feet, Keturah's eyes opened. They rolled lazily in their sockets for a moment and then settled, staring at him. The .380 hole in her forehead was clearly defined, and the dark within showed it had penetrated the skull. She couldn't have survived it. It wasn't possible. So much wasn't possible.

She smiled at him, a sneering, triumphant rictus, and she said something, but the syllables were thick and liquid, and Carter couldn't have reproduced the sounds her throat made if he had heard them a thousand times. Her eyes rolled up in her skull and she lay still. Then Carter noticed her chest moving slow and rhythmically. She had been gutshot, headshot, had bled out more than she should have had in her, and she was breathing.

Shaken, he got to his feet and backed away from her.

"Did you find a phone?" asked Lovecraft from the dark.

"I got a Zippo," he said, working hard to keep the shakes he could feel in his legs and his guts out of his voice. "It'll have to do."

He climbed over the lip of the hole and into the darkness.

Chapter 28

THE HUNTED IN THE DARK

Lovecraft and Carter moved as quickly as they dared in the uneven and claustrophobic tunnel. Lovecraft had taken the Zippo to guide their way, but the metal casing grew hot quickly and she could only use it for a minute or so before plunging them into darkness while the brass grew cool enough to handle again. The tunnel was not at all regular in its construction, but wound both left and right, and sometimes up and down. They had lost the slightest glimmer of light from the tunnel entrance in the first minute of crouched scurrying in the low, oddly organic tube cut through the bedrock of Waite's Bill. Carter noticed and then purposefully ignored the curious walls of the near circular tunnel, how there were no obvious tool marks but only fine striations marking the surface like ribs, as if some unimaginable machine had melted an inch or so of the tunnel and halted to get rid of the molten debris before repeating the process again and again and again. The enforced moments of stillness in the dark were unwelcome and unnerving for them both; all it left them was the sound of their breathing, the touch of the striated wall against their palms as they steadied themselves, and a faint chemical smell, musty and acrid, unlike anything else in either of their experiences.

Carter thought of the tunnel as "organic" in the first instance because of the indiscipline of its path, but presently he realized that when he thought of the "something" that had made it, that "something" had ceased to be a machine in his imagination and become a living creature. Somewhere the excavated rock had been dumped, and he feared that when he saw that spoil heap it would have more in common with a worm casting than a heap of rubble.

The flint grated, sparks flew, and the dark fled from them to await its next chance.

"Did you feel that breeze?" said Lovecraft. "Please, God, let this thing open out onto the beach. Somewhere."

The last word told Carter she was having the same misgivings as him; Waite's Bill was not large, yet already they had been walking as rapidly as they could for six or seven minutes in between moments of dark. Even allowing for the winding of the path, they should have passed the edge of the spit of land by now. That meant they *must* be underwater, but there was no sign of it, no coldness in the air, no condensation or water leaking through the bedrock. They might as well have been wandering beneath the Gobi Desert as the Providence River.

Then the tunnel split. It did it as easily and, yes, as organically as an artery forking.

"Keep tending left?" said Lovecraft, and went down the left-hand path without waiting for an answer.

Keeping moving was obviously the right thing to do; they were being pursued. But were they? In the quiet of the halts both keened their hearing as much as they might, yet neither ever heard the least sound behind them.

"You know what's worrying me?" asked Lovecraft during the second break in darkness since they'd taken the left-hand fork.

"There's so much to choose from," said Carter. "Okay, what specifically?"

"The reason they don't seem to be chasing us. I have, like, a mental image of a scene from some shitty 1930s B movie. You know the kind of thing—Fay Wray and some hero with a firm chin have escaped from the bad guy and run off into the forest or caves or a jungle on an alien world. The bad guy's guards—they all wear silver clothes and stupid helmets—are going to chase them, but the bad guy—I'm thinking of someone like Leslie Banks here—says, 'No. Those woods or caves or whatever are home to the voracious snorkfangs. Leave them to the snorkfangs!' And then he laughs, and all his guards laugh because it's in their job description."

"Snorkfangs?"

"Or whatever."

"You think they're not following because there's something in these tunnels already?"

"No. I was just saying it's like those movies where . . . Shit, you don't think something's in here with us, do you?"

"No. I don't." He forbore to mention his concerns over whatever had made the tunnels. There was no point in frightening Lovecraft.

"Well, something made these tunnels," said Lovecraft. She didn't sound frightened, only angry and determined. "Wish I had my Mossberg. It would be awesome in a tight tunnel like this."

"You're handling this well," said Carter.

"I have a little trick. I'm doing my best to pretend this is all some sort of live role-playing thing. It's all special effects and makeup. You're handling it pretty well, too. What's your trick?"

"I don't have one," he said, and as soon as he said it, he realized it was true; he didn't. The realization startled him. He was accepting it all; the Perceptual Twist, Colt's ability to take advantage of it, the man who wasn't a man on the riverside, the Waites and their inhuman nature, the tunnels cut by something other than human tools. He acknowledged it all, accepted it all, assimilated and then acted on it all. It concerned him, but only in the same way as if he'd found out Colt and the Waites were dealing crystal meth and were prepared to kill to protect their trade. The danger was there, and he reacted to it as he would any danger. Its origin seemed not to trouble him at all.

"I don't know how that works," he said. "I should be freaking out, shouldn't I?"

"You're a descendant of Randolph Carter," said Lovecraft. "I think there's more to that than just taking his name. In the H. P. L. stories, Randolph Carter's special. He's a dreamer in a technical, practical kind of way, and he sees some pretty fucked-up stuff, but he always keeps his sanity. Randolph Carter was a very special little snowflake, and maybe you are, too." She sparked the lighter into life, tapped Carter on the nose, and grinned.

The injured man and Keturah had been taken up into the main body of the house to be tended to. The man would be fine. Keturah's brain had been disrupted by the passage of a .380 slug into the skull, where it lacked sufficient energy to escape and had instead ricocheted around inside the brainpan, causing massive damage as it did so. It might even have killed her; she was lucky to survive. They put her to bed in a dark room and left her there. It would take a while, perhaps as long as a couple of months, but her brain would re-form completely and her memory would be patched by the RNA analog stored in her bones. The Waite women were not fragile in any sense.

In contrast, the injured man was only human, but extended contact with the women was rectifying that. He had to be prevented from trying to push his finger into the bloodless bullet holes, marveling at them as a child does at the socket of the first lost tooth. He would not obey a command to leave them alone, so finally they restrained him, strong leather restraints being a household item on Waite Road.

Keturah's place was taken by Charity Waite, who had so recently visited the neighbor Owen Worley to persuade him he had never seen Kenneth Rothwell coming out of Waite Road. Her "persuasion" had been more in the manner of an erasure of the memory, and she had caused Worley much disruption to the workings of his mind and his personality, but that was acceptable. His wife had since separated from him while he "pulled himself together," but that was never going to happen. He spent his days watching the isthmus now, standing slack-jawed and dead-eyed on his untended lawn, waiting for a sight of Charity. Maybe she'd marry him, she thought. She was, after all, over the age of consent. Far, far over.

Charity looked around seventeen years old, perhaps a little more, perhaps a little less, right up until the moment one looked into her eyes. They were not the eyes of a young person. If one looked closely enough, they were not the eyes of a person at all.

She'd sent another of the men down into the cellar room first, the men being both less bothered by damage and generally more expendable. He'd come back with blood on his shoes to report that both Keturah and Richard were shot, and the Lovecraft woman and the Carter man were missing.

"They're in the tunnels," Charity said to Colt. He was sitting on the sofa, clutching a glass of water and shaking. "We're goin' t'have to go after them, y'know?"

"You don't need me for that," said Colt. The surface of the water rippled with his tremors. "Send your men after them. You've got guns."

Charity smiled as if she were talking to an adorably stupid child. "Yeah, we got guns. Trouble bein' that they're probably goin' t'end up at the Fold. You really want a shootin' match in there?"

"Twist," said Colt, glancing up at her. "It's called the Perceptual Twist."

"Semantics, darlin'. They'll find it, jus' like they seem t'find every one of our little secrets. They're special, y'know."

"There's nothing special about them."

"We kinda think there is. They're descendants of the folks who made the Fold . . . *so* sorry . . . the Perceptual *Twist* back in the day."

"They're not mathematicians. They can't—"

"Billy, Billy, Billy. We ain't mathematicians, either, but we got by with it all these years. It's not always down to the numbers. Some folk can just feel their way 'round The Twist. We can, and 'less you can tell me how Daniel Carter didn't die in your house, I'm guessin' he can, too. Better than us. What if he finds The Twist and ties it up tight, huh? That makes life bad for us, and it turns you back into just another number monkey again. You wanna carry on being a god, you better get your ass down those tunnels and stop them."

Only Colt's mother had ever called him "Billy." He bridled at Charity's use of it, but not as badly as at the sudden fear of Carter and Lovecraft somehow strangling The Twist. Charity was supercilious and patronizing, but he forgave her these aspects because she and her extended family had welcomed him here when the indicators—he could hardly call them "clues"—he deciphered from the cube first led him to Waite Road.

They had known why he had come, had seemed to understand and even anticipate his oblique references to an interest in the history of that little tongue of land. The men were of no use—he was barely aware of the names of any of them, an interchangeable mob of Daves, Bobs, Johns, and Eds—but the women were not the landed trailer trash they first appeared to be. They showed him books, memoirs and diaries, some very old indeed, that told of the land's past. The women guarded these books with the care they would have given their children, a distinct absence on the street. Colt started to understand the nature of the Waites quickly, and that there never had been and never would be a new generation. At least, not in the conventional sense.

It should have shocked him, or even just surprised him. But the revelations of the cube had spoken to him and his horizons had not merely broadened, but disappeared. He stood at the precipice above the infinite, and then saw even the precipice was only an illusion. He stood above everything on a pinnacle of self, and he felt secure on that needle, one of only a handful in the world who might, and who had the intelligence and talents to understand what he was seeing and how to manipulate it. The chances of the cube being discovered and by a convoluted path coming to his attention or somebody else like him were infinitesimal. Colt understood that, but it didn't disturb him. After all, the effects of the Perceptual Twist made a joke of probability, so he didn't think long or hard upon the subject. It was nothing but a retrograde effect of the causal ructions he had inevitably made, the anthropomorphic principle writ large in that the observation and the interpretation of that observation were joined at the hip. It had happened because he had used it because it happened.

Charity did not see fit to tell him the more mundane, and far more horrifying, truth: one of the Waite men, still a Waite if no longer entirely a man, had placed the cube in the deep sea trawl while it was deployed.

The captain had passed it on to the college because he had been told to and knew far better than to question any orders coming from that quarter. If he had, the best he would have suffered was empty nets until bankruptcy. The worst was the love of a Waite woman, where the terms "love" and "woman" are euphemisms. Contingency plans had been laid to bring it to Colt's attention if need be, but his natural curiosity and arrogance had led him straight to it. Then it was purely a matter of waiting.

Charity's thought processes were in no way human. Where a human mind would pursue a single thought in a train of association and examination, Charity and her sisters maintained a glowing hum of cross-referenced cognitive processes that constantly mapped and modeled possibility and contingency. Elegant and alien, a system once inadequately represented as a frozen moment on a wall in Red Hook. Charity had known there was no possibility of Colt failing to use the knowledge of the cube to his own advantage; she understood him far too well. Once it and he had crossed paths, they only needed to wait until the inevitable day when a red Mazda3 made its way across the isthmus, and William Colt started asking questions. They answered freely, because he never even thought to ask the right questions. They knew he never would, until it was far too late.

"Fine," said Colt. He said it in the peevish tones of a man bullied into doing the washing up. He picked up the cube from the table with markedly less enthusiasm than he had shown in the past. "Fine, I'll go after them, but I'm not going alone."

"Course not," said Charity. She smiled and his flesh crept.

Lovecraft had been dismayed when she found she couldn't turn the Zippo's flame down. "Why the hell not?" she had said as she looked for some sort of control. "Every lighter I've ever seen had a little doohickey on it. What the fuck, Zippo?"

"Those are propane or butane," said Carter, who used to smoke. "That's a naphtha lighter. You can't control it the same."

"I never thought my life might come down to what kind of lighter I could get my hands on," said Lovecraft. The flame was dying. There couldn't be more than a minute left in it.

"We need to keep moving," said Carter.

The flame flickered.

"Wait, wait, wait," said Lovecraft. "That was a breeze. That was a breeze, right? That's not just it running out of gas?"

Carter looked into the darkness. He could smell salt water. He tried licking his finger and holding it up. The pad felt cold after a moment. "There's a breeze," he said. "Let's go."

His sense of direction was completely shot. He'd always flattered himself on keeping track of which way was north even on cloudy days when he couldn't see the sun, but this was like a funhouse maze. The tunnel had split, split, split again, and if he had met the fucking Minotaur coming the other way, it would not have surprised him.

The floor sloped up and down, and he was confident that it

could easily have gained or lost—he had no idea which—enough depth to be crossing back over itself for all he knew. The feel of cool air was something new, however. Unless the Waites had left their front door open and the breeze was coming in from the cellar, then he knew he was heading away from them. That was good. That there was a breeze was also good; that meant they were above the water level and, he guessed, heading for someplace-out-of-doors. He hoped they were off the spit and would come out in somebody's backyard. That would be the best.

Then they saw light ahead, gleaming from the smooth, glassy surface of the melted rock, and Lovecraft clicked out the guttering Zippo with a sigh of relief. Carter signaled her to halt for a moment while their eyes grew accustomed to a natural light far brighter than the Zippo's flickering flame, then to follow as he advanced, the Beretta braced in both hands, leading the way along his eyeline.

The tunnel jinked and they suddenly saw the exit. It wasn't the ending of the tunnel, but more as if the tunnel had grazed the surface, leaving a gap in its wall. Carter once again thought how organic the way had been, and how it did not feel like a human tunnel—a way of getting from here to there—but instead the by-product of the passage of something else, something he did not even care to make conjectures upon because he doubted he would like any solid conclusion that might form from the evidence.

Besides, it didn't matter. There was a way back to the surface, and that was all they needed. They could get out into the city, make contact with Harrelson, and formulate a new plan. Carter liked the idea of filling the back of a pickup with Molotov cocktails and burning every fucking house on Waite Road down to the foundations.

They made their way to the exit cautiously, both because the light of the day was so intense on their eyes and because there was a good chance the Waites knew about the exit and might have people waiting.

At the edge of the opening Carter paused, his back braced

against the curved wall of the tunnel, his eyes wide to become as accustomed as possible to the light, then narrowed them as he swung out suddenly, gun up, safety off.

He looked at the cityscape before him. There was no sign of the Waites.

"Oh, shit," he breathed.

Lovecraft looked fearfully at the expression of frozen horror on Carter's face. "Are they there?" she asked in a loud whisper. Carter didn't answer, so she risked a peek. What she saw made her freeze, too.

They were on the edge of the city. It just wasn't *her* city. It was hard to believe it was *anyone's* city. It sprawled like a spreading infection under a daylight moon, and even that was a terrible blight upon the heavens. Clumsily bisected as if by the action of a petulant, idiot god, the two halves of the moon clung together by their mutual gravity and tumbled slowly across the sky of an alien Earth.

She ducked back into the tunnel. The tunnel she could deal with, just so long as she didn't think too hard about how it might have been made. The city, though . . .

"I've seen it before," said Carter in an undertone that Lovecraft could only just catch.

"It's *wrong*," said Lovecraft with furious emphasis, as if it were Carter's fault that the wrong city was outside. "It's all wrong. The proportions, it's . . . What do you mean, you've seen it before? In what fucking nightmare did you see that ants' nest before?"

"When I . . ." He hesitated. He'd seen it twice, hadn't he? Once when he first visited Waite Road and again when he escaped Colt's house and ended up at Waite Road again somehow. It was hard to be sure. The sensation of it, the experience had been so similar, and so alien, on both occasions he had done what he could to remove the memory by inattention, just like he tried to erase his dreams. It hadn't entirely worked; the edges were gone, but the aberrance of the sight still seeped through his mind, liquid and electric. There was no mistaking it now, though. It wasn't a dream.

It was real, and Carter fought to stop the sensation of everything he thought he knew about the everyday act of existing sheering away from him like a panorama made from jigsaw pieces, caught in a hurricane.

"We can't go there."

"No," said Lovecraft. She had made no further attempt to look at the city, anomalous in so many ways. "We can't."

Both of them meant that they shouldn't, that they mustn't.

Carter spotted movement in one of the long unglazed windows of a twisting tower.

"We should go."

Chapter 29

MEDUSA'S COIL

They returned to the tunnel and left the exit behind them, because it was no exit at all: only an entrance into something that would complicate their already complicated lives beyond any human ability to deal with.

The Zippo refused to light, its reservoir finally dry, and they were compelled to travel blind, Lovecraft volunteering to go first, arms waving, one foot tapping ahead, afraid of a sudden drop. Carter walked close behind her, his left hand on her shoulder and the other pointing the Beretta ahead. If something happened, he would pull her back and fire, the muzzle flash providing him with an idea of what the danger was and leaving him with a single round with which to deal with it if need be. It was a shitty sort of tactic for a shitty sort of situation, and Carter felt like he was a kid again, playing War with the neighborhood kids and coming up with stupid tactics that sounded pretty cool to a seven-year-old.

"It's not a natural tunnel," muttered Lovecraft under her breath, "so there shouldn't be any sudden drops." But she kept testing ahead with one foot anyway.

She thought she was developing some sort of sixth sense—she was prepared to believe almost anything by this point, slippery slope for her mental stability though it was—when she saw the tunnel curve ahead of her, the bend rimed in the dimmest light. Then Carter asked, "Is it getting lighter again?" and she didn't know whether to be relieved or annoyed that, despite everything else, she wasn't developing extrasensory perception. Or, if she was, so was Carter, and where was the pleasure in that?

The tunnel opened out dramatically, and the neat striations in the wall became chaotic and smeared, as if whatever had excavated the way so far had been reduced to running around and around to create the larger space. It still looked organic, and it was far from perfectly formed, the floor being a rolling surface like the slow heave of a lake suddenly turned to stone.

The chamber showed three or four other exits; it was hard to be exact since some gaps in the wall might have been the beginnings of new tunnels or just a redundant extra opening into a tunnel that had another farther along. The chamber had in no way been designed, not even in the impromptu way of miners. It was an abscess in the earth, boiled around the glowing thing in its center.

"Oh," said Lovecraft as she saw it, "what is that?" She said it in a faint tone of complaint, as if to say the universe was simply being unreasonable now and she would like a return to some sort of decorum.

Carter couldn't say. He didn't want to look at it, but he also knew he couldn't look away. It was some twenty feet tall and too complex for his eyes to parse as an object. The one thing that surprised him was that the Perceptual Twist actually looked twisted. A mass of splintered and extruded light, it stood like a piece of a tornado, equal in width at top and bottom, although it had no particular top and bottom but instead bled into light and variation at each end. It neither moved nor stood still, slicing and rolling every iota of sensory data it carried to the observers. Under the liquescent flood of the blistering probabilities, the cortices of Carter's and Lovecraft's brains started to misfire, and synesthesia spread through them like roaring-rough blue tear gas.

Carter was overwhelmed first. He couldn't understand what he was looking at, what he was experiencing, and his brain had no safety mechanisms built into it to tell it not to even try. More and more of it was assigned to comprehension in a way that brains simply are not supposed to behave, and as it committed to the hopeless task, he became helpless as the higher brain functions were starved of cerebration, his muscles locked, and his heart slowed and stuttered at the edge of fibrillation.

As his life moderated, his mind quickened. He was standing at the window in the Suydam house, watching the omega, the ending of all things roar toward him with some unseen alpha assuredly traveling in its wake, and he finally understood The Twist, at least a little.

Colt was wrong. Colt was so very wrong. It was a shame, Carter concluded, that he was going to be snuffed out by the realization before he ever had a chance to tell Colt to his face what a total dick he was.

Then he was falling, and he blinked reflexively, and he was saved. Lovecraft lay on top of him, slapping him, saying angrily, "Do *not* look at the Medusa!" as if it had been a considered decision.

He liked how, at such a time, she could use an allusion like that and realized he was perhaps a little bit in love with her.

"I'm okay," he said. His heartbeat settled. He was aware of the feel of fresh air being drawn into his lungs with every breath. He could sense the skin of his lips lying against each other, warm and smooth. He took such landmarks of normality and used them to build a bulwark against the unknowable, an inner campfire within whose circle of light he felt safe and stable, and without those defenses, the other things that threatened his very mind and soul could—with his most sincere best wishes—go fuck themselves. "I'm okay," he said again, and he was. "You didn't look?"

"I did for maybe a heartbeat. That was long enough for a lifetime. Then," she added pointedly, "I shielded my eyes because I'm not a moron."

She helped him to his feet, and he shocked her by immediately looking back at the thing.

"Man! What are you . . . ?"

"It's cool," he assured her. "I get it now."

There *was* a Perceptual Twist; Carter could see that now, and he appreciated the irony. He was experiencing it right now, but the difference between him and Colt was that he knew it. Using it, he could look at the thing and not die, or go insane, or be turned to stone or a puff of steam or any of the other things it could probably do if you perceived it incorrectly. He liked to think he could look at it without ill effect because he was smart and perceptive, but he had a strong sense that he was kidding himself. You could probably walk a hundred smart and perceptive people through that chamber and ninety-nine of them would end up dead or as good as. The hundredth would be him. There was something else that saved him, and it probably had to do with his ancestor. Carter made up his mind that, if they ever got out of this place, he would read H. P. Lovecraft's stories of Randolph Carter, because he could do with every little bit of help he could get.

The thing was bearable now that he had twisted his own perception to underestimate it. Now it was just a very nice special effect. He had to be careful not to consider it a movie special effect, because that would undermine his own confidence in his existence as anything more than a fictional construct. He didn't want to think about that; he mustn't think of that. The thing was fractious and might be responsive to even passing whims and random conceits such as that. What if it rendered himself as fictional as he'd thought Randolph was? Was that what had happened to Randolph when the world was twisted all those decades ago?

What would happen to Dan Carter when the tale was told and the book was closed?

No. The thing was an effect without context; as a collection of pretty lights and moving lines he could look at it, even admire it, and still deal with it. It took a mental effort, and the cognitive sensations it caused were new to him, untrained muscles getting their first ever workout. There was a skill developing here, a knack at least, and he remembered Lovecraft—Emily Lovecraft— referring to Randolph Carter as a "practiced dreamer" like it was a job, or a vocation, or even a calling. Daniel Carter, Private Investigator and Practiced Dreamer. He'd need new business cards.

He was still deliberately distracting himself with such thoughts when Colt and the Waites arrived.

William Colt did not seem happy to be there. Another of the Waite women was with him as they emerged from one of the tunnel mouths on the far side of the chamber, and she, by contrast, seemed pleased enough. She carried an air of languid malevolence with her that made Carter think of a cat, although she was as rangy and raw as a cowgirl in Wyoming. She and Colt were backed by two of the Waite men, dead-eyed and disinterested. Both were armed, one—to Lovecraft's outrage—with her Mossberg.

"Give me my gun back, you fucking thief," she demanded.

It was a bad start to negotiations, or it would have been if everybody in the room hadn't already been so polarized in their opinions of one another. As it was, the Waite man looked at the shotgun in his hands as if he hadn't noticed it before. By a mental process telegraphed through brow and shoulders, he decided the gun was definitely his now and returned it to a position of readiness.

"Motherfucker," said Lovecraft.

"Well, you found it, Dan," said Colt. He was smiling, but it was a weak smile on a wan face. Carter hadn't conducted more interviews than he could number without being able to read Colt's distress easily.

"Yeah," he said, "I found it. This is the big deal, huh, Colt? This is what you used to kill a couple of guys and fritz some slots? Wow. What a colossus among us you are."

"Slots?" said the woman. She looked at Colt with inquisitive contempt.

"It was practice," said Colt. He was sweating, rolling his copy of the cube nervously between his hands. "Probability manipulation. I was just practicing."

"Is this what you showed Ken Rothwell?" Lovecraft was speaking, avoiding looking directly at The Twist. "Is this what you did to him?"

"Rothwell?" Colt was astonished by such an idea. "You think I'd show some politician something as beautiful as *this*? No, Miss Lovecraft. Your boyfriend never came here."

"Your boyfriend?" said the woman. That smile on her face, that damnable smile, that fucking smile. "Why, he didn't mention you when he lay with my sister."

"Shut your mouth."

"We didn't expect him to be so weak, honey. Men break easy, but . . . why, he just *shattered*. We were all so surprised. That wasn't the plan at all." Her eyebrows raised in false sympathy calculated to infuriate. "Sorry. So sorry."

"I will *end* you," said Lovecraft.

"Like you did with my sister? Yeah, Keturah was the one who played with your boyfriend, darlin'. She's not functionin' so well at the moment—the second shot, the one to the head, was just rude, so you know—but she'll be fine soon enough. Then I can tell her what we did with you and Dan here to cheer her up." The smile was gone. "You can't 'end' us, Emily. You don't know how."

"I do." Carter said it and, when he had their attention, he slid his eyes to the thing that shouldn't be in the center of the chamber.

"Holy shit," said the woman. She was deadly serious. "Billy. The Fold isn't fazin' him. How's he doin' that?"

"The Twist," said Colt, correcting her in an irritable tic. He shook his head. "That's impossible."

"That sounds pretty fucking ironic coming from your lips, *Billy*," said Carter.

"If it isn't fazin' him," said the woman, "what if he's *understandin'* it?"

"Shut up, Charity," said Colt.

"Charity?" said Lovecraft. *"Really?"*

"What if I am?" said Carter. "What if I understand it as well as you, Colt? Better, maybe?"

"You can't," Colt said, his face taut. His was the face of a jealous lover seeing his woman walk away on the arm of another man. "You *can't*. How can you? You're just some ignorant, stupid cop. You can't understand anything, never mind something as beautiful and profound and mathematical as—"

"How about if my great-great-great-uncle used to do this shit for a living, Colt? What if it's genetic? What if math is the idiot's way of doing it?"

"Carter." Charity said it under her breath. Then louder, *"Randolph* Carter? That was your . . . ? Oh, fuck! Fuck, fuck, fuck! Billy! Stop him!"

Carter found the change in her expression from comfortably in control of the situation to full panic gratifying. He would have found it more so if he had the vaguest idea how to actually do what he had just suggested he could. The man with the Mossberg raised it to fire at Carter, but Charity knocked the muzzle down with the flat of her hand.

"Not in here, you fuckin' moron! You'll kill all of us!"

Carter wasn't clear whether she meant it was a bad place to fill with shot or hitting The Twist might cause problems, but he was fine with it either way. He had two bullets and four targets, three of whom might as well have been coated in six inches of Kevlar for all the good Lovecraft's Beretta would do against them. He considered shooting Colt instead, but he couldn't easily bring himself to kill an unarmed man like that. Fool he might be, but at least Colt definitely *was* human.

And Colt was staring at the thing, The Twist, except it wasn't.

He was focused and concentrating on it, and Carter realized what he was doing.

"Don't call me 'Billy,'" said Colt in a disconnected monotone.

"Don't do it, Colt," said Carter. "You've been lied to. That thing's not what you think it is."

"That's weak," said Colt in the same monotone. The Twist shifted under his gaze. "It's exactly what I think it is."

"Only because you think it. Do you understand what I'm talking about? Colt! Do you understand?"

"I understand it all," said Colt, and so demonstrated he understood almost nothing.

Carter glared at The Twist. He could feel his inner landscape bleeding out, but this time, he let it. The Twist was relaxing, releasing phenomenological and probabilistic shrapnel as it did. Colt sucked on it, not a god but a parasite, an addict at a glory hole. Colt had reified himself a golden calf out of reality's undercoat and could see it as nothing else. Carter would have pitied him but for Colt being a self-serving fucking idiot.

For his part, Carter wanted nothing of it. Every iota of ontological radiation The Twist emitted was an indication of growing danger, danger of a kind he was too wise to guess at.

"For Christ's sake, Colt! You don't know what you're doing!"

It was meant literally, but Colt took it as a challenge, and that error would change everything.

"No?" shouted Colt over the growing sensory roar they felt and heard and tasted and saw and smelled and that made the pineal glands in their skulls ache under stimulation they had never experienced before. He glanced briefly at the cube in his hand and tossed it to one side; he didn't need it anymore. "Well, let me show you."

And Colt destroyed the world.

Chapter 30

THE NIGHT OCEAN

William Colt reached into the Perceptual Twist. Not physically—
nothing so gross as that—or even psychically—nothing so gross
as that, either—but conceptually. He looked at a vase and forced
himself to see two faces. He looked at an old hag's portrait and
saw a full-length rendering of a pretty girl. He saw two different
shades of gray and perceived them as the same. Lines of perception flowed one way, and were reinforced by stanchions of actu-
alization passing the other. The Perceptual Twist untwisted a little
further, sending differences of potentiality and probability outward and in, eddying along the seams of Colt's will.

"No." Carter raised Lovecraft's Beretta and fired twice at Colt's
head at a range of less than five feet. He couldn't possibly miss,
but possibility wasn't what it was, the laws of ballistics had been
hacked, and the bullets fell to the striated floor directly beneath
the gun's muzzle.

Colt smiled, because he perceived himself to be the victor. Carter snarled, because he knew they were both the losers.

"You stupid *dick*," said Carter. These were the last words of any importance uttered in the world, and summed it up well.

The Perceptual Twist uncurled, loosened, and potential flowed. Colt laughed at the pleasure of empowerment, what felt to him like natural justice, the mark of a superiority that had been evident to him ever since he was old enough to realize that he was an individual and that he was surrounded by idiots. Now, flanked by two men whose mental processes ran like cold fat, he was the biggest idiot in the chamber, and too much a fool to know it.

Carter had to stop him. He had no idea how. Bullets hadn't worked, and he doubted he could get close enough to punch the man; the Waites would be on him before he had a chance. There was only a single chance, and it was no chance at all. Carter looked at The Twist, saw it for what it really was, found sliding planes of reinterpretation on which to lean his mind, and pushed back.

Colt's smile vanished instantly. He said nothing—the time for that was passed—but sought to reestablish control of the Perceptual Twist. He bent himself to the task, physically leaning forward as he brought his concentration up.

Lovecraft was going to a lot of trouble not to look at the warped thing that was the pivot of all worlds, so instead she was looking at the Waite woman Charity and her two kinfolk. She was the only one to see Charity's expression of horror at the discovery of Carter's ancestry fade into a deeply satisfied smile. Charity tapped the two Waite men on the shoulders and walked out, going back through the tunnel from which they'd emerged.

Lovecraft was unsure what to do; Carter and Colt were both staring at The Twist and she was the only one not enthralled by it. Whatever the Waites were up to, it stank, and she was the only one left with her consciousness largely intact to deal with it. With forebodings—and a feeling that such forebodings were pointless because she and Carter were already deep in a world of shit, so how much worse could this get?—she made to follow Charity and her men.

She left Carter and Colt doing their weird staring match and ducked into the tunnel Charity had retreated along. She no longer needed the Zippo; the tunnel thrummed with light. At least, she thought it was light. She could see, but the colors were not ones she could easily identify and they made her forehead hurt. The black was almost red, and there was a pale green marking out the detail that was occasionally indistinguishable from purple, or perhaps orange. She couldn't remember what those colors looked like anymore, in any case. She tried to remember what an orange looked like to help her recall the color, but her memory only offered her a cluster of related labels and associations, all devoid of immediate sensory recall, and it was like having an orange described to her over the phone.

"I'm seeing in the dark," she muttered under her breath. The sound of her own voice helped ground her, so she continued. "Kind of cool. Okay. It's cool. I'm down with this. I like seeing in the dark. I'm just not going to think about how I'm doing it. I think I need new words for colors."

The light wasn't stable, however. It pulsed and raced. Lovecraft knew it was something else, that the tunnels, that the *world* was emitting light that was not light in the sense that she understood it. Light that was not light that she was sensing in a way that was not seeing.

Her forehead hurt badly, but it didn't feel like any sort of headache she had ever had before. She had to ignore it. Catch up with Charity Waite. Get her gun back. Save the day. Somebody had to do it, and she wasn't convinced Carter was going to be the one. Staring contest. Whoever stares at the thing in the chamber longest wins. Yay. Macho bullshit.

Lovecraft had never made any great claims to her navigational talents and so did not care much that she had no idea where she was. Despite which, whenever she reached a junction she made a choice of which way to go without hesitation and felt sure, truly positive, that she was following the path taken by Charity Waite. "Just follow the smell of bitch," she said to herself.

The tunnel twisted abruptly, and she was entering a chamber, but it wasn't the chamber of The Twist, or even the cellar beneath the end house. It was immense, and she was standing on the rocky beach of a vast subterranean lake, perhaps even a sea. She looked up and saw there were stars, but that was impossible. She was in a cave. They couldn't be stars. They were stars. There couldn't be stars in a cave. She rationalized it away, put it down to the strangeness of seeing in the dark. They weren't stars, merely artifacts of her new way of seeing. It was a lie, she knew it was a lie, but it kept her mind working and what she needed more than anything else in the world right now was not to piss herself with terror and curl up into a fetal ball. That was a bad thing, she told herself fiercely. *Stay focused, Emily Lovecraft. Stay focused, stay sane, find Charity Waite.*

And there she was. On the bare rock escarpment that led down into the sea that was a subterranean lake because it had to be, and *fuck* those stars because they're nothing. Charity Waite was naked, her clothes cast aside, detritus from an existence she was shedding as a spider sheds a skin. The two men were also undressing, but slowly and awkwardly; Lovecraft had a feeling they were usually helped to get dressed and undressed. They fumbled with shirt buttons and belt buckles and it was painful to watch. Charity could have helped, but she did not, and ignored them in their patient incompetence.

"It's beautiful, ain't it?" she said over her shoulder at Lovecraft. "The world before. Like turning a page in a book and a pressed flower leapin' up into life right there in front of you."

Lovecraft ignored her. Her Mossberg was lying discarded on the rocky edge; she grabbed it, shouldered it as she'd been taught, and aimed it square at Charity. She could hear her instructor's words: "Never aim at something or somebody unless you intend to shoot it or them."

Fucking A, thought Emily Lovecraft.

"You're wastin' your time, darlin'," said Charity, unafraid of the weapon. She looked back out to sea. *To the* lake, Lovecraft reprimanded herself. *It's a lake. An underground lake.* She ignored the stars that were becoming clearer. She ignored the clouds that shifted across them.

"What have you done?" she demanded of Charity Waite. "This was never about helping Colt and getting on his right side, was it?"

"Billy? Oh, no, no. Billy the pocket god. He's a sweet boy, but . . ." Charity glanced at her kinsmen. One of them was having trouble getting his jeans off, and fell heavily to the stone floor. There he continued to writhe and squirm out of them. "Men are stupid, y'know? Your pal Danny isn't as smart as he thinks, either."

"Dan's worth twenty Colts."

Charity looked back at her again, smiling. "Why, Emily. So quick to defend. You got feelings for that boy? Well, I hope you're happy together. I do, truly. And, yeah, Danny's worth at least twenty Billys, but given Billy is a piece of idiot shit, that's not such a big deal now, is it?"

Loathsome as Colt was, Lovecraft had never been anything but impressed by his intellect. She was going to argue, but then started to understand what Charity meant. "He's very smart . . ."

"No, Miss Lovecraft. He's *intelligent*. Intelligent in a particular way, too. That was good for us. But he ain't smart, he ain't clever, and he sure as fuck ain't wise. That was good for us, too. Your boy Danny's smart and he's clever. I can't speak for his wisdom, but he ain't so intelligent. Put them together in the same room and it's like two dogs fightin' over a chew toy."

"Dan's a good man."

"That's good for us, too, because Billy's what you might call evil. Those are those moral absolutes you guys buy into, ain't it?"

"*You guys?*"

"Y'know." Charity shrugged. "Humans."

Somewhere out in the lake that was not—absolutely *not*—a sea, something huge moiled and shrugged beneath the surface. A hump of water heaved away from it, turning to a wave as it reached the shore.

"There's my boy now," said Charity. "I've missed him." She started to walk down to the water's edge, the men now finally naked and walking with her. Lovecraft made the mistake of glancing at them and then looked quickly away again, not because of their nakedness but because they had sloughed their humanity and what walked with Charity Waite were no longer men at all.

"You planned all this?" shouted Lovecraft at the receding forms. The shotgun felt useless in her hands, and she lowered it.

"Nope," called Charity back to her, "but we have common interest with so many. Somebody else got this thing rollin' and I played along."

"Who are you? Really?"

Charity Waite stopped and turned. She was radiantly beautiful and terrifyingly monstrous. She was the sea and of the sea. If Lovecraft hadn't been frozen in horror at the sight of the slick skin, the writhing hair, and the eyes that held her in a thrall of exquisite terror, she might have fallen to her knees and worshipped Charity as the goddess she clearly was, not like the tawdry dime-store deity Colt aspired to be.

"I have many heads. You shot one earlier, but I'm seeing my lover again after all this time, so I've no mind to be vengeful 'bout that. Clever girl like you, you can work it out, I'm sure."

"Dan will stop Colt. He'll stop you." Lovecraft managed to croak out the feeble few words of defiance.

"Darlin'," said the god that had once pretended to be a piece of trailer trash called Charity Waite, "think of what happens to something when it gets bent back 'n' forth, back 'n' forth a few times. There's no stopping us, 'cause we already won."

The men had already slipped below the water. Charity walked into the sea . . . the nightmare lake . . . the *ocean* as a queen enters a bath. The vast ocean was too small to dwarf her. Lovecraft realized she was weeping as she watched the goddess return to her domain to join her lover. Emily Lovecraft felt so inconsequential it was hardly worth breathing. She might as well just die there and be done. There wasn't a person in the world worth a second's contemplation by the forces now finding their liberty. It was all a joke. A ghastly unfunny joke.

Then she thought of Charity's words and some part of her pushed against the shock that was crushing the very soul from her and reminded her of two dogs fighting over a chew toy, back 'n' forth, back 'n' forth. Charity called it the *Fold*, not The Twist. Back 'n' forth.

Lovecraft sucked in air as if she'd just been brought back from the dead. In a sense, she had; the hopelessness fell away as she found purpose. She was crying, and she was more furiously angry than she had ever been in her life before. Nothing had ever mattered this much before.

"Not done yet! We're not done yet!" she shouted at the sea. She ran toward the tunnel mouth, clutching the Mossberg fiercely. Its weight felt good.

"Fucker!" she shouted over her shoulder at the uncaring waves, and ran into the tunnels.

Logic against instinct, nuance versus principle, Carter and Colt fought an indefinable battle in a non-Euclidean battlefield. Neither knew how long they had been fighting, time becoming just another thing without limits or metric. There shouldn't have been time enough to draw breath, yet still worlds could have turned to dust, as they presented move, countermove, feint, and block. Colt had discovered a new mathematical argument and bore down upon Carter with it, a juggernaut of brutalist rationalism in a melt of discarded rationales. Carter fended it off and evaded, holding The Twist with difficulty, swaying and sweating and swearing while probability grew heavier and heavier upon him. Then he remembered himself, sidestepped, and the weight became light and blinded Colt long enough for Carter to throw his shoulder back against the door and push. But it wasn't a door, and it wasn't a Twist, perceptual or otherwise, though it was closer to a door than the other thing and Carter wondered how they could ever have thought—

Then Lovecraft was there, she had a shotgun, and she was telling Colt that if he didn't stop doing what he was doing *right this fucking second* she would *blow his fucking head off.*

He ignored her. She fired.

They all saw the densely packed cloud of pellets and fragments of cartridge padding travel as slowly as pebbles in honey toward Colt, saw them glow red, white, cherry pink, and turn to vapor that hung in heavy tendrils, falling slowly in fanciful metallic curlicues as they cooled.

Lovecraft mouthed something angrily, and swung the gun toward Carter. She communicated that she liked him a lot and she wasn't enjoying pointing a gun at him, but if he didn't stop doing what he was doing *right this fucking second* she would *blow his fucking head off.*

He didn't ignore her. He relaxed his mind and stepped away from The Twist.

Colt was taken entirely off guard and off balance. He was still pushing, and pushing hard; he'd been expecting Carter to carry on their battle just as he had when threatened by Lovecraft. The Twist unfurled. Too much. Far too much. The potentials held back within it slipped out like dust, first in a wisp and then in a drift and then in a blizzard. He saw Emily Lovecraft grab Daniel Carter's arm, shout something at him, start pulling him away.

Carter looked Colt in the eye, and Colt saw pity there. Then they were gone, and Colt was all alone with the Perceptual Twist.

He looked back to it and started to bring it back under control. He'd done it before; this was more of a leak of potentiality than he'd dealt with before, but the principles remained the same. He anticipated no problem . . .

Except there was a problem. His perception was twisted and the Perceptual Twist no longer seemed to be a twist in perception. He scrabbled backward mentally from it. He had to stay in control. He had to see it as he had always seen it if he meant to control it, but it was too late. Like a nagging thought or an earworm, the realization that The Twist was not and had never been simply that had taken hold of him. He had failed to understand it all.

He thought momentarily of the old story of a group of blind men trying to identify an elephant by touch alone. One embraces a leg and declares it to be a tree, another finds the tail and says it's a snake, and so on.

Just like one of those blind men, Colt had profoundly and utterly misunderstood what he was perceiving.

It wasn't a twist untwisting. It was a fold unfolding. There was no perceptual liberty to be had at all; there was only one truth, only one way to see, and as he saw what was obscured, what had long lain hidden and partitioned away from the world of men and women, of ephemeral lives and TV dinners, of love and money and lazy days and religious genocides, there lay a reality that brooked no glib reinterpretations or alternate points of view.

William Colt looked on the pure stuff of the universe, the pervading omega, the incandescent alpha, the binary of that which is and that which is not, and his synapses turned to mercury, the axons of his brain to glass, his eyes froze in his skull, and his heart liquefied in his chest. The everything and the nothing poured through him and his scream lasted forever.

It was confusion and certainty all boiled together. As in a dream where you have something *so* important to do, but the situation and the people keep changing and sometimes the important thing to do becomes a different important thing to do, they ran through the tunnels. Sometimes it was to escape whatever was coming, sometimes to reach a place for reasons other than safety.

Lovecraft spluttered words, but Carter already knew what she was trying to tell him. The Waites had used Colt. They had tried to use Carter. They were always intended to war there, to fight over The Twist that was a Fold. They were always intended to damage it in the fight, to release what lay beyond. That which

Carter's and Lovecraft's ancestors had placed under a fold in reality, as one hides a smudge on a bedsheet, or a note upon a piece of paper.

Both sides had lost. Both sides had won. Coup could only be counted in individual cases, by individual standards. Right now not being in the immediate area, as the Fold unleashed an angry reality that had suppurated like a boil for the past several decades, would and could be all they hoped for.

They found themselves on the riverside. Lovecraft's car was nearby. An old blue and white sneaker lay on the grass. They did not remember leaving the tunnels. Above them the stars whirled as in a planetarium and roared as they sped across the night sky. The river shuddered, and the close Atlantic raged, and even the earth rippled and swept beneath their feet. It might not do any good to run. The whole world might die that night, but they could not stand and not even try to outrun the epicenter of the world's end, for that is human nature and human nature was not one of the things that had lain pinned beneath the Fold.

They ran. They ran to the car, and Lovecraft slung the Mossberg into the footwell, started the engine with the key the Waites had not bothered to take from her, and pulled away in a shower of earth even as Carter was dragging his door shut.

They got as far as the isthmus, where they almost crashed into Detective Harrelson coming the other way. He opened his door and half got out, yelling, "Where the fuck have you been? What happened?" Lovecraft was waving at him to reverse out of the way and he was starting to obey when—above them and unseen—the stars became right, the omega erupted, and the world was destroyed.

Chapter 31

Death felt a lot like being in bed.

Carter finally decided that nothing could feel quite so much like being in bed without actually being the experience of being in bed. He would have to do something to ascertain the truth of that and he settled on opening his eyes, which seemed to work.

He was in bed and, as far as he could see, was not dead at all. He was in the bed in the apartment over Hill's Books and the world had therefore not ended, unless he was wrong about eternal souls and this was some sort of version of Heaven, or Hell, or maybe Purgatory. Then he remembered that there is no such thing as an eternal soul, and he remembered why he knew that, and he sat up in bed breathing hard and with a cold sweat squeezing from his pores.

The room sat around him, continuing to look willfully mundane. Carter closed his eyes, centered himself, and looked again, but this time he *looked*. It was just the apartment. His apartment, the one he'd inherited. He could detect nothing *twisted* or *folded* about it at all. Clean, comfortable, and completely unthreatening.

He decided to take it at its unspoken word. He rose, showered, and made himself an omelet for breakfast, washing it down with orange juice and coffee. It was as he was finishing his breakfast that he noticed his shoulder holster lazily slung over the back of the chair opposite. His Glock 17 was in it.

Hadn't the Waites taken it from him?

He wasn't usually so cavalier with firearms as to leave them littering up the place like that, but it wasn't unknown when he was tired and securing the weapon properly looked like taking a minute further away from sleeping that he wasn't prepared to give. He secured it now, checking its load and discovering it was un-fired. His Ruger holdout was lying in its ankle holster on the chair's seat. This, too, had not been fired.

He locked them in the safebox he'd fixed to the floor of the closet as a temporary measure until he could make something more secure and checked his watch. It was almost half past ten on a weekday, but there was no sound from downstairs. Lovecraft was punctual, always punctual, and the store always opened at nine.

Carter was somewhere in the uncomfortable hinterlands be-tween acceptance and denial. The world had ended, and now he'd had an omelet. It wasn't something he'd thought he'd ever enjoy after the destruction of the world.

He went downstairs, shrugging on his jacket as he went. The bookstore looked much as it ever did, right down to the political biographies near the door. He went behind the counter and found the Mossberg there. He checked that the chamber was empty and cautiously sniffed the muzzle; no scent of gun smoke. Not that that proved anything; a good cleaning would lose the smell. He also noticed the ammo tube was unextended. Frowning, he replaced the shotgun in its hiding place.

Nothing was different. Was Colt still out there? Was The Twist or the Fold or whatever the fuck it was called still active? Did all that ever happen? Carter would have loved to shrug and say in a faraway voice, "It was all a dream," but he knew damn well it wasn't. He'd experienced something, although he was prepared to accept it might be some sort of breakdown. That was preferable to it being true.

He noticed a vinyl figure on the shelf behind the counter and his frown returned. He didn't recognize it at all. He didn't remember it at all. Didn't there use to be a little vinyl Cthulhu there? He picked up the figure and studied it. It was of a serious-looking, heavily built fantasy knight in fanciful black armor. Carter looked at the base. Along with the manufacturer, copyright, and trademark information, he read, *"Randu the Swordmaster as created by H. P. Lovecraft. Masters of Fantasy Series No.31."*

Carter had never heard of Randu the anything. Based on Randolph Carter, maybe?

Across from the counter he found an encyclopedia of fantasy and looked up "Randu the Swordmaster."

Lovecraft's major creation, Randu the Swordmaster was the protagonist of twenty-nine short stories and two novellas published from 1925 until Lovecraft's death, the final story, "The Funeral Bride," being published the following year. Randu predates Robert E. Howard's "Conan the Barbarian" stories (c.f.) by some seven years, although—despite the friendship between Howard and Lovecraft—the stories seem to have influenced Howard only slightly, the character of Randu having more in common with Michael Moorcock's "Elric of Melniboné" stories (c.f.), a tragic hero apparently inspired equally by Lord Dunsany (q.v.) and the Nordic tales of Ragnarok.

Carter felt cold again. He flicked through the book to the entry for *Lovecraft, H. P.,* and skimmed it. He didn't find what he was looking for and forced himself to read it more slowly, taking in every word.

There was no mention of the Cthulhu stories. He checked the index. There was no mention of Cthulhu at all.

A scrabbling of metal against metal, tumblers thrown, and

Lovecraft swung the store's door open. She sagged against the frame and looked despairingly at Carter.

"We did the right thing, yeah?" she said. Her tone was pleading. "We did the right thing? We didn't fuck up?"

He left the book on the counter and came to her. "We didn't fuck up," he said, trying to calm her. "Colt fucked up, we stopped it being worse. Things have changed—"

A small voice, as quiet as a fading memory, whispered to him, *Didn't you have a Glock 19?*

Lovecraft laughed at his words, a pitying, hopeless laugh. "—but nothing too big. Colt opened the Fold, but I don't think it opened all the way."

"You think?" She was smiling, but such a sad smile, as if she were an ace from crying. "You think that?" She held out her hands, and he took them. She drew him out into the street.

Providence had gone.

The street was entirely different in character. The buildings were old, the roofs gambrelled, the frontages colonial, the aspect brooding. The city looked far more European than it had any right to.

"What the fuck?" said Carter in an undertone.

People walked by, cars drove past, all seemingly blasé to the fact that their whole city had been replaced.

"What happened to Providence?" he asked. "Did we do this?"

Lovecraft reached in her bag and took out a newspaper. It was some local rag running on ads and press releases as the Internet sapped the life from the print business. It looked like a thousand others across the country.

But this one was called the *Arkham Advertiser*. The lead story was about a pay dispute between faculty and campus staff at Miskatonic University.

"These . . ." Carter's throat was dry. He swallowed and tried again. "These are from H. P. L.'s stories, right?"

"No." Lovecraft shook her head and was silent for a moment. Her attitude to Carter seemed to be one of grief. "Turns out, no.

I think the stories were his way of remembering his old town. The way it was before he and Randolph changed out that reality and put in one where Arkham never happened and a town called *Providence* did." She shook her head and giggled, a little desperately, a little hysterically. "All those poor scholars who were *so* sure Arkham was based on Salem. He must have changed the details to fit the market. Maybe to hide the truth." She looked at Carter, the wan smile fading. "We *did* do the right thing, didn't we?"

"I think so," said Carter. He felt desperate and directionless. "I don't know. I think the Fold's still there. We stopped fighting over it . . . it wasn't destroyed. It shouldn't be destroyed. I'm sure it wasn't."

"You're sure. Awesome."

"This has got to be reversible. It must be."

Lovecraft wouldn't look at him anymore. She looked at the street, full of good citizens of Arkham.

"Randolph Carter and H. P. Lovecraft fixed this once," Carter persisted. He needed a rock. He needed a path. "We can do it again. Somehow. Somehow we'll do it again."

Lovecraft looked at Carter.

"That is such bullshit," she said.

They did not notice the bookstore sign above them. They did not see that it, too, had changed.

Now, the sign read *Carter & Lovecraft*.

Epilogue

THE STRANGE HIGH HOUSE IN THE MIST

There was a heavy mist rolling in from the Miskatonic River, drowning the lower-lying streets and burying the roof ridges in thin tendrils of curling white.

From his top-floor office beneath the penthouse suite at the highly reputable law firm of Weston Edmunds, Henry Weston watched the mist advance. It wouldn't last long, he knew; from his vantage point, the sky was clear and blue, and the sun would soon burn away the mist. Still, it was a pretty enough sight, and he enjoyed watching the panorama below, the ancient city spread out before him like a quaint model town. It was an exclusive view, after all; the Weston Edmunds building was eight stories high, one of the highest in Arkham, a city that took its skyline seriously and was not keen to see it cluttered.

Weston had missed Arkham. Providence was all very well and he hadn't disliked it, exactly, but it simply lacked the character of its predecessor, vanished from space, time, history, and human recollection but for the writings of H. P. Lovecraft, and it was partially Lovecraft's fault it had vanished in the first place. Weston didn't blame him for that, though, nor did he blame Randolph Carter for his part in the affair. Weston was not the sort to hold grudges.

Still, he was glad it was done with now, in as far as he understood the concept of gladness. He still remembered Providence—that was in his nature—and it seemed likely Daniel Carter and Emily Lovecraft might, too, if they had survived Waite Road. But they would be alone, and Weston would never admit to knowing a city called Providence had ever existed there. Why should he when one never had? A moment's concentration, and almost a century's history was peeled away from his memory to be replaced with the correct version.

There. Much better.

Not that he would entirely dispense with the memory of those phantom decades, of course. He had learned useful things during the period and, in any case, it might transpire that there was unfinished business to attend to. He hung up the memories in a rarely used closet in his mind, and closed the door upon them.

Henry Weston decided he would indulge himself with a walk through the mist-haunted streets and got as far as reaching for his coat and hat when he heard a sound he had not heard in a very long time, a metallic purr so high that it would have troubled few dogs.

With a small sigh, he returned his hat to the hook. First things first, of course.

He locked the door and called through to his assistant that he was taking a personal call and was on no account to be interrupted for the next hour. Then he climbed the flight of stairs to his penthouse and secured its door after him, too.

From a locked drawer in the desk in his penthouse study, he removed a wooden box six inches deep by a foot square and placed it on the desktop. It wasn't exactly six by twelve by twelve inches, of course; it had not been built by artificers who used inches, or even centimeters. No dendrologist would have succeeded in identifying the wood used in its construction, either.

He made to lift the lid, but remembered himself in time. How could he speak to the others through something as crude as a mouth? This life had made him habituated.

Henry Weston, attorney at law, smiled a very human smile, dug his fingers into the synthetic flesh of his neck, and proceeded to tear away his face.

ACKNOWLEDGMENTS

The opportunity to develop and write *Carter & Lovecraft* came to me from Brendan Deneen via the good offices of Peter Joseph, my editor at Thomas Dunne Books. I enjoyed writing it, and I'm grateful to Peter for suggesting me to Brendan. I am also, as ever, grateful to my literary agents—Melissa Chinchillo of Fletcher & Company in New York and Sam Copeland of Rogers, Coleridge & White in London—for fighting in my corner during negotiations.

My thanks also go to my editor, Peter Joseph (yes, he gets thanked twice; disgraceful, I know) and copy editor, Ivy McFadden. While I flatter myself on turning in manuscripts that are reasonably polished, the text is a great deal shinier due to their efforts.

This book is dedicated to the memory of my father, Noel, who never had a chance to read it. This is just bloody typical of obstreperous fate, as it's the first novel I've written that I think he might have enjoyed, being that he was not a great fan of fantasy, horror, or science fiction. My dad enjoyed detective stories a lot, though; he bought me my first Sherlock Holmes book and lent me his Ed McBains. I think he might well have enjoyed reading of the travails of Dan Carter, PI, and Emily Lovecraft. It pains me that I shall never know for sure. Literary interests aside, he was also a good man, and whatever is good in me came from him and my mother. I miss him a lot. I owe him a lot. Thanks, Dad.